Hope

A Books on the Beach Anthology

AMY DAVIES | ARIZONA TAPE | C.N. MARIE | CARRIE AUSTIN-MALONE | D J COOK | ELLE M THOMAS | EMMA LUNA | ERIN O'KANE | H.A ROBINSON | K A KNIGHT | K J ELLIS | K M LOWE | LAURA GREENWOOD | LYNDA THROSBY | MARTIN FERGUSON | MELODY WINTER | PAULA ACTON | POPPY FLYNN | R.M. GARDNER

Copyright © 2022

All rights reserved.

Hope: A Books on the Beach Anthology

No part of this book may be reproduced in any form or by any electronic or mechanical means, including information storage and retrieval systems, without written permission from the author, except for the use of brief quotations in a book review.

This is a work of fiction. Names, characters, businesses, places, events and incidents are either the products of the authors' imaginations or used in a fictitious manner.

Any resemblance to actual persons, living or dead, or actual events, is purely coincidental.

Cover designed by Eleanor Lloyd-Jones at Shower of Schmidt Designs
Formatted by Lizzie James at Phoenix Book Promo

CONTENTS

Burning for Us by Amy Davies	1
The Fairy Festival by Arizona Tape	51
With Fate by My Side by C.N. Marie	83
Declan's Salvation by Carrie Austin-Malone	129
The Last Day by D J Cook	169
The One by Elle M Thomas	203
I Was Always Yours by Emma Luna	249
Finding Hope by H.A. Robinson	295
Life Before by K A Knight	337
Life After by Erin O'Kane	381
When Hope is All you Have by K J Ellis	431
Don't Hold a Grudge by K M Lowe	479
The Pastry Warlock by Laura Greenwood	525
Hope is The Dream by Lynda Throsby	565
Perfect by Martin Ferguson	605
True Love by Melody Winter	655
When All Seems Lost by Paula Acton	681
Choosing Hope by Poppy Flynn	731
Did it Hurt by R.M. Gardner	781

A Note to the Reader

Hope is a collection of short stories arranged together by Phoenix Book Promo. This anthology is collated for Books on the Beach Events.

This anthology features nineteen authors bringing together different stories and genres that relate to the second chance romance genre.

All proceeds from this anthology will be donated to Macmillan Cancer Care.

All stories are written with the below quite in mind by the magnificent Christopher Reeve:

"Once you choose hope, anything is possible."

Foreword
by D J Cook

Some of you may know me as D J Cook, however, I write this foreword as just me, Danny.

Nine years ago, my heart broke into pieces as I watched my mum struggle to live with cancer until she couldn't battle it anymore. I was twenty-one years old, had three younger siblings and no father to depend on. The whole time, Macmillan Cancer Support was there—not just for my mum, but for me and my siblings, too.

Macmillan supported us as my mum received chemotherapy.

Her Macmillan Nurse was at our beck and call when my mum was so ill she could barely speak.

Macmillan were able to provide financial support so we could have our last family day together to make memories.

Macmillan were on hand to help wipe debt that HMRC tried to pass to me.

Macmillan helped source counselling for me and the rest of the family when I was in too much pain to look for myself.

I write this, after bringing up my three siblings, all while juggling a full-time job, volunteering for Macmillan and writing books.

After hearing my story, many people say that what I did at twenty-one years old was noble and something not many others would have been able to do in my position. My response? I wouldn't have been able to do it without my incredible friends, inherited family and an amazing group of professionals, including Macmillan Cancer Support.

Three years ago, I decided to give back, so I set up West Cheshire Macmillan Committee with a group of friends. We volunteer our time to fundraise and raise awareness of the incredible work of Macmillan Cancer Support.

I was overwhelmed when the wonderful Lizzie James asked if she could raise funds for Macmillan via this anthology and the amazing Books On The Beach Book Signing. Lizzie, thank you for recognising the importance of Macmillan in my life, and the lives of so many others, and for doing whatever it takes to raise funds for people living with cancer.

To the authors of this anthology: you should feel immensely proud to be part of an anthology that will contribute to the support system that so many people with cancer rely on. I'm proud of all of you.

Finally, thank you to the readers for buying this anthology, and for supporting this charity and the talented authors who have given up their time to weave words and write stories for your pleasure. I hope you'll enjoy them as much as I have.

Macmillan are there to do whatever it takes to support people living with cancer, but they can't do it without your support, so thank you. I can say, hand on heart, they did just that for my family and continue to do that for so many others.

All my love,
Danny xoxo

Burning For Us
by Amy Davies

Chapter One

APRIL

After slicing up the last of the watermelon, I place the plate on the kitchen table, along with the other plates and bowls for breakfast this morning. I know to some it may seem like much—to have pancakes, freshly cut fruit, pop tarts and even bacon every morning—but my kids deserve the best.

They are my life, my world, my air.

Picking up my coffee mug, I walk over to the bottom of the stairs and call up.

"NELL. LEO. Get a move on; breakfast is on the table."

I hear them scatter, then smile, moving back over to the kitchen counter to top up my coffee. Leaning back, my two kids step into the room smiling and looking hungry. Both of them have always had a great appetite.

"Mom, this looks yummy," Leo says as he sits on his chair.

"Thank you, baby," I reply to my nine year old.

Nell, my darling twelve year old, rolls her eyes, as she

slips some watermelon onto her plate while Leo piles on the pancakes and bacon.

"Even though he's annoying, he's right. This looks great, Mom." I wink at her with a smile.

While the kids dig in, I scroll through my very limited social media. I only have it to keep up to date on my friends from high school and college. I smile when I see their careers, achievements, and families.

I love seeing them smiling and being happy.

I had all of that once. The husband who loved me, the kids who made us complete. The two story house with the front and back garden, and the white picket fence.

Then our world came crumbling down.

One day, Kent, my husband, wasn't feeling very well; headaches, achy muscles. Then he passed out at work and got rushed to hospital, where after hours of tests and waiting, we were told he had lung cancer. It was aggressive, and it was already spreading.

Within months, Kent was bedridden, and within two months after that, he passed in his sleep, with his kids and family surrounding him. Some didn't agree with Nell and Leo being with him, but we felt they deserved to see their dad to the end.

That was four years ago.

It was hard for me for months after. Hell, it's still hard for me on some days, but I stay strong for the kids, and for me too. I know that if I let myself crumble, then I will never piece myself back together.

Me and the kids moved back to Hope Falls a month after Kent passed. I sold everything we had, except the house. I let a young family rent it at a very low rate. They needed a place to build a family without the added struggle of money for rent or a mortgage. I can only hope that they build as many memories as we did in that house.

When Kent's life insurance came through, I almost had a heart attack and got buried next to him. Let's just say that I don't have to work a day in my life again. He made sure that myself and the kids were set for life, with zero struggles. That's why I wanted to pay it forward with the young family.

Everyone has to have hope that one day, they find some solace; they get that helping hand, that simple smile that changes the world for them.

Kent was my everything. He wasn't my first love, but Kent had my heart just as much. They say you can't love two people the same. Well, I did. Still do, to some level.

Thinking of my first love, I know that today will be a challenge to get through. The man who owned my heart first is back in town. When I heard he was moving back, my heartrate became fast, and I don't think it has slowed.

This man was my first everything, and I mean everything. We were high school sweethearts; the one couple everyone thought would get married, have kids, and grow old together. Then one night, a barn caught fire at one of the farms on the outskirts of town.

It was that night that he caught the firebug. He wanted to do more, help more people. Have that rush of adrenaline that Hope Falls couldn't give him.

After being together most of my teenage life, he broke my heart, telling me that he was leaving for Boston. He needed more of the rush, and our sleepy town couldn't give him that. He wanted bigger, better.

So after a kiss on the cheek, he left and never looked back.

I was like a zombie for weeks, even months after. Even

his family was shocked that he left me, but they also had to stand by his decision. Though they still supported me. I still see them every day. Well, I kind of have to since his little 'oops' sister is the same age as Nell, and they are besties.

When I moved back home, I couldn't have asked for a better support system, that included the people of the town.

Now he is back. After almost fifteen years, I'm going to see my first love, and I'm not entirely sure how I feel about that. It will be strange seeing him, especially since he has never come back to Hope Falls since he left. His sister told me that he refused to return home because it held too many painful memories.

Well, hell, buddy, we all hold painful memories, but unlike you, most own up to them.

Today is the day I meet the new Fire Chief of Hope Falls.

Today is the day I see him again.

Ezra Hale.

Chapter Two

EZRA

The buzzing of my alarm goes off, dragging me from sleep. Pulling me from a dream about the past. Groaning, I scrub my hands over my face and get out of bed, stretching my back.

Looking over my shoulder, I chuckle at the rumbling snores coming from my border collie, Barnaby. He's a rescue dog. We got called to a house fire where the elderly couple didn't make it. He was only three months old at the time they adopted him.

I took him in, and he has been my sidekick ever since.

Moving into my bathroom, I turn the shower on, letting the water heat up before I climb in. Looking in the mirror, I check out the bruise that was my going away present from the lovely fire starters of Boston.

During my last shift, my house was called to a fire at a rundown strip mall. The fire destroyed four of the stores. Hell, it almost took me with it. The roof caved in, just as we pushed through the back exit. I caught a chunk of wood to the left side of my body, my collarbone and neck taking the brunt. Nothing broke, just bruised, thank fuck.

I jump in the shower, have a wash, then hop out. Wrapping a towel around my waist, I stand in front of the vanity again to trim my beard. I never used to have one, but having facial hair not only keeps my face warm on the cold days in Boston, but it also brings the ladies.

I get that done, then move into my bedroom and slip on a plain navy t-shirt and some jeans. Once my Chucks are on, I go downstairs, with Barnaby in tow.

His claws clatter against the hardwood flooring I have throughout the downstairs. When I bought this house, it was the back side of the property and the garden that enticed me. When the confirmation email came through that I was the new Fire Chief, I had my sister, Donya, to help me find a place, and this is what we found.

Flicking on the coffee machine, I fix Barnaby's breakfast, before making myself some pancakes.

Watching the smooth mixture in the pan heat up, turning a golden brown, I flash back to my past, when I was last in Hope Falls.

It was the time when I was always over her house for breakfast before we walked to school, or we rode on my motorcycle. Her parents hated the bike, but they trusted me.

With her arms wrapped round my waist, I felt like the king of the world. No fucker could touch me. I had the girl guys wanted; the girl other girls envied because she was so sweet and kind and willing to help anyone out.

It took one night to blow it all to hell. To break both our hearts.

It left us both in misery, but in my heart, I believed it was the right thing to do.

HOPE

The fire out at the old Maynard barn, where I stepped in to help the local firehouse put the fire out, changed me. I helped handle the equipment, even held the hose. I was eighteen and watching this building burn to the ground, the flash of orange and yellow filling the sky, mixed with black smoke–and I knew what I was going to do with my life.

I was filled with adrenaline; the rush flooded my veins. It stuck with me for days after.

I started looking into what I needed to do, even spoke to the Fire Chief at the time, Chief Schmidt. He gave me all the information needed, and I started the ball rolling. Within weeks, I was expected into the academy and had the painful task of breaking my girl's heart.

The night I told her, we had just made love. It was bittersweet because I knew it would be the last time I got to touch her, to kiss her.

But my heart was with the flames.

The next day, I left, pushing the images of her crying out of my head.

I've had to do that for close to fifteen years. Even when I was with someone else, I would picture her. Her face would haunt me in my sleep. I would even smell her on occasion, and it would send me into a spiral of women and whiskey.

I hated thinking about her with other men; having a life that didn't include me. When my family came to visit, they weren't allowed to speak her name. I wanted to know nothing about her. I wasn't prepared for my heart to crack open any more than it was, so they kept her name out of their mouths.

I knew I had no right to feel all the hate and pain, because I was the one who left her, but in my heart, I knew it should have been me who gave her the special moments of her life.

I shake off my thoughts. I need to get a coffee and make my way to the firehouse to get some paperwork finalized before I start work on Sunday night.

Tapping my thigh, I call Barnaby.

"Come on, bud. Let's go. Might as well get this over with."

Knowing I need to face her again, I get Barnaby clicked into his harness in my truck, then pull away from my house. I turn the radio up and listen to some classic rock on my drive.

I park outside the bakery, the one everyone goes to for their morning coffee and pastry. Something to get you in a wicked good mood to start the day.

Climbing out of my truck, I help Barnaby down, then turn to look at the large, elegant sign spread across the building's two front windows.

'*Sweet Hope*'

My heart is going a mile a minute. My palms are sweating like I'm about to step into my first fire.

Licking my lips, I pull in a deep breath, hoping the fresh air gives me the strength and hope to survive seeing her again.

My first love. April Bennet.

Chapter Three

APRIL

Smiling at the gentleman I just served, I go into the back to check on the fresh batch of bagels. We sell out of them like they're going out of fashion.

When I started working here at Sweet Hope, which is owned by my aunt and uncle, Carrie and Vance, they helped me and the kids get settled back in. They love babysitting. So the least I could do was work at the coffee shop when one of the girls had to leave for college out of state.

It helps pass the time, and all the money they pay me because they refused to let me work for free, I donate to a charity that helps spouses who have lost a loved one to cancer.

Pulling the tray out of the oven, I breathe in the deep, heavenly smell of the cinnamon and apple bagels people love so much.

Placing the fresh batch on the counter, I let them cool before I take them out front. Stepping over to the fridge, I remove the lemon bars that are also a huge hit.

I add the white readymade citrus icing, then the little lined pattern of the yellow icing. Picking them up, the image of Ezra pops into my head. He used to love my lemon bars.

Placing the tray back down, I flatten my palms on the counter and close my eyes, dropping my chin to my chest and breathing in a deep breath. I know that at some point, I'm going to see him. No doubt today, because Carrie asked him to stop in for the treats for the firehouse.

Pulling my big girl panties up, I nod and straighten my shoulders.

"I can do this. This man can't get to me again. I mean, I bet he looks hotter—you know, looks better with age," I mutter to myself.

"Talking to yourself again, I see," comes a voice.

I yelp, turning my head with a glare, I look to my uncle.

"That was mean, you know."

He chuckles, stepping into the kitchen. Coming to my side, he kisses the top of my head, because yes, he towers over me. Crossing his arms, he looks at me, his soft smile in place on his delicious mouth.

"What?"

"You know what." I shrug at his reply, smoothing my finger over the marble pattern on the countertop. "You can't avoid him forever. You know that, right? He's here to stay. Taking on the Fire Chief position is a huge commitment."

I nod, knowing what he's saying is true.

"Let me get those. You make me one of your special coffees." He winks at me.

Shaking my head, I walk out in front of him. The special coffee he's talking about is a simple black coffee with some cinnamon added.

HOPE

With my back to the room, I make his coffee in his favorite Harry Potter Slytherin mug. He's as mad about Harry Potter as Nell is. Adding some cinnamon, I stir, making sure it's fully dissolved.

I set that aside and pull my mug down, one that says, 'I'm a bookaholic and I regret nothing.'

After making my coffee just the way I like it, I turn to hand my uncle his—only to let out a little yelp. I jump nearly an inch off the floor when I see Ezra standing by the counter.

My first thought is damn, he looks handsome. Ruggedly handsome.

He gives me one of his cocky smirks, and my heckles shoot up. He doesn't get to smirk at me like that anymore.

"Hey, Blossom," he greets. I hear a gasp but keep my eyes fixed on him.

"Chief." I calm my breathing, before setting the mug behind me and turning back to face him. "Also, don't call me that."

The smile drops from his face, before he quickly recovers from my scolding.

"Still feisty as ever, I see."

"What can I get you?" I go into professional mode, not wanting to be in any other mode with him.

Nope. Not happening. Even though he is looking damn fine, with his neatly trimmed beard and muscles. He's bigger than he was when we were eighteen. He definitely grew up.

I have no doubt the ladies in Boston loved him strutting around in his fire gear.

"They did actually." I blink and look at him.

"What?" I ask, frowning.

Giggling sounds to the right, and I look over, seeing my aunty and her friend.

"You spoke out loud, honey," my aunty tells me.

My cheeks heat up, my skin turning red no doubt. Damnit.

Shaking it off and completely ignoring what I just did, I look to the man who makes my heart race, my stomach tighten, and causes a layer of guilt to settle over me. I know it's not his fault, but this is what he makes me feel.

Ezra has always been able to make me feel things I'm not ready for. Even when we were younger, he wanted to take the next step, but I was cautious, until we talked and decided it was the best thing to do, and I never regretted that—until the day he left me.

"What can I get you, Chief? You came into a coffee shop, wanting coffee, I presume. So what can I do to you—I mean, do *for* you?" I keep my eyes focused on his, in a way daring him to call me out on what I just said.

I hear giggles and some murmurs, but I focus on him, not giving them the satisfaction of knowing I'm flustered to Hell and back right now.

"I will have your famous black coffee, please," he asks.

"No can do. That's for Uncle Vance only. Pick again." I fold my arms, popping my hip, even though he can't see it because of the counter height.

Ezra leans forward, resting his palms on the countertop. My breath hitches at the sudden closeness, and it gets me thinking about expanding the worktop, to keep people further away.

"I remember you giving me anything I wanted." He smirks at me.

Now is the time to shut this *cocky* guy down. He was always this cocky, and in high school, I loved it; his swagger, his confidence... Who the hell am I kidding, I like it now. But I push down how my body is responding to him being in my space.

"And I remember you walking away. Coffee or not?" The smirk drops from his face. The room has gone deathly silent.

I may have won this battle, but I know winning the war is far from over.

Ezra orders his coffee. I get to it quick-sharp, so he can get out of my atmosphere. I need to breathe, and not breathe him in, because he smells as good as he did back in the day.

Sliding his coffee over to him, he goes to pull his wallet out, but my uncle stops him.

"The firehouse don't pay here, man."

Ezra says nothing. He looks at my uncle, giving him a nod, then he brings his gaze back to me.

"It was good seeing you, April."

I nod, saying nothing, and watch him leave.

As soon as the door closes behind him, I sag against the counter, letting out the breath I was holding.

It's going to be tough with him around here, but I'm a strong woman. I can do it.

Right?

Chapter Four

EZRA

Parking my truck outside my parents' house, I shut off the engine, before climbing out, calling to Barnaby to follow. He leaps down, then rushes to the front door. It opens, and my father is standing there, smiling. Bending down, he makes a fuss of the attention-seeking whore of a dog before even looking at me.

"Wow, don't I feel the love today. First April, now you," I jest.

My dad smiles as he looks up at me.

"Oh, come on, you get enough attention from the ladies, so don't act like you're deprived of it, son." He grins, pulling me in for a hug.

"Get in here, you two. Dinner will go cold," my mom bellows from the kitchen.

"Like her food would ever go cold. She has every damned piece of machinery known to a professional kitchen. Believe me, I know, so does my bank account." He winks.

HOPE

"EZRA," my baby sister screeches as she runs into the room.

She throws herself at me. I catch her and hug her tight. Inara is the 'oops' baby. Mom and Dad had a shock when they fell pregnant with her, since I'm thirty-three, Donya is twenty-nine, and Inara is only twelve.

It was a high-risk pregnancy, but my mom is one tough cookie.

"How is my sweet girl? School okay?"

She nods vigorously. "Yeah. I love school. Nell and I are going camping at the start of summer. We will have our own tent, sleeping bags, and goodies," she says, the last part quietly.

I've heard her talk about Nell before, but my parents always cut the conversation off.

"Who is Nell?"

"Come on, you two," my dad calls, and I groan, knowing they don't want me to know who the hell this Nell kid is.

We sit and eat, talking about Boston, Inara's schooling, and how Donya and her job is going. My parents explain how they are looking to expand the family business profile. In Hope Falls, we own the convenience store, the gas station, the bar and a hardware store.

The family may have more money than most in town, but we never throw it around. My parents are all about Hope Falls, about creating jobs, keeping the townspeople in the green and happy. We bring in a lot of tourists, so we need to keep the place looking lively and peaceful.

"So I saw April today," I blurt out.

No one says anything. I look to Inara, who is staring down at her phone, no doubt talking to this Nell girl.

"Why do you all cut me off when I bring up Nell?"

Inara gasps, her head snapping up, her wide eyes locked

on me.

I look to my family and cock an eyebrow.

"Tell me what I'm missing. I'm back to stay now; I need to know things. Does this have anything to do with April?"

"The thing is, son, you told us not to talk about her around you."

"Ez, brother, you hated it when I spoke her name."

I sigh and sink back into my chair, nodding. "I know, but now I'm back. I need to know everything. Give me the cliff notes at least."

Donya shifts uncomfortably. Dad just looks at me, then nods.

"Inara, go to your room, please?"

"Yes, Ma'am." With that, my baby sister leaves.

I track my sister's steps. As soon as she's out of the room, I bring my gaze back to my parents.

"Talk."

"Before I start, I need you to understand this was on your order, Ezra. You were so damned adamant that we not talk about April. You cannot get pissed, hurt, or angry at us. Do you hear me, son?" My father's voice holds a firm tone, so I know he's serious.

I also know he's right. It was my choice to keep her out of my life, because I knew it would hurt too much. Seeing the looks on their faces right now, I know they pity me, but I also know how much this is going to hurt and make me angry.

"You left. April went to college. While there, she met Kent." I nod, my gut tightening. "They dated and fell in love. A few years later, once they got college out of the way, and got really good jobs, they got married."

It's like I've been sucker punched in the stomach. The wind is knocked out of me. My head and heart are trying to catch up with this piece of information. I look down at the table, tracing the tablecloth pattern with my eyes, trying to regain some control.

They have gone quiet, but I want this over with.

"Go on," I state, looking back to my family.

"Oh, Ezra. I know this is painful, but you do need to hear this. We want it to come from us, rather than you being caught off-guard while in town," my mom says softly. I nod.

"A few years after they got married, April got pregnant." I see my father's eyes flick over to the door Inara exited. And it dawns on me, like a ton of bricks.

Not only did the first woman I ever loved get pregnant by another guy, said child is close to my family.

"Nell," is all I say.

"Yeah." My father nods. "They are best friends; non-biological-sisters, they say." I see a ghost of a smile on his mouth.

I nod. "Good. I'm glad she has a friend she's close to. Any more?"

They all nod. I see Donya has tears in her eyes.

"When Nell was three, April fell pregnant again. Her and Kent had a baby boy, Leopold."

My chest tightens around my lungs, my stomach knots, and I think I'm going to suffocate, or puke.

My body goes hot and cold at the vision of April with another man, wearing his ring, carrying his babies.

I did this.

I did this to us.

It should have been my ring, my babies.

I get to my feet, suddenly the room closing in on me.

My father calls my name. Stumbling over to the patio, I step out, dragging big gulps of air into my lungs to help the tightening ease. Resting my hands on the wooden railing, I drop my chin to my chest, close my eyes, and breathe in deeply.

I fucked it all up.

I threw her away and another man caught her. Supported her. Gave her everything she wanted.

"Son." Opening my eyes, I turn and lean against the wall.

My mom and sister have joined us.

"I lost her," I choke out as tears build. "I threw away the best thing that ever happened to me."

"No, you did what you thought was right, Ezra. Was she hurt? Yes, but April made a life for herself. She had to, son."

"Is she happy with him?" I look to my parents and sister. They all share a look, having a silent conversation. "What?"

"When Nell was Nine, and Leo was five, Kent passed away, honey."

"What?" I reply to my mom's statement. "How?"

It's like a ton of cement has been dumped on me again. My body feels heavy with emotion.

"Cancer. It took him hard and fast," Dad explains.

I think back to all the times they came to visit me, and they never said a thing, then I remember the promise I made them make.

"That week you came and stayed the weekend with me, you were all sullen. I even caught Inara crying on the back deck. That was when Kent died, wasn't it?"

"It was," is all my mom says.

That made the night shift in a direction I didn't see coming. I spend the rest of the night at home, in a dark room, thinking about my past and future. Maybe, just maybe, with a little hope, we can find a new ending.

Chapter Five

APRIL

Smiling, I hand over the white paper bag containing the lady's order.

"Thank you. Please, spread the word that Sweet Hope has some new treats on sale." The lady smiles at me, then walks away.

I step over to the side, taking a drink of my water. As I scan the area, I see Ezra, in all his glory. He is wearing black boots, navy cargo pants, and a navy crew neck t-shirt with the firehouse logo on the breast. The material sculpts to his upper body.

I lick my lips, watching as he talks to some kids that are buzzing with excitement over the firetrucks.

Like he can sense someone watching him, Ezra looks around, his gaze landing on mine. His lips quirk into a sexy smirk that I love seeing on his handsome face. My body heats up at being caught staring at him. I mean, who wouldn't? He's one delicious man to look at.

Since losing Kent, I haven't once looked at a man like I'm looking at Ezra right now. It always made me feel guilty; moving on while Kent can't. He lost his fight to breathe on this earth, so I always had it in my head that I should be happy that I had his love for as long as I did, and he gave me two wonderful children I love and adore.

Ezra winks at me. Oh boy. My cheeks heat up, and like he can see the reaction he's causing, he chuckles, before turning his attention back to the kids in front of him.

Damn it all to the clouds and back. This man is making me feel things I'm not sure I'm ready to feel. I know Kent told me he didn't want me to be lonely, but can I move on with Ezra?

My first love. My first everything.

Wouldn't that be a betrayal on Kent's memory?

Shaking away my thoughts, I get back to it. Today is about raising as much money as we can, so the town can help out the many charities we have selected this year.

It doesn't take long for Nell and Leo to come back to the tent, bouncing with excitement.

"Mom, Inara told me her brother is letting people sit in the firetruck. Can I take Leo over? He would love it." Nell bounces on her toes.

I smile at her excitement and love how innocent she looks, how happy and free.

"Yeah, come on, Mom, let me show them the truck," comes Ezra's voice.

My gaze moves over to him, to see him smiling wide at me. He seems so carefree, his eyes bright, his smile wide. It was one of the things I loved about him; his smile—hell, his mouth in general. Now add in the sexy beard and his hotness level has gone up tenfold.

"Please, please," Leo chants, jumping up and down.

HOPE

Ezra keeps smiling at me, like the heartache he caused is something of the past. And in some cases, it really is. He moved on and so did I. Seeing him here after all this time, it makes me think that our painful history has to be left behind.

His smile is infectious, and I nod.

"Fine. But you listen to Chief Hale, okay?"

Both of my kids nod before looking up at Ezra. He looks down at them, grinning.

"Go and tell Paddy I sent you over. He'll give you the good treats. Let me speak to your mom for a second and I'll catch up with you guys." They nod and run off.

Ezra nods to the end of our tent. I walk over to meet him and step out of the tent.

"Hey," he says.

I lick my lips. "Hi." Damn, why do I feel like a teenage girl again?

"They seem like good kids," he states, and pride hits me in the chest.

This man, who I thought I would have kids with, praising me for my own kids, is heartwarming.

"They are. The best," is all say.

An awkward silence settles between us.

"Listen, I—" he says.

"What can I—" I say.

We both laugh and smile at each other. His smile drops, his eyes soften, and I see lust looking back at me. My heart speeds up, my body becoming aware of how close he's standing in front of me. I look down at the floor to break the intense connection between us.

Fingers are placed under my chin. Bringing my head up so I can meet his gaze, his other hand gently tucks a few strands of hair behind my ear. The small contact of his fingers makes me shiver.

I lick my lips, and his eyes drop to the little movement. I swear I hear him moan, but surely I'm hearing things. Ezra takes a minor step forward, bringing him even closer to me.

He lowers his head, bringing his nose to the crook of my neck, and inhales, and this time, the groan he lets out is clear as a blue summers sky.

"Damn, you still smell good. Like sugar and cherry blossoms." His voice has gone deeper, sexier, which makes me shiver.

"Ezra," I pant.

"Fucking love you saying my name like that, Blossom." He kisses my cheek, letting his lips linger for a little longer than decency would allow, before stepping back.

With a grin on his face, he speaks. "I'd better go and see what your two munchkins are doing to my firetruck. Later, babe." With a wink, he leaves.

I lean against the tent's support pole, panting like a dog in heat. Reaching to the side, I find one of our flyers and use it to fan my face. Damn, that man is fine.

It's been years since anyone has called me 'babe' or 'baby.' Kent always called me 'honey' or 'sweetheart.'

I'm acting like a teenage girl gushing over her high school crush, except Ezra was my high school crush and my boyfriend. He was my whole teenage world.

My gaze lands on him and my kids. They are all laughing, smiling. Nell and Leo look so happy as Ezra shows them the lights and sirens. I watch as he shows them all the different buttons.

He jumps down from the truck, turning to look at me, and he finds me watching him. Throwing me a wink, I shake my head at his cockiness with a smile, which makes his grin wider.

Moving back into the tent, I get back to work; which is why I'm here, after all, not to eye-fuck old boyfriends. Today is about raising money for people who need that little extra help.

Chapter Six

EZRA

Who would have thought I would be here, showing my ex-girlfriend's kids the way around a firetruck. The one woman I thought I would have my own children with.

She has done an amazing job with Nell and Leo. They are kind, respectful, and well mannered.

I climb down off the truck and let them hit the buttons. The engine is off, so they can't do any damage. I look over to the tent where I know April is helping to sell the sweet treats she makes with her aunt.

She's watching me, no doubt making sure her kids are safe with me. I wink at her, and one of her beautiful smiles graces her face. She shakes her head and turns back to the customers.

Images of a very pregnant April gets me thinking that I could have that with her. Would she be opposed to starting something new with me?

I never thought I would want to settle down, especially

after I ruined things with her, but now, knowing that I have a second chance, I have to take it and run. But I know I have to tread carefully, because her husband has only been gone for four years.

Some people take years and years to grieve and move on. But if I know April and the people she allows in her life, I know her husband would want her to move on; to have a father figure in his kids' life; and to keep his woman safe. I know I would.

I want April. I want to be in Nell and Leo's life. It's crazy how much your life can take a new direction after learning some new information. When I was informed I was coming back to Hope Falls, I knew that if I saw April and she was single, I would try again; that seeing her would make all my suppressed feelings break free, and just that happened.

Time to do what I should have done years ago.

Chapter Seven

APRIL

I flop down on the sofa and sink into the cushions, careful not to spill the glass of wine I have in my hand. I take a sip, before turning my head to look at my bestie of many, many years; so many that I don't want to think about it because it makes me feel old.

"You know I'm right," she says in a condescending tone.

Right before I was forced to refill my glass, thanks to her bestie intervention, she was telling me that Kent would want me to find love again. He told the kids he had all the hope in his heart that I would find the right man for me, someone I trust with not only my life, but theirs.

When we left the town festival two days ago, Nell and Leo didn't stop talking about Ezra; how he was so cool, and didn't speak down to them, and talked to them like they were grown-ups. Their words, not mine.

Even now, two days later, when I dropped them off at Carrie and Vance's house, they were still rambling on. It seems my ex-boyfriend has made a lasting impression on my kids.

Thinking about Ezra making an impression on the kids, it reminds me of one of the last things Kent said to me.

"I want you to love again. Your heart is so full of love and loyalty that it needs to be spread around. Do that for me. Let other people feel the same love that you shared with me. Fix what was once broken. Leave impressions on those around you. Make amends, honey."

His words have always floated around my head over the years. He passed later that night, with me and the kids with him.

Thinking of Kent's words and Ezra coming back into my life, it's like he knew that one day, Ezra would come home.

"I know, but it's hard, Evie," I reply to my best friend.

"You will always love Kent. It isn't like you're just going to forget him, April. Those two kids are a sweet reminder of him every single day. You are still young, and you can find love again."

I nod, because I know what she's saying is true. Seeing Ezra for the first time in so many years has made my feelings for him surface. Would I have felt the same if Kent was still alive? Maybe, but I never would have acted on it, and I know Ezra would never have pursued me.

I take another sip of my drink, looking at the picture of the four of us that is sitting on the fireplace. We took the kids to a cabin near a lake, and we had the best week ever. They played in the water, met the family next door. It was a break we needed. Little did we know it would be our last family vacation.

We sit and talk over amazing memories of our pasts; school life and love. Evie is married to one of the guys who works with Ezra. They are also high school sweethearts who actually went the full hog. Married, kids, a dog, and a lovely house with a white picket fence.

I had all of that with Kent. Could I have it again with Ezra?

It's easy to think we could have lasted, but everyone grows up. They develop as the years pass. For all I know, Ezra could have stayed and grown to resent me over time because he didn't become a big city firefighter.

Everything happens for a reason. That is one thing I live by.

There are so many emotions in the world that we need to embrace them, let it all out. Tucking things away is toxic. It will fester and build until there is no going back.

Maybe it's time to let my feelings for Ezra back out. See what happens. Evie is right, I am young enough to love again. My kids deserve all the love in the world, so maybe more from Ezra, who clearly adores them even after only a few hours, would be a good thing.

Smiling to myself, I look to my friend, who is smiling back at me like she knows what I'm thinking.

Nudging her shoulder against mine, her smile widens.

"Go get him, tiger."

Oh, I plan to. But I will go into this with a guarded heart. I need to protect myself as well as my kids.

Chapter Eight

EZRA

Saving the form I was just working on, I sit back in my chair, stretching my aching back. That's what you get when you do all the paperwork in one go, rather than doing them as they come in. Lesson learned.

Muffled voices come from the floor below me. Getting out of my chair, I stand and walk out of my office, then head down the short hall that leads into our kitchen area. I bypass the large wooden table, leaning over the railing to see our visitor.

My heart jumps when I see who is here, in my firehouse. A smile crosses my face as I skip down the two flights of stairs.

There, in all her prettiness, in a floral dress and summery wedges girls love to wear, her hair perfectly curled, her make-up light, is April, the woman of my dreams.

Jimmy is standing too close for my liking. They're both

smiling at each other like they're overly familiar, and I fucking hate it.

No fucker is getting with April, except me.

I know she's single, thanks to Inara getting me the information from Nell. These kids are sneaky as hell these days.

I hit the bottom step, and April looks over Jimmy's shoulder. The smile she was giving him, brightens, and holy shit... My heart skips a beat. The smile she was giving him was friendly, but the one she's giving me means so much fucking more.

"Morning," her sweet voice greets me.

I can't help myself. I step closer to her, my hand touching her hip, as I lean in and kiss the corner of her mouth in my own greeting.

"Morning, beautiful."

A delicious blush covers her cheeks, making my dick take notice in my work pants.

"My aunt asked me to drop these off for you and the guys." It's then I see she's holding a large container filled with cookies and pastries.

"Jimmy, take them to the kitchen."

"Aw, come on, Chief, it's not every day a beautiful woman brings me treats."

"And today is still not your day. Move it," I say in a harsher tone. The smile on his face widens, with a hint of cheekiness.

"But she loves me tasting her treats, don't you, April?" He winks at her. "I even got an extra sample too."

"Fucking move, Jimmy. I swear, if you don't stop flirting with my woman, you will be on washing the trucks and changing out the equipment for a month." This time, I snarl at him.

"Jimmy, behave." April giggles. Her hand rests on my chest, and I look down at the contact, loving the warmth coming from her.

Moving my gaze back to her, I see her smile is wide again. Her eyes dance with mischief. Nudging her head to Jimmy, she says, "You know that Jimmy crushed on my bestie in school, Evie?" I nod.

"Yeah. You two were as thick as thieves, but Jimmy was the nerdy guy who could speak to girls." Looking at him now, you would never have guessed.

He's built, packed full of muscles. He got a growth spirt and is as tall as my six-foot-two.

"Well, after you left, someone decided to join the gym and start running, and got Evie's attention," April explains.

I look to Jimmy, who is smiling like a loon. He winks at April before looking to me.

"I married Evie, Chief. Got myself a stunner of a wife and two adorable babies to go with it."

My eyes bug out. How the hell didn't anyone say anything? Fuck, how the hell hadn't I clicked on when the guys were talking about their families?

I was so focused on April that I missed vital information. Damn it.

"You're shitting me?" He shakes his head.

"Nope. April is our kids' Godmother, and we are the same to her two hellions."

"Hey, I take offense to that, you cheeky shit." April hits him on the stomach, making me laugh. He bends over for dramatic effect before looking up at me.

"Damn, Chief, restrain your woman."

Hearing him call her my woman sends my heart racing and my dick throbbing.

It has been too fucking long since I've been inside a woman, and even longer since I've been inside April.

"Don't say shit about my kids then." She pats him on the head, then takes my hand, leading me away.

I look over my shoulder at Jimmy, and he winks at me. Shaking my head at him, I flip him off, making sure April doesn't see it.

We walk down to my office, still holding hands. My skin prickles with anticipation at what she wants. I know what I want. I can only hope her wants and needs are the same as mine.

Even though I have only been home for a very short time, I know I need April back in my life. Her two kids are an added bonus. I will never try to take the place of Kent. He is their dad and always will be, but I hope they will accept me in their mother's life, and possibly give them another brother or sister.

We get to my office, and April walks in and leans against my desk. She looks like a fucking wet dream come true. After locking the door behind me, I walk over to the double windows, closing the blinds.

Turning back to April, she licks her lips and watches me as I step closer to her, bridging the gap that has been too big for far too long.

Taking the last step, I place my feet on the outside of hers, caging her in. To my surprise, her hands come up to rest on my hips, her thumbs brushing back and forth over my work uniform. The heat from her palms sears through the material.

"Why does it feel like no time has passed between us?" Her voice is soft, showing her emotions.

Bringing my hands up to her face, I cup her jaw, my thumbs moving in the same motion as hers. Her eyes focus on me, and it's like I can see right into her soul. See the girl I fell in love with all those years ago shining back. I see adoration, but I also see pain and sorrow. Uncertainty, yet lust.

"I know how you feel. When I came back to town, I was dreading seeing you with another guy, and I knew that it was very likely you was with someone else."

Her eyes go wide. "You didn't know I got married? Or had Nell and Leo?" I shake my head.

"No." I sigh. "I made my family promise not to talk about you. I didn't want to hear of you being with someone else. And before you freak out on me, I know it was my fault. I was the one who left."

"Oh, Ezra." April stands, making me take a small step back before I drag her against me.

"I'm an idiot, I know. I'm so sorry about Kent."

"Thank you. I loved him, Ezra. That's one thing you need to understand. He will always be part of my life. He's my kids' father," she says, and my heart grows for her exponentially.

"I would never ask you to forget him. You know I'm not that type of person, babe."

Unable to wait any longer, I lean in, taking her lips in a sweet, soft kiss. The ones she used to love me giving her, that always lead to us getting hot and heavy.

Her hands snake around my neck, holding me to her, and my arms go around her waist, one hand sliding down to cup her ass. Growling into her mouth, she giggles.

"Damn, I've missed that ass. And that giggle."

"We need to go slow, Ez. I'm worried how the kids will take me dating again." I smile wide at her words, making her frown then cock an eyebrow at me.

"What?"

"I'll tell you later. I'm about to start a new pattern of shifts, but I'm off Friday and Saturday. Let me take you on a date and we can talk more."

We make plans and she leaves, letting me get back to work when a call comes in.

Friday, she is mine. Hell, she is mine from today on.

Chapter Nine

APRIL

It's Friday night, and I'm a nervous wreck. Ezra is due to arrive in ten minutes, and my stomach feels like it's filled with a thousand butterflies. When he text me yesterday to arrange the date, he told me to dress snazzy because he was talking me to the next town over, to some fancy restaurant.

He knows I don't like overly fancy places, but he said we would go this one time.

So I went and got my hair done once I dropped the kids off at my parents' house, after a long talk with them about me going on a date with Ezra. They understand that he used to be my boyfriend before their dad and seem okay with me possibly dating him again.

I did inform them that Ezra would never replace their father, but he would want to be in their lives if we pursued this between us.

Thankfully, I waxed my lady parts a few days ago. I got

my nails done, all on the push from my mom and best friend.

It has been four years since I've been on a date, so all this pampering is making me nervous. I can only imagine the type of women Ezra dated in Boston. Models, slim, big-chested.

I still have my big boobs, but now I have hips, and some love handles, as Kent used to call them. He told me they were perfect, and my body was the most beautiful thing he had ever seen, because it was the body that carried, fed and protected his children.

Stepping over to the tall mirror, I give myself a once over. I take in the black dress that is off the shoulders, with long sleeves and a deep 'V' that gives a nice amount of cleavage. The material reaches just below my knees, with a split up the middle, but just a few inches. I slipped into a simple pair of black, heeled pumps.

I kept my hair down, just added some soft curls to it. My make-up is a little daker than I'm used to, but this is a date after all, and possibly the start to something new.

A knock on the door makes me almost jump out of my skin. Closing my eyes, I pull in a deep breath and reach for the door.

My breath hitches in my lungs as I take in the sight before me.

Ezra is dressed in brown shoes, navy pants and a matching blazer that fits him like a glove, and a white shirt with the top few buttons open. Damn, he looks damned fine. Boston gave him some fashion sense.

"Damn," I mutter under my breath. Ezra laughs, stepping forward.

"Shouldn't I be the one to say that?" He grins at me. "Fuck, baby. You look stunning. Ravishing. Do we really need to go out? I'm sure I can whip us up something to eat, then I can eat you."

By the time he's finished, he has me pinned against the wall, his lips on my neck, with me panting like a dog in heat.

This is what I have missed for four long years; intimate human contact.

But it has been so much longer longing for his touch. To feel his lips on my body again. For him to kiss me and make me come apart just like he did years go. The way he makes me feel beautiful.

"I'm okay with that," I pant, my fingers digging into his hair.

I hear him growl, before he kisses me one last time, then he pulls away. His eyes are dark, full of lust. I did this to him.

Biting my lip, Ezra moves in, slamming his mouth onto mine. His hands go around my body, cupping my butt, pulling me even closer to him as his erection presses into my stomach.

Damn, I forgot how big he was.

"I had hoped you would want me as much as I want you," he growls when he breaks the kiss.

"Even with the years apart, my body recognizes you, honey. I want you, like you wouldn't believe."

He nods, leaning in to kiss me again, before he takes my hand.

"Grab your purse and let's go. We're going to my place. Fuck the restaurant. I need to taste you and bury myself in something I have deprived myself of for so fucking long," he growls.

Damn, the sound makes my pussy weep with need. My panties are already soaked because of the kiss.

I pick up my purse, making sure everything I need is in there, then I'm locking the front door, being lead over to his truck. Ezra helps me in, because that's just the kind of man he is. With another kiss, he climbs in the driver's side, and we are off.

My body buzzes with sexual and nervous tension, but it's a welcome feeling. I want this. I just hope he doesn't hurt me again.

CHAPTER Ten

EZRA

The drive to my place is fucking torture. My dick is permanently marked with the pattern of my zipper. I'm throbbing in my pants, and I can't fucking wait to have my girl again. As soon as I pull up outside my house, I shut the engine off and rush out to help her out on her side.

I don't waste any time. As soon as I we are inside, I slam and lock the door. No fucker will be stopping me from burying my cock deep inside her pussy tonight.

"Fuck, you feel so good in my arms again, Blossom," I say to her, as I spin her around and unzip her dress, letting it pool at her feet. As April steps out, I kick off my shoes and strip down. April stands in front of me in a strapless black bra with matching panties.

Unclipping the bra, it falls to the floor. She shivers, looking over her shoulder at me, following me down as I drop to my knees. Hooking my fingers in the material of her panties, I pull them from her body.

She squeals in delight when I lay a kiss on her luscious ass. Getting to full height, I spin her again, pulling her to me, then we crash down on my bed. We have wasted enough time apart. There is no more waiting.

We kiss, hands roaming over each other, getting the feel of each other again. It's like we were never apart. I suck on the part of her neck that makes her mewl in pleasure. My hand latches on her tit, while my mouth bites and tugs at the other.

"Oh, God," she pants, arching into me more.

I smile against her, before moving down her body.

"I need to taste you, baby."

Spreading her thighs, I delve right in, lapping at her juicy pussy. Her flavor has changed, but she still tastes so fucking good. My dick throbs as I rub against the bed to get some relief, but I know it won't come.

Speaking of coming, I slide two fingers into her warm pussy, making April scream my name as she comes all over my face.

Not waiting for her to catch her breath, I move up her body, making sure to kiss and nip at her flesh on my way. Reaching over to the bedside table, I pull out a condom and roll the latex over my throbbing cock.

April goes up onto her elbows, smiling salaciously at me.

"Shit, that was so good. I forgot how good you are with your tongue." I grin back, before leaning down to kiss her again, letting her taste her climax on me.

Positioning my cock at her entrance, I slide in, making her gasp. My eyes practically roll into the back of my head from how tight she is.

"Fuck me, baby, you are tight."

"It's been a long time for me, Ez," she moans.

I look down at her, and we lock gazes as I move in and out of her.

This is what I have been missing for the last fifteen years. This right here. The love that is emanating from her, aimed at me... The adoration between us...

Her hands go to my face, holding me in place while I make love to her; rolling my hips, making sure to drag my pelvic bone over her clit. April gasps, her eyes going dark with lust.

"Yes. Don't stop. God, Ezra, I've missed you," she pants out.

I nod, before dropping my head to kiss her. Then I pull back because I want to see her face when she comes. It was one of the things I used to love doing, because she was never shy about her orgasms.

Before I know it, we're both panting heavily as our climaxes build.

"I'm going to come. Go harder," April cries out. So I listen.

Pulling out, I slam in, once, twice... then she's coming.

Like a glove made just for me, my cock gets sucked in as her muscles clamp down on my shaft. That tight feeling makes my balls explode, coming deep inside of her.

Holding myself off her, I lean down to kiss her lips. Her harsh pants push her air against my lips, but I take it all. We are both sweaty, but I don't give a fuck right now.

We're both where we belong. Where we should have always been.

"That was amazing," she pants as she lies next to me.

Pulling her closer, her leg moves over my thigh. I hook my hand behind her knee, holding her there.

"Hell yeah, it was. There is more to come, baby. We have so much time to make up."

She gives me a sad smile, then kisses me.

"We do. I may have found another love and had kids with him, but you, Ezra, will always be my first love. There was no stopping that. When Kent passed, I hoped I would find love again. Our future may have taken different paths, but we are here now, like this was how it was supposed to be all along."

Fuck me, she hit the nail on the head.

"I love you, April."

"I love you too, Ezra."

Who would have thought that when I moved back home, I would see the one woman who owned my heart, let alone have both our feelings of love resurface.

Like she said, our paths took a different turn, but we are here now. In each other's arms again.

Both ready to make a new life with each other, like we always planned.

Epilogue

APRIL

Today is my wedding day. Ezra asked me to marry him just a week after we got together. He stated that we had wasted enough time apart, and that we would marry in a month. As it turned out, it was the same date we had planned all those years go.

So it seemed fitting.

Nell dances around the dancefloor with Leo and Inara; the girls wearing matching dresses and Leo in a suit that matched Ezra's.

When it came to changing my name, we decided I would double barrel, because I still wanted to have the kids' surname in mine.

So as of today, I am April Mayberry-Hale.

Seeing the way my babies connected with Ezra was heartwarming. They clicked with him, and he with them. They all seemed to be on the understanding that he was allowed in their lives without taking over from their father.

I often hear them telling Ezra stories of their dad; the fun times they had with him before he passed.

Ezra also told them that they can do the fun things they did with their father, and they have also loved trying out new adventures with Ezra.

Bringing the glass to my lips, I sip the sparkling water, then look down at the ring on my left hand. Ezra did good, but he did confess that Donya helped him out. In all its sparkly glory, is my beautiful wedding ring.

The vintage daisy oval halo engagement ring is white gold and sits perfectly. Ezra has a white gold band with four small diamonds imbedded on the top, but when he goes back to work, he plans on wearing a silicone ring, or like Evie recommended, he could have a ring tattooed on his ring finger.

Arms slip around my waist, and I lean back into my new husband. One I plan on keeping until it's my time to leave this earth.

"I love you, wife." His voice is smooth and deep, making my lady parts quiver.

"I love you too, husband." I rest my hands over his, which rest on my currently flat stomach. I smile at the secret I'm about to tell him.

Turning in his arms, I kiss him. His hands find my butt, and mine go around his neck, toying with his hair.

"I have something to tell you." He cocks an eyebrow at my statement.

"Go on."

"What would you say if we added to our little family?" He frowns at first, making me smile at his confusion.

His eyes go wide, his eyebrows almost hitting his hairline as it registers what I just said.

"Are you fucking kidding me?" he gasps out.

"No. I'm pregnant. Eleven weeks."

"Fuck yeah." He kisses me. "God, I love you, April. You are mine until my last breath."

We kiss, knowing we are where we belong. The hope that I find someone to grow old with, was always in the stars.

I just didn't know who was in the stars with me.

The End

Also by
Amy Davies

Standalones

Let Me Love You

What Are The Chances

This Time Around

Defeating The Odds

Christmas at Paradise Meadow

The Phoenix Boys

Rafe

Ryder

Reeve

Castle Ink

Dex

Jay

Ivy

Unforgiven Riders MC

Claiming Mine

Protecting Mine

Taking Mine

Getting Mine

Keeping Mine

Reckless Angels MC

Twisted Steel

Santa's Naughty Helpers – Unwrapping Mine

Twisted Steel Second Edition: NOMAD

Twisted Steel Third Edition: Preacher

Rebel Hype

Creed - Heart Beats Anthology

Rugged Skulls MC

Magnum

Opal

Slide

Sarge

Rookie

Edge

Rugged Ink

Zeb

Lee

Rugged Skulls MC – Next generation

Royal

Finan

Riot: Road Wreckers MC #4

Fighting for Una: Royal Bastards MC

The Fairy Festival
by Arizona Tape

Chapter One

The distinct sweet scent of fairy pollen greeted me even before I got off the train. I breathed in deeply, savouring the lightly floral scent that mixed perfectly with the greasy air of fried food.

I couldn't believe I was actually here.

The Fairy Festival. The entire town was decorated with colourful flags and lanterns in preparation for the annual event. Children with large balloons followed their mothers and fathers around, chattering excitedly while eating fairy ice cream and candy.

"I'm so excited we're here!" Julie sighed dramatically. "I could actually die. I've been wanting to see fairies bloom forever."

I nodded, sharing the sentiment. It was a truly special event that wouldn't have been possible if the local conservations hadn't worked tirelessly to restore the cocoon fields so the fairies could hatch here.

Rashid and Larissa agreed too and the four of us started our walk to the town square were the festival was held. It was nice that I didn't have to go alone after Tina cancelled on me, crowds weren't really my thing and there was a big one here. The enthusiastic chatter of my classmates blended seamlessly with the general atmosphere of excitement and joy. I could feel it sitting in my chest too, the growing anticipation for this annual event.

Plenty of the roads were closed off to the public to ensure the emperor fairies growing in the surrounding fields weren't disturbed. That would truly be catastrophic. Luckily, most people were happy to oblige and enjoy their time at the festival. Drunken chatter surrounded us even though it was only just past noon but the sunny weather brought out people's best moods.

I briefly paused under a large advertising poster with a picture of a blooming fairy abandoning the flower it had claimed as its temporary host. The six wings shimmered slightly and its curly antenna gave it an elegant and inquisitive look.

"Why are you looking at the poster?" Rashid asked, encouraging me to keep walking. "You'll see the real thing tonight."

"But not from this close-up though," I rebuked. "I'm not that lucky."

He chortled as we caught up with the others. "You should use your luck to get into the internship you want. Which one is your first choice again?"

"The Griffin Sanctuary. I've loved that place since I was a kid and working with the unicorns would just be a dream come true."

"Yeah, you'll need that luck. That place is impossible to

get into unless you're from one of the all-star universities like Glyzen Hall or worse, Evergreen."

"Evergreen isn't that bad. The campus was amazing and they had some fantastic facilities. I wanted to go there." We passed a stall making fried doughnuts and the addictive smell of the sugar had my mouth watering.

"Well, I'm glad you're here," Rashid said, pulling me away from temptation. "Those snobs wouldn't have appreciated you."

"You're just bitter because your sister got in and you didn't," I teased.

"Touché." He chuckled. "Anyway, it doesn't matter, I'm happy at Ashway. Did you know our Zoology program is actually seventh-best in the country? And percentage-wise, over half the students that graduate from Ashway find jobs in relevant fields within five years. That's actually pretty high."

"When did you become a school rep? Chill, I'm already here, aren't I?"

Larissa called us, urging us to hurry so we didn't get separated. In a full crowd like this, it would be all too easy.

"Wow, it's really busy. I didn't realise this many people were interested in seeing the fairy bloom," I mused, scanning the sea of heads.

Rashid shrugged noncommittally, his thick eyebrows rising slightly. "I think a lot of people are here for the festival, not the fairies themselves."

"Probably," I agreed. "If people cared about the fairies, they wouldn't have gone almost extinct."

The festival came into sight, the rows of stalls and booths decorated with colourful flags and lanterns to match the emperor fairies.

"What shall we do first?" Rashid asked the group, rubbing his hands together like he was ready to tackle it all. "Food?"

"We've just had lunch," Larissa pointed out. "I think we should do stalls first so we don't waste all our budget on snacks."

Julie agreed enthusiastically. "I saw a stand with just plushies. I *need* one."

We all snickered at her comment and Rashid voiced the thing we all thought. "You and your plushies. Don't you have like a thousand already?"

"It's not collecting if I'm not constantly adding to it." Julie looked expectantly at me. "What do you want to do, Charlotte? Food or merch?"

"Food," I answered without hesitation. The various smells were already making my mouth water and I wanted to try all the local specialities. Who knew when I'd have the time or money to be back. If the repopulation efforts of the conservations in the area didn't work, there wouldn't be anything to come back to either.

"Guess we're splitting up," Rashid declared decisively. "Meet up back here in an hour or so?"

The other two girls nodded and flitted to the nearest stall that sold plushies.

I turned to my classmate. "What are we trying first?"

He sniffed the air demonstratively, a dopey grin stretching across his face. He gestured to a nearby food stall with a moderate queue selling fairy cakes. "That. Come on, Beaver."

I cringed. "Do you have to call me that?"

"What? It's a great last name."

It wasn't.

Not wanting to get into it, I shrugged and changed the topic to what we were going to order from the cake stand.

Ten minutes later, I bit into the lightest fluffiest confectionary I ever had. I felt slightly guilty ruining the delicate icing and decorations that depicted the six-winged emperor fairy but it was just too delicious.

Rashid practically inhaled his. "I could literally eat fifteen of those."

"Without throwing up?"

"I didn't say that."

We strolled past more booths, mostly ignoring the stalls selling trinkets and souvenirs. I spotted one of our professors hooking ducks and cheering when he won prizes. He was always chill in class and it was nice to see it wasn't an act. It wasn't a surprise to see him or some of our other lecturers here either. The Fairy Festival was renowned around the world and people travelled a long way to see the fairies bloom. Anyone interested in mythical creatures was here, all eager and desperate to see a fairy and get sprinkled by their magical dust.

Plenty of vendors were selling miniature pots of it to naive tourists but I had no doubt they were just filled with sawdust or commercial glitter. Real fairy dust was practically impossible to bottle and would certainly not be available in these quantities, not even in the largest bloom area of the country.

"I want winged dogs," Rashid announced, dragging me to a food truck that smelled like caramelised onions and greasy meat. The vendor was making the typical open-faced sandwiches at a rapid pace and the gleeful looks when someone took their first bite was the best kind of advertising he could've had.

We joined the queue and I checked my phone to see if I

had any new messages.

"Tina?" Rashid questioned, catching on to what I was doing.

"She said she was busy," I replied, forcing myself to smile as I put my phone away. "It's fine. She's just not an animal person so this probably wouldn't have been fun for her."

He gestured around. "It's a festival, what's not to like?"

"Well, yeah this part is fine, but the waiting for the fairies to bloom is kind of boring, I guess. Honestly, I'm not upset. I actually don't mind doing things without my girlfriend."

"Do you think it's boring?" he asked, eyebrows raised. "Cause I don't."

"No, me either." I scanned the menu list, trying not to cringe at the outrageous prices. I knew it was normal for festivals but it still hurt. I turned to Rashid. "What kind of winged dog are you getting?"

"Hmm, they all sound good so I don't know yet. Maybe the spicy one?"

"I think I'm going to take the one with triple cheese." I stared at the list, my thoughts snapping back to the previous topic. "Do you think it's weird that Tina doesn't care about animals? Like, at all?"

Rashid shrugged as he ordered his winged dog. "I don't know, I personally wouldn't want to be with someone who doesn't understand and appreciate what we do. But hey, love is more than shared interests, right?"

"Yes, true. And we do love each other, a lot." I handed the vendor my money and we moved along to pick up our food on the other side of the truck. There was no denying that I wished my girlfriend shared some of my enthusiasm for mythical creatures, but it was fine without. It was good to have our own interests, our own life.

"See, there you go," Rashid nodded, accepting the winged dogs and passing mine over to me. The savoury smells were delightful and despite being already quite full, I was determined to eat it all like a greedy caterpillar in honour of the fairy festival.

Chapter Two

After trying out every possible snack at the festival, Rashid and I desperately needed a break.

"I'm so full," I complained, barely able to remain upright on the picnic bench.

Next to me, Rashid released a pained gurgle. "Me too. I should not have eaten those pollen drops. That was just too much."

I groaned while pushing myself up. "We should find Larissa and Julie and go to the viewing arena so we'll have a good spot for when it gets dark."

He grumbled in agreement, huffing and puffing as he got up. He clutched his bulging stomach and sat back down. "It's too late for me. Save yourself."

"You're so dramatic." I pulled him up by his sleeve and pushed him in the direction of the tent we agreed to meet the others at. Even though it was still a couple of hours away from twilight, getting a good viewing spot in the middle of the predicted path of migration was important. The last thing I wanted was to come all this way and not get a proper view of the bloom.

Larissa and Julie were already waiting at the tent, the latter carrying a massive emperor fairy plushie. It even had the signature curly antenna and the six shiny wings it was renowned for.

"Wow, didn't have anything bigger?" I joked, gesturing to the newest addition of the group.

She beamed, her arms tightly clutched around its blue belly. "I won the jackpot from a stand, you better believe I was going to pick the biggest one they had."

Larissa chuckled, shaking her head in bemusement. "You should've seen her, she was like a woman possessed. Not going to lie, it was kind of freaky. She made a little kid cry."

I had no doubt. Julie was well-known for her competitive spirit, something everyone in our class was well aware of. It was no surprise that she had the best grades of us all in most classes. If anyone from our crappy university was getting into an internship in one of the top sanctuaries or zoos in the country, it was her.

We made it down to the village square where the arena was hosted. To my surprise, there was no queue and we skipped right to the ticket booth where Larissa took the lead. I couldn't hear the conversation from the back except Julie's fiery response.

"What do you mean we can't buy tickets?" she shrieked.

That got my attention. I shuffled closer, determined to figure out what was going on.

The man in the booth shot us an apologetic smile. "I'm sorry but we're already at capacity."

"How's that possible?" She gasped when a small group of guys with Evergreen sweaters stopped at the adjacent booth and were allowed in. "Hey, why do they get to go in?"

"Evergreen University reserved part of the arena for their students, they do that every year," the ticket guy explained. "Look, I'm really sorry but you should've got here sooner."

Rashid gently pried Julie away from the booth and with good reason. She looked like she was five seconds away from strangling the man with his own tie. Fuming, she ranted the whole way back to the picnic table.

"This is outrageous!" She kicked a bin, her chill demeanour from earlier completely gone. "I hate Evergreen! They're so effing pretentious."

Larissa sighed and shot us a helpless look. "What are we going to do now?"

"I don't know," I admitted, trying to mask my disappointment. If I'd known the viewing arena was so hard to get into, I'd have queued the moment we arrived. I didn't care about the festival, I just wanted to see the fairies.

"We should have an okay view from here too though," Rashid attempted, glancing worriedly at Julie. "The fairies will be visible from everywhere, we just won't be straight under it."

"That's so lame." A mischievous twinkle filled Julie's eyes. "I have a better idea."

I already had a bad feeling about this.

"You know where we'd have a great view of the bloom?" She gestured over her shoulder. "Up in the cocoon fields."

"We're not allowed up there, there are signs everywhere to warn people from disturbing the fairies."

Julie rolled her eyes. "Yes, but those are for dumb

tourists and stuff, not people like us. We know how to respect mythical wildlife, we won't be a disturbance. We'll just settle in a nice spot and watch the bloom from up close."

Sensing the discomfort of the other two in the group, I spoke up. "I don't think that's a good idea. The slightest disturbance could cause some of the emperor fairies not to hatch from their cocoons."

"Yes, I was at the lecture too," Julie bit back. "Well, I'm doing it. I came all this way to see the fairies and I'm not going to miss out because some rich snobby school threw money at the organisation."

"The organisation actually donates all the proceeds from today to a local charity that preserves the breeding grounds of the emperor fairy," Rashid commented softly.

"I don't care." Julie heaved the giant fairy plushie over her shoulder. "I'm finding a way to sneak through. Who is coming?"

"Not me," I said decisively.

"Me either," Rashid added, turning to Larissa who'd been suspiciously quiet. "Don't tell me you're approving of this crazy plan. You could get arrested."

"I came here to see the emperor fairies," she said emotionless, avoiding looking at us.

Rashid looked crushed and I couldn't help but wonder if something was going on there that I didn't know about.

"What if you get caught by security?" I argued, my last attempt to stop them from making a stupid mistake.

Julie shrugged, her arrogance shining through. "Then I'll just use my charms. See you later, cowards. We're going to see the fairies!"

The two of them took off, their departure leaving a bitter taste in my mouth. That was not how I expected

HOPE

today to go and while Julie had never been my favourite person, I'd never realised she was this reckless and selfish.

"Should we go after them?" Rashid wondered, concern colouring his voice.

"Nah. They're adults, I'm not going to babysit them," I said stubbornly. I wasn't going to waste my time chasing after my classmates and keeping them out of trouble. Besides, what would I even say that I hadn't already? "Let's find somewhere for us to wait, surely there'll be other good viewing spots besides the arena."

He hesitated, scratching the slight stubble on his cheek. "Yeah, let's go. Did you bring binoculars? They've got stalls around if you didn't."

I patted my pack. "I've brought my trusty pair, I've had them since I was seven. Birthday present."

"Nice." He gestured to his own backpack as we walked down to a less-crowded area. "I got mine when I was nine, good grades. Best thing you've ever seen with them?"

"Pretty sure I saw a beacon phoenix when I was fifteen. I went on this excursion with school and my friend and I got lost. We found this hill overlooking things so I pulled out my binoculars to see if I could spot our class and I saw it flying by. It only lasted a second and nobody believed me but I know what I saw."

"Did it have the white crest?"

I swerved to avoid a stroller. "Hmm-hmm. And the winged tips too. I did some research into sightings in the area but never found anyone else who saw it. I think it might've just been passing through."

Rashid's eyes shimmered. "That's wicked. My first sighting was my best. A gaggle of haggis rolling down a hill. They were going so fast, I don't know what species they were, but that's the day I fell in love with them."

"Ooh, I've always wondered why you're so fond of them."

"That's why."

We continued exchanging our favourite mythical creature stories in the search for a good spot to wait for night. Plenty of people around us didn't seem in any sort of hurry and were still hooking ducks or buying snacks. Rashid had been right earlier, only a small sliver of the visitors were actually here for the fairies.

After a short walk around the festival, we decided to retrace our steps to the train station to see if there was anywhere calmer that we could wait. Seeing the fairies mattered to me but nothing ruined the experience as people trampling on my feet and screaming in my ear. I could definitely see the appeal of trying to find an isolated spot in the meadow but the damage it could cause to the fairies was too high of a price to pay. We were supposed to protect them, not selfishly do whatever we wanted.

I wondered if I could report Julie to our university for that kind of behaviour. It really wasn't fair that someone like that would be allowed to work with animals. Then again, I didn't want to tell on her like we were toddlers.

Life was just unfair and that was something I had to deal with.

"Hey, this looks like a good spot," Rashid said, gesturing to a small park with some benches. People were picnicking and some kids chasing after balls or each other.

We settled on a free spot in the grass, both having to sit on our sweaters. I stared up at the pearly blue sky, doubt flitting through me. "Do you think the weather will turn?"

"I hope so. The fairies need a good gust of wind to get airborne," Rashid said, checking his phone. "My app says it'll be sunny for two more hours but there's a storm planned."

"So perfect weather for a fairy bloom."

"Hmm, it should be but you never know. We could sit here all night for nothing."

I really hoped not.

Chapter Three

Nightfall came and the excited bustling of the day quiet down into a more contained lull of quiet satisfaction and joyful contemplation. As expected, plenty of people had already left without bothering to wait for the main event of the festival. The real reason we were here.

"It's quiet," Rashid observed, his hands folded under his head as he stared up at the sky.

I sat up to rearrange my jacket under me. "No breeze yet."

"It'll come."

"You sound confident."

"You can feel the storm in the air. It's got a distinct smell," he said, a boyish grin stretching across his face. "It smells quiet."

I had no clue what he was talking about but I hoped he was right. Without the perfect breeze, the fairies wouldn't be able to take flight and get the start they needed for their journey across the world.

My phone vibrated in my pocket and I pulled it out, hoping it was Tina.

"Larissa," I concluded, trying to hide my disappointment.

Rashid hummed. "Yeah, I got one too. She's asking if we've made up our minds cause they've found a way to sneak past security."

Temptation laced through me but I shook my head. "No, I'm good here."

"Yeah, same. I'm sure it'll be fine. The viewing arena is slightly downhill from here so we'll have a decent view." Rashid returned his gaze upward. "Do you believe their dust brings good luck?"

I contemplated his question as I counted the stars. "No, I think it's foolish to attribute human qualities like that to animals. The dust is meant to fertilise the plants so they'll be there when they return to lay eggs. It has nothing to do with luck."

"Dry," he remarked.

"That's just how it is." I sat up and gasped. "I think I felt a drop of rain."

"What? No. It's not supposed to!" Rashid desperately tapped his phone to check his weather app. "Nooo, the wind turned and there are clouds coming our way. No, no, the fairies won't bloom if it rains."

Unmeasurable disappointment flooded through me but I tried to bite it back. "It might pass."

Another cold droplet fell on my forehead and I'd never hated it more than right now. I waited with bated breath for another one but the world around me seemed unmoved by the sudden threat. A minute passed without another drop and I breathed a sigh of relief.

There was still a chance that everything would turn out alright.

"Someone's calling me," Rashid said, sitting up again. "It's Larissa."

"I'm not breaking the rules and going past the fence," I said decisively.

"I know." He swiped to answer. "Hello? What? Are you serious? No way, shit. Hold on, where are you? Okay, yeah, we're coming. Okay, see you in a bit."

I glared at him as he ended the call. "I told you, I'm not going."

"No, they got busted climbing over a fence and are currently being detained by security."

"I don't see how that's my problem," I said calmly, a slight feeling of glee rising in me. That served them right and I didn't even feel bad for them. They shouldn't have tried to sneak in, the signs and restrictions were there for a good reason.

Rashid crawled up and shook the grass off his jacket. "Well, I'm going to make sure they're okay. Are you really not coming?"

I shook my head. "I'm not going to miss out on the fairy bloom because they thought the rules didn't apply to them. Play stupid games, win stupid prizes."

"Alright, I guess I'll see you back in class." He left without much else, the displeasure clear in the way he held himself as he pushed through the crowd.

The slightest twinge of guilt flickered through me and I wondered if my response was too cold. It was good to care about people but I wasn't going to miss the first fairy bloom in a decade because my classmates were idiots. They didn't matter, *animals mattered.*

Refusing to let my day be ruined by Julie and her dumb antics, I shot a quick text to Tina to let her know I wished she was here. It wasn't that I minded being on my own but these things were always better shared.

I leaned back down, staring up at the darkening sky. The moon was bright and rising rapidly, casting a silver glow over the surrounding area. It was quickly getting later and later and there still hadn't been a single fairy sighting. Various families around me with small children were gradually packing up and leaving, not having the patience or time to wait.

At least I didn't have anywhere to be. I was going to sit here all night and nothing could stop me.

Another cold droplet hit me in the face and I sat up, my hands held out. Surely not...

Rain pattered down, a light mist that quickly grew heavier. It wasn't long for the ground was dotted and people were packing up their stuff and running for shelter. I remained still, the stubborn part of me refusing to move.

Water streamed down my face, soaking into my clothes and cooling me down. With a frustrated groan, I gathered my stuff and ran for cover too. Clearly, it wasn't letting up any time soon so sitting in the rain and catching a cold wasn't going to make a difference.

Why was everything going wrong today? This wasn't fair but I knew there was nothing or nobody to be mad at. This was simply the nature of things.

The covered bus stop was packed with people, their grumbling and complaining an echo of the dark feelings inside me. I shared in the collective disappointment, wishing desperately that the rain would stop.

Gradually, people gave up and rushed out into the night, swallowed by the curtain of rain. After an hour, there were only half of us left, stubbornly holding still in the hope that the weather would turn.

I didn't know a single person there but I felt a certain kind of kinship with them. Their determination matched mine and even without knowing anything about them, we shared something in this moment.

"Anyone got a light?" a man with a deep voice asked.

A girl about my age held out hers, smiling politely.

The group of singletons fell silent again as we waited out the rain, hope dwindling with every passing minute. The smoke from the man's cigarette prickled my nose and I contemplated sheltering somewhere else but there wasn't much around. It certainly beat standing in the rain.

The man lit up five more times, always borrowing the girl's lighter. Each of his buds ended up squashed out into the ash tray compartment of the bin, their bitter smell lingering. A text from Rashid arrived to let me know they were catching the train back home.

The rain kept falling.

"It's never going to let up," the smoker eventually said, pulling his jacket over his head and running out into the rain. Two others followed suit, taking the number of determined people down.

The park was completely abandoned and I couldn't help but wonder what the arena and festival were looking like right now. Were the people there giving up too? Or were they waiting for something that might never come, just like me?

Chapter Four

By the time the rain stopped, it was well past midnight and there were only seven others stubborn enough to have stuck around. I stepped out into the night, a shiver running down my spine. It was a good thing I brought a jacket with me after all, not that I was going to admit that to my mother.

The park was dead silent but slowly, more people appeared from underneath small ledges and surrounding houses. It wasn't nearly as busy as before but I was certainly not alone in my insanity.

I briefly wondered about going back down to the festival and seeing if I could get into the arena. Surely, plenty of people had vacated so that should've opened up space.

Deciding it couldn't hurt to check, I set in motion down to the village square. The road was slightly slippery and littered with abandoned cups, cardboard plates, and leftovers. It was clear that people left in a hurry.

I did not envy the people who were responsible for clearing this all up.

The street grew busier the closer I got to the festival and hesitation set in. Less people left than I expected and the arena still looked rather crowded.

I paused at the ticket booth and hopefully placed some cash down. "Hi. Just one person, please."

The woman nodded and pushed a ticket through a slot.

Grinning from ear to ear, I quickly hurried through the gate before they could change their mind or tell me they made a mistake. Nobody stopped me and I couldn't quite believe I managed to secure a place after all that. All the benches were wet so I remained standing. The arena was pleasantly full and not surprisingly, plenty of Evergreen University students were still here. Their signature green jackets with the obnoxiously big logo made it easy to recognise them.

Since they had the best view, I chose a spot next to a girl around my age with long blonde hair. Her gaze was glued up at the sky, her eyes shimmering with hope and anticipation. Some of her friends were still conversing but she was ignoring them all, captivated by the promise of the fairy bloom. I could see the admiration on her face, a deep reverence that I understood perfectly.

I wondered if that was what I looked like too.

A faint gust of wind made me shiver, drawing attention to my soaked shoes and socks. I wouldn't be surprised if was sick tomorrow. How shitty.

It took me a moment to realise what the cold meant. A breeze.

Hopeful, I looked up at the sparkling sky. With the rain gone, it was a perfectly cloudless night and suddenly, perfect conditions for the fairies to bloom. A sweet smell filled the air and my heart beat faster, the anticipation and excitement almost too much to take.

Someone behind me gasped and I turned, hoping to find what they were looking at. They pointed in the air and I followed their gaze, my heart leaping.

They were here. I could cry. They were actually here.

A lone fairy fluttered over the arena, bravely flapping its purple and pink wings. It swerved back and forth, almost like it was showing off its majestic beauty. It was so close, I didn't even need my binoculars to see its culy antenna or the delicate stripes on its wings.

It disappeared into the night, leaving me and everyone around me in awe.

Hope blossomed in my chest as another fairy flew over my head, and another, and another. More appeared from over the horizon, passing directly over the arena as predicted. There were so many, they replaced the stars and cast playful shadows over the ground. It was a full bloom.

The sound of tens of thousands fairy wings flapping through the night sky created a rhythmic noise that I would never be able to forget. It was so much louder than I expected and I could only watch in quiet admiration. The wind turned and carried the beautiful creatures on a wild chase through the air. Their wings sparkled in the moonlight and the lanterns around the park, blinding me in a whirlwind of colours that took my breath away.

The noise changed to a faint rattle as the fairies shook the rainwater off their wings and a shower of droplets containing rainbows fell down on me, the cooling water imbued with the same floral scent from before.

Magical. Absolutely magical.

Fairies of varying sizes and shades of pink, magenta, and purple flew past. It was a majestic display, one that matched their name. Despite only just having hatched, they knew exactly were they were going. That remarkable determination and instinct was what kept their species surviving the cold winters and what brought them back here in spring to lay their eggs in the same meadows where they were born. It was an absolute shame that fewer and fewer returned every year and that soon, the fairy bloom might be a thing of the past.

At least I was able to witness it just once. A once-in-a-lifetime event, just like working at the Griffin Sanctuary with mythical animals would be.

A sudden silence took me off guard and all the fairies hovered mid-air, their blue bellies glowing bright. They held eerily still as they released their coveted dust. A rain of golden flecks showered the people and the surrounding plants, covering everything in a thin shimmering sheen.

Stunned by the moment of beauty, I watched the specks on my hand. It disappeared almost in an instant and left nothing but a slight tingling on my skin like it had never been there in the first place. But I knew what I saw, what I just experienced. It was as real as the fairies fluttering above my head, flying to warmer coasts to survive the winter.

A warm glow spread through me as I recalled Rashid's words. Maybe fairy dust didn't bring luck or fortune but getting to see this, being a witness to this miraculous spectacle of nature made me the luckiest person in the world.

As quickly as they came, they vanished and the night grew quiet once more. A collective silence hung in the arena, a shared trance from the fairy bloom.

Someone released a triumphant cheer and the bubble burst, laughter and excited chatter swelling. My chest felt like it could explode from the excitement and I joined in, fist-pumping and cheering. Even though I was celebrating on my own, I didn't feel alone. This was a victory for us all and I knew that every single person here was glad they stuck around. Some things were worth waiting for, worth fighting for. The fairy bloom was undoubtedly one of them.

Epilogue

I sneezed loudly, almost hitting my head on the back of the wall from the sheer force.

"That's what you get for staying out all night in the rain," Rashid chided from the other side of the cafetaria table.

"Mworth it," I snottered, grabbing a tissue so I could blow my nose.

"Was it though?" he asked, sounding sceptical.

"Totally. The fairy bloom was the most amazing thing I've ever seen. You really missed out. It was absolutely magical. I'm going back next year, for sure."

"Hmm-hmm." Not looking up from his phone, he groaned. "Damn it, another rejection."

"Where from this time?"

"Creek's Animal Park. They said we're not a good fit and they wish me good luck. Such empty words."

"I know." I sighed, checking my phone for new notifications. "Oh, hang on. I got a reply from the Mythic Alliance.

Aww, nope. They appreciated my application but— Ah, they don't believe we're a good fit and they also wish me good luck with wherever I end up."

"See, empty," Rashid said, mindlessly dragging his thumb down his screen to refresh his emails. His phone chimed and he gasped. "Oh, shit. I just got accepted. To—"

"To?" I prompted.

"The Mythic Alliance." He grimaced. "Sorry."

"Don't be. That's amazing, I'm excited for you," I said, only slightly jealous of his acceptance. That was a really good place to do an internship and he'd learn a lot there. As pleased as I was for my classmate, I wouldn't be able to celebrate until I had all my responses. I briefly worried what would happen if every place rejected me but that seemed like a cruel joke from the university considering our internships were part of our course. One of these places *had* to accept me.

Another rejection arrived in my mailbox and I deleted it. This was torture. Digital torture. I'd rather stand in the freezing rain for hours than refresh my emails obsessively.

"And?" Rashid asked, still beaming from ear to ear.

"Nothing yet."

"You'll get something good, I know you will. Your grades are amazing."

Easy for him to say. He just got into one of the most desirable programs. I grimaced, reminded of Julie and how resentful I'd feel if they picked her for the Griffin Sanctuary and not me. Although it was much more likely that nobody from our university was getting accepted there.

My phone vibrated again and a new notification popped up. My heart leapt in my throat. "It's from the Griffin Sanctuary. Fuck."

"Open it," Rashid urged.

"I can't, this is too scary. I've been dreaming of working here since I was a child. I can't." I stared at my screen, the email's subject line not giving anything away. I couldn't open this, a rejection from them would crush me. My second and third choice had already declined so the only other places remaining were pretty mediocre. I needed this.

Gathering a breath, I opened the email. I was so nervous, my eyes danced over the text and I needed to read it twice to fully register the words. "I got in?"

Rashid gasped, gaping at me. "What?"

"I got in! They accepted me for their unicorn program!" I shrieked, bouncing out of my chair, my cold totally forgotten. Not only had I just seen the fairies bloom, I was going to work at the Griffin Sanctuary, one of the leading experts in mythical animals. And even better, I was going to work with my favourite animal in the world, the silver blush unicorns.

Maybe fairy dust brought good luck after all. Or maybe my hard work finally paid off. Whichever it was, I couldn't wait for the next leg of my journey and what ever wonders it would bring. It was impossible to know and that was the beauty of working with mythical creatures.

Thank you for reading The Fairy Festival. I hope you enjoyed meeting Charlotte and seeing the fairies bloom. If you love mythical animals and you're intrigued about what it's like to care for them, you can read all about Charlotte's internship at the Griffin Sanctuary where she'll take care of the unicorns: https://books2read.com/theunicornherd
There are also phoenixes, kitsunes, and dragons in the sequels if those are more your thing!

Also by
Arizona Tape

The Griffin Sanctuary - The Afterlife Academy - Queens Of Olympus - The Samantha Rain Mysteries - My Winter Wolf - The Hybrid Festival - The Forked Tail - Rainbow Central - Sapphire Bay Billionaires - Twisted Princesses

With Fate by My Side
by
C.N. Marie

Prologue

INDIE

"Once you choose hope, anything's possible."
- Christopher Reeve

I'd never thought four letters could symbolize so much in my life. I'd always been obsessed with my career, striving to be the best, the one person who everyone hoped to book for an event but barely had a chance to grab a meeting with as her waiting list was too long. Now none of that mattered. Only one thing did. My life, and the people that surrounded me. My support network; my man and his four-legged best friend. I'd always been someone who'd kept themselves isolated away from society and the prying eyes of the world. I know you're thinking how- seeing as I'm forced into the watchful eye of every celebrity across the globe. I mean, a facade works within my industry too. I'd ensure my clients thought I was their best friend if that's what I needed to do to make them stand out from the other events planned that week or even month. It didn't matter if his Royal Highness was celebrating a birthday. My job was to make every guest forget that he'd even been born. After all, a spread in the next fashion magazine or mention on prime-time television could be the next million in their back pockets. It was always about the investment and how much revenue is produced in return. The moment I was alone though, I turned into a recluse, a nobody and hid the real me away, enjoying the silence of my own thoughts away from the noise of the media. The white noise was essential to my healing process before the next big celebrity started to flash the cash for my services. I'd burn it all in a bonfire now though, every last dollar, because money meant nothing in comparison to what I'd been through.

Hope isn't the first four-lettered word that normally sprung to the forefront of someone's mind; it was love. I'd always gone with the majority, but now I forged my own path and instead I preached the four-lettered word of hope in abundance. The fact it was an opportunity for a second chance. Something that I grabbed hold of with both hands just to ensure the world as I knew it was spinning in the right direction on its axis.

The problem was, it never would be the same again. I had my eyes freshly opened, just like when you'd been fitted for a new pair of prescription glasses. The picture in front of me was clearer, more polished, and brighter. An image though that would never dull for me going forward, ingrained into the depths of my mind. I'd cherish every second of my life as the road ahead was about to push me to limits like nothing ever had before. But I was strong, a fighter, and I'd use everything I could to win this battle because I chose to hope. Not to have a defeated attitude, but to hope for a future. Nothing else would do because with hope, anything is possible, especially when I have Bryce and my four-legged friend, Fate, by my side every step of the way.

Something that before this journey, I'd never have had. The support of a loving man and my savior. A solid reason to live for.

Chapter One

BRYCE
2 YEARS AGO

"Josh, I've not checked my emails yet," I mumbled down the line after I'd lost count of the amount of calls my business partner had attempted in the last fifteen-minute period. I squinted and leant forward in an attempt to read the time on the wall, but it was pointless. The slow rise of the sunlight filtering through the blinds told me it was early as my hand hit the bedside table in search of my glasses. "Got them."

"Got what?"

"My glasses, douche. I want to know how early it is." I winced as I placed the dark-rimmed frames in place and allowed my eyes to adjust as I stood up and stretched my aching muscles. "Josh, it's before 6am, why would I have even logged on yet? I mean, you do know people have a morning routine?"

"Chloe woke me up again crying the place down, third time this week. I couldn't settle once she'd gone back down and was too excited to not call you.

2 YEARS AGO

"Is she still not settling very well, man?" I asked with a pinch of guilt. I felt such an insensitive ass. Josh was still struggling with Chloe's night terrors of late since he'd revealed the truth that Caroline, her mother, wanted to travel the world rather than be tied down with a child. If Caroline had her own way, she would've thrown her into care last year at just seven years old, but Josh stood up and told her he'd fight her for custody. It ended up a non-starter, scared of losing all her precious travel money, so she signed her rights away to Josh and has not seen the precious girl since. "What was so exciting?"

"That Indie Webster person emailed again, but it's different. More direct and forceful. Do you think that it could be *The* Indie Webster, as in the event coordinator to the stars and I've made a huge mistake?" Josh quickly asked back cautiously.

"The sexy minx that you know I'm obsessed with and *not* a hoax that you said you were certain it was." I felt the bubble of sickness whirl in my stomach at the thought that I'd bypassed the woman of my dreams for the last six months. "Why would she want to meet with us?" I stood up and tried to keep my composure in check, thinking Josh was just over-exaggerating the urgency in this email. He must have made a mistake. So many people try to impersonate celebrity personnel nowadays to get five minutes in the spotlight. The checks he'd done originally must have shown something, or he wouldn't have thought to bypass her. "We're just two nobody web designers."

"Take that back," Josh huffed.

"Which part?" I chuckled, "the web designers?"

"Don't get cocky with me, Bryce. It's too early." Josh yawned down the line as I balanced the cell between my ear

CHAPTER FIFTEEN

and my shoulder as I precariously fought my way into a pair of clean boxers one handed and my tracksuit running bottoms. My balance was not as on par as I thought as I fell backwards with my trousers locked around my ankles.

"Fuck," I dropped my phone on the comforter as Josh's muffled concerns could be heard quietly in the air whilst I sorted myself out and rubbed the back of my head where I banged it against the wall. *Fucker deserved radio silence for a moment.* Damn, that hurt as I fought to reign out a full list of expletives as long as my arm instead of just the uttered one.

"Josh, I've now got a banging head. My mind is fucked from the news you've thrown at me. I've not had my coffee yet and I need to go for a run. Let me blow the cobwebs out and think this through..." I hissed at him, "we need to figure out *if* this is her or not. We need hard proof now."

"That's why you're the voice of reason," he uttered quietly, but I knew his mind was deep in thought of how we'd achieve that. After all, he was sure this was all fake. What if he was wrong? What could this do to our business? Our careers?

"And you're my pain in my ass, but I wouldn't have it any other way. Be at mine for ten am," I replied, as I heard the telltale scuttle of paws against the laminate floor, "we'll brainstorm a plan. Gotta go. Fate is up."

"That dog of yours gets more attention than your best friend. Are you sure I shouldn't be worried?" Josh sniggered as I wished he'd been here, and I could have given him a clip around the head.

To think about it, I was shocked that he wasn't already outside my apartment, in a state of desperation, banging the door down with Mrs. Phelps across the hall coming out in her baby pink robe and curlers playing hell at the racket he'd caused.

"I'm sure Fate will smother you in kisses later Josh, so you don't get too jealous," I countered.

"Fucker."

"Don't you know it? See you later, mate." I placed the cell down just as Fate made her presence clear.

"Come on girl, give me two seconds to get ready," I yanked my t-shirt over my head and pulled it down over my chest as the muffled words left my mouth and the swish of my Labrador's tail hit my thighs. "I know you're excited to go for a run, but I still need to get my trainers on yet and grab my water bottle."

I scratched behind her ears and gave them a massage as she turned and licked my hand before I headed out of the room with my loyal companion on my heels. It was our daily routine, a twice daily run and damn did I need it with Josh's bomb he'd just thrown at me. I needed to be realistic and be the decision maker of the pair of us without allowing the potential of a name to influence my decision. If this wasn't a game, it could destroy Josh's and I's livelihood and I wasn't about to let that happen.

It had taken blood, sweat and tears, constant reinvestment, and pitches to companies to take a chance on our designs to get to where we could stand on our own two feet. We'd even decorated my pokey back bedroom and turned it into our office space. It was ours. Our dream. Illusionize your Designs, a place to create the world you want on a website and broadcast it across the Internet to fit your brand. I knew a good run would help refocus my mind and what options I had to figure out the true identity of this person without hiring a private investigator and hacker.

"Right, girl, you ready?" I grabbed her lead and slipped

CHAPTER FIFTEEN

my feet into my trainers as she nuzzled my calf with her head and let out a bark of enthusiasm. "Let's go then."

I opened the door of my apartment and took the steps two by two until I reached the main complex door and waved to Ritchie, an old family friend who happened to be my local postman who'd just loaded up his van across the road for the day.

"You're out early today, Bryce. Don't normally catch you out at this time." He chuckled as he shut the back doors and walked around to the driver's side. "Who or what has got you running now? I bet it wasn't young Fate."

"I always run in the morning, Ritchie," I snapped before I ran my hand through my hair, "but you're right, not at this time. Josh, that's who."

"That guy wouldn't know how to tell the time if you paid him to make the sun rise and fall. His body clock must be a mess. He'd be perfect for helping me out. I ain't getting any younger." I raised my brows and crossed my arms, making Ritchie laugh at me.

"Stop trying to steal my business partner," I replied, dropping my arms. I started to stretch my muscles and Fate bent, stretching her hind legs in response. "He just got worked up over something, that's all."

"Sure, would be a big thing if he needed to wake you."

"Yep, that's why I'm out here. Better go Ritchie before Fate gets restless," I said as I gave him a wave, glad to have escaped his interrogation.

That's the problem with family friends. I'd have my mom or dad straight on the phone asking questions that were none of their business in a panic. It didn't matter that I was a thirty-two-year-old grown man with his own business and apartment living in the small town of Jacksonville, Oregon. I'd long ago left the large city lifestyle of Florida

93

2 YEARS AGO

that I'd been brought up in, but it hadn't stopped me moving close enough that I could drive home easily if I was needed. Josh joked I was a mummy's boy through and through. I'd never admit that he was probably right.

I took my normal route straight to the Forest Park and headed directly for one of mine and Fate's favorite trails, The Hanna Park South Trail. I got my entrance fee out and waited patiently with Fate by my side as I gave her a squirt of water from a sports bottle. I was at first surprised by the number of hikers, bikers, and other walkers with dogs around this early in the morning, but then, it was a popular trail people frequented here for its easy layout and beautiful large flowers. People could take the trail at any speed and enjoy it thoroughly through its beauty. Each time you visited, you always seemed to spot a new delight you missed the time before. A real treasure in the midst of a small town.

It made the time we hit the beach more of a relaxation than a workout as Fate normally ran straight into the water and shook the spray of the water across me. I couldn't wait. Maybe I really needed this today. I hadn't had a chance to visit Forest Park in the last week and had eluded for runs around the block instead. It was as if my mind needed relaxation as much as my body.

I took a step forward in the queue, nodded as I gave across my money and ruffled Fate's ears as we walked through the entrance.

"Ready girl."

"Woof," Fate barked back.

"Good, Let's..."

"Bryce Woods?" a delicate, toned female voice shouted my name, interrupting me. I turned around to face them,

CHAPTER FIFTEEN

wondering who could want to talk to me now. *Would I ever get to just run since everyone thought I shouldn't sleep?*

When I saw one person, I never thought would step foot in a small town like Jacksonville, let alone be standing wearing tight fitting running gear and a florescent pink headband with matching arm and foot warmers.

"Indie Webster. Fuck."

Chapter Two

INDIE

I didn't know what to do after Bryce Woods and his partner Joshua Lewis had ignored my emails for the last six months. I'd never been rejected before. Never. I had a proposal for them which could catapult them to places they'd only dreamt of, but they had the audacity to think it was acceptable to just ignore me. I was flummoxed by it all. It meant taking the situation into my own hands.

It was after my last client's wishes and the dreams he'd aspired from my event that I realized enough was enough. Celebrities or, in this case, a washed-up reality television star knew what buttons to press to get what they wanted, but extortion was a first for even me. It made me sick knowing that this guy wanted me to become his piece on the side to transport him back along with his A-list pals from the past, and my event would be a celebration of our love. Fuck that shit.

All because he'd got wind of my plans of a new venture - my idea to create an events management team package online. A way to give a small town a pop-up event on a shoestring budget. He'd even found out about Illusionize your Designs and was determined to out them to the world. I couldn't have that on my conscience, and I knew I had to work fast before Quince Aston got to Bryce and Josh first.

That's when I decided Jacksonville, Oregon, was as good a spot to use my vacation days up as any. Zena could travel alongside me and figure out the best way to approach one of them and I'd prepare them for the shitshow that could happen.

I just didn't expect fate to contribute to my plans.

I'd always been active. A runner and loved the great outdoors, so when Zena had told me about Forest Park and The Hanna Park South Trail, I felt like my dreams had been answered. I just couldn't believe my eyes when the outline of the guy I'd been researching stood in front of me, with a gorgeous young black Labrador.

"Bryce Woods?" I questioned timidly, hoping not to attract the attention of too many people. I mean, my face was recognizable, but I'd tried to disguise myself with florescent pink headgear and my hair tied up in a less than normal polished appearance.

I didn't expect for him to turn and trip over his feet when he saw me and speak my name. I rushed forward and grabbed his shoulders, brushing him down.

"Sorry, I didn't mean to scare you." I felt the heat on my skin rise up my neck and was certain it would have left a pinkish blush behind.

"I just didn't expect to see you here. Are you going this way?" he pointed down the dirt tracks as the beautiful dog lifted her head and rubbed it against my calf. "Fate, leave her alone. You'll molt all over her."

"Don't worry about a bit of hair, Bryce. She's beautiful,"

I scruffed her ears, taking in the pink collar and lead as her tail wagged in appreciation. Fate gave us a spin, causing her lead to get tangled up and making us both laugh. "I am going this way. Do you mind if I come with you?"

"Not at all."

The early morning run turned into a casual stroll, with Fate being let loose off the lead and constantly running ahead a few meters before running back to our sides. We'd gotten past the awkward moment of why I was here in Jacksonville and that deep down I did want to discuss an opportunity with him, but I decided to hold back on the Quince Aston issue. I didn't want to scare the guy any further.

He'd already turned into a bumbling mess the moment he'd seen me, but the moment he spoke, my heart fluttered. I expected him to trip over his words, with his crimson face that shone back at me, but if anything, he was strong and powerful. I couldn't fault him for his dashing looks. He was cute and sexy with his short brown windswept hair and a single lighter streak at the front, deep hazel set eyes, and those dimples that I couldn't stop staring at when he smiled. I mean, if I'd thrown anything else at him, I'm sure he'd have run off straight to talk to his business partner Josh about the shitshow I'd brought to their doorstep. I know he'd have been less than pleased with Zara telling me he had a daughter to care for. The media was certainly not a place for a child. It would've been true, but still he needed to get used to my presence first, it seemed.

"What plans have you got for the rest of the day?" I asked casually as I pulled my hair out of the messy bun and whipped the headband off to mop the fine mist that had formed off my face. "Reply to my last six months of emails?" I chuckled.

I watched his face wince and his shoulders scrunched up.

"Six months? I didn't realize. Josh is the one who deals mainly with correspondences," he admitted, as we pulled back to the beginning of the loop and the entrance. "He was certain that the emails were from a hoax source. If he'd - we'd - known..."

"You'd have reached out, would you?" I interrupted him, holding the headband on my wrist and placing my hands on my waist.

"Absolutely, who wouldn't want the opportunity to have a proposal of work from the great Indie Webster," he blushed again and dropped his head as I took a step forward and tilted his chin up, so he'd look me in the eyes.

"I'm just like any other girl, Bryce. I talk the same and look the same."

"Woman, Indie. You're a fucking ravishing woman and don't forget it." Bryce held his head up as I felt the tremble from the tip of my finger pulse its way all the way down to my throbbing core of body. Fuck. "Meet me at the office, say twelve. It gives me time to fill in Josh. He may collapse from this news."

"I could just turn up and surprise him. See the look on his face?"

"That would be a picture. Damn, I've not got my business cards on me." He winced.

"Bryce, I know where your office is. See you later."

Chapter Three

BRYCE

"It wasn't just a nightmare," Josh spouted the minute I cracked the door open, and I saw his little princess curled in his arms wrapped up in blankets asleep. "She's got a fever and been sick."

"Josh, you should've stayed at home. I could've dealt with this. Chloe obviously needs rest." I grabbed a few cushions and placed them at the top of my wide lounge sofa for her head. The moment Josh laid her down onto it and she snuggled with moans into the fabric, my heart sighed.

"It's okay sweetheart, you'll feel better soon." I kissed her head and directed Josh away from the living area and watched as Fate took a spot by her side. Her head lopped onto the little girl's hand and nuzzled her skin.

I looked up at him and the worry lines marked across his brow as the soft sound of a snore filled the air. "She'll be okay. Don't worry. Fate won't leave her either."

"I just panic, you know. I knew if I was here, you'd help

and plus, your text said you had urgent news. You never have news," Josh uttered, before he filled the kettle and turned it on like he was at home. "Want a cup of coffee?"

"Yeah, please," I joked at the reverse logic of the situation, being served a drink in my own place. "I'll grab the biscuits and we'll take a seat before I tell you about my eventful morning at Forest Park."

"Now I can't wait, do go on." Josh tapped the sideboard impatiently as he waited, but I just ignored him by mimicking a zipping motion over my lips and taking a seat at the breakfast bar. "Come on, how long does a kettle take to damn boil? I hate waiting for information. You know that better than anyone, Bryce. It's pure torture."

"It's worth it. I promise."

The moment Josh sat down and placed his hot steaming cup of coffee on the coaster, I allowed the words to spill from my mouth about meeting Indie "sex kitten" Webster. I'd never taken such pride before in seeing a person's jaw slacken so quickly and become useless in those moments. Josh wasn't someone to become speechless, and I'd done the impossible. No, Indie had done that. The moment I mentioned she was dropping by round noon, the color disappeared from his face and he turned a garish pale shade.

"Indie Webster, ran with you?" Josh finally spluttered out; his hands gripped tightly to the edge of the wooden breakfast bar. I was grateful it wasn't the hot coffee.

"Well, technically, we walked and talked together. Fate was the one that ran off." I blew the steam that lingered on the top of the hot nectar in my hands. I peeped over the top as I took a sip and let out a sigh. Damn, that was good.

"You invited her here. Have you seen the place?" Josh quickly babbled out of his mouth.

I looked around the apartment, at the blanket thrown in a pile in the corner and scattered cushions out of place, the plates in the sink and the half dead plant in the corner and shrugged my shoulders. It was a typical apartment, well loved. Well, I tried with the plants, I really did. I winced though when I turned and saw the opened office door and the state of my workspace. I was ashamed. I'd been so lost in my designs online that the paper trail had become an overgrown mess of chaos. With paperwork strewn across the desks in the office and every surface possible, I knew I was in trouble.

"Think I've time to cancel?" I turned to face Josh and put my cup back on the breakfast bar. "I mean Chloe is ill."

"Unlikely. Have you seen the time?" Josh ducked his head to avoid my eye as I caught the clock on the wall behind him.

"Ten minutes. She'll be here in ten minutes. Shit. Help me."

I never felt my legs carry me so fast into the office before. I loved my job, but this was different. I wanted to show I was a good candidate after Josh's email fuck ups. My hands moved to gather as many pieces of paper as possible as I heard the bell to the apartment.

"Shit," I headed straight toward Josh who'd just loaded the dishwasher and closed it too, slamming the pile of papers into his arms, "hide them in the bureau, under the cushions just anywhere Indie Webster isn't likely to go or isn't going to snoop."

I headed straight toward the door and quickly blew out a breath of composure to calm myself as I placed my hand on the handle and peeped through the keyhole. Damn, she was fine. I was taken aback though. She wasn't alone. I took a quick glance at Josh and noticed the pile of paperwork now missing and a quick nod and raise of his brow, wondering what the hell I was doing making her wait out in the corridor.

I opened the door and greeted her with a kiss on each cheek, as I felt the heat rush to my own face as she introduced her assistant Zara and I introduced Josh. The awkward moment we shared as we danced, unsure whether to give each other a hug as old acquaintances or shake hands as strict partners, was comical and, in the end, we both just let out a laugh and shrugged it off.

It was at that moment my breath caught at the back of my throat and my full attention went to Indie and I couldn't break my gaze. It was like I'd forgotten how to formulate basic words and turned into a primal baboon. I didn't want to be that uncertain man whose skills looked good on paper but in person was a letdown. It was when Chloe coughed, and Fate barked, that the tension between us broke, and all focus turned from us to her.

"Sorry, I should've mentioned I had to bring my daughter Chloe with me. She's laid up on the sofa poorly," Josh muttered as he made his way toward her with her bag off the side, searching for something. "Where did I put it?"

"Side pocket, Josh? You always put the thermometer in the side pocket. Take a breather."

"I did wonder where Fate was," Indie piped up, as the dog's head lifted at the sound of her name and her tongue lolled out. "Is she always such a sweetie and protective of people?"

"Yeah, she'd never touch a fly. So caring and loving," Bryce replied, "I'd never let her near a child if I thought otherwise. She'd just lick her to death, more than likely."

I watched Josh go to Chloe and Zara follow behind,

103

placing her hand on his shoulder in support, and let out a smile.

"Why don't you guys get to work and talk through this proposal?" Josh questioned as he helped Chloe sit up and give her a few sips of water from her water bottle.

"We'll be fine. I may raid your cupboards though, Bryce, and make this little one some soup to help get some nutrients in her. If that's alright with you Indie?" Zara asked sheepishly, the bright red tinge apparent from the far end of the room. "I just don't think I'd be much help at the moment."

"Zara, there's no need to justify yourself," Indie interrupted, "Bryce and Josh will begin to think I'm a hard ass and run a tight ship." I laughed so hard as a huge grin spread across her face. "It's a sweet thing to offer, and it gives Bryce and me time to talk. I say that's perfect."

I looked up and smirked and indicated the direction to my office.

"This way, Indie, and Zara, make yourself at home." I gave her a wink and left her to it.

Chapter Four

INDIE

What had I just witnessed? Zara had gone from her normal strict and strategic self to a woman who'd been struck by Cupid the moment she'd entered the room and spotted Josh hidden by the breakfast bar. In the past, children and a sickness bug had always sent her running in the opposite direction with the hand sanitizer pulled from her bag and dowsing herself in the stuff, but this was different. She'd told me and Bryce to work. I was in charge, not her. I was gobsmacked. Then for Zara to throw in she was going to cook a meal for Josh's daughter. I honestly thought she'd had a knock to the head or something. It was the most unusual thing ever, but I'd got the scoop later on once we were alone.

Bryce and I got straight down to work. It was as if we just clicked. The moment I'd gone into the details of my proposal, he was able to fire back ideas of how we could achieve my vision without losing my brand that I was known for and how I could also incorporate the new clientele. I couldn't have it looking like it was meant for high-flyers when I wanted my clients to be the everyday person. It was a fine line and Bryce knew exactly the path I wanted to go without the constant renegotiation and hand holding of so many people I've used in the past. It was like I'd taken a breath of fresh air after being stuck in a broken-down elevator, too scared that the oxygen would run out and slid down the wall to the floor to consume every molecule. The moment the doors opened, and you saw the light, the tightness and panic disappeared immediately, and the moment seemed like a bad memory until you glanced over your shoulder and shuddered. It has always been my life. A consumed fear, but for some reason, it didn't exist here with Bryce.

"How are you two doing in here?" Zara asked as she appeared at the door. "Are you ready for some chicken noodle soup?"

"Soup? How long have we been here for?" I glanced across at Bryce, who just shrugged his shoulders and stood up from his chair, offering his hand out to me to stand.

I grabbed his hand to stand and smiled, the warmth of his palm sending tingles up through my arm and straight to my core as Zara coughed and interrupted us.

"Sorry, chicken noodle soup sounds good," I said as I dropped my hand away from his and made my way out of the room without a backwards glance.

I knew if I turned around and Bryce's face showed an ounce of what I felt inside, I may have risked mixing my professional life with pleasure. An issue I've never once battled since I started working in this world. I've always found keeping the two worlds separate really easy, that was, until Quince Aston's demands, of course, and my own thoughts towards Bryce. Now Bryce made me want to delve

HOPE

across to the dark side and leave professionalism in its wake, fuck him, and hope that relieved my obsession with constantly researching the guy since I met him. When I'd first seen his picture I'd searched for everything I could find about him over the last year when I first had the brainwave and possibility of needing to find a web designer in a small town. It took a six-month debacle of toying with my decision and finally picking Illusionize your Designs as the correct company to lead my vision but when I met Bryce in person a few hours earlier it was as if the light had been turned on inside my head. The guy had illuminated my whole fucking world.

I took a seat at the dining table in front of the steaming bowl of soup and pitcher of iced lemonade sat in the center. I smiled at Bryce as he took the seat opposite me. Zara and Josh mysteriously headed back to Chloe, who was now propped up and sat on the corner of the sofa with a tray balanced by her side, chatting away to the pair of them.

"She seems to have perked up?" I whispered to Bryce as I brought the spoon to my mouth and blew the hot liquid before placing it into my mouth.

"I am thanks. Who's your friend Uncle Bryce?" she spoke before sneezing and reaching for the outheld tissue in Zara's hand. My hand flew to my mouth in mock shock at her reaction as she rolled her eyes at me, and Josh rolled his eyes at the pair of us.

"This is Indie Webster."

"Indie as in events Indie to the stars? Do you think she may be able to take me to one of her events? I'd be the talk of school. Dad..." Chloe pleaded, fluttering her eyelashes in hope.

"Chloe!" Josh reprimanded. "Apologize to Miss Webster

now. I'm so sorry for her lack of manners. It must be the fever."

I couldn't help but let the laugh leave my throat, "Josh she's a little girl. I'm honestly flattered."

I pushed the chair away from the table and stood up, careful not to knock the table, and made my way across to the sofa. The last thing I wanted to do was to spill hot soup or lemonade everywhere as a memory flew into my mind of Quince doing the exact same thing, but with coffee on a celebrity's lap on live television. I could feel Bryce's gaze penetrating my back and Josh's and Zara's from the other side. I just hoped I wasn't overstepping my mark and making a huge mistake. I didn't want this little girl to feel shame or hurt for wanting to reach out and admire someone. I wasn't that type of person, even if I did want to shy away from the crowds.

"Chloe," I bent down by the side of the little girl and knelt on the thick shaggy grey carpet, "I'd happily take you along with me as a special guest one day to an event but maybe you could be my guest of honor. You're just as special in your Daddy's eyes," I looked up at Josh and saw him turn his head quickly to wipe a tear he thought I hadn't seen from dropping down his cheek, "even in your Uncle Bryce's eyes." I felt the warmth of his palm on my back circle away. "These celebrities have an image they want to portray, but in truth that's why I'm here. I want children like you, everyday people, to have the experience of what they have. The people who deserve it. Not the people who flash the money to do so."

"Do you really mean I could have a ball with flowers and drapes and..."

"If your Daddy and Uncle Bryce don't mind," I interrupted, "you can be our first client. You can be what we base our designs off. A small-town princess' birthday. The girl who deserves everything."

"Indie, but..." Josh started to try to find the words as Zara just stood in shocked silence. I stood up and the warmth of Bryce left my back. "Are you sure?"

I knew Josh felt uncertain about what to say to me. Chloe's smile was shining across her face even though her washed out features were apparent, and this illness was wearing her down. I could see the signs of tiredness and knew she'd succumb only too soon.

Zara indicated with her head that we were just going to head back into the kitchen, as Josh tucked Chloe back up onto the sofa and encouraged her to rest her eyes.

"The more sleep you have, ladybug, the sooner you'll start to feel better."

"Thanks, Dad," Chloe mumbled before her soft snores filled the air.

I had to say it before anyone stopped me. "I hope I didn't overstep by suggesting the event to Chloe without consulting you first. It was just, I just thought it was a perfect way to make a little girl's day." I quickly tagged onto the end, "I also thought that it would form a great connection between both businesses."

I waited for the fallout. The fallout always came. Whether it was a client or Zara, someone had something to say to normally disagree with me, but it never came.

I knew that Zara and I should've left then, but we stayed and talked, not about business, though. It turned into relaxation time, but instead of doing it as I'd always done in the past, alone, I craved to be with this small group of people. I wanted companionship, and I wanted to be alongside Bryce and curled up in his arms.

Chapter Five

BRYCE

I couldn't believe it's been nearly a month to the day since I'd seen Indie Webster. I'd never been so antsy to see someone in the flesh in my life. The dreams of those soul-searching ocean blue eyes and her long, brown, sun-kissed hair as I bunched it up within my fist and held it at the nape of her neck as I bruised her lips with my mouth was what saw me through the lonely dark nights. I had to conduct some images to help relieve the hard length in my pants every moment she struck my mind. She'd become my addiction and did Josh and Zara know it. I'd only spent one day in her company, and lightning had hit me.

The radio silence after a few days had me in a panic. I kept thinking that I'd made a fool out of myself that day with her. I kept trying to recollect what we'd spoken about and my actions. Had it been the fact I'd loved pineapple on my pizza, and she'd just played along with it being her favorite too? Then I remembered Zara and her face pulling and splitting a slice of pepperoni with Josh. Had I had one too many beers and made her uncomfortable when I slid my arm over her shoulder when she snorted, and her drink came out of her nose? If anything, she'd turned a lovely shade of red before she turned into my chest and fired back a retort to knock Josh a peg or two down. It was perfect.

Nothing was abnormal, so when Zara phoned me, I was taken aback at the announcement that Indie had Chloe's illness and was holed up in bed and wanted to apologize for being absent.

Apologize to me. I felt I'd been knocked over by a feather.

The moment Indie got better though, I ended up having to head out and placate my parents' concerns yet again. I tried to rearrange, but after Dad revealed he'd had a conversation on the phone with Ritchie, they felt they had to see for themselves that I was looking after myself. Josh was fantastic and took Fate for me whilst I spent the couple of weeks making my parents see sense yet again. My parents kept questioning me about when I'd find a woman to settle down with and find happiness like they had, but I wasn't about to reveal I thought I'd already found her. I was a grown man and not a child who needed to be led in life. I could make my own mistakes and whether they liked it or not, it was my choice to make.

My gut screamed though something else was going on with them both. A panic laid in the pit of my stomach, but unless they talked to me, I couldn't help, and I wasn't one to push them. They knew I wanted to stand tall on my own feet, but that never stopped me from still being there for them. I just hoped that for once it didn't amount to anything.

The moment the wheels of my car passed the sign for Jacksonville, I drove straight to Josh's place. I didn't want to waste more time than needed. The sooner I got Fate, then I could get home and invite Indie over, not for business but for dinner. I don't care if it was insane, and she thought I'd lost the plot, but I hoped she'd enjoyed my company enough the last time we spent time together that she'd agree. I didn't want to talk about fonts and shade preferences for the website tonight. I wanted to talk all about her.

"Hey mate, it's me. Will you let me in?" I pressed the buzzer long and hard to Josh's apartment with a chuckle, knowing it was only mid-afternoon so he shouldn't be too busy, as Chloe would've been at school.

I tapped my foot impatiently and checked my watch on my wrist as ten minutes later a ruffled blond-haired Josh finally opened the door with his striped blue lounge pants on and bare chest showing.

"Decided to have a nap instead of work, man?" I nudged him in the chest with my elbow as I pushed my way into the apartment and Fate ran toward me full of her typical bounce, attempting to knock me backwards as I bent down to greet her. "Missed me, girl?" She began to lick my face full of gusto as my ears pricked up at the sound coming from the bedroom.

"Josh, have they gone?"

I turned to look at him and smiled, grabbing Fate's lead, and headed toward the door as Josh clapped his hand together in a pleading motion as I opened it, but I couldn't resist.

"See you later Zara. I'm off to grab Indie." I chuckled as I shut the door to the sound of the expletives that began to leave his mouth. *I'll pay for that later.*

The moment I got in the apartment, Fate settled and nestled in her favorite spot by the fireplace. I fired off a text message to Indie, too scared to call her in case I turned into a bumbling fool, or she rejected me, and I grabbed a beer and got comfortable for the rest of the day. The warmth of the fire and quiet was just what I needed after the journey back and the constant chatter I'd endured the last few weeks from my parent's. A little silence was a welcome reprieve until a knock at the door disturbed me.

"One minute," I shouted as I got up and made my way over to the door and glanced through the peephole to see who was there. I shouldn't have been so shocked. I know I'd invited her over, but she'd actually come over. She could've been busy or anything, but less than twenty minutes, and she was outside my door.

I opened the door in haste, thinking Mrs. Phelps would love to quiz Indie after finding out she'd missed her when she last came over. I wouldn't put anyone through that torture. She was mainly harmless, but once she started talking, it was hard to get a word in, let alone escape. I reckoned deep down it was a mix of loneliness and wanting to know what was happening in other people's lives.

"I hope this is, okay?" she said timidly, with one arm wrapped around her center and the other holding a bottle of shiraz.

"I texted you, Indie. I was desperate to have you here," I admitted coyly as I realized she was still standing in the doorway. "Shit, where are my manners?" I opened the door wide and indicated for her to enter the room as she passed me across the bottle of wine. "Go and make yourself comfortable and I'll grab a couple of glasses. Fate's over by the fire."

"Let me just slip these heels off first. My feet are killing."

I couldn't help but turn and get a glance at her fine ass as she bent over and undid the straps that held the heels around her ankles. Fuck. I blatantly rearranged my hard length in my trousers as I caught her peeking at me in the mirror. Minx. With her heels off and her ass swaying, she made her way to the sofas as I grabbed both wine glasses by the stems and began to head towards them.

"Fate, I've missed you, girl," Indie piped up with a bounce in her tone. "You been good for..."

Fate's growl and tone changed before it turned into a menaced rumble of aggression.

I dropped the glasses, and they smashed to the floor. Fuck.

"Fate, what's wrong with you?" I pulled her back by the collar toward me, but her strength was fierce as she pulled against me. "It's Indie, remember, this isn't like you. Let's take you into the bedroom and I'll give the vet a call."

"I'm sure it's nothing, Bryce. She's not seen me in a month. Maybe she's forgotten who I am?" she replied.

"Maybe." I tried to guide her to my room, but she forced all her weight on her hind legs before I lifted her in my arms. "You're too big for me to do this now, girl."

I walked across the room, careful to avoid the edge where the glass had smashed. I knew from experience it always seemed to scatter far and wide and I'd need to do a deep clean. I'd only taken a few steps when Fate jumped out of my arms and pounced straight back toward Indie.

"Fate," I warned. My feet carried me straight behind her as her paws jumped up and her head nestled straight under Indie's arm, sniffing away at her, encouraging her to lift it higher.

"It's okay, Fate. I know you don't know me that well. It's fine if you need to smell me." She patted her head in encouragement.

It all happened in slow motion from that moment on. The blood-curdling screams. The pain in my chest of placing Fate into the bedroom with her belongings wondering what had happened to make her lash out like that. The pale peach blouse Indie had worn was torn with a huge visible bite mark near her breast. The text to Josh that I was on the way to the ER with Indie.

I bundled her into my arms and took her straight out of my apartment, and strapped her into my car.

"I've got you, sweetheart; I've always got you."

Chapter Six

INDIE

What had happened? I looked over and saw the pain-stricken face of Bryce driving and winced at the pain next to my right breast. Fate.

I don't know what came over her. Neither had Bryce. I mean the caring, considerate young Labrador that splashed through the water when we walked on The Hanna Park South Trail and then dried her coat on us both. The same youngster who barely left young Chloe's side through being sick had turned into this jealous, overbearing dog who'd bitten me. Could that have been it? Fate was upset at the connection between Bryce and me and saw me as competition. I shook my head and stopped almost immediately at the shooting pain that spread down to the wound. Fate knew she was loved. She'd seen plenty of people share Bryce's attention, but something had happened to set her off like this. Just what?

"Bryce," I grumbled, hating to admit I was in pain, "where are you taking me? I need to let Zara know."

"Providence Medford Medical ER. I've let Josh know... Zara's with him," I admitted. "We need to get that checked out. See if you need any treatment and figure out a plan with Fate."

"Fate? Is she alright?" I asked as we pulled to a stop at a set of red lights. Bryce's eyes flashed in wonderment at me, as he tipped his head to the side and ran his thumb across my knuckles before a horn honked at him and he set off again.

"I've never met anyone so selfless before, Indie. I mean, Fate bit you and you wanted to ask how she was," Bryce stated, his gaze firmly fixed on the traffic and the fact our next turning was for the ER.

"Something had caused her to react that way that wasn't her usual self. I don't blame her, Bryce, so you can get that thought straight out of your head," I admitted to him in a firm tone as he parked the car in a space that had just become available.

"Thank you, Indie, that means a lot," he whispered as he made his way around to help me out of the car.

"There's no need, Bryce. Honestly," I uttered as I kissed him on the cheek, close to his mouth. "I'll save a proper one for when we're in a more romantic place."

"Okay."

Bryce was a superstar by getting my arrival registered at the front desk. I took a seat and prayed that the overcrowded waiting room soon cleared away. I was sick of the constant glares and snaps of cameras that shouldn't even be turned on in here. The signs are plastered everywhere when you arrive in a reminder that when you enter you must turn your phone off. So much for discretion. I hated conspiracies, and this was just like a waiting game for the news crews to arrive out the front door in anticipation of a story. It didn't take the nurses and doctors long to slide me into a side room to wait. I heard the distinct muttering between them about it being better for me, but I knew that was bullshit. They just didn't want to deal with a media frenzy.

I knew I'd still have to wait to be seen, but I just prayed that it wouldn't be late into the night. I normally had a high pain threshold for some reason. I seemed to be handling this like a baby and I couldn't understand why. I wanted Bryce's comfort and protection and was glad when he reappeared, and he'd not just left after telling the front desk everything. He was the stable force I needed not to crumble into a real spectacle mess. I knew if people had spotted my ripped blouse, accusations would have already been made of how they'd happened just because I was a well-known name. I hated it. All I wanted was to live my own life and to be a nobody now.

A few hours later, a sharp knock at the door disturbed us after Bryce had done everything to keep me distracted from the pain. He'd done a good job with tales of his parents meddling and the obsession of him not being able to stand on his two feet, too, how he and Josh met. Bryce went across and opened the door.

"Indie Webster," he nodded, keeping his soul focus on her, "I'm Doctor Forbes. Would you like to follow me, and we'll have a chat about what happened?"

"Can Bryce come along with us, please?" I asked the young male doctor as I looked across to Bryce, hoping I wasn't overstepping the mark. "Of course, that's no issue at all."

Doctor Forbes led the way as we followed behind. I watched as Bryce pushed his glasses back up his nose and he reached for my hand in moral support. It was as if he could sense my trepidation and fear surrounding the place, combined with the level of pain I was in. Bryce just knew exactly what to do to support me and I didn't want to leave him in that side room whilst I dealt with this alone, no matter how embarrassed I may get. I mean, the bite was next to my breast. I'd have to reveal naked skin. It hadn't been the way I'd thought he'd first see parts of my body.

"I didn't mean to make you think you had to come with me," I leant toward Bryce and whispered as I squeezed his hand before we took a right down the corridor ahead.

"I wouldn't prefer to be anywhere else. Trust me," Bryce admitted, as his hazel eyes watered. The quick swipe of his sleeve as he rubbed them dry made my heart clench that bit tighter at how emotional I'd made him. "I just wish it hadn't happened, that's all."

"I know, but no one's to blame, Bryce."

Doctor Forbes disturbed our conversation as he stopped at a door and led us into the sterile examination room and asked me to take a seat on the bed before indicating the chair to the side for Bryce.

"Miss Webster, I believe you've come into the ER today as you've been bitten," Doctor Forbes said, as he took off his stethoscope and placed it on the table beside him. He quickly logged on to the computer next to him and brought up my records before he turned back to face me. "Can you elaborate to me about how this situation happened, please?"

"Of course. I was visiting my friend..." I looked into Bryce's gaze and saw his nod to continue, "when his dog bit me."

"Has this ever happened before?" Doctor Forbes asked, standing up and grabbing his stethoscope, "can I see the area please?"

I took my top off, allowing the cold air to fall onto my bare skin as Bryce handed me a gown and passed it to me to cover the opposite side.

"Can you lift your arm for me?" Doctor Forbes asked as I nodded with a sharp wince to the notion of grabbing Bryce's hand to help try to relieve the pain. "Has the animal ever shown any indication of violence before?"

The tears that threatened my eyes became too much, and I allowed them to fall down my cheeks as the Doctor prodded the flesh around the wound.

"Doctor Forbes, Fate is an amazing animal, the sweetest, kindest Labrador I've ever known. She lies with a child when sick, snuggles your leg for a cuddle, and barely makes a whimper throughout the day." I forced the words out through my sniffles as Bryce pulled a clean packet of tissues out of his pocket. "I mean I'd been ill and then Bryce had been away, so it's been a month since I've seen Fate and the moment she saw me she wanted to get under my arm. Desperate to get my arm up and to this skin." I pointed to where Doctor Forbes was just about to press.

The moment he did. His eyes widened.

"Miss Webster, I'd like to grab a couple of scans as well as get some strong medication into your system. I'll get the paperwork and admittance forms sorted now." Doctor Forbes stated quickly, before he headed towards the door, "I'm glad you came in today."

I was in shock. I didn't have time to question Doctor Forbes. All I knew was my gut was swirling around in a deep state of panic.

Chapter Seven

BRYCE

Indie and I had been in the medical center for a few days. I mean, how uncomfortable are the chairs in places like this. I know I should've been kicked out and sent home, but then money talked, and, in this case, it meant a quick upgrade to a private room. Luckily, I quickly lost the chair and got an upgrade to an extra bed to keep Indie comfortable.

"Zara, are you sure you're okay keeping everything running with Josh at the moment?" Indie questioned, as she snuggled into the pillow after the latest biopsy that had drained her.

"Shh, you. No business talk. I told you, we've got this. If we have any problems, we'll go to Bryce. I promise you everything will be fine. You're more important than work," Zara replied, as she grabbed her bag from the chair and headed over toward the door.

"But Quince..." Indie piped up before shooting a pained look at me.

"Josh and I have dealt with that piece of shit. Trust me, he won't be bothering any of us, let alone you, Indie," Zara confidently replied. "I've got to get going. Keep me informed of any changes."

"Do I need to go and talk to someone, kitten?" I asked, heading straight toward the side of her bed and reaching for a lock of her hair between my fingers.

"No," she uttered, closing her eyes too, before allowing them to reopen and latch onto mine. "If Zara says it's sorted, then I believe her."

"Okay," I hushed, kissing the top of her head as the tiredness took hold and her restless body struggled to settle.

I'd have preferred to have taken her back to my place to recover, but Doctor Forbes insisted we wait until the final tests results came back today. We'd all been on tenterhooks after the initial scans had progressed into more aggressive ones. Something didn't sit right with us both for just a simple dog bite. We thought a bacteria could have settled into the skin, but then we came straight to the hospital. What else could it be?

We didn't have long to wait.

Doctor Forbes turned back up in our room an hour later with a full team of specialists and news that we'd never have imagined.

Indie had breast cancer and Fate had caught it in its early stages.

He'd given us a plan of action and a world of hope.

With a four-legged friend named Fate, who'd given me the chance of love with the one woman of my dreams, anything was possible. Especially - hope.

Epilogue

INDIE
PRESENT DAY

Today marked the day of change. I was strong enough for my double mastectomy. I'd battled a tough road to this point and originally refused to even consider losing my breasts. I'd thought having the surgery would mean it would make me less of a woman. Who was I kidding?

I was Indie 'sex kitten' Webster and no-one would take that away from me. Bryce had made me realize I was all woman in more ways than one. Two mounds attached to my chest didn't signify that at all. He'd been my rock. My savior. My Hope.

I knew I could do anything I'd put my mind to. The limelight to home life had been a complete flip of a coin. The media couldn't keep their hands off my story of my diagnosis, but that didn't mean they knew how I discovered my fate. I wasn't about to throw Bryce and Fate into the limelight. I was going to protect them at all costs. Thank god for Doctor and Patient confidentiality agreements.

PRESENT DAY

I once thought I needed solidarity in my personal life, but if anything, I now knew I was wrong. I'd just not found the group of people I needed to keep close back then. Now I had them. I wasn't letting any of them go, ever.

"Are you ready to go?" Bryce asked me, before kissing me softly on the lips.

"Absolutely," I replied as Josh stood at the door with my bag in hand.

Zara gave me a huge hug and whispered in my ear, "I'm so proud of you," as she grabbed hold of Chloe's hand, who handed me a pink glitter hat and scarf.

"Just to keep your head warm," she replied. "I don't want you getting ill on the way."

"Thanks, Ladybug, that means a lot. Will you do me a job whilst I'm gone?" I asked Chloe as she dropped Zara's hand and gave me a hug.

"Anything for you, Aunty Indie." I smiled, a huge grin across her face as Josh wrapped his arm around Zara's waist.

"Go and start planning that big party for when I'm home. Let's go for Christmas and don't forget the dresses," I said before kissing the top of her head. "I'm sure Josh and Zara will love to help. Fate needs a special collar too, don't forget."

"Really?" Chloe beamed as she bounced up and down. "I'm going to start planning right away."

"Thank you," Josh mouthed as Bryce reached for my bag from him and grabbed my hand with the other. "Keep us updated."

"We will," Bryce replied.

Just as Bryce opened the door, I felt the familiar nuzzle against the side of my leg and looked down.

EPILOGUE

"Now then, girl. You thought I'd leave without saying goodbye. I think your daddy was just too ahead of the game." I ruffled her fur at the scruff of her neck as she moved closer to me. "Thank you, Fate. Thank you for giving me hope for the future. I'd never have had it without you."

The End

Also by
C.N. Marie

Standalones

Alone With You

Confessions of a Bossy Protector: Frat House Confessions

Life is Guarded: Perfectly Stated

Make Me Want You

Stocks and Lies

Tempted by Fire: FireHouse 13

The Mistaken Bet

Lot in Between Series with Lizzie James

The Lies of Gravity

The Sins of Silence

Declan's Salvation

by

Carrie Austin-Malone

Chapter One

Rubie sat waiting at her favourite table, tucked away in the back corner of Arturo's. She checked her watch; her childhood friend Stephen was late as usual. She had watched the lunchtime diners come and go as she waited for him to show his face. She liked to sit with her back to the wall and people watch. People rarely wanted her favourite table or the one closest to the kitchen as people came here to be seen as they ate great food. But not her. She just came for the spaghetti carbonara and the chocolate mousse. The chef always made the mousse for her, even though it wasn't on the menu anymore. If Stephen told Arturo she was in town, she would get chocolate mousse.

Stephen always bought her to Arturo's for her birthday or if he needed a favour. He knew it was the only way to get her to come to London's West End near where they had grown up, unless it was for business, as most of her corporate clients were based in the city. She glanced around the restaurant. It was pretty much still the same as it was when Stephen and their friend Declan had first taken her there for dinner on her eighteenth birthday.

She sipped her water and popped one of the olives into her mouth that the waiter had left for her earlier.

The colour scheme had been freshened up since her last visit. The walls were now painted a rich cream, with light oak panelling on the bottom half of the walls around the whole of the restaurant, and met either side of the cocktail bar in the far corner near the kitchen. She caught her reflection in one of the large ornate mirrors as she glanced around the restaurant. The mirrors were spaced evenly along the back wall to make the small restaurant look bigger than it was. The wall nearest the bar had autographed framed photos of famous clientele from the past and present. Apart from the food, she loved the small but beautiful crystal chandeliers that hung over each table. They sparkled as they caught the sunlight coming through the windows that faced the street.

Not that she wasn't happy to meet up with Stephen, it was just that Rubie rarely felt the need to leave her home in the little seaside village of Rainmouth on the Essex coast. She'd bought a little fixer-upper nearly six years ago and had built a new life there, away from the hustle and bustle of London. She had Felix her German shepherd, and friends. Cathy, her best friend from her old job, had introduced her to the area her family lived at the other end of her street. George lived opposite and ran a small boarding kennel and rehomed failed working dogs. His grandson, Ryker, had moved in with him several years ago and never left. She'd continued with the Tai-Chi and weapon classes that she'd started as a teenager and now taught self-defence classes in the local church hall.

She checked her phone again. No messages. Where was Stephen? Her house had been a labour of love and helped her heal the broken heart that Declan had left her with. Her house sat high on the cliff road at the edge of the village, where she had a great view from the back of her house overlooking the sea. She hadn't thought twice after seeing the house Cathy had told her about. Being in London was too hard, especially knowing Declan was living there. The house hadn't even been placed on the market; it had been a wreck but had good bones and she needed a project to focus on keeping her thoughts away from Declan and the what ifs. It had needed a complete remodel, including plumbing, electrics, a new roof and windows. It had been the best decision for her. She'd got a bargain when prices were low, due to the work needed as it had sat in probate while the distant family of the previous owner had fought over their estate for a couple of years.

Being a detached house, she'd extended it and now had an open-plan kitchen diner leading to a large living room, three double bedrooms, and a converted loft that contained her office. She was also now debt-free. She'd worked her arse off, living in her home as it was renovated. Thanks to her scholarship and working part-time, she'd left university with no student debts or loans. She'd spent wisely over the years and was now finally able to pick and choose her jobs. She loved the work she did for Stephen. It was more interesting than going through cheating spouses' accounts for the law firms she contracted her services to. His business had been growing and when he needed help to investigate someone's finances, he went to her. He'd also taught her to do background checks and help with investigations. The job was the perfect fit for them both, but this must be a big favour if it was in person and at Arturo's.

Stephen had been her best friend since she was five years old and he was seven. He was more like an older brother she'd never had, being an only child. They'd grown up together as neighbours before they'd been joined by their friend Declan when he met Stephen in class a year later. Their mums had become friends. As single parents, their mums had helped each other out. They'd spent a lot of time together and were always in each other houses. Their friendship had survived Declan's dad returning to his life when he was fourteen and moved Declan and his mum into his home with him. They had stayed close even after she'd headed to university. Stephen had gone into the Navy like his two older brothers and Declan had joined his father's property investment company, or so she'd thought.

Rubie tried not to think about Declan as it made her sad. Being at Arturo's made her sad, like today when she was in their restaurant and the memories hit her like a Tsunami. Arturo's had always been their place, for all three of them, but there was nowhere she would rather eat when she came to London. It was the first proper restaurant the boys had taken her to for her eighteenth birthday. She played with the thin silver bracelet they'd bought her for her twenty-first birthday with the ruby, diamond, and sapphire representing their birthstones and bond. She rarely took it off, as she felt naked without it.

It had been seven years since she had seen Declan, since their relationship had ended because he had cut her out of his life. He had given her hope of a future with him. They'd talked of marriage and children. She had been so naïve back then. If she was honest with herself, it hurt more because he had been her friend first and first everything, first kiss, first grown-up love, even if it had been one-sided. According to his father, Declan had played her; he had used her to rebel against his father's wishes. The whole time he had been with her, Declan was to marry his business associate's daughter and had been engaged to Gisella Marconi.

Now at thirty-one, she knew it was time to move on; she had built a good life for herself, but now she wanted a family to fill her home. She'd been researching sperm banks and IVF as she wasn't sure if she wanted to go it alone. She'd dated other men since, but she had built a wall around her heart. She wouldn't let another man hurt her the way Declan had. Rubie sipped her water. As checked emails on her phone. She heard the bell above the door ring, she lifted her eyes to the door as Stephen walked into the restaurant, waving to her, before removing his coat and handing it off to the waiter.

He strode towards her as she stood to greet him, "Sorry I'm late sweetheart," he leaned in and kissed her cheek as he pulled her into his arms. "God, I've missed you, Rubes. It feels like ages since I've seen you. Video meetings just aren't the same. How's my boy Felix?"

Rubie laughed as she took her seat. She opened her phone and passed it to Stephen to show him the latest pupdates, the way someone would show friends pictures of their kids. "I've missed you too, but you keep me busy. Felix is good, spending the night with George and his dogs."

Stephen flicked through the photos. "My boy's come a long way since you adopted him. He's grown into those ears." Handing the phone back to her, he picked up the menu.

Rubie laughed. "Why are you looking at the menu? We always have the same thing. I placed our orders when I arrived. As soon as you walked through the door, the chef started cooking, and I'm starving. Why were you late?"

Stephen sneaked a peek at the clock above the bar. "Let's eat first and catch up. We can talk shop later."

Stephen watched as she tucked into her pasta carbonara as though she hadn't eaten in days. He grinned as he cut into his Steak Pizzaiola. Rubie scowled. "What? You kept me waiting, and I skipped breakfast. I keep trying to replicate the recipe at home, but it's nowhere near as good. Arturo won't give me the family recipe, although he gave me the one for the chocolate mousse for my thirtieth birthday. I told him I'd marry into the family, but he's still holding out!" Stephen coughed. If only she knew Declan now owned Arturo's.

They chatted together, catching up on each other's news. The restaurant had slowly emptied until they were the last two left. The waiter refilled their glasses and removed their plates. Stephen looked at his watch before he spoke, watching the wait staff prepare the tables for the evening at the other end of the restaurant.

Rubie wasn't usually nervous, but then again Stephen wouldn't usually have waited to tell her the reason for the lunch. "How big is this favour if we're sitting in Arturo's? The only time you bring me here is for my birthday or if we have something to celebrate? It's not my birthday for three months and we're not celebrating anything that I know of?"

Stephen shifted in his seat. "Rubes, an old friend needs our help?" He wondered how he was going to tell her that Declan was the old friend.

Rubie looked at him warily as she sipped her drink, unsure as to why he was being so reticent. "That doesn't tell me much?"

He pulled a file from his briefcase and passed it across the table. "Someone killed Declan's father, along with Roberto Marconi, last month. They used to meet in a park that bordered their territories and were shot at point-blank range by someone on a motorbike. Declan told me there's been peace amongst all the London families since the late eighties and every family has a seat on the council. Declan senior and Roberto Marconi were better than some of the other family heads. They looked after the people in their territories. They didn't extort money for protection and didn't deal in drugs or prostitution. The council is investigating, but so are Declan and Gisella. The council have given them time to investigate and report back, to ensure their own families are not involved."

Rubie was conflicted, but couldn't help herself. She opened the file. The first thing she saw was the crime scene photos. She reviewed the usual summary page of the case that Stephen always provided and saw a USB stick in a plastic wallet she knew would be encrypted with the password they shared if the job contained sensitive data. Closing the file, she took a sip of her water, trying to compose herself, but couldn't. She looked from the folder to Stephen as she pushed it back towards him.

Her face flushed with anger; she spoke quietly, not wanting to bring herself to the attention of the staff. "Are you fucking kidding me? You want me to find out who killed the heads of two crime families? How can you ask me to help with this, you're supposed to be my friend!" No lunch was worth this, and she wasn't even going to get her chocolate mousse, she thought, as she rose from her chair, she grabbed her bag from under the table.

Stephen stood, stopping her from passing him as he reached for her hand. Squeezing it gently, he slipped the

USB stick into her palm. She closed her fist around it and placed it in her pocket. "Please think about it, no matter what happened in the past he trusts you, he's given you access to files, not even his inner circle has seen but I'll understand if you say no. He wouldn't have asked for you if he didn't need our help."

Rubie stared at Stephen, speechless for a moment as the waiter bought her coat. "He cut me out of his life. He promised to come back for me, but he didn't. I'm not even sure if he deserves my help."

Stephen watched Rubie leave. Picking up his phone, he dialled Declan's number. "Well, will she do it?" Declan enquired.

Stephen looked out of the window as he watched Rubie get into a taxi she'd hailed, glaring at him through the window as she mumbled to herself. "She's gone, but took the USB stick, so I'm taking that as a good sign." He sighed as Declan ended the call.

Stephen closed his phone as he heard the doors to the kitchen swing open with a creak. Declan strode into the restaurant; his two cousins Ryan and Sean flanked him on either side as he made his way to Stephen's table. Taking the seat Rubie had vacated. Declan sat down. "She still looks amazing. Is Ryker still her security?"

Stephen sipped his beer. As he assessed his friend, gone was the relaxed playboy persona he used to wear. The man who sat in front of him looked tired and harried since becoming the new official head of the O'Bannon family. "Yeah, he's stayed on here since your dad first sent someone to check on her. George, her neighbour, looks out for her too and considers her family. When I explained our concerns to him, he offered Ryker a room and a cover as his grandson and installed cameras on his property to watch hers. I get weekly updates."

Stephen continued. "George is a good guy, introduced himself to me when my brothers and I helped with the renovations on her house. He was checking me out by the questions he asked, and I did the same. He's a retired dog handler and dog trainer. He fosters failed working dogs, and he helped her adopt Felix and trained him to protect her when she goes running."

Declan poured himself a glass of water from the carafe that had been left for Rubie after the waiter had bought him a fresh glass. "I stayed away because of my father. You know how ruthless and possessive he was. Now he's gone. Nothing is standing in the way except seeing if I can make amends and get her back, but I don't want her caught up in my family drama, especially if a war is brewing."

Chapter Two

Rubie returned to her hotel; she'd planned to go shopping after her lunch but wasn't in the mood. She considered going home, but knew George would be concerned about her change of plans. She'd talked about her trip to London for weeks, as she'd been looking forward to seeing Stephen. She dropped her bag on the bed as she entered her room, kicked off her shoes, and removed her coat. She pulled her laptop out of her bag and booted it up, having argued with herself the short journey from Arturo's to the hotel as to the reasons why she shouldn't get involved, she knew she would. She inserted her encrypted key password into her laptop and started up her program. Her laptop began downloading the data to be reviewed as she input her search parameters.

She couldn't help herself and added her name to her search criteria. There were thousands of pages of data, from bank accounts to call logs and bank accounts from the O'Bannon inner circle and extended family. Stephen must have got the information, as it was exactly what she needed to start her investigation. Stephen must be part of Declan's trusted inner circle. There was no way the O'Bannon's would've handed this information over otherwise. Leaving her program to do its job, she ran herself a bath.

As she soaked in the bath, she tried to relax and listened to her favourite playlist of country songs on her phone. Why now? She was comfortable; she was moving on and had made a good life for herself. They had all stayed friends until the night of the accident.

She reminisced about happier times as she soaked in the huge tub. She'd looked forward to Declan's visits while she'd studied for her degree in business and computer science. Stephen's visits had been less frequent as he'd been away at sea. They had been each other's shadows, and she'd missed them so much. Declan visited often, especially when he needed to get away from his dad or London. He'd told her she was his anchor and kept him grounded.

When she'd returned home and started a job in the city, they'd continued their relationship, they'd taken things slowly. He'd been patient and loving during their time together, taking care of her feelings. He'd made her feel special. He'd taught her nothing had been taboo if they both enjoyed it. He'd even taken her toy shopping. He'd moulded her into the lover he wanted and needed, and the one she wanted to be. It still made her blush, thinking of their time together. She missed the sex, no that was wrong. She missed the **great** sex. Every man she'd dated since hadn't come close. No man had got past the third date or near her bed, as the thought of being with someone else left her cold.

Her world had been turned upside down when they had been out for the night. The guys had insisted on celebrating

Rubie completing her accountancy exam and her promotion to the Forensic Accounting team at Fox, Reicher, and Smyth, one of the largest accountancy practices in London. She'd worked her arse off to get that promotion. She'd been looking forward to not feeling as though she worked twenty-four seven and getting to relax for a while. Studying and working had taken over her life when she wasn't with Declan or Stephen.

They'd gone to Arturo's and then onto a club owned by Declan's family where they'd danced until the early hours, they'd been having a great time. Declan's father had lent them his limousine and driver for the evening, so they could relax and have fun. She'd been sitting in between Declan and Stephen, laughing and joking. Opposite sat Declan's cousins Sean and Ryan, who had always travelled with him at his father's insistence after they had received threats. Declan wouldn't explain why because he hadn't wanted to worry her, he'd said. He just assured her she was safe with him always. As they were driven towards Declan's apartment where they were all staying. Ryan had noticed a car kept trying to overtake them. She had felt the tension build in the car, as Ryan warned them and their driver. Declan had pulled her to him and held her tightly. The car hit theirs and forced it into the roadwork barriers.

Panic hit her as the car rolled onto its side, but Declan hadn't let her go. He'd held onto her tightly. She'd felt scared but protected. They hadn't been thrown about the car thanks to their seatbelts. Stephen had hit his head and was unconscious. She'd checked he was still breathing, even though it hurt to breathe as she moved. Ryan checked on Declan as he'd removed his seatbelt. Sean was on the phone shouting and pushing at the passenger door closest to Declan when they'd heard shouting and gunfire. Ryan and Sean pulled guns from beneath their jackets. The passenger door was forced open from the outside. Turning to Declan, she saw him struggle as he was pulled from the car. Blood trickled down his face. She'd screamed until she realised it was his father and another man pulling him out, thinking they had come to rescue them. As she yelled at Declan's dad not to move him, the glass from the back window blew into the car. Ryan covered Declan as Sean went for her.

Of course, their priority had been Declan. Even though she'd heard him yelling her name as he was pulled away from her and forced to release her, he had promised he would come to her. She'd felt devastated then anger as they'd driven off, leaving her and Stephen behind surrounded by carnage. The last thing she heard was police sirens before she blacked out from pain. That night had changed her life. She'd spent a few nights in the hospital and was visited by the Metropolitan Police organised crime unit. The detectives had asked the same questions repeatedly about Declan and his family. How did she not know his father wasn't just a wealthy businessman, and that he was the head of a crime family?

She still couldn't decide if she'd been stupid or naïve. Had she only seen what she wanted to see because she'd loved Declan? As she got out of the bath, she wrapped the warm fluffy towel around her and glanced at herself in the mirror as she cleared steam from it. She studied her reflection, touching the scar on her forehead close to the hairline she'd received when bullets had sprayed the back window. She'd insisted on keeping it as a reminder not to be so trusting in the future. She'd never heard from Declan again; his number had been disconnected and his social media accounts had disappeared. She'd thought her anger had faded until today. She was sure if she'd wanted to, she could have tracked him down quite easily and confronted him, but her pride hadn't let her.

She had seen an obituary for his father online. She'd felt sad for Declan and his mum but felt nothing for his father's passing, after all, he'd threatened her life. Rubie thought she had gotten on well with his family until his father had sent lawyers to the hospital, they'd passed on the family's concern for her health and offered payment for any private treatment and recompense if she signed an NDA, but she'd refused when they wouldn't answer her questions about Declan.

The final straw had been after refusing to take his money. Men started paying her visits. The first visit had been to her office. The last had been late one night at her mother's house. She'd woken with a man's hand over her mouth before she'd bitten him and fought him. He'd slapped her in retaliation. While the man with him continued to hold her down, Declan's father had stepped out of the shadows. From what she'd learned, he would never have gotten his hands dirty unless his business was personal. He'd told her Declan had been using her to rebel against him as though he were an unruly child, that he had a fiancée, Gisella Marconi, the daughter of a friend. He warned her she would die, and that no fatherless whore would mess up his plans for his son. He'd left leaving an envelope next to the bed, she'd opened it and seen a cheque. The amount of money was life-changing, but she wouldn't be bought off. Her silence had been her final gift to Declan, and she'd never uttered his name again.

She'd done what research she could on suspected crime families. She wanted to make sure she was safe when she'd moved to Rainmouth. Occasionally she'd searched the web for news on the O'Bannon's when she needed a little motivation to move on. His father kept a low profile, his son not so much as he became the face of their company O'Bannon Properties. A few years ago, Declan had been in the top thirty under thirty in the business news and had never been pictured with the same woman twice, except for Gisella Marconi in the early days.

Rubie stood and stretched; realising she'd been working for several hours, her stomach rumbled in protest, having not eaten since lunch. It had gone 2 am and the hotel kitchen was closed, but she knew there was a 24-hour diner open down the street. Looking out of her window, she surveyed the street from her second-storey window. She was drawn to an expensive range rover sitting opposite the hotel. Two men sat in the front, watching the hotel. She checked the registration from the files she had been given access to.

She drew the curtains; her laptop was still searching the documents looking for patterns. She texted Stephen, confirming she would help, she sent him a photo and told him if Declan was in the car outside to send him home and tell him to meet them at Stephen's office the next morning, she'd need to ask questions only he could answer.

She'd reviewed some of the data Patterns were starting to appear. Everyone had them, from spending to money transfers or phone calls. She started a list of what she'd need and would suggest he check the security and access at Declan's head office and home if he hadn't already. If she was right, someone had hacked one of the families or sold them out. It could have been done any number of ways or one of the families went after Declan senior and Marconi in hopes of taking over their territories. She'd read some of the background information on the USB stick Declan had given her. He had given her access to his life. She'd looked at documents where her name was mentioned first. His father had kept an eye on her. There were pictures of her with George and Cathy, even her credit history. She'd seen why Declan had cut her from his life, to protect her. The man had been a little obsessed. She wasn't sure if she was ready to forgive Declan or if he wanted her forgiveness. The only thing he'd asked for was her help.

She changed into her workout clothes, wishing Felix was with her, her protector against shadows and left to find food.

Declan sat in his car with his cousins and trusted bodyguards Sean and Ryan Maguire, right now he only trusted his mum's side of his family, because they had always had his back, as they watched the entrance of Rubie's hotel, his phone rang. "Stephen, what's up!"

Declan looked out of his car window. The street was quiet, being a weeknight. "You've been spotted. She sent me a picture of your car outside her hotel and wants you to leave. She's agreed to meet with us at my office tomorrow afternoon and said she had questions for both of us, oh she said to stop by Arturo's as you own it and bring her the lunch you ruined?"

Ryan turned from the front seat to get Declan's attention. "We have a problem. One angry Rubie is heading this way."

Declan looked across the street. "Shit! Stephen, I've gotta go." As he quickly hung up and got out of the car.

Rubie stepped up to the car. He could feel the anger radiating off his little spitfire. Even though she tried to pretend she wasn't and spoke calmly, he felt his cock come to life. "No! Get back in your car and fuck off! I don't want to see you anywhere near me until tomorrow, bring me lunch and don't skimp on the mousse. I deserve a double portion."

Declan stared down at her, a grin slowly rising on his face, realising she was really going to help him. "Who do you think you're talking to, little girl?"

She could tell that he was laughing at her by the glint in his eyes. That just riled her up more, as she felt the colour rise in her cheeks. "Fuck you, arsehole. You know what? Don't bother coming to the meeting tomorrow. Just send your girlfriend instead!"

Rage took over her body as she stomped off towards the all-night diner. Declan went after her, grabbing her wrist. He pulled her to him, catching her other wrist as she turned to take a swing at him.

He pulled her close and held her hands behind her back. "You know she's not my girlfriend. You've still got a potty mouth when you're angry and need to eat. Do you need to eat baby, let me feed you?"

Rubie wiggled, trying to get free as she lifted her knee to his groin "Let me go!"

Declan blocked her knee. He couldn't help himself. His heart felt lighter. He'd missed her, especially when she got all feisty. It made him hot and his dick harder, if that was even possible; he wanted to throw her over his shoulder and take her up to her room and keep her there for a week, show her who she belonged to. He looked around and pushed her back into the nearest closed shop doorway, holding her close. He ran his fingers through her hair, pulling gently, tilting her head up towards him as their eyes locked. "I've missed you, baby. I always planned to come and get you once it was safe."

Rubie's heart skipped a beat. He gave her a second to see if she'd pull away. He leaned in, kissing her gently on the lips, nibbling on her bottom lip. Shifting her body slightly so there was no way she could strike him in the groin and do him a mischief, he wanted so much more. He wanted the dreams he'd had of her to be a reality. He ran his fingers along her ribs with a featherlight touch. As she gasped, he deepened the kiss as his tongue delved into her mouth. She tasted of peppermint toothpaste. He knew Ryan was at his back. Facing the street, he stood at the doorway, blocking anyone's view from the street.

Declan looked down at the only woman he'd ever loved. "Do you know how long I've waited to kiss you, hold you, have you naked beneath me again?" he whispered as he took her earlobe gently between his teeth, nipping to get her attention as he moved his lips to the sweet spot just behind her ear that made a shiver. "Seven years, seven fucking years I stayed away!"

Rubie groaned and tried to push at his chest, but he didn't move. "No one asked you to stay away. I'm sure you consoled yourself with one of the many women you've dated over the years?"

He pulled her body to him so she could feel his stiff cock against her stomach. "There's been no one in my bed except you, and I know no other man has been in yours. Those women were a smokescreen, so my arsehole father wouldn't go after you. If you couldn't be scared off or bought, he didn't like it. You became his obsession. If he thought I was happily playing the field, he'd think I lost interest."

Declan loosened the hold he had on her, taking a breath to calm himself, as none of this was her fault. This was all on dear old dad. She hadn't moved, waiting, watching him as though he was a bug under a microscope. "What do you want to eat, I don't want you wandering around late at night, I'll get one of the boys to go grab us something to eat from the Diner up the street, we'll eat in the car or we can eat in your room!"

Rubie grumbled to herself. She couldn't believe the way he was behaving, as if he hadn't disappeared from her life. "Go away. I can get my own food. Wait, how do you know no one's been in my bed?" Screw this, she thought, as she shoved past him. She wasn't sure she wanted the answer.

He'd wanted his family drama out of the way before going after her, but knew his time was running out to try and he needed to win her back. He couldn't walk away from his people or family. That wasn't an option. Death or prison were the only options in his world. It didn't matter that all his businesses were clean now, and he planned to keep it that way. The people in his territory needed him. He wouldn't lie to himself. He'd thought of taking out his father, but he knew there would be fallout if he had. He'd die before he would let anyone take over his territory. His father was nothing like him. The community elders and business leaders in his territory had placed their faith in him when they'd come to him, having heard rumours about his father stepping down, wanting to offer their support. None of them had wanted to come under his uncle. When his father had been murdered, they had come to him with information and help, which had narrowed down the suspects.

As he watched her storm off, he followed behind a short distance. Ryan walked next to him as he watched the street.

Ryan was telling him what a stupid idea it was and to just throw her in the car. Sean sniggered from the car as he followed slowly behind. Hearing the roar of the motorbike, Ryan looked up the street. A motorbike with two riders headed towards them. The pillion pulled and aimed a gun. Ryan pushed Declan. "Down!" Sean pulled in front of them to use the armour-plated car as a shield. Declan pulled Rubie to the ground as he felt his arm burn and rolled her beneath him. He heard bullets ping the car as another bike came from the other direction.

Declan held Rubie close. "Shit, stay down, move to the car when I say run, run, the boys have this." Thank God the road was quiet; no doubt the police would be on their way. Someone must have heard the shots.

Declan's only thought was to protect Rubie as he covered her body with his. He couldn't and wouldn't lose her again. Not while there was breath still left in his body.

Chapter Three

Rubie looked around as Sean drove them into a small street, passing security guards at the end they were ushered through to a private residential cul-de-sac, shaped like a horseshoe with large upscale houses each with gates, manicured landscaping and large driveways. In a van behind was Declan's backup team, who had been watching the rear of the hotel, in case she'd tried to sneak out. A driver, Declan, Ryan, and one of Declan's other men who'd had medical training. She'd wanted to go with Declan, but he'd insisted she stay with Sean, in case there was another attack. His favourite car may be full of holes on one side, but it was still safer than the van.

Sean had blasted a message to men he'd trusted in Declan's inner circle, as he'd driven through Declan's territory. Sean pulled into the drive of the largest house at the top of the horseshoe as the van went into the garage connected to the house.

Sean placed his arm around her shoulder and lead her

into the house. As he nodded to people on the way, one handed him an earpiece, she heard a commotion and looked around. "Don't worry, there is a back entrance into a small medical centre. We have our own medical team on standby. Let's get you settled. Stephen is on his way. He's checking out for you and bringing your things here."

He took her to a guest room. "Declan's mum leaves clothes here for when she visits and the clothes in the wardrobe are hers. This was originally his dad's house. I'm sure she wouldn't mind you borrowing something. You can clean up in the bathroom over there. When you're ready, come join me in the kitchen."

Rubie went to the kitchen wearing a pair of Declan's mum's lounge pants and one of Declan's shirts she'd found in his room when she'd been snooping. Stephen had arrived with her overnight bag and stood by the kitchen counter drinking coffee and chatting with Sean as he prepared sandwiches.. Sean spoke into the security earwig he now wore as he scrolled through his phone. "Keep trying to get information from him. I want to know this fucker's life history and who hired him." He ended the call, turning to Stephen. "Can you check our security cameras to make sure there are no blindspots or if cameras have been moved please?"

"No problem!" Stephen glanced down at his friend as he pulled her into his chest and hugged her gently. He spoke quietly. "Declan and Ryan are both in surgery to remove the bullets, but they should be okay. Declan took a bullet to his arm; Ryan took two bullets, one to the back of the leg and one in his shoulder."

As Stephen left to check security, she noticed several sheathed knives sitting on the worktop. Sean waited for her reaction to the knives, seeing her eyes light up even though the tiredness was clear to see. "Wondered when you'd notice them. No playing with knives until you eat something, so sit, eat and then you can decide which knife you want. They're all different weights, as I didn't know your preference."

Rubie put her best innocent face on. "What makes you think I know how to use a knife?"

Sean smiled that 'I know a secret' smile he'd used on occasion back in the day. "Who do you think Declan made responsible for watching over you when his dad got obsessed after the accident? I know where you like to run, that you switch up your routes and the days you teach self-defence. I know that you go to London to train with your Martial Arts teacher from when you were a kid on a Saturday morning before you meet your mum for lunch. I kept your secret, didn't tell him about your weekend classes, thought it could be a surprise, but please refrain from slitting his throat. I know he can be an arsehole, but he's family."

Rubie dropped her eyes to the floor and took a seat at the table, thinking whether to be honest, this man had watched over her on occasion. What was that saying? *The truth will set you free.* "After I got less angry, I always hoped he'd come back for me as he promised. In my mind, I'd given him until my next birthday, otherwise I'd move on completely because I want a family. I wanted to be the woman he needed. To protect him when it came down to the wire. I find some people underestimate women and I've been taught to use that to my advantage."

She could hear voices coming from Sean's earpiece. "His

uncle and his cousins are on their way. They should be here in the next thirty minutes. They heard Declan had been hurt." He called Stephen. "Declan gave you the approval to check all phones and calls made. I want his spy."

Rubie sat back and pulled out her laptop and waited. She just needed Declan to be okay so she could kick his arse. Had these people never heard of Kevlar? At least finding the spy would give her something to do while she waited. "I can do that. Just keep the coffee coming."

Sean had chatted with her while she worked on the information Declan had given her, adding questions to her list. He answered her questions as far as he was allowed and filled her in on some events since he'd last seen her. Declan hadn't lied. There had been no one else, and he'd stayed away for her sake. He and Gisella were just friends. They'd faked their engagement to give them time to talk their fathers into a business deal, to take their families down more legitimate routes and out of their stupid marriage idea. They had set up a company building and managing resort-style hotels and they'd made a lot of money. According to Sean, the fathers met in the park regularly to shoot the breeze and complain about their lack of grandchildren. She couldn't understand why he couldn't have got a message to her. She would have waited, however long it took for him to come for her, since he'd nearly taken too long.

It was time for her to step up. He'd protected her from his father, and now it was her turn to protect him. She glanced up at Sean, standing by the door, watching her. She glanced back at him. "You guys need to invest in Kevlar. I'm buying you all vests for Christmas."

Looking back at her laptop, she carried on working. "Do you trust me, Sean?"

Sean laughed, "Yes, why?"

"Ryker is one of yours, isn't he?" she smiled. "George forgot he told me he didn't have any grandkids when I moved in, then a grandson came to visit and didn't leave."

Sean grinned, looking over at Stephen as he walked back into the kitchen. "Nope, not mine, his."

Stephen refilled Rubie's coffee. "Who's mine?"

She stood glaring at him, hands on her hips. "You put Ryker on me?"

"Of course, Declan insisted, about a year after you moved into your house. George had noticed a stranger coming around asking questions and came to me. Declan checked and found his dad hired a private investigator; he was checking up on you. Kept threatening you to test Declan."

"Why didn't you tell me? Don't forget I know when you're lying!"

Embarrassed, and slightly uncomfortable with the way she was staring at him. "Don't look at me like that. You wouldn't allow Declan's name to be mentioned after the car accident. Declan kept in touch when he could and found out his dad had broken into your mum's home and threatened you. He went ballistic. Sean and Ryan had to stop him from killing his father as he would have died too."

Rubie glared at both men. She was surrounded by alpha arseholes. She and Declan were going to have words when he woke up. He'd cared enough to protect her, but not to reach out. She sat with her head in her hands. She would never understand men. If he hurt her again, she would cut out his heart. She needed to think his uncle would be here soon. "Sean, tell me who takes over if he dies and do you have men you can trust?"

He thought for a moment, looking at Stephen as he

nodded towards the door. "Leave. What I need to tell her is family business. Declan told me he planned to marry her so she's technically family in my eyes and this could get you killed."

Stephen shook his head. "Nope, not going anywhere. We've been friends since we were eight years old and she was six. Consider me adopted."

Sean glanced back and forth between them, deciding how much information to give them. "His uncle inherits as Declan doesn't have any children yet. You'll need to work on that when you get married. You're both not getting any younger, you know. His uncle gained his territory before the council was put in place. The council agreed territories stay within a family unless the council proves a family was involved in a family member's death. It's complicated and Declan can explain it."

He continued. "We're related to his mum, distant cousins, but our mums are close. She married his dad as part of an arrangement to build bonds with the Maguire's out of East London and to get access to the docks. His mum ran when Declan was five, Declan Senior had been sent to prison, she knew she and Declan wouldn't be safe with his uncle in control but couldn't come to us. Declan's uncle's territory was smaller than his dad's, their father had split the territory into two, the larger part went to Declan Senior and the smaller part went to his older illegitimate half-brother, neither of his sisters could step in as it wasn't done back then and their children were too young. His uncle stood in for his dad until he got out, so she changed her name and appearance and hid on the council estate where you all grew up."

As Rubie listened and continued typing, Sean poured more coffee into her now empty mug as he carried on talking. "His Dad went crazy when he found out they'd disappeared, but by the time he'd gotten out, his territory was a mess. His brother had told people he was following his instructions from prison, and he tried taking over his territory in his dad's absence. He was extorting protection money from small businesses, running brothels, drugs and a variety of underground clubs, including bare-knuckle fighting and gambling. His uncle wanted what he thought should be his as the older brother and was skimming the books, taking money for his own territory.

His uncle is ruthless, and his sons aren't much better. They're abusive and Declan was building a case to take to the council. They think Declan is too soft for wanting to look after the people in his territory like the Maguires do. You don't bite the hand that feeds you is a saying we live by. They don't want to work for their money and when they found out Declan made more money legitimately than they did illegally; they were jealous. We were made part of his security by his mum when he was sixteen. She always had Declan senior's ear. He listened to her advice, another thing his uncle didn't like. When his dad died, she moved to the States to live with family for a while and gifted this house to Declan."

Rubie paced, thinking as she walked back and forth. "Right then, when they get here, can I suggest letting them in? I'll greet them, which will piss them off. If anyone asks, his sources are wrong. Declan is fine, and he's looking for the shooters. We need to pretend he's okay and if anyone asks, only Ryan was hurt. I want people you trust with me. I'll also deal with the police if they come asking questions. It's my turn to protect him."

Sean smiled as he reached into his pocket. Pulling out his phone, he began texting. "I always knew you'd make him a good wife. I'll go get your ring from Declan's safe. If anyone asks, you're his fiancée. Stephen, I'll stay with her while she meets them. I need you to give me updates on Declan and my brother."

As Stephen and Sean left, discussing strategy, she closed her eyes for a moment and said a silent prayer as she went to check out the knives.

Chapter Four

She guarded Declan as he slept. He mumbled her name. She spoke quietly as she sat next to him and held his hand. He would settle for a moment and then move around again. "It's okay. I'm here, we're all OK, we're with you." Hoping that by repeating it over and over to him, he would hear her as he came through the layers of the anaesthetic as she watched the numbers on the machine he was hooked up to while they beeped.

Ryan was still in the small medical facility being monitored as he'd hit his head when he went to the ground. The doctor had explained both men's injuries and the surgeries. For now, they'd need rest.

Stephen and Sean had been looking at the data she'd collated in Declan's office. The bikes had been stolen and dumped. The riders disappeared, with one shooter dead and the other in their custody. It was a matter of time before he spilt his guts. He was a contractor with no affiliations to any family that they knew of yet.

The hotel had given Sean the camera footage. She hadn't known it was one of Declan's and Gisella's boutique hotels. Fortunately, there was no working CCTV on the street. According to Sean, it kept breaking. Rubie suspected they used a jamming device whenever they were in the area, so the police couldn't see them.

Rubie sat waiting for him to wake and continued working. Stephen walked into the room. He didn't look happy. "Ryker is on his way and bringing Felix. George is watching your house and one of my team is heading there to increase your security. Sean showed me footage of you and his uncle. Declan is going to lose his shit that he laid hands on you and don't think I didn't notice you provoked him?"

Rubie gave him a slow smile. "He slapped me and called me a whore; don't think I won't make him pay if he's responsible for this."

Stephen snarled, "You provoked him! Are you trying to start a war?"

"I'm trying to end one. He was lucky I didn't slice his throat; I was being fucking nice!"

Declan slowly woke. Warily, he waited as he listened to the sounds around him. His arm hurt like a bitch and he could feel a weight on his chest. He slowly opened his eyes, looking around the room. He realised he was in his own bed. As he looked down, he saw Rubie resting her head on his chest, snuggled into his side.

Stephen moved from his position by the door, Felix moved with him. Speaking quietly, not to wake her. "Hey mate, how are you feeling?"

Declan couldn't take his eyes off as he lifted his head

Rubie moved slightly. He pulled her closer, as her hand moved up his body slowly and it stilled when it reached his chest. She'd gotten into bed with him and was wearing his shirts. "Is she okay? How long have I been out?"

Stephen pulled up a chair next to the bed. "Too long for her. It was only four hours, but she has your men eating out of her hand, stepped in as though she was made to be a boss's wife."

Declan smiled as he stroked her hand resting on his chest and brought it to his lips. He noticed a large diamond on her ring finger. Looking again, he realised it was his ring. He'd had it since the day of the accident when he was going to propose.

Not wanting to wake her, he looked at Stephen, then back at the ring. His heart jumped. He mouthed his message to Stephen to read his lips. "What the fuck did I miss?"

Stephen grinned. "Meet your fiancée, don't screw it up. They removed the bullet from your arm. Ryan's still out. His operation took longer. We were going to wake you, but she wouldn't let us. Threatened to castrate us if we did. Just so you know, she has a knife under her pillow, oh, and she pulled it on your uncle."

He was shocked that his woman had confronted his uncle, rendering him speechless.

Stephen continued with his update. "She wasn't hurt, but she is angry you got hurt. In between looking at the data you sent us and taking on your uncle, she's been researching body armour and kept mumbling that you all need Kevlar suits. If she wasn't wearing the ring that Sean gave her for you, I think you'd have a battle on your hands."

Declan smiled. He would not let her go now that she

was wearing his ring. "You better fill me in on what I missed."

Stephen whispered, not wanting to wake Rubie. "Word reached your uncle that you'd been hurt. We're trying to find his spy. He rocked up with his sons. Insisting on seeing you saying he was concerned you'd been hurt. She was all class man, but she provoked him, so don't kill him yet!" Chuckling, he pulled up the video recording and handed Declan his phone.

Declan was intrigued as he watched the video of the standoff between Rubie and his uncle in the foyer of his house. His uncle had walked into his home with his men as though he owned it. He'd tried to push past her, thinking he'd knock her to the floor. She'd pretended to stumble and tripped him; he'd seen her use that move before on a school bully. She pulled the knife from the sheath hidden in the bottoms she wore and held it to his throat. He watched the tension between his uncle's and Sean's team as they stood, guns drawn on each other. She'd got them all to calm down and holster their weapons. She'd even offered the fuckers tea if they wanted to wait until Declan was free to talk to him before his uncle had tried to push past her. He was in awe of his woman, watching as she'd sat on his uncle. She'd leaned in and whispered something; he'd nodded his head and she let him up. His woman had skills, his uncle had stormed out, he'd been embarrassed by a woman. Declan knew he wasn't going to let that slide. He was going to have to ask Sean to find a female bodyguard for her.

He felt his erection grow. He'd missed her so much, he'd wanted to go to her so many times, but couldn't and stopped himself, not knowing who was watching him. Now he wanted nothing more than her beneath him, naked. He had a lot of time to make up for.

Sensing his mistress was waking, Felix jumped onto the bed to check on her, pushing at Declan to move so he could squeeze between them. He rubbed his nose into her neck as she woke. "Back off Declan, I'm still not happy with you."

"It's not me, sweetheart."

Rubie opened her eyes slowly as Felix nudged her arm. "Hey boy, I missed you."

Ryker stood by the open door, assessing the room. "You okay Rubie? Cathy packed a bag for you. I'm ready to go when you are and we have a safe house until this is sorted."

Declan's eyes narrowed as he waited, not realising he was holding his breath. Would she go with him? Rubie waved her hand at Ryker, showing him the rock on her ring finger. "I'm staying." She turned and smiled up at Declan, leaned over, and kissed the top of her head.

"In that case, I'll go see if Sean needs an extra man." Ryker and Stephen left the room, taking Felix with them as they closed the door quietly behind them.

Rubie went to get off the bed as Declan pulled her back. "Are you really staying?"

Rubie sat back on the bed. "Yes, for now, you need me, or at least that's what everyone is implying. I'll help find who took out your father and Marconi."

"Give me time, please, to convince you to let me back into your life. I promise I'll never let you down again. I love you, I always have."

She'd waited seven years to hear those words again. Rubie was still apprehensive, but being close to him made her body hum. It had been so long since she had felt that way. It had always been him. She didn't want anyone else. He could see her brain ticking over as her eyes moved around the room. "Okay, but there will be rules."

She moved next to him, getting comfortable. She

cuddled close to him as he rolled her beneath him. "You need to rest Declan."

"No, I need to be inside you." He looked at her the way he used to when they'd made love. She knew there was no arguing with him whenever he got that look.

He held her gaze as his blue eyes went slightly darker. He moved in to kiss her. She reached up, touching his face gently. She held his head in her hands as her lips met his. His lips were gentle at first, taking care as he caught her bottom lip between his teeth. She could feel his cock. She slowly pulled at his pants to release it. She took it in her hand, stroking it gently as he groaned. He ran his fingers along her throat to her breast, unbuttoning his shirt as he went. It was one of his favourites. His uncle had stopped in his tracks when he had seen her wearing a man's shirt and ring. He would have known it was one of his, that he'd never let her wear another man's shirts, wear another man's scent; all the O'Bannon men were possessive arseholes, himself included. He needed to stake his claim. He needed her now, naked, to feel the softness of her skin against his. He had waited so long for her.

He watched as Rubie removed his shirt, throwing it on the chair next to his bed where he'd placed his underwear. All he wanted to do was taste her and drive his cock deep inside her, take her over and over so she would never doubt his love or who she belonged to. He wanted her to feel as though he was still inside her every time she moved. He kissed his way down her body to the little landing strip of hair that covered her pussy. He parted her legs. He wanted to make sure she was ready for him. He could smell her arousal and cocoa butter. The heady mixture was intoxicating.

He parted her folds, his tongue played with her clit.

Before he pushed two fingers into her pussy before adding a third, as cried out. Tasting her cream, he continued his onslaught as he moved with her to the bottom of the bed. As her leg hung over the edge of the bed, he wiped his mouth on her thigh and his heart beat faster. If he was still wearing the monitor, his heartrate would be calling his medical team.

"Please don't stop," she cried as his fingers continued to pump inside her. She was ready for him. He licked her cream from his fingers. "Do you know how good you taste to me right now, Rubie?"

His fingers entered her again as she groaned. "No."

Declan released his fingers and held them to her lips. "Taste it. This is what I've been missing."

He leaned over her body, Rubie took his fingers into her mouth, and sucked. She tasted cocoa butter and herself. He ran his fingers down her body, gripping her hips. He lifted her body off the bed, pulling it towards him, her legs hooked around his waist. He entered her an inch at a time, pulling out and pushing back as he went deeper, stretching her pussy until she was full of his cock. All he could hear were their groans, all he could smell was sex. When his cock was finally up to the hilt, he stilled. She groaned.

"Declan, don't you stop. I need you now."

He grinned, entering her again and again in one full stroke as her pussy clenched his cock when he tried to move. "I'm not sure you deserve to come. In fact, I think you deserve to be spanked! Don't think for one moment that I didn't know you provoked my uncle." As he pulled his cock out of her body, she moved her hips to his waist, pulling him towards her.

"Fuck me now, spank me later or I swear to god I will get a gun from Sean."

Declan gripped her hips, pumping his cock into her pussy as her legs gripped his waist. He played with her clit. "more please," she repeated until she screamed his name and he emptied his cum into her.

She pulled him down on top of her. Sated, they both lay holding each other. Declan went to move to clean her body, but she wouldn't let him go.

"Who said we were finished, Declan?"

Declan smiled to himself. Investigations could wait. There was no place he'd rather be than here with Rubie.

The End

Also by
Carrie
Austin-Malone

Hiraeth: An Indie Love Anthology

The Last Day
by
DJ Cook

Chapter One

I stood looking out at a world I'd tried to hide from, mumbling to myself as the wind muffled my words into silence.

I'd had a lot of time to think about my life over the past few months. In fact, there wasn't anything left for me to do other than to think anymore. I'd thought about the next time I'd eat, when I'd be able to get an uninterrupted night sleep in a warm bed, but mostly, I'd dwelled on everything that I'd once had—incredible friends, a boyfriend, a home—and how it was all gone.

I'd contemplated everything I'd lived through that overshadowed all of the good. The only things left were the pain of my past and the uncertainty of my future.

A year ago, I'd had a normal life—normal to me, anyhow.

I hadn't had much of a family, my father having been an

excessive drinker, spending his days muttering to himself more than he would ever speak to me. We'd had nothing in common to begin with, so telling him I liked men and not women had been the nail in the coffin for us.

But my dysfunctional family had never been a reason for me to not excel, so I'd finished college and had been eager to head to university.

Until I wasn't anymore.

Until I met Shane: a tall, slim guy with light greys woven through his hair and beard, whose voice was as tender as his touch, and whose words wrapped me in a euphoric bubble.

We'd met online, had a few dates, and things had moved fast for us. Shane was much older and more mature than the eighteen-year-old me, and I'd welcomed the commitment as I hadn't been able to wait to move out of my father's home. It had never felt like my home, and although my life didn't turn out as planned, I didn't think I would ever be in a position of wanting to go back there.

I hadn't needed to work: Shane had had enough money to fund a lavish lifestyle for the both of us—city breaks, shopping sprees and meals in the most sought after places —that to any other person my age would have been merely a dream.

Six months ago, I'd had friends who wanted to hang out with me and would message me constantly.

Until I didn't anymore.

A few of those friends hadn't agreed with me dating someone so much older, and the ones who hadn't cared, I'd pushed away without even trying.

With Shane, the hands of time had moved so fast, and I'd never made time for those friends who'd once held importance in my life. I spent all of my time on Shane, because I was utterly in love. Being with him meant I needed no one else in the world.

I hadn't known at the time how far from the truth that was.

Three months ago, I'd waited for Shane —the only person I cared about, until I didn't anymore—to come home from work.

"Toby, I'm home."

I could still hear his voice so vividly in my mind, despite how many times I'd tried to forget. He'd left me with nothing, taking pieces of my heart, pieces of my life, until there had been nothing left.

I knew all of that now, but I wished I didn't.

Part of me wanted to turn back time and naively soak up more of him before he turned my world upside down, but mostly, I hoped I could just forget.

That weekend when Shane had thrown me out onto the streets, I'd had no one to turn to. I'd quickly packed a bag of my things with enough tears to make my eyes bulge and then wandered around town to try to keep myself busy and out of the cold.

I'd spent the first two nights in a twenty-four hour supermarket, where I took residence in a toilet cubicle, lightly sleeping, sitting upright on the toilet and waking up every time the sound of the toilet door made me jump. It hadn't been ideal, but at least I'd been warm and not slumming it on the wet and windy streets where I could have been seen by those friends who had once meant so much to me. That would have been embarrassing.

Those two nights had allowed me to prepare for the

inevitable, as it hadn't been long before I was caught and forced to sleep on the streets.

I'd ended up leaving town with what little money I had left and hadn't once looked back—not because I hated the town I'd grown up in but because of the shame. I'd never imagined I'd be banned from entering the local supermarket I'd visited nearly every lunch break while at college.

It was embarrassment that had made me get on that train to Edinburgh.

I'd lived day-by-day, not once thinking about the next, because there were times I hadn't believed there would be a tomorrow. There were nights I'd shivered in the cold where I'd felt as though my body was shutting down, and as my eyes had shut, part of me hadn't woken up at all.

The cold of the concrete slabs I'd slept on left a sharp agonising pain that bled deep through my skin, attacking my nerves and numbing my muscles, but the days had grown longer and things had got a little better.

At first, I'd hid myself away from the bustle of the city streets, and only spoke to others who were homeless, trading everything other than the clothes on my back for food and a sleeping bag. It wasn't until I'd had nothing left to trade that I'd had no choice other than to sit within the middle of the city centre and beg for money.

The first few times, I hadn't stopped crying—I'd cried through a lack of dignity, disgusted in myself and by what I'd allowed to happen to me—and then I'd spent the rest of the time crying because of the kindness of strangers who had passed by.

I think a lot of them had taken pity on me because I'd looked young.

I may have been young, but with each day I'd spent on

the streets, I aged physically and mentally more than I ever should have.

I stared across the city in the spot I liked to think and where I didn't feel so alone, everything seemed to be put into perspective for just a short minute. All I'd ever known and everything I'd been through almost didn't seem to matter as I watched the heavenly sunset above the horizon.

My eyes darted across the sky to all the colours—an artist's canvas, a work in progress—merging into an ongoing masterpiece as the evening drew to a close. The sky seemed to change with each blink as the wind rushed into my eyes and my eyelids shut to protect them.

As I stood on top of that bridge—my past having led me there on that beautiful night—I glanced to my left, along the road that led back to the streets I'd come from, where I'd slept for the past few months and where I would continue living a life full of uncertainty and pain.

I looked to the right where unknown streets lay in front of me. Could I dust myself off and try to piece together the parts of my life I had control over? I didn't think I had the energy to pick myself up, and turning right seemed to be the hardest choice of them all. . I couldn't deal with more pain—my body had felt enough of it to last a lifetime, being at the top of its threshold for so long. I had become used to the world of discomfort, the only reprieve coming after the occasional time I'd allow myself to drink away my sorrows. I was in a cycle I couldn't get out of, and maybe I'd found a little comfort in that.

I considered going to my left again and shook my head.

I had one more choice.

I straightened my back and lifted my head up to the now dark sky. I shivered with cold as I stood gazing out at the concrete jungle in front of me.

I wondered if people could see me all the way up here. I wondered if my pose resembled a superhero overlooking the streets that weaved themselves under the shadows of the bridge.

I'm no superhero. I can't fly, but I can jump.

Chapter Two

My feet, once cemented to the bricks of the bridge, became light as I readied myself to not feel anymore.

The world slowed around me and I took one final deep breath, holding it in until, gasping, I dragged in another—one I didn't want to breathe.

A silhouette appeared next to me, carving a shadowed outline on the streets below.. I turned to find a woman standing a few columns away from me, her eyes shut and her arms spread like she was on the bow of the Titanic. She embraced the wind as it battered her face, just like it did to mine, like it was the only thing stopping her from jumping—stopping both of us from jumping

And suddenly, I was presented with another choice...

I could let her jump, or I could save her.

I hopped off the edge of the bridge as if I wasn't inches away from my own death and raced over to her.

Her arms had flopped to her side like she didn't have any further energy to fuel her body.

The traffic below drowned out any sound she was making, other than the occasional silence between the noise of cars revealing her small sob's.

"Are you okay?"

Have you ever said something and instantly regretted your words? Of course she wasn't okay. The sound of my voice so close behind her startled her, forcing her to look at me before she turned swiftly away, shaking in the bitter wind. If I'd brought my sleeping bag to the bridge, I would have wrapped it around her.

"Is there anything I can do for you?" My voice cracked. I'd not said that many words out loud in a long time.

"Go away," she said fiercely, sounding angry at the world—angry at me.

"The way you're feeling right now—" I wanted to tell her that what she was feeling was temporary, but who was I kidding? If I hadn't been focused on the thought of someone else in pain, I'd still be standing on the ledge of the bridge. Nothing about these feelings were temporary.

"How can you even fathom how I'm feeling right now?" she yelled, looking directly at me, her eyes a bright red colour under the dim street lighting. "You have no fucking clue what has led me to this point in my life, you scruffy prick."

Ouch.

She was right, though. I was scruffy. I couldn't remember the last time I'd had a bath or showered with hot water from a pipe instead of cold water from the sky.

"You're right. I don't know how you're feeling, but I know how I feel. I was standing right on that ledge just a minute ago. When I saw you, I got down."

"You still don't understand. Just go, leave me alone." She was no longer angry, she looked defeated. I couldn't give up like she had, I had to try harder.

"Then let me understand, whether that's now or in a week. Let me be there for you." I paused for a second, looking into her eyes. "Please don't jump. Please don't let my last memory of this world be seeing you give up. Please don't say I got off that ledge for nothing, because getting back up there after you will be really damn hard." I choked at my words.

She didn't speak. Instead, she rubbed her eyes and wiped her hands down her dark T-shirt, that had the crest of a famous band on the back, and then stepped steadily off the ledge, placing her a few feet from me.

"Happy now?" she said sarcastically, not acknowledging that I'd been ready to end my life as well.

I didn't blame her for that. She clearly had a lot going on in her head.

"Over the moon." I was fluent in sarcasm, too, and it helped: her shoulders dropped as she realised I was just as human as she was, just a scruffier male version.

"You look cold. Do you have somewhere warm to go?" I asked, knowing full well that if she didn't, I wouldn't be able to save her any more than I already had.

She nodded, her emotions still in full control of her body—one minute angry and the next crying like there would be no tomorrow. If only that were true.

"Good. Would you like me to walk you there? You shouldn't be wandering around this late by yourself."

"I think that would be a good idea. If I'm not ending my life tonight, you're certainly not. I'm not leaving you on this bridge." She grabbed my hand without hesitation, no thought to the dirt that lingered on my skin.

"I guess that settles it then. Nobody is dying tonight." Together, we walked to the right, off the bridge.

I could tell we were different from the moment we met: she seemed angry, full of emotion, as if whatever had happened to her was still raw and she was still processing it; I'd had a whole lot of time to understand what had happened to me, although I was in pain, I was sick of living a life of neglect—a life I no longer wanted to live.

"I'm Toby," I said looking to the floor, conscious that my breath could probably boil acid.

"Siobhàn." She pulled me closer, and I desperately wanted to pull myself away. I'd not had this much human contact since Shane. To say I'd missed it would have been an understatement, but I was embarrassed. The way I looked and smelt made me feel uncomfortable. I hated what I'd become, but for some reason it didn't seem to faze Siobhàn one bit.

We didn't speak for the rest of the journey, and I spent most of it feeling awkward, second-guessing everything I wanted to ask and say. I was out of practice at talking to people, and Siobhàn seemed too out of sorts to even consider small talk.

"This is me." We approached a semi-detached house just outside the city centre. It hadn't been much of a walk but my feet ached in my shoes, if that's what you could call them: worn, and discoloured with an unacceptable number of holes.

"Are you going to be okay?" This seemed like the only suitable question, even though I knew that she needed time.

"At least for tonight. You're coming in, right?"

"What? Are you sure?" I looked at her house, craving the warmth that was just metres away from me.

"Of course. I wouldn't have let you walk all this way for no reason. Besides, I could do with the company."

I smiled and walked up the narrow path lined with bushes that hadn't been pruned in years, following her to the front door. As she turned the key in its lock, she turned to me once more.

"Thank you, Toby."

"For what?"

"For saving me."

I smiled and prepared to not feel the cold outside. Maybe I was a superhero, after all, and maybe she was mine.

Chapter Three

I didn't know if it was my stench or her need to be the best hostess that led me to being in the shower just a few minutes after entering her house. I liked to think it was a combination of the two and not just the first.

It was like I had jumped off that bridge, died and gone to heaven as steam filled the cubicle and the hot water ran against my skin. The shower even did a pretty good job at hiding my tears, too. as an overwhelming feeling of happiness filled me.

For the first time in months, the numbness was gone. Was a shower—something so many people took for granted every day—really all it took to fix me?

I must have spent more than half an hour in the shower, using every soap, shampoo and potion in sight in order to rid of the smell of the streets that always seemed to linger on me.

I didn't want to get out, but the thought of leaving

Siobhàn downstairs by herself a moment longer made my stomach turn.

I dabbed myself dry with the towel she had given me. It was the softest cotton that had ever caressed my skin, like a hug for my senses. The only downside was putting on my old clothes that were sodden. I had told Siobhàn I'd be happy changing into her clothes, but she thought I was joking.

"That was incredible. Thank you so much," I said with a smile. It had been so long it almost hurt to move my face in such an unnatural way.

"You're welcome. How long has it been since you've had one?"

"Honestly, I stopped keeping track a long time ago. It's easy to lose all sense of time and days when the only tell-tale signs are the rise and fall of the sun and the changing of the seasonal items in the shop windows. I've not had one since at least Christmas."

"That's months. I'm sorry," Siobhàn said and naturally grabbed my hand, comforting me as best as she could.

"You have nothing to be sorry for, and that shower means more than you'll ever know." I smiled once more and allowed my other hand to hold hers.

The television flickered in the background, filling the room with intermittent bright light. My eyes had a hard time adjusting to a screen at first, but within an hour or so, I found myself feeling comfortable—on the sofa, and in Siobhàn's company.

After all this time I'd had no hope, but Siobhàn had set aside her feelings and unknowingly come to my rescue, and I may not have had the smidge of hope I did. I may have been nothing at all.

"Do you want to talk? I'm all ears." I spoke softly, not wanting to push her.

"Shall we talk tomorrow? I think we could both do with a good night's sleep."

I nodded, hesitantly pushing myself off the sofa and making my way towards the front door.

"What are you doing?" She looked confused. "Did you really think I was going to kick you out onto the streets? You're not going back there—not if I have any say in the matter. I'll go and grab you a blanket and pillows."

I couldn't speak. If it had been possible, tears would have escaped through my mouth as I dropped to a crouch.

I muttered, trying to say thank you—trying to tell her how much I appreciated it—but it was all inaudible.

"Come on, you." She wrapped her arm around my shoulder as we made our way upstairs to an old boiler cupboard that stored her spare bed linen. With a handful of bedding, Siobhàn gave me a brief tour of the upstairs, reminding me where the toilet and shower was as well as her room, but shuffled past another door that was shut and walked downstairs. I couldn't help but not look back at the room she hadn't shown me and wonder why she avoided showing me it.

"Here you go, a nice comfy sofa turned into a bed. I'm not working tomorrow, so I'll make you a nice warm breakfast and we can talk about life, okay?" She placed the linens neatly on the sofa and gave me a hug before wishing me sweet dreams and heading to her room.

I looked around the room, really taking in my new surroundings before turning off the light. There were half filled mugs of coffee sitting on the coffee table along with magazines that had dog eared pages. There was a picture of a young child and a woman, both smiling. Either one of them could have been Siobhan.

I switched off the light and stumbled to the sofa, banging my foot against the frame as I climbed onto it. I immediately sunk into the cushions, and my muscles ached with pleasure, making my heart beat that little bit faster.

It wasn't long until I drowned underneath the heavy duvet with a smile and fell asleep.

The next morning, I woke just as the sun was creeping above the horizon, its rays shining through the small gaps around the curtains. I stretched while still lying on the sofa, each of my bones and muscles thanking me for the best night's rest in a long time.

I put my head through the same old T-shirt and walked up the stairs, across the hallway and towards the toilet, trying my best to tiptoe past the light snore coming from Siobhàn's room.

Once I was done, I perched myself back on the sofa, looking at the mess that had started to accumulate. I started by putting the heap of magazines into a tidy pile and then folded a pile of clothes that had been left in a pile on the table.

I carried the plates and mugs that had been left around the living room into the kitchen, trying not to make a sound. It was difficult to find a place for them, as there was barely any room left on the counter tops. The only thing left to do was to wash up, so I did, trying not to allow the crockery to clink together to avoid waking Siobhàn.

Thirty minutes had passed before she came down the

stairs, startling me as I was just finishing up washing the dishes she'd allowed to pile up.

"Oh you scared me!" I smiled and wiped the last of the mugs.

"What are you doing?" Siobhàn said, flicking the kettle on as she simultaneously grabbed a clean mug from the cupboard.

"Washing up. I thought I'd help you out. It's the least I can do really for letting me stay here. I tidied the magazines and folded the pile of your clothes that were left on the table, too." I said as Siobhàn stopped in her tracks.

I thought she'd be happy, but the expression on her face said otherwise. She ran her hands through her hair and her head fell bac. She didn't speak to me, not even a thank you.

"Is that okay? I'm sorry if I've crossed a line. I just wanted to show you how much I appreciate you."

"No. Yes." Her words were muddled at first. "I appreciate it, I really do, but those were my mum's clothes, not mine. She died a few days ago and I've just let things pile up. I've not stepped foot in her bedroom either. I know eventually I'll have to sort through her things, but I guess I'm not ready to let her go just yet."

"Oh my god, I'm so sorry. I shouldn't have touched them."

"No, it's fine. I'm sorry, I should have told you last night. It's my own fault for leaving things a mess."

Siobhàn sat down, so I continued to make her coffee plus an extra one for me.

"That's understandable. How did she... pass?" I said as my fingers and thumbs intertwined each other.

Siobhàn looked at me, her big blue eyes filling with tears and burning sadness into my soul.

"She had a cardiac arrest," Siobhàn said, taking in a

deep breath. "It happened at night. I was working, and when I arrived home, she wasn't breathing." I placed my hand on Siobhàn's shoulder after putting her coffee down on the kitchen table. I couldn't say anything to take the pain away. No words of mine would have helped her in that moment. She had to cry. This was another chance for her to let go of some of the emotion she was bottling up—the emotion that had clearly led her to the bridge last night.

"This is why you were on the bridge, wasn't it?" I pulled a chair as close to hers as I could to her.

"Yes." She sniffed, wiping tears from her eyes. "I feel so empty without her—so lonely. I've been signed off work, so I'm not seeing my people, and the worst thing about it is, if I hadn't been at work that night, maybe I would have heard her—maybe I could have done something to help." She was feeling guilty for living her life, but she couldn't have planned for this.

"You can't and shouldn't live your life in regret, believe me. I've lived in regret, too, and look where that got me." I rubbed my hand across her back, seeing she was being consumed by her own thoughts. I tried to distract her. "What do you do for work?"

"I'm a care assistant at a nursing home. The thing is, as much as those residents need me, my mum needed me that night, and I wasn't there for her." She took a large gulp of coffee, her hands shaking as she rested the mug back on the table.

"I'm here for you," I said.

My words were simple.

Four words that made Siobhàn smile.

Perhaps they gifted her a reminder of the warmth her mum had provided for her in abundance before she'd passed away.

She mouthed 'thank you', took another sip and then wrapped her arms around me.

It was at that moment, I knew we were friends and that we would both rely on each other. It was as her body pressed against mine that I knew there was hope for both of us.

Chapter Four

The following few weeks had me euphoric as things seemed to be turning around.

I had a large comfy bed in a room that was warm in a house that had a roof—things only those who didn't have them would appreciate. I had a friend who listened to me talk about the pain of having nowhere to go, no one to turn to, and what led me to being homeless in this city—all because I'd been manipulated by love.

Speaking to Siobhàn was a pivotal point in my road to recovery because it allowed me to start reclaiming back parts of my life I thought I'd never get back as they had been irreparably broken. If my trajectory hadn't changed, and without Siobhàn, I may not have seen that little ray of hope—that light shining as bright as it could in the darkness. Maybe feeling clean and having my first friend in a city I'd called my home for months also contributed to a rush of elation, leaving me feeling like I could take on the world and everything else it had to throw at me.

HOPE

I helped Siobhàn clean her house along with my new room, taking our time to sort through pieces of her mum's life. With each item she held on to, like brass ornaments and six years worth of magazines, happy memories and laughter made the process as easy as it could be. The stories she told brought her mum back to life right in front of my eyes, and I learned so much about her, something I believe brought us closer. Afterwards, I was stricken with grief knowing the lady who raised Siobhàn was no longer with us. I had no clue what Siobhàn was feeling.

Once Siobhàn had taken some time, she returned to work, but not before pushing me to continue to thrive.

I was the happiest I'd been in a long time, but she knew I had more potential.

It all had to start with using her computer to write a CV, dropping it off at businesses around the city.

But I heard nothing, not even a call to Siobhàn's landline that I waited beside for days, hopeful that something would come up.

My light was fading.

I'd been given more than I could have ever asked for, but I couldn't help wanting more: to be an adult, to earn my own money and start paying my way living with Siobhàn.

The phone rang as Siobhàn and I sat in front of the television eating a late lunch after she'd woken from sleeping after her late night shift.

I immediately jumped and almost knocked the plate off my lap, making sure to answer the phone within three rings in case they hung up.

"Hello. Toby speaking," I said, trying my best to be professional.

Silence.

"Have you had an accident that wasn't your fault? Then you..."

I placed the phone down, straightened my back as a sigh escaped me and then placed my plate back on my lap before tucking back into the bacon sandwiches.

"Are you okay? You don't seem yourself."

I could have lied, but what would have been the point? Clearly not having a job after finishing college and no experience was destroying my chances of leading a proper life. I could have blamed it on Shane, but I knew I could have stood up for myself—I could have used all that ambition and drive I once had and put it into something of use.

I was disappointed in myself.

"Honestly, I feel like I'm driving myself crazy. I've barely moved from the sofa waiting for someone to take a chance on me, but it's not happening. How am I supposed to get a job that wants me to have experience if nobody is willing to give me experience in the first place? It's so frustrating," I said in between bites of my sandwich, wiping red sauce from my lips.

"Right. Tomorrow you are coming to work with me. We have volunteers that come in all the time. You can volunteer. I know it's not paid, and it's nothing like what you want to be doing with your life, but it will stop you from moping around on my couch. I'm not okay with seeing a Toby-shaped arse print on my sofa."

Crumbs fell from my mouth with each snort of my laughter. One of her super powers was making me laugh, and she knew exactly how to do it.

"Okay, I'll volunteer."

"That's the spirit, Katniss," she said, forcing orange juice out of my mouth.

HOPE

"What if they don't want me to volunteer? What if I'm not what they're looking for?"

"Puhlease! They are crying out for staff. Believe me, you have more skills and life experience than half of the staff there—me excluded, obviously." The cheekiest smirk grew on her face as she finished her sandwich and then she proceeded to flick through the television channels.

"Obviously," I said, playfully.

The thing was, she was so much more than someone with skills and experience: she was fast becoming my best friend.

That following day, I awoke to birds chirping outside my bedroom window. I pushed open the curtains allowing a steady stream of light to fill the room. The hatchling's mother swept in and out of the tree, dodging branches as it flew around the nest.

For a long time I would have been saddened at its sight, envious of the hatchlings and all they had, but not anymore. Siobhàn was unknowingly filling all the empty spaces in my life. I hoped I was doing the same for her.

It was going to be a hot day, so the news channel had said the day before. The sun was already radiating against my skin through the window pane, I could feel my body tingle underneath its warmth.

I pulled on my new backpack after getting dressed—the one that Siobhàn had treated me to along with a whole host of new clothes ready to immerse myself into the world of working. I wasn't going to be earning yet, but I assured her that the moment I had money, my debts would be paid.

"You ready?"

"As ready as I'll ever be," I said, wiping the sweat from my palms on my new pair of skinny jeans from Primark.

Before leaving the house to head to her place of work, I looked in the mirror, taking in my appearance. My skin wasn't dirty or dull, and my eyes weren't worn or tired. I was rested and was getting used to the smile that was appearing on my face more and more often. I felt invincible, and when I stepped off the doorstep and into the sunlight, I had back the determination and drive Shane had stolen from me.

As I approached the care home with Siobhàn by my side, I expected to see a hospital building painted in a dirty magnolia with a bench or two outside for the elders to sit and smoke on. I certainly hadn't been expecting the clean, modern building with as many windows as an Apple Store, nor the countless butterflies that fluttered around the flowers planted and pruned in and around the care home gardens.

"This place is lovely," I said as I ran my fingers through my wind-swept hair to tidy it after catching my reflection in one of the windows. I needed to make a good first impression if I was ever going to be welcomed back, and I was already keen on that idea.

"It is, isn't it. The residents are lovely, too, but they will talk your ear off. They will want to know your life story and I'm sure a lot of them will tell you theirs, so fair warning. Oh, and just wait until you try the food."

We walked in and the smell of freshly cooked bread lingered in my nostrils—a smell so good my stomach growled.

"Hi Paul," Siobhàn said as she walked behind reception and into the staff room, where she placed her bag down and promptly flicked on the kettle.

"Hey Sob, how're you doin'? Ah, you must be Toby. Great to meet you, lad." His thick Scottish accent was the strongest I'd heard and made Siobhàn's unapparent. "Sob said you were gonnae come in and help our residents. Ya ken we aren't gonnae let you escape?"

I laughed out loud, using the time to decode his dialect and decipher what he was saying. "I'm really looking forward to it, and don't worry, I'm sure I'll give the residents a run for their money. I can talk the back legs off a donkey if I try."

"You'll fit right in then. I'll leave Sob to show you around, but if yer need anything, I'm here." He took my hand in his large one—that could have wrapped around mine twice—with a firm grasp and shook it.

We walked out of the office and made our way through different corridors as Siobhàn showed me around, introducing me to a few of the residents here and there. She wasn't supposed to have favourites, but I could tell who they were.

"Why does he call you Sob?" I asked, after she'd introduced me to Maria, a patient with Alzheimer's. Talking to her transported both of us to a simpler time, where she would have parties in the street with her neighbours. They had been her friends and they'd known everything about each other, meeting up for a coffee or chatting on the way to the shops instead of over the phone or the internet because it had been the only way they knew.

"Because when he first interviewed me, he kept mispronouncing my name to see if I had the grit it takes to work with the elderly. Six years on and I'm still here and the name kind of stuck." She smiled. I could tell she was happy to be back at work around the people she loved. She was reliant on those around her, just as I was reliant on her in order to keep living with this new lease of life she'd given me. If her work friends had been around more during her period of absence, I wondered if she would have even ended up on the bridge that cold evening and if I would have met her, but I dismissed the thought quickly because I couldn't imagine my life without her.

The day seemed to disappear before my eyes, and before I knew it, I was sitting with Siobhàn on my lunch break, devouring potato and leek soup along with homemade bread, which turned out to be the chef's speciality. I was going to like it here. Very much so.

Chapter Five

A few weeks ago, I'd felt as though I was the loneliest person in Edinburgh. A few weeks ago, I'd had no hope—no one to rely on, no one to care about.
No one.
How my life was different.
Not only did I have Siobhàn, who had become my rock, I was making friends with the other staff as well as the residents. I had a lot in common with many of them: we didn't have a family to rely on, nor did many people care about us. The residents gave me purpose, something I'd lived without for so long, and I never wanted to live without my newfound friends ever again.
That morning started out like any other in my newly obtained routine. I pulled on my backpack and walked to work with my best friend. We'd battled all types of weather —pouring rain, bright sunshine and the bitterest wind— however that day seemed calm. Trees held up their

branches still and birds flew without making a sound. It was as if our surroundings were in mourning.

I picked up my shoulders that had started to slump under the weight of my backpack and took in a deep breath, not speaking, and grasped Siobhàn's hand tightly.

In the safety of work and surrounded by my favourite people, I released her hand, leaving beads of sweat behind. Both of us immediately wiped our clammy palms on our trousers, placed our things in the staff room and parted ways until our routine lunch break and our favourite part of the day.

I flicked on the kettle and turned to wait for Siobhàn. She was late, as usual, but I forgave her. When she eventually arrived, she slumped on the sofa in the staff room, not saying a word, looking more tired than usual.

I took her packed lunch from the fridge, a new addition to our routine as she said she was putting on too much weight from all the delicious food at the canteen. Damn, I missed that soup and homemade bread.

"What's up?" I asked, sitting next to her and ignoring the kettle that had just finished boiling.

"Maria passed away." She ran her hands over her eyes like she was trying to stop seeing the pain. "I had to call her family and tell them, but I don't even think they care. They almost sounded relieved. She had no one by her side and I…"

"You were there for her, more than you know. You were Maria's family." I wrapped my arms around her, kissed her forehead and then reboiled the kettle.

Siobhàn picked up the day's newspaper.

"Oh my god," Siobhàn said, looking physically sick as her eyes followed the words on an article near the front, salty tears puddling in them as she tried to stop her hands from shaking and the newspaper rustling underneath her movements.

"What is it?" I finished pouring a coffee and sat beside her, placing our mugs in front of us on the coffee table.

She pointed to a headline that made my stomach lurch.

"When did it happen?"

"Two days ago," she said, passing me the newspaper to read for myself.

Scanning the words sent shivers down my spine, knowing that the person who had jumped from the bridge could have been either one of us. Reading that the girl deciding to take her own life had been only fifteen only kept the shivers coming. She hadn't had anyone that evening to give her the hope she'd needed to pull through.

For the rest of the day, Siobhàn wasn't the same. In fact, in the short time I saw her during our shift, I was reminded of the day I'd first met her: high levels of emotion and grief but doing her best to bottle it up and putting a brave face on for everyone around her.

What she didn't know is that I could see through it.

We'd walked to work in the calm before the storm, we'd braved some of the wind and now, in the eye of that storm, all I wanted to do was shelter her from feeling anymore hurt.

"Where's Siobhàn?" I asked Paul, who was busy typing away on his laptop in the office.

"I sent her home about two hours ago."

"Why?"

"She said she wasn't feeling well. Did she not come find

you?" I caught a glimpse of Paul's expression as he finally looked up from her laptop, concerned.

No. She didn't.

I ran out of the office, past the trees that rustled in the ever-building wind, and scrambled to our home. My heart raced as the door wouldn't open, so I pulled the key from my pocket and shook as I tried to fit it in the lock.

I swung it open and yelled.

"Siobhàn? Siobhàn!" Each time I screeched her name, my voice grew higher and louder.

Nothing.

I continued to shout as I ran from room to room, taking a quick look in each before running out of places to look.

"Where are you?" I questioned out loud, vocalising my thoughts as my brain was too full to keep them inside.

Scenarios ran through my head, some I didn't want to picture, sending me physically sick—scenarios that made me heave and all leading to Siobhàn being back to the bridge.

I didn't think twice before running out of the house and up the cobbled streets.

I was out of breath, panting, with sweat dripping uncontrollably off my forehead.

There she was.

On the bridge.

I couldn't see her properly as it was the busiest I'd ever seen it. People were walking past her, not stopping or even thinking about the woman all alone and silently screaming for help.

The closer I got to her, the more I could see the emotion on her face. Tears rolled off her skin like it was waterproof, yet their salt left her face red and puffy.

HOPE

"Don't jump!" I screamed at the top of my voice as she approached the column where she once stood.

Siobhàn turned her head and smiled through the tears before walking towards me with a look of embarrassment as everyone around began to stare.

Those two words had been necessary for those strangers to even begin to care.

"I'm not going to jump," she said as she buried her face into my left shoulder and wrapped her arms around me.

"Then what in the hell are you bloody doing on this bridge?" I panted in between words, still out of breath from the exercise.

"I'm putting up these." She held up a laminated sheet of paper which read, *'You're not alone and things will get better'* and then began to show me the rest. Each one she'd made herself, all different, and each one as powerful as the next.

"You made these because of that young girl who jumped?" My heart ached at how much I loved this incredible woman in front of me.

"Yup. Not everyone will be as lucky as I was to find my very own superhero."

I pulled her in for another hug, partly to show her how much I appreciated her, but mostly to hide my tears—tears of happiness I never thought I'd cry.

I stood on that bridge with Siobhàn and helped her put the rest of the signs because she was right: sometimes, all you need in life is a sign that things will get better—that things won't always be the way they are. It's hard to be hopeful if you can't see past your pain, but one small gesture can be powerful enough to give you hope, whether that be a ray of sunshine in a sky full of clouds or someone reaching out to grab you on the darkest of your days.

Siobhàn had been my sign.

"What if someone takes them down?" Siobhàn asked, adding the final sign on the last column.

"Then we will keep putting them back up."

We walked off the bridge together, hand in hand like the night we'd first met.

"You know, I think my mum sent you here on the night I wanted to jump. You had been homeless for months, your life in ruins for a long time, yet you chose to give up at the precise moment I did. I think you're my guardian angel, you know?"

I squeezed her hand that little tighter, knowing how lucky I was to have Siobhàn in my life—knowing how lucky I was to still be alive and living a life that made me so happy.

"I could say the same about you."

Also by
D J Cook

The TLC Series

Tamsin

Liam

The One
by
Elle M Thomas

Chapter One

My life had always been quite simple. Easy. Happy and familiar. I had grown up with the people who still meant the most to me. My parents were fairly easy-going and as the baby of the family, I was a little spoilt. I had a few good friends, but for most of my life it had just been them. I had been protected by them. Overprotected by them. *Them* was my brother, Dom and his friends, Jack, Mickey and Rayner. My first alcoholic drink, well the first legal one had been with them, and every couple of weeks they'd taken me to the pub with them and guarded me, meaning any boy who showed any interest was quickly scared off.

As a schoolgirl, nobody had messed with me as they all knew of my older brother and his friends. I had seen it as a curse and seen them as a pain in the arse, but now I missed that. I missed them, especially Dom and Rayner. I had moved to a city a couple of hours away five years before, and in those same five years, the boys had gone on to be discovered and were now huge rockstars. I had spent years listening to them play in my parent's garage, and although I had always thought they were amazing, now the rest of the world did too. The straight women in that *rest of the world* also seemed to be willing to do just about anything to land one of them for a night, a week, a year or a lifetime. The tabloids were often full of speculation, photos and far too many kiss-and-tell recounts. I avoided all of it where I could, especially if they involved my brother, but more so Rayner.

Rayner had been every girl's dream man. I once did one of those things online where you have a certain amount of cash to spend on designing your own boyfriend and when I had finished, I had made Rayner. Loyal, broad, funny, muscular and a good lover. The truth was that Rayner ticked every bloody box I could ever draw, and I wasn't the only one to notice. While he and his friends took every opportunity to scupper any possibility of any kind of romantic liaison for me, Rayner had no such qualms for himself and over the years I watched on as dozens of women passed through his life. Passed through quickly and often with a loud and dramatic protest, and that was before the fame.

At least I hadn't been one of them. I hadn't been loud nor dramatic when he had dumped me. It had all happened one night when a boy I had managed to sneak under their radar had tried to push things too far with me. I wasn't ready to go farther than kissing and touching, but he was. He'd got heavy-handed with me and literally pushed for more. We'd been at his student house, and I had managed to get him to hear me, to understand that my no really did mean no. He had hurled all kinds of shit at me, but when he asked what I was waiting for, the answer sprang to mind

205

immediately. Rayner. I'd left his place and knew I would never see him again and was absolutely fine with that.

I had found myself at Rayner's place and just hoped there wouldn't be some woman in barely any clothes on the other side of the door when I knocked on it. I wasn't entirely sure why I was even there. What was I going to say? What did I want or expect beyond his big brother routine?

There had been no woman there, just a shocked looking Rayner. He'd invited me in and poured me a glass of wine that I drank as I told him about my night.

"Are you okay?" Rayner's fists balled at his side, his anger rolling off him at the thought of anyone hurting me.

"Yes. It's over. It wasn't right."

"And this is why you need us to protect you," he said as he ran a hand through his hair whilst pacing the room. "He wasn't good enough for you."

I laughed. "Nobody would be good enough for you guys."

He didn't disagree. "I still want his name and address."

"And you're not getting it. Look, Rayner, it wasn't that he wasn't good enough, but he wasn't enough. He wasn't the right person for me."

He nodded and came to stand in front of me. "The right person is out there for you, Zee. You just haven't met him yet."

I didn't know if it was the wine, the night I'd had or the words, maybe all three, but getting to my feet, I responded. "I already have. Met him," I clarified for a confused looking Rayner. "It's you."

He leapt back as if I had thrown a bucket full of ice-cold water over him. "No! Not me, it can't be me. I am not the right person for anyone, least of all you!" His earlier anger was replaced with something else. Fear.

I stretched out to touch him, and he recoiled.

I had messed this up. He didn't like me like that and now I had ruined everything. Nothing would ever be the same again. Feeling awkward and embarrassed, I turned and grabbed my bag before walking to the door. "Sorry. My mistake. Blame the drink and we can forget this." I wasn't going to forget this. Ever. "Maybe I should go back to my date's house, apologise for not giving him the right chance because of my crush on you."

My hand was turning the door handle, opening it a fraction, when it was forced shut again.

"No!" A single word announced as I was spun around.

Looking up, the heat and want in Rayner's face was unmistakable.

Before I knew what was happening, I was being hauled up in Rayner's grasp. My back pressed against the door putting me eye to eye with him, and then his mouth met mine in a kiss that was more than I ever imagined it might be, and I had imagined it countless times. This was my fantasy, but this was now real. I just hoped it lived up to my imagination and more than that, I hoped this wouldn't be the biggest regret of either of our lives.

"Shit!" I jumped as my phone sprang to life. My mum's name lit up the screen which was unusual as she was a creature of habit, and her time for calling was between eight and eight-thirty on alternate nights between her soaps. "Mum," I told my friend and business partner, Fran.

"Then bloody answer it." She was as alarmed by the call as me since we lived together, and she knew my mother's calling routine as well as I did.

"Hi, Mum, you okay?"

I listened to the words and although I understood them, they weren't sinking in. Already on my feet, I gathered my belongings and still listening to my mother, headed for the door. Fran, hot on my heels, knew our suspicion of something being wrong for the cause of my mother's call was correct.

Chapter Two

"How much longer?" I knew I'd asked the same question a dozen times or more, but it was all I could focus on. How much longer before we arrived. How soon before I could find out what was happening and how they really were?

"Soon, I promise. They'll be okay." Her words were intended to be reassuring, but they were anything but convincing. This was bad, she knew it and so did I.

Twenty minutes later, we pulled into the car park and fought our way through the press and paparazzi to enter the main hospital. We were about to be turned away when security spotted me and pulled Fran and me in.

"This way." The huge guy before us led us to an elevator that took us several floors up.

"The press got wind of it then?" Fran asked and stated at the same time.

"Yeah, it was only ever a matter of when. I mean, it's not every day that the biggest rock band of modern times are involved in a crash in their hometown, is it? And the crash was a big one. . ." His voice trailed off.

"Are they okay?" I was desperate for someone to give me an update.

"I'm unsure." The guy turned his back to me as the lift came to a standstill, and he led us out.

My parents came into view, as did Jack and Mickey, then Noah, the newest member of the group who I didn't know particularly well, and through a mist of tears, Dom appeared looking bruised, battered with his arm in a cast, but he was alive. I scanned the room as they all approached me, but I couldn't see the person who was missing. I couldn't see Rayner.

As I disappeared under arms and embraces, I felt claustrophobic and retreated a little until I stood opposite my brother, who reached forward and brushed away my tears.

"Rayner?"

Dom looked around at his friends, all of whom looked suddenly nervous and emotional. "He took the brunt of it," my brother told me. "He's in a bad way." His voice began to break.

"Can we see him?" I was unsure why I'd said we because what I really meant was me.

Jack shook his head. "Not yet. The doctors are with him still."

I felt the scowl crease my brow as I wondered what that meant. *Still with him*. What were they doing? In my own mind I knew what that meant. They were trying to save him. Oh God! What would I do if he died? Rayner and I were complicated, but I never imagined not getting a chance for us to make it right. To see him, speak to him. If I was completely honest, I always imagined a time when we might get a chance, a second chance to do it right.

The tears falling were nothing compared to the cry I heard leave my throat, howl after howl as I imagined this being the end of Rayner, the end of Rayner and me.

"Come on sis," Dom said, leading me to a bank of chairs.

It was then that I noticed he was in a hospital gown and when he took his seat, it was in a wheelchair. "Are you okay?" I asked nervously.

"Yeah. Bit knocked about and I might need a few nights in this place, but I was lucky."

We sat for hours and during that time, people came and went. My parents eventually left, happy in the knowledge that Dom was okay, although, my refusal to leave the hospital had delayed their departure. Once they knew and accepted I wasn't leaving, they did. The guys in the band remained behind, and there were managers and PR people sorting out press releases in an attempt to keep the media at bay.

Fran sat with us for a while and then by daybreak, decided to go and check into a hotel. Dom sent the same security guy who'd brought us in to make sure she got out and was unbothered by the press.

A nurse appeared just as Fran left and stood next to Dom. "Your time is up, Mr Partridge."

Dom groaned.

She shook her head in response. "We had a deal. You were allowed to be out here until your next meds were due, and then you agreed to come back to your room, get into bed, take your medication and rest."

"But—"

The nurse cut him off. "No, a deal is a deal, so easy way or the hard way?"

I watched on as my brother gave her his best dirty blond, rockstar, panty-melting, swoon-inducing smile. She arched a brow that suggested she was unaffected by it, but I wasn't convinced.

Dom grinned up at her. "If I was working at full capacity, I would be taking the hard way." He got to his feet and moved towards her. "The hard way is always more fun and far more rewarding when you reach the climax."

Oh my God! I had a ringside seat to his flirting. He was talking about shagging this nurse and eye fucking her while I watched on.

They were almost toe to toe and she now stepped closer to him. "Unfortunately, you aren't working at capacity, meaning the easy way is the only option you have. So," she all but whispered. "How about you be a good boy, sit back down and let me do all the work."

I sat, mouth gaping and eyes wide as this weird kind of porn scene played out before me.

Dom cocked his head before returning to the wheelchair. "You're seriously fucking sexy when you're in control."

The nurse flushed. "You haven't seen anything yet."

"Neither have you," he fired back.

She told us all where Dom's room was, and with us all promising to keep him in the loop, he disappeared.

I stared across at the other guys, who all laughed at me.

"Welcome to the world of Demonic Dreams."

"Is he always like that?" I struggled to reconcile the man who had just left with my brother.

Jack laughed. "Yup!"

"Shit! I may have to have one of you guys check that the coast is clear before I go in his room."

They all laughed.

"You're not in Kansas anymore." Mickey smiled across at me as he toyed with a packet of cigarettes.

"No shit!"

Before anyone could say any more, a doctor appeared. "Rayner Philips?"

Chapter Three

The world stopped and I held my breath as we all listened to the doctor explaining the details of the injuries Rayner had; broken bones, organs damaged and ruptured, swelling on the brain and possible long-term, life-changing effects. He talked about likely surgeries but not immediately unless Rayner's condition forced their hand. The realisation that what was being said wasn't even the worst prognosis hit me like a train when the doctor began to speak about the following hours being critical; four hours, twelve hours, then twenty-four hours.

A sob caught in my throat. What wasn't being said was that death was a likely outcome for Rayner.

The doctor asked who his next of kin was and when his family would arrive. Everyone looked around at each other, but nobody spoke.

"Me, us . . . he doesn't have blood relatives. We're his family." I had no clue where those words had come from, but they were all true. Rayner and I hadn't seen each other for a while, and our last few meetings had been fleeting and in the company of others, but we were family.

"You should all go home. There's nothing you can do," the doctor began, and the boys and I all began to voice our objections when one of the management team or PR or whatever she was spoke.

"Guys, I know you don't want to leave while Dom and Rayner remain here, but the media are beginning to speculate that this is a vigil, and if that rumour builds pace, we're going to have a complete media frenzy here."

The guys all looked at each other.

"Seriously," the tall, willowy redhead continued, "You can come by each day, and we can release a statement and underplay Rayner's injuries unless we have to come clean."

Fuck! She meant if he died.

"I'm staying!" I announced.

The PR woman barely acknowledged me. "Well, she can let you know of any changes and keep tabs on Dom and Rayner." She looked at me now and smiled. "If you're happy with that."

I nodded.

"So, I am going to prepare a statement to deliver downstairs, and you are all going home."

They still looked ready to object.

"She is unknown to the press and even if they figure out who she is, they'll know she's visiting Dom, and in the morning, we can release an update on Dom with a photo or a wave from a window."

It didn't make complete sense to me, but the boys all nodded and began to move away.

The doctor was about to excuse himself when I grabbed his arm and gained his attention. "Can I see Rayner?" I could see he was about to object. "Please. I really need to see him. We were close." I had no idea why I had revealed those final details, but they along with fresh tears seemed to have the desired effect.

"Okay. Give us about half an hour, and someone will come for you."

Once the guys had all checked and double-checked that I was going to be okay, I watched them leave. The woman who had coordinated their departure, whom I now knew was Skylar, left me her number and also ensured that everyone else left. A TV I hadn't noticed before was on the wall and showing news of the boys' crash. As Skylar had said, there was a lot of speculation that there had been significant, if not life-threatening injuries to one or several band members.

The sight of the tour bus they'd been travelling in appeared on screen and all the air left my lungs. How the fuck had three members of the band walked away from that unscathed? How had Dom escaped with relatively no injuries, and certainly none he wouldn't recover from. But Rayner, he hadn't been so lucky. He had borne the brunt of it, and now, his life literally hung in the balance.

"Miss Mason, Zara?" The doctor from earlier appeared.

When I noticed a nurse accompanying him, I panicked, assuming she was his reinforcement for delivering bad news. My face must have betrayed my fears as he hurried to reassure me.

"This is Tania, she's going to take you to Mr Philips."

I released a huge breath and happily followed her until we arrived at a rather uncomfortable looking chair next to a door that separated me from Rayner.

"Just give me a few minutes and I'll take you through."

Taking the seat, I made myself as comfortable as I could and in an attempt to distract my mind from imagining what might await me when I entered the room behind me, I focused on the Rayner of my past.

Chapter Four

That night, five years before, had been one I had never forgotten.

From the second he had stopped me from leaving, it had seemed inevitable. One of the young men who had been my protector, was gone and he had been replaced with someone who wanted me. Everything about him was filled with desire, his look, his breathing, and his touch. He seared me with his lips and his hands that brought me to life in a series of strokes, grazes and holds. The back of the door was where we'd remained for long moments as our mouths became acquainted and our hands began to explore.

By the time we reached the bedroom, I was drunk on desire and staring up into Rayner's big brown eyes; I was pretty certain he was too. I'd somehow missed the shedding of my jacket and T-shirt but had found myself lying in the middle of his bed wearing jeans and a bra. It had been difficult to believe we were really there together and that I wasn't dreaming. I'd had this dream a hundred times before, but the reality was something else.

Rayner stood over me, his own jeans hanging loosely with the button undone and the zip already at half-mast, while his top half was bare. Bare, bronzed, and although not as defined as it would become, it caused a hitch in my breathing. He was beautiful. Perfect.

With a half-smile, he leaned down and his body covered mine. He kissed me again, his lips moulding mine until we worked as one and then he made a path along my jaw to my ear, where he began to whisper to me, telling me how beautiful I was and how he was going to savour every second of our time together.

I was far from experienced, but I didn't need to be to know that this was what I wanted, that it was right and perfect for Rayner to be my first. He kissed his way down my body, divesting me of my bra and jeans as he went. He'd teased and aroused my nipples to hard points that ached for his touch before continuing until he came to rest on his knees between my thighs. My underwear had gone at that point too, and that is when he spread my thighs and feasted upon me. The feel of his tongue there was like nothing I had known. The way he alternated between licking and lapping, probing and dragging the length of me, almost had me seeing stars. My fingers became lost in his hair as he drove me closer to pleasure and release. Then, just when I thought it couldn't feel any better, I felt a finger slide inside me and a second.

Rayner had looked up at me several times as he had devoured me, but with two fingers buried inside me, he'd stopped.

"Zara, you've never done this before?" His use of my full name startled me initially, he rarely called me Zara. He had phrased his words as a question, but he already knew the answer.

I shook my head. "Sorry."

He began to withdraw. "This should be special. You should be with someone who deserves you."

I had no idea how I would move on from this if he rejected me before we'd done this. I'd thought I would at least get this one time. Sitting up slightly, I looked into his eyes and was briefly distracted by my arousal glistening on his face.

"Rayner, I want you to be my first."

He looked startled.

"You know I've always liked you."

He smiled the perfect smile, a mixture of happiness and downright cockiness at my words.

"Please, don't stop. I know it's going to hurt, but I want it to be you. I could have done this earlier tonight, with someone else, but I didn't want to, not with him, but if you don't want me, I will have to find someone else."

"It's nothing to do with not wanting you."

I could feel him withdrawing a little more.

"You said it should be special. It will be. Nothing could make this more special to me. I have never trusted anyone else to do this with. Rayner, I trust you."

He still hadn't looked entirely convinced until those last three words. He had kissed my inner thigh. "Okay. I'd be honoured."

With his mouth back on me, the storm of arousal began to gather immediately until, with the fingers inside stroking me and his lips drawing my clit into the heat of his mouth, I was literally seeing stars and crying out in sweet, torturous ecstasy.

"Zara," Tania, the nurse from earlier, called my name and if I didn't leap from the seat.

She looked panic-struck to have startled me, but the truth was, I had been locked in the memory of my first time so tightly that I hadn't even been aware of my surroundings, all thoughts of the injured Rayner forgotten.

"We're ready for you if you're ready."

I nodded and smiled at the reassuring hand she placed on my shoulder.

"When you first see him, it will be a bit of a shock. He is quite badly battered and bruised, and there are lots of machines attached to him, and they make noises, so please, don't be alarmed."

I nodded and took a deep breath.

"If you need a moment—"

I interrupted her. "No, I'm fine. Really."

I should have taken the moment or maybe a lifetime of moments because I wasn't ready for the sight that greeted me, and neither was I fine once I saw Rayner.

The white sheets provided a stark contrast to the myriad of blues, blacks and purples of Rayner's skin. Machines were everywhere, and the beeps and pings were almost deafening. He was literally sprawled out flat, lines, drips and tubes everywhere. He was unrecognisable as the person I knew, or indeed a man at all. Even the dark lines of the tattoos he now had were almost impossible to see due to the amount of discolouration on his skin.

When the comforting rub against my arm registered, I realised I was crying again. I had cried more tonight than I had in a very long time. This amount of tears hadn't been shed by me since Rayner had dumped me five years before.

"It's a lot, right?" Tania said with a tone that did begin to make me feel reassured.

"Yeah. Can I sit with him?"

"It's supposed to be just a few minutes, but so long as you let us do what we need to, I don't see why not." She ushered me into the hospital's idea of a comfy chair and retreated to a table at the end of the bed to do whatever it was she needed to.

Time went so slowly as I sat and literally watched Rayner breathing, grateful that he continued to do so, even if it was with the help of all the equipment. I watched as Tania did her checks and then, when she retreated, I allowed myself to consider how we had gotten here, Rayner and me.

That night at his place, had been the best of my life, and not just because of the hot sex. It had shown me that we got on, just the two of us. After the sex, we had laid together, got up, ate and talked, really talked. We had also laughed, a lot.

Previously, it was rare for it to be only us, in fact, I was unsure if it had ever happened. There had been moments when nobody else was around, but they were rare, and yet, in a crowd, a group or a family gathering, I had always sought him out. That realisation was jarring. My crush was so much more than that. It may have started off like that, but over time it had changed and grown. If it hadn't, I was unsure if I would have given up my V card to him, but I had. I smiled to myself, remembering his conflicting feelings when he realised that I was still a virgin.

I loved Rayner Philips. Had for as long as I could remember, and now, when he needed me, I was going to be there for him whether he wanted me to be or not. In fact, I decided in that second that the accident was likely to be life-changing for us both because no matter what the outcome for Rayner, I was going to be around and make him see that this, us, was meant to be. My feelings couldn't still be there after all of this time if it was nothing, could they? Every man I had ever known before and since him had meant nothing to me, not really. Even those I'd developed feelings for had never advanced. It was as though my emotions and my heart weren't fully available. That they would let someone in, and then things would hit a certain point and just fade. Nobody had ever been Rayner. Nobody ever came close and whilst it was never a conscious decision, I had compared each and every one to him, and they'd all been found wanting. So, now, I just had to hope. Hope that he would pull through this so I could tell him exactly how I felt and hope he felt the same.

Chapter Five

The day was beginning to break on day four, or was it day five? I wasn't sure as I was starting to lose all semblance of time in this place. There had been no change in Rayner's condition since I'd arrived in this room, and I had barely left it. The others came by each day and checked on Rayner and Dom, who was due to leave today. We had spent hours chatting, Dom and me. He came here early morning, sent me to eat whether I wanted to or not and then we settled in for the day. Whoever visited first brought stuff for lunch, and the last visitors brought more food for dinner. When my parents arrived to see Dom, they would check in on Rayner and me and also bring me some clean clothes, using the opportunity to encourage me to go home, at least for the night to sleep. I didn't. Even if Rayner didn't need me here, I needed to stay. The thought of him waking up and nobody being here for him horrified me. The idea of him slipping away alone absolutely terrified me.

Gazing across at his battered and broken body, I

thought back to the crash. I still didn't really understand what had happened, and although there had been reports on the news, I had stopped watching them because they were traumatic, to say the least.

The night shift became the day shift and by eight in the morning, I became aware of someone entering the room behind me, Dom. He still looked battered and bruised, more so than when I'd last seen him, but the bruising was still coming out; however, the main thing was that he was still very healthy, if a little weary.

"Hey." He leaned down, kissed my cheek and pulled up a seat. "How is he?"

"Same. How are you doing?"

"Okay. I had a lucky escape." He sounded guilty.

"What?" I turned and gave him my full attention.

"About ten minutes before the crash, we swapped seats. Rayner was in the aisle seat and chatting to Mickey on the other side of the bus. I was hanging out of my arse, and watching the road roll by through the window was making me feel sick, so, after bitching and moaning, Rayner swapped seats."

Hearing my brother's voice break with sadness, grief and guilt broke my own heart a little. Launching myself towards him, I pulled him in for a hug, even if my arms struggled to wrap around his huge ones.

"There is no reasoning to an accident and no room for guilt. You aren't to blame, and he will say the same when he comes to." I gestured towards Rayner.

"You really believe he'll be okay?"

I nodded, but the tear sliding down my cheek betrayed my own doubts. "He has to be, Dom. I can't lose him."

Dom shook his head. "You love him."

"I love him." There was no point denying it.

"Like kissing and doing dirty stuff, love him." He pulled a pain expression that had nothing to do with his injuries.

I nodded.

"Shit!"

"Sorry." I wasn't sorry for loving Rayner; my apology was for having kept it a secret from my brother. "I'm sure he doesn't feel the same. I mean, why would he? You guys hit the big time and have travelled the world several times over, had women throwing themselves at you, and five years ago must seem like a lifetime ago to him—" Shit! My brother's face, as I rambled until what had happened between one of his best friends and me dawned on him, was conflicted.

"You. It's you! My own sister." He looked across at Rayner and addressed his unconscious friend. "If you weren't struggling to stay alive right now, I would kill you."

I watched on as tears formed in my brother's eyes, and then he pulled me in close for a hug.

"I don't know how to feel about this, but the truth is that I don't want him to die. I'll even forgive him and you."

We sat, huddled together for a few minutes. I replayed his words, over and over. "What did you mean, it's me?"

"What?"

"When you figured about us, you said, *you, it's you.*"

"You're the one. For Rayner, you're the one."

"I don't know what that means." I hoped what I thought it might mean was correct, but it couldn't be, could it?

"About five years ago, you left town to take that really awesome job in fashion. I didn't think anything of it at the time, and it coincided with a record label executive coming to see the band play at Bernie's."

I grinned at the pride and awe in my brother's voice at

being discovered and propelled into the stratosphere of rock band stardom.

"We literally had the world at our feet. Money, drink, drugs, if we wanted them, we didn't before you get twitchy, and women. God, they were everywhere, guys too, if that was your thing. We all drowned in the sea of women, but here's the thing, for Rayner, they were only ever a one-night thing. Some of us had regular hook-ups, a few became girlfriends, and Mickie even got engaged. However, for Rayner, they got one night and no more. Ask me why?"

"Why?"

"He didn't want any of them beyond the single night of sex. We thought he was living his best life until about six months later in a hotel room when we were all very drunk. One of the guys was seeing a girl and had become a little pussy whipped—"

"Nice, Dom! I wasn't even sure that was a real term!"

"It is," my brother said, quickly recovering from my interruption and chastisement. "We took great pleasure in teasing him, and Rayner really got involved, so much so that it soon turned on him. We all joined in and asked why he was so opposed to trying things more than once. Honestly, I thought he was going to say something like *too many girls so little time*."

"He didn't?" My curiosity was beyond piqued now.

"Nope. He told us there was a girl. Someone he had known and cared for. That despite him knowing it was a bad idea and fighting it, he had slept with her, and she was more than he had ever thought possible."

My eyes were drying at that information, but Dom looked slightly uncomfortable too.

"I was just sick in my own mouth, thinking about that . . . thinking about you. Anyway, he told us there would never be anyone else. That she was everything, and nobody would ever come close. That he had loved her and lost her, and he hoped she'd find her way back to him, somehow, some day, because if he couldn't have it all with her, he wouldn't have it with anyone else. She was and would always be, and I quote, *the one*. You, my beautiful and slightly annoying baby sister are his *one*."

I was not expecting any of that, my brother telling me, but more than that, I had never dared dream that what had happened between us had meant the same to Rayner as it had to me, but it had. He had hoped for the same things I had, and now, I had to hope for the both of us. Hope he pulled through this. Hope he would be okay if he did survive and hope he still felt the same.

Silent tears ran down my face as I stared at Dom. "Fuck!"

He laughed, and then we both stopped dead and turned to Rayner. Alarms and machines began to sound while the nurse calmly approached the bed.

"I think sleeping beauty may be coming to," she told us with a smile as someone else joined her.

Dom took my hand in his and gave it a reassuring squeeze.

Chapter Six

Dom and I were ushered out as the room filled with people. I had considered protesting at my ejection, but Dom had escorted me out with words about me not being in a position to help Rayner yet.

Yet. Three letters that made up one of the most insignificant words and right then, it had meant everything. One, that was another three-letter word that had also climbed the ranks of importance once my brother had told me I was Rayner's one.

We sat in a small waiting area, and the other guys from the band appeared. Dom went and sat with them for a while as they took the piss out of my brother's daily headlines as their management strived to ensure rumours of the boys' demise was kept low. There had been speculation about Rayner, but with statements confirming he had sustained the most serious of the injuries and was undergoing several procedures and intensive therapy, the rumour mill had been quashed slightly.

I tuned them out and tried to focus on what was happening with and to Rayner. Was he conscious? Was he breathing unaided? What if something had gone wrong, and he had taken a turn for the worse? Surely life and fate wouldn't be so cruel as to bring me back here, ready to make my move, knowing our time together had meant as much to him as me, only to snatch it all away? I hoped not.

Needing to push negative and increasingly dark thoughts from my mind, I went back to that first night. I had never seen a man completely naked before, and with little to compare it to, I was sure any man would have seemed a daunting prospect, but Rayner, he was something else. He moved up my body until we were lost in kisses that quickly grew heated. His mouth carried the taste of something foreign, something I quickly figured was my own arousal. Unsure if I liked it or not, it still turned me on, and it wasn't long before I found myself wrapping my legs around his back while his erection rubbed and nudged against me.

"You're sure?"

"Absolutely."

Slowly he'd edged inside me, my own body objecting to his invasion, but with a few pushes, lots more kissing, words of praise and encouragement, a painful sting and a garbled cry, he was inside me.

"Shit! You feel better than I ever thought you might."

I stared up at him, unsure how to react to the knowledge that he had ever thought about this.

"You good if I move?"

I nodded, unsure if I was or not, but as soon as he did move, I was way better than good. After the initial discomfort dissipated, I only felt pleasure, physical and emotional as we locked eyes and shared this intimate moment. Within what felt like seconds, I could feel I was ready to come again, and with a few words from Rayner, I was falling apart beneath him. He followed soon afterwards, and if I hadn't been ruined for all other men before that, I was after it.

We remained cocooned in our exclusive bubble for only a matter of days, but they had been the best days of my life until, one night after we'd made love, Rayner told me it was over. That he should never have allowed himself to succumb to the heat between us and that it could never happen again, and for my sake, he was letting me go.

I had been stunned and the pain was like nothing I had ever known, at least not until I had learned of the accident and his injuries.

Soon after that, on the back of being ignored, avoided and cast aside by Rayner, I found a job a couple of hundred miles away working for a company of party planners. It wasn't something I'd been especially interested in, but I'd had no idea exactly what I wanted to do. I'd applied, got the job and moved away within the month.

When the boys had made it big a few months later, they had begun travelling the country and then the world. That allowed me and Rayner to move on from each other and with our lives, not that I really had, and the truth was that I didn't think he needed to because I was sure he'd never been as invested in us as I had been.

And now, here we were, and if my brother's words were true, this might be our one and only chance for a do-over and this time, to do it right.

"No!" Mickey's single-word cry startled me back to the present.

Looking up, his eyes, as were those of the other guys, were firmly fixed on me.

"You!" Mickey accused, although a smile was on his lips.

"Do we need to beat his ass for touching the baby of the gang?" Jack's question was aimed at Dom.

Dom shook his head. "I don't think he can take another beating, but maybe when he's back on his feet.

They all laughed, but Mickey still stared at me. "You're *the one*."

I smiled at that little word again. "Yeah, so it seems, but he's also *the one*."

He shook his head before we all turned at the sound of footsteps. The doctor was back.

Chapter Seven

Knowing Rayner was on the other side of the door but awake this time, was daunting. I was literally holding the door handle, and the guys were all behind me, eager to see their friend. I was nervous. This would be the first time I had seen him since discovering his feelings for me, but what if the guys had got it wrong and I wasn't the one he'd been referring to. I felt sick. That was without taking into account how his injuries may have affected him physically, emotionally, and his memories. I didn't care how long it took him to recover, nor if he carried scars, but I knew Rayner would struggle if he couldn't rediscover his previous physical prowess and the ability to play the drums just as well.

"You okay?" Dom stood directly behind me.

"Yeah."

With a deep breath, I opened the door to find Rayner Philips, still battered, bruised, slightly broken, but awake, propped up on pillows, looking the worse for wear, but then he looked at me, saw me and after an initially blank expression moved through confusion and concern, he smiled.

Without any thought, I rushed towards him, landing against his chest with a thud that caused him to groan.

"Sorry." I pulled back, concerned that I may have hurt him. What was the matter with me? I knew he was injured, had almost died and here I was launching myself at him.

Rayner reached for my hand and pulled me closer. "It's okay. I wasn't sure you weren't a mirage or my entry to heaven until my ribs stung."

The sound of coughs, pretend sick noises, and at least one snigger reminded us we weren't alone.

Dom appeared at my side. "We need a conversation about you and my sister, but for now, I am seriously pleased to see you awake."

"You know about that, huh?"

"She's the one," called Mickey from behind us.

"Yes, she is," Rayner replied but allowed me to withdraw to let the boys have their reunion.

The next couple of days passed by in something of a blur. People, lots of people came and went, including my parents, who still tried and failed to make me go home. My reasons for not leaving Rayner alone may have changed, but I was determined to spend my time with him. A photographer came, and with all the other members of the band assembled around the bed, the press release was finalised. That helped remove most of the media circus outside of the hospital. Dom had been discharged as planned, which come evening, left just the two of us.

The first couple of nights had seen Rayner fall asleep immediately, but tonight as the last visitor left, he was awake. With most of the machines, drips and lines removed, he had more freedom of movement and was currently shuffling to one side of his bed.

"Come up."

I stared at him from the chair. "What?" Even I heard the nervousness in my voice.

He laughed. "Zee . . ."

I loved when he called me that, always had.

". . . I am in no fit state to launch any kind of seduction right now, but the nurses here, they talk, and I know that you haven't left this place in almost two weeks, and you have barely slept, and when you have, it has been in that uncomfortable chair, so get your ass up here and let's talk."

I didn't hesitate in climbing up beside him. "What do you want to talk about?"

He laughed. "Everything. But first, I want to say sorry."

I stared into his eyes and saw the apology clearly reflected there.

"I shouldn't have treated you the way I did. I panicked. I had always had a soft spot for you, and then it developed, and that night when you came to me, well, it was every dream I had come true. Those days we had were the best of my life."

I sniffed back tears. "Mine too."

"I fucked it up though. The guys, Dom, your parents, I loved them all and didn't want them to think I had taken advantage. I was planning to suggest we start again, open, honestly, and I would have spoken to your parents and Dom."

I watched as he ran a hand through his hair, and even with the bruises and injuries, he looked hot.

"But you didn't."

"No. I went to your house and when I got there, I was all pumped up for it. Ready to face whatever their reactions might be. Dom was buzzing when he opened the door about some record company executive being interested in the band and that they were sending people to check us out, to meet with us. It was a once-in-a-lifetime opportunity, but I thought you might be too, but I knew I couldn't subject you to a life of me being on the road and groupies and long separations, so I had to choose."

"I see." I did see. He had made a decision there and then and chose the band—the opportunity. I wasn't sure if I was hurt or not or whether I completely got what that was all about.

"There hasn't been a day that I haven't missed you, thought of you and kind of regretted it."

"Kind of?" Those words didn't sound like he'd missed and thought of me.

"Yes, kind of, because if I hadn't ended things, I don't know that we would have survived it, but now."

"But now?"

"This is our second chance, Zee, and we have to take it with both hands. It might not be the best of circumstances that brought us back together, and I'm a little broken..."

His voice trailed off, an uncertain expression creasing his face. Instinctively I moved in closer and cupped his cheek. "You're not broken, not really, and you can get better again. If you'll let me, I'll help you."

No words were needed, with one of Rayner's hands cupping my cheek, mirroring my own movement, he leaned in as he pulled me close, and then he kissed me. A soft, gentle, tender kiss that gave me a clearer answer than any words might have.

Chapter Eight

It had been a month since Rayner had woken in the hospital and two weeks since he had been discharged. My parents had insisted that he should stay with us to recuperate, something he hadn't put up too much of a fight over, although he was beginning to get itchy feet for his own place now. I knew part of that was down to one or both of my parents constantly walking in on us. Not that we were doing anything beyond holding hands or kissing, but still, it was awkward. We lay together for hours in the evening, and as much as he pleaded for me to spend the night with him as I had ended up doing in the hospital those last couple of weeks, I didn't. Couldn't. We were under my parents' roof, and I knew they'd disapprove, not that they disapproved of us being together, they didn't. They loved Rayner, and the idea of us being together thrilled them.

"Time for your physio."

Rayner scowled at me.

I moved into the middle of the home gym that was now in my parent's garage and sat opposite Rayner on the bench. "Come on. You want to get back to your peak, right?"

He grabbed for my thighs and easily pulled me along the bench, then wrapped my legs around his hips until we couldn't get any closer.

"There are several peaks I think I could already reach."

I laughed at him and smacked his chest gently. "You are so cheesy."

"No, Zee, I am horny."

I laughed again, but as his hand slid into my hair and prepared to pull my lips to his, the amusement disappeared.

"I don't want to hurt you." I really was concerned that sex would be too much for him, and I could wait.

"You're not going to hurt me. A permanent stiff dick, that is going to hurt me."

The laughter was back.

"You need to do the physio to build your strength and stamina, and the speech exercises to ensure you get full movement back in your jaw or whatever it was that got dislocated, and some yoga for the core strengthening and flexibility."

"Okay, the physio, I will do. The speech thing, I will do. I will even do the yoga, but we need to move out of here, and we need to have sex."

"Are you trying to bargain your way to sex?" I pulled back to observe his expression fully.

"Too fucking right I am because otherwise, I am going to lose my mind. Having you so close, close enough to see, touch, smell and taste and somehow unable to do all of those things, it's torture, so let's strike a bargain here."

"Okay." I leaned in and landed a gentle kiss on his lips. "You stick to the plan for the next two weeks, and you can move back home."

"You have to come too."

"You want me to live with you?"

"Absolutely."

I was unsure if this was happening too quickly, but the truth was that I wanted to be with him all of the time. "Okay, but I will need to pick up more work because Fran has carried me long enough."

"Deal, but we need a work conversation soon."

"Okay. After you move back home, you keep up with the plan for six weeks, and we can partake in some heavy petting or making out."

He scoffed loudly. "You're going to live with me for six weeks and expect that to be sex free. Never happening."

I prepared to protest.

"Look, Zee, you're over-planning. I know that's your job, planning, but stop. I am not a job or a project, I'm me, Rayner. We move back in two weeks, and then let's just see how things go."

"No plan?" I was uncomfortable without a clearer idea of what was happening and when.

"No plan," he confirmed. "That way, if after two days, I wake you up by making you come on my tongue, no deals will have been broken. Then, after two weeks, if I join you in the shower and fuck you against the wall, no broken deals. If after a month, I tie you to the bed and fuck you for hours on end until you're begging me to stop, no broken agreements."

I stared, my eyes drying and my jaw hanging. He grinned.

"And in case you're wondering, if you beg me to stop, I'm carrying on."

"Okay." I heard myself say, but at that point was unsure just what I had agreed to.

Two weeks later, we moved into Rayner's place. The same place he had lived in when I was last here. I thought he might have bought somewhere bigger, fancier, but he hadn't, and I loved that.

We spent our days going for short walks, watched TV, hung out together, talking and laughing and between it all, Rayner kept up with all of his rehabilitation programmes. By the fourth week, he was already moving easier, his reflexes were quicker, sharper, and he didn't ache for as long afterwards. That was backed up by just how handsy he was becoming, not that I was complaining, and our kissing and curling up together was becoming increasingly heated.

The sixth week came and went, and I could really see the improvement in Rayner, physically, mentally and emotionally. We had fallen into our own routine, and although we slept together every night and woke wrapped up in each other every morning, we still hadn't had sex. It was getting harder not to give in to our passion and desire, but I think we both knew that Rayner wasn't quite up to it, and once we gave in to it, there'd be no stopping us.

My business was beginning to suffer because of my absence. Fran was working flat out, and everything that could be done remotely was done by me, but it wasn't the same. It wasn't enough. I needed to speak to Rayner about it. In fact, he had been the one to suggest a conversation about work some weeks before.

He had walked through the door, sweaty from his run, when I seized the opportunity. I followed him to the bathroom, where he was stripping off. Turning to see me watching him, he began to put on something of a show. His muscles were looking more defined, and his tattoos glowed with a combination of sweat and a natural glow he wore. I stared at the glory that was Rayner Philips. He was magnificent. Pushing his track bottoms and then his boxers down, his already semi-erect penis sprang free.

I leaned on one hip and with a cocked brow, smiled. "Pleased to see me?" I had not come in here to flirt and possibly embark on some sexy time, yet here we were.

"Always."

Before I could process it, he had pulled me to him and was beginning to push my t-shirt off, then pushed my shorts down.

"Rayner, are you sure." All thoughts of conversation were gone.

"Absolutely." He leaned in as if to kiss me. "If you're sure?"

I immediately went back to our first time. "Yes. I want it to be you, always have."

He grinned briefly before his lips took mine, and his tongue breached my mouth. We were heading for the shower that had filled the room with steam, however, I think the heat I felt was all us.

The water was just the right temperature as it rained down on us. Neither of us showed any sign of wanting to get clean. I felt Rayner's hands cup my behind before lifting me up and pressing me against the cold, tiled wall. I shrieked into his mouth at the shock of it. He simply laughed as he broke our kiss. We'd already had the contraception discussion weeks before, so knowing we were both clean and I was on the pill, I anticipated his entry, but he had other ideas.

His mouth dropped to my breasts and as he licked, sucked and nipped at my nipples, I was already seeing stars.

"Touch yourself, Zee, make yourself come," he commanded, and although I had expected him to do that, the idea of doing it while he watched excited me. "As much as I want to bury myself inside you and fuck you hard, I don't want to hurt you if you're not ready."

I nodded. Dropping my hand between my currently spread legs that were wrapped around him, I began to circle my clit, slowly at first, but as the sparks of pleasure began to ignite, I moved faster.

"That's it, baby, for me."

He returned his attention to my nipples, and as the sensations there caused my clit to throb, I knew it was going to be intense. My sex clenched around the emptiness there, but not for long. A finger or a thumb pierced me at the exact second Rayner bit down into my nipple, and my own fingers pressed down into the flesh around my clit that I still circled and then, accompanied by heavy breathing, panting and a sea of stars and cursing, my climax arrived. I had barely come down from the first orgasm when Rayner gently nudged his way into my body, but once inside me, any gentleness ended. Driving into me hard, he pounded away, his body grazing my clit each time he drove inside me. I was moaning and crying within what seemed like seconds, and as I pulsed and tensed around him, Rayner came at the exact second I did.

We lay in bed together afterwards, the silence surrounding us as we absorbed the intensity of what had happened between us. We hadn't put it into words, but we both knew that the other had felt it, the emotions as well as the physical reactions.

"That was seriously fucking hot!" Rayner eventually said.

I laughed at his choice of words.

"Intense, but yeah, hot."

"And now I have proven my fitness, we will be doing that a lot."

"How do you feel about a long-distance relationship?" I blurted out the question and knew it wasn't going to go well when I felt the previously relaxed man next to me tense.

"For other people fine, but as you are no more than a foot away from me, we don't have one of those."

"I have to go back to work."

"You can work from here. You have been working from here."

"Rayner, I need to go back and pull my weight."

"Are you giving me the brush-off?" He sounded nervous of my answer.

I moved so I straddled his middle, gazing down at his sad and serious expression. "No. Never. I want to be with you. I don't know what will happen with the business long term, but Fran and I are business partners, so I need to be there for her, and now you're on the mend . . ." I let that sink in. "I presume you and the guys will go back on the road, so you won't be here either."

"Zee, I want to be where you are whenever I can be, but

yeah, I guess if we're realistic, there will be separations, not that the band are going anywhere any time soon."

"Come with me."

He looked sceptical. "Don't you and Fran live together?"

I nodded and then laughed. "Okay, maybe not, but you could visit."

He shook his head. "I don't want to visit. I want us to be together. So, if you go, I go, and we'll find a place."

"You'd do that?"

"Of course. I lost you once, that won't happen again. I won't let it. I love you."

I couldn't fight the grin spreading across my face. "You love me."

"Yes."

"I love you, too, always have."

"Snap. What can I say? You are and have always been *the one*."

Also by Elle M Thomas

Standalones

Disaster in Waiting

Revealing His Prize

Falling Series

New Beginnings

Still Falling

Old Endings

Love in Vegas Series

Lucky Seven

Pushing His Luck

Lucking Out

Valentine's Vows

Winter Wishes

Revelation Series

Days of Discovery

Events of Endeavour

The Carrington Siblings

One Night or Forever

Family Affair

The Nanny Chronicles

Single Dad

Pinky Promise

I Was Always Yours

by Emma Luna

Chapter One

EMMALEIGH

Hope is a word I stopped believing in a long time ago. It's one of those words that people throw about so casually. Hope you are well. Hope you have a great day. Hope you feel better soon.

But what does it really mean? For someone like me, hope is a pipedream. It's something I gave up believing in a long time ago, a bit like Father Christmas. As my dad used to say—once I finally stopped believing—"There's only one fat man who brings presents to this house... me."

I know I probably sound depressed, and you would be right. I believe my doctor's files say something along the lines of *moderate depression, generalised anxiety disorder, and suicidal ideation*. Basically, I feel exactly the same as most people do at some point during their lives. But that's the thing, this isn't just a passive phase, this is my permanent existence now.

I once had it all. High-flying career as a surgical nurse, long-term boyfriend who I saw great potential in, friends I enjoyed spending time with, a loving family who all live nearby, financially self-sufficient. I even had my own fucking car. On paper, my life was perfect, until it wasn't. Until the day hope became nothing except a wish.

Nine years ago, my life changed forever. I stopped being Emmaleigh Wayward, and I became the girl with Multiple Sclerosis—or MS for short. I lost everything and gained a shitload of symptoms, hospital visits, and medication that I didn't ask for. As each day passed, I stopped hoping for a better life, for a cure, and started hoping it would all be over soon.

I still remember the days when I didn't know what MS was, when I just thought my body was failing me. I remember wondering what was happening, and would my life ever be the same again? This is the story of how my life turned dark, and how I reached the stage nobody should ever have to reach. Until a bright bolt of electricity zapped me back to life.

Chapter Two

EMMALEIGH

I know this probably seems like a stupid message, but I just wanted to clear something up. I really did want to meet you and go on a date. When I said I couldn't go because I broke my foot, that wasn't an elaborate cop-out. A way to get out of meeting you. It's the truth. I have loved talking to you, and think we could get on just as well in person. But I know you are dating someone else now, so I wish you all the best. Was nice talking to you, Carlos.

Fuck. Could I sound any lamer?

Without thinking too much about it, I press Send. I don't normally send such desperate, pathetic sounding messages. But at the present moment, my life literally can't get any shitter.

It's three in the morning. I'm sitting in a bathroom that screams 'owned by a guy' while his cum dribbles down my legs.

I wish I had some incredible sex story to share, that I could tell you all about how he had magic fingers he knew how to use, but it was nothing compared to his dick. That I saw stars and couldn't catch my breath as I came so many bloody times.

Ha. I fucking wish. Let me tell you what really happened. I was stupid, and I made the mistake I kept telling myself I needed to stop making.

Drew, the guy who I can hear snoring from two rooms away while I cower in his bathroom, is one of those people that looks fucking gorgeous. He exudes bad boy, with tattoos on top of his lean muscles and a perfectly sculpted face to match. His short, spiky black hair, that admittedly featured far too much gel, and the cocky smirk, round off that bad boy vibe. They were the idealistic things I focused on when I stupidly hoped—there's that word again!—that I could change him. So I ignored the fact that he wore tracksuit bottoms everywhere, smoked roll-ups, which I fucking hated, and he didn't want any kind of sexual activity to take place while he was watching reality TV. They are just the everyday issues. The other ones were even worse. Still, I ignored all this and the shit times I'd had before with him, hoping this time would be different. That maybe, just once, I will be the one to cure the bad boy.

News flash... I'm not that girl. Then Drew took his dickish behaviour even further and I think back to the beginning of the evening, wondering how the hell I got myself in this position.

- Earlier That Evening -

"Emmaleigh, I need to ask you something, and I expect you to be honest. Are you dating anyone else?" asks Drew, and instantly my mind travels to the text I had been sending Carlos, whose real name is Lee—it's a long story. We had been texting a lot, but we never met. We had been talking about it, until I went and broke my stupid fucking foot with my clumsy, off-the-chart bad balance. I think he thought I was blowing him off, as so many people who meet on dating apps do, but that wasn't the case here, and it hurt he didn't see that. He went on a date with someone else, and he likes her, which is why he messaged me this morning to let me know we couldn't talk anymore. I haven't been able to reply yet.

How do you tell the guy you had started to fall for over a damn dating app that it's okay if he moves on? It's not okay. Out of all the guys I've talked to on this shitty app, he was the only one I could ever hold a conversation with, who asked me about my day, and who didn't send me a dick pic —winner in my book.

Instead, I found myself back here, sitting on Drew's shitty old couch, wondering how much lower I can stoop.

We had been seeing each other on and off now for the last few months. Nothing serious, just the odd hang-out and hook-up. Other than the first time we met, we've never even been on a real date, and to be honest, that's okay. We have zero in common, and I don't think I could stand a date with him.

I can already hear the judgement. If this guy's such an ass, why are you still meeting him? Worse than that, why are you still fucking him?

And the honest answer is so fucking depressing to admit. I'm using him to make up for my shitty, low self-esteem. He's hot, and I'm in a place right now where I hate everything about myself. I can't even tell you how often I feel like my body fails me. I'm exhausted all the time. Sometimes, for no reason, I can't feel my leg, or my vision will go blurry. Doctors say I'm just stressed, but I can't help worrying it's something more. The more my body fails me for no reason at all, the more depressed I get. So, when this hot guy started showing an interest in me, I jumped on it. I ignored the fact that we have nothing in common. He's dull as dishwater, and he wouldn't know a clitoris if it whacked him around the head. Still, I keep showing up at his apartment late at night so nobody can see me making another big mistake.

Tonight, I'm probably the lowest I've been in a while. I know you shouldn't get your hopes up with guys you meet on a dating website, but I honestly thought Lee was different. I thought we had great potential. And even now, as I'm sitting on another guy's sofa, all I can think about is him. But when Drew asks me if I'm seeing anyone else, I can answer honestly. If I'd arranged to meet Lee, I would have told Drew right away. I don't believe in leading two guys on, or dating two people at once—even though I'm definitely not dating Drew. I still only sleep with one person at a time.

Trying to put all thoughts of Lee's message out of the way, I answer Drew honestly. "No, I'm not seeing anyone else. I thought we talked about that the other week and agreed that if we ever wanted to go on a date or fuck someone else, we would tell each other. We aren't exclusive or dating, but it just feels polite to tell each other when it gets to that stage. I would have done that anyway, but it was you that suggested it."

Drew shifts his gaze to the floor, and thankfully for him, his reality show starts up again after the commercial break, and he clarified that we can't talk while his show is on. I should have run the minute he enforced this rule on date number one. I'm such a twit for still being here.

I zone out for the next half an hour, playing with my phone, rereading Lee's message and trying to think of an appropriate reply. I'm pulled back to the room when the show's theme tune blasts out of the television speakers, and Drew talks again. "So, are you looking for us to be exclusive?" he asks, as he turns the television volume down—not off, just down!

"I don't think I said that specifically. What I said is that I won't sleep with someone who is fucking other people. We don't have to be boyfriend and girlfriend, and do all the soppy shit. I just want to know that the person I'm with isn't with someone else, too." I don't think that's an unreasonable request, and when Drew lowers his eyes, looking down at the cigarette he's rolling up, I should have been suspicious, but I'm not. Or maybe I am and I'm just choosing to ignore the obvious?

"You know I don't do girlfriends. I don't like to be tied down. But I'm happy to just see one person," he states as he takes a drag from his cigarette, lounging back on the opposite sofa.

"Okay," I add, not really understanding why he's bringing up something we hashed out weeks ago when we first started sleeping together.

"Good. Now, why don't you come over here and give me a blow job?" Fuck, is that romantic?!

I know I should read between the lines, questioning him on why he would bring up something like that when we sorted it out a while ago. But, I guess the saying *ignorance is bliss* really is true.

"I thought this time you were going to go down on me, show me the magic fingers you tempted me with when we first started talking," I ask, remembering all the messages we sent over the dating app. He was hot, sexy, and kept telling me exactly what I wanted to hear. All about his magic fingers that could find my G-spot without even trying, and about how much he loved to lick pussy. Not to mention his giant cock and the fact that he liked to get rough and dirty when he fucked. That was exactly what I was looking for. A guy to throw me around, spank my ass, and call me his slut. So, when we first had sex, to say it was a let-down was an understatement. I gave him the best blow job of his life and got him nice and ready, but then a few pumps in doggy and it was over. I barely had time to think about getting wet, and my G-spot was nowhere to be seen, let alone an orgasm. I didn't even give a shit that he lied, and his penis was just average-sized. I've been with men who are average, and if they know how to fucking use it, that's all that mattered. Yet, Drew neither had the size he boasted about nor had the skill.

I can hear the screams again. *Get out of there. Why are you back for another round?* What can I say, I'm an idiot.

"I will do, but it has to be the right time. I have to be in the mood. So, why don't you help me get in the mood with that fucking amazing mouth of yours?" he asks, his voice taking on that low husky tone he gets when he's horny.

I drop to my knees, feeling the last drop of self-esteem fall to the floor with me, and I crawl towards him. By the time I'm sitting in front of him, on my knees, he has his sweatpants and boxers off, and his cock is standing to attention, pre-cum dripping from the tip. Pushing all thoughts of my dignity to one side, I lower my mouth around his cock and am rewarded with a loud groan as he thrusts his hips upwards until his dick hits the back of my throat. I suck hard, bobbing up and down the shaft, twirling my tongue around the head and along the vein on the underside—that really drives him wild. He threads his fingers through my hair, but doesn't take control, so I continue sucking the way I know he likes.

It's not long before his hips thrust frantically, his breathing becomes more erratic, and his cock pulses in that telltale way. I know he's close, and so much to his disappointment, I pull away from his cock. "Nooo. Em, what the fuck?" he groans, as he slams his hand down on the sofa next to him.

I look up at him, hoping he can see the annoyance clear on my face. "Because, Drew, if you come in my mouth now, you won't be able to fuck me. You will fall straight to sleep, and I will have hobbled all the way over here with a broken foot just to blow you."

He looks at me with a face that says, 'and what's wrong with that?' I shake my head and stand up, making my disapproval clear, thanks to my glare. I'm sure he rolls his fucking eyes at me, but thankfully he stands and pulls his t-shirt off so he's fully naked. Without saying a word, he walks towards his bedroom, just expecting me to follow—which I do—stupid me!

Upon entering his bedroom, I try not to look at all the mess around the room. I'm sure underneath all the laundry there's a carpet to be seen. There's just crap everywhere, over every surface, but thankfully his bed looks clean with new sheets. As soon as he turns his bedroom light on, and the fucking hideous red bulb coats the room in a crimson glow—reminding me of the Red Light District in Amsterdam—I remember why I usually tell him to keep the light off. I already feel slutty, without a fucking red light adding to it.

He doesn't make any move to undress me, just sits in

the middle of his bed, stroking his cock in one hand while pointing for me to join him with the other. I slowly remove my clothes, although why I'm dragging this out is beyond me.

"Come on, baby. Get on your hands and knees," he purrs, and I feel disgust ripple through my body. Shocker, of course, he wants to go for doggy style again. I should have known.

Crawling onto the bed, naked, I get onto my hands and knees the same as always. I feel him shifting into position behind me when the bed shifts beneath me.

I feel his finger lightly stroke through my slit, and for just a second I get my hopes up that this might be the start of some foreplay. Instead, he simply uses his fingers to part my lips so he can aim the tip of his cock. Unfortunately, he doesn't aim it too well and the first couple of attempts bounce off my perineum.

"Open up for me, baby." *Argh, it's not a matter of me opening up. It has a lot more to do with you hitting the right fucking target.*

Realising he needs a bit of guiding, I reach around and take hold of the tip, guiding it to the right area. I expect him to ease into it, to get me ready first, but he doesn't. He plunges his cock straight into my dry pussy, and I yelp from the burning sting of skin against skin.

As soon as his cock bottoms out, he doesn't wait for me to get a little more ready. He just continues thrusting in and out at a ridiculous speed. I realise then that doesn't have a care in the world about if I'm enjoying it or not. I'm literally just a hole for him to use to get himself off, and the more that realisation sinks in, the shitter I feel.

It's over all too quickly—although at that point, I didn't exactly want to prolong it. I don't think I even have a chance to consider getting wet, let alone for it to actually happen. I feel him pull out, and as I feel his cum trickle from my pussy, I spin around so fast, my eyebrows draw together as I look at him with venom in my eyes.

"Why the fuck didn't you use a condom?" I snap. I didn't check with him before we got started because I didn't think I needed to. We'd had this conversation weeks ago when we first slept together. He knew what I expected, and he'd never done it without one before.

Shrugging his shoulders, he leans back against the headboard and lights a roll up that sends a billow of smoke into the room, and the smell causes my nose to wrinkle. "I ran out of those latex-free condoms you bought, and I went to buy more, but they are so fucking expensive, so I just bought normal ones. I figured we could just not use any, since I know you aren't fucking someone else, and you're on the pill."

There's so much wrong with that fucking sentence. I don't know where to start. I feel like I should start by punching him between the eyes for deciding by himself about something that concerns us both. I don't give a shit that I'm on the pill. I never wanted to have sex without a condom until I was in a long-term, committed relationship.

"I'm so fucking pissed at you right now," I fume, as I try to roll off the bed. At first I'm trying to do my best to not drip cum everywhere, but then I think, fuck it. It's his cum, he will have to deal with it. I pick up his t-shirt and pull it over my head, trying desperately to ignore the nausea-inducing cigarette smell that clings to it. "How dare you make a decision like that, and not at least discuss it with me?"

He shrugs his shoulders, and that blank expression remains on his face as he snuggles further into the bed, pulling the duvet cover up, like I'm not even there. "Chill out, babe. We can talk about this later. I'm tired now. Come on, just go to sleep."

I get ready to argue, but there's no point. He isn't even listening to me, and within minutes, he rolls over and begins to snore. I'm just about to head out to the bathroom when a buzzing rings from on the bedside table where Drew carefully placed our phones before we had sex. There's definitely no all-consuming passion where we can't hold it in any longer and we rip off each other's clothing, letting them fall where they may. Even the act of getting naked is boring and dull.

I go to pick up my phone, until I realise the vibration wasn't in fact from my phone, it came from his. I would never normally read another guy's phone without his permission, but it's just sitting there, the message preview staring at me, tempting me to look. All I can see is it's a message from someone called Tiff, and she enjoyed...

Well, that's more than enough of a reason for me to open the phone and read the rest. The idiot doesn't even have a passcode on his phone. That's how cocky—or stupid —he is.

Tiff: I enjoyed hanging out with you last night. That thing you did with your tongue was amazing. I know you said you are seeing another girl and can't get serious, and that's okay with me. I don't mind being the other woman. But, when you say she gives the best blow jobs, I'm determined to prove I'm better. Then maybe one day you can get rid of her for good. But for now, this is fine. What do you say, can I be your dirty little secret on the side?

Fuck! My mind whirls as I try to take in all the fucked-up things with that message. Looks like the reason he wanted to clarify that we were still only fucking each other was because he was secretly fucking someone else. And, by the sounds of it, he actually showed her a good time. If I felt like shit before, it's nothing like how I feel now.

I know if I look further into his phone I will find more. I don't know how I know that, I just do. I guess maybe it's something I knew all along but just wanted to ignore. The bad guy never changes, and the short, curvy girl never gets the guy.

Picking up my phone, I head to the bathroom, and that's when the message I've been trying to send all day finally comes to me. I message Lee, using our joke name of Carlos, and I bare my soul. I tell him I thought we had a connection, and that I really wasn't trying to blow him off, that my broken foot is real. I wish him all the happiness in the world with this new girl, and as I press Send, I know in the pit of my soul that I don't mean a single word. I can't explain it, there's a pain there that hurts more than all of Drew's deception. The idea that this is the last time I will ever speak to Lee physically hurts me. There's a part of me, I think it may be my heart, telling me that Lee is important and that I shouldn't let him go. But therein lies the problem. I haven't let him go. He left me. He decided to date someone else, just like they all do in the end. After all, who wants to date a short, curvy, sarcastic girl with an incredible ability to fall over a leaf and break her foot? There's nothing about me that screams 'date me, love me'. I'm one hundred per cent forgettable, or replaceable.

I clean myself up, and as quietly as I can, I move around the flat, picking up my clothes so I can get dressed and leave this fucking shithole, never to return. Once I'm fully dressed, I debate waking Drew up, but there's no point. We don't need to have a conversation, it won't go anywhere. I just need to forget all about this little mistake and accept I'm going to grow old with hundreds of cats—or maybe dogs, since cats scare the shit out of me. There's no denying that one day a cat is going to rise and take over the world. Just look at them. They have that evil dictator look about them—all of them.

It's three in the morning, but I order a taxi on my phone. Opening the front door, I'm shocked to see the person in the flat opposite is also coming out of their door too. I hadn't expected to see anyone. My hair is all messy, my make-up smudged, and my dress is all wrinkled from when I threw it on the floor. It's obvious I'm making the walk of shame, and to be honest, that wouldn't be a problem at all, if it wasn't for the fact that I recognise the person coming towards me.

"Emmaleigh, what are you doing here?" asks Neelam—my boss!

"Erm... I-I was just... visiting a friend. Now I'm heading home." Yeah, that doesn't sound suspicious at all. I watch as her gaze travels over the slutty dress I'm wearing, and the big boot I have on to support my broken foot.

I suppose now would be a good time to mention that I work in the hospital as a nurse, and of course, given the broken foot, I'm currently on sick leave. "This is an odd time to be leaving, Em. Should you be on your foot at all? I don't want you injuring it further," Neelam states, and I can hear the tone of disapproval in her voice.

I mumble my response, trying not to act like a child being chastised by a parent. "I'm just heading to the taxi. I have my crutches at home. That's part of the reason I'm going home. My foot hurts. What are you doing here?" I turn the tables on her, although she doesn't look like she's making the walk of shame. She's in jeans and a t-shirt, and honestly, she looks as perfectly put together as she always does at work.

"This is where I live. I'm on call, and they are short-staffed on the ward, so I'm just going in to help." I can't help but wince, thinking I could be responsible for their staff shortage. I try to visualise my off-duty schedule in my head, and I let out an audible sigh when I remember I definitely wouldn't have been working tonight anyway. So, technically, it isn't my fault, but I still don't enjoy hearing that my colleagues—my friends—are struggling. We work as a team on our ward and I hate that my body means I am letting them down.

"Oh well, hopefully things will get better." What else am I supposed to say? I can't exactly help at all.

Neelam gives me a small smile. "Make sure you rest, please. Then when you get back to work, you can tell me all the gossip about why you are sneaking out of a boy's apartment at three in the morning."

She gives me a small wink as she walks past me towards the door that acts as an entry for the whole block of flats. I follow behind her, hobbling at a slower pace, trying not to wince. Fuck, I'm really regretting not bringing my crutches right about now.

Before I even have time to think of a response to that, she jumps in her car and my taxi appears. I wave her off and I feel my body sag. Typical that she spotted me at the worst moment of my life. I can't really get much lower. A girl so desperate to be loved that she will settle for something as fucking disgusting as Drew. I think now is the time when I really need to concentrate more on loving myself than on finding a man. Which is a fucking good job since I'm out of options. My mind wanders to Lee, and I can't help but think about what we could have been if we'd just had our chance.

Chapter Three

LEE

"Ugh, I had the worst date ever last night," I groan as I flop down onto my best friend Craig's rumpled double bed. It's well after two in the afternoon, yet it still looks like he's just rolled out of it because he knew I was on my way over. Not that I can comment too much; my bed remains unmade at home.

"Which one was this?" he asks, as he munches on a chocolate bar he had on his computer desk. I can see he has a few, but he doesn't bother to offer me one. Typical. I almost roll my eyes at him.

Our friendship has never really been any different. Don't get me wrong, he's still the closest thing I have to a best friend, but that doesn't make him very good at it. We've been friends since we first met in school, around the age of five, and we have been close ever since. But the thing about Craig is that he's flaky as fuck. It's almost like if he sees something new and shiny, he will ditch me for a bit while he goes to play with that. I've come to learn that the newness always wears off, and eventually he always comes back. What I've never quite understood is why, each and every time, I let him.

"Is this the one with the massive tits?" he adds, as if that helps to clarify the situation.

Shaking my head. "No, that was the singer I met the week before last. This was the babysitter."

Craig has this lightbulb moment when he suddenly remembers who I'm talking about, and as he gets a mischievous glint in his eye, I remember why. "Oh fuck, yeah. Please tell me you fucked her and spanked her ass for being a bad babysitter," Craig jokes as he stands up, puts one foot onto the edge of the bed, and begins thrusting his pelvis while spanking his own ass.

Rolling my eyes, I push at his chest, not wanting his gyrating hips anywhere near me, thank you very much. "You watch too much porn, man," I chastise, before explaining that if I'm not her boss, I can't treat her like a bad babysitter.

He ignores me, like he never heard a word I said. "Okay, so you didn't have sex, is what I'm hearing?"

I can't help releasing a groan as I pull my fingers through my short jet-black hair. This is what every failed date boils down to with him, and honestly, we are twenty-one years old, so I don't fucking blame him. But still.

"Look, I'm not like you. I have to get to know them slightly before I fuck them. And every date I've been on lately has been so monumentally fucking bad that I just can't get past their shit to even kiss them, let alone go for more," I explain, trying to hold in the groan as I think back to all the horrendous dates I've had over the last few months since I joined that fucking awful dating website.

They say that it's the men on there that are sex mad,

and we're all sending dick pics within the first few minutes, talking dirty instead of asking how they are. But, in my—albeit very limited—experience, the women on there are just as horny. I've had pics of nipples, cleavage, and pussies sent my way all before I'd even asked how they are. So, as much as men get a bad rep on those sites—and it's probably well deserved—there are a few women that are just as bad.

I can feel my balls shrinking the more I talk about wanting to get to know a woman, and if I'm being honest, I'm not looking for a long-term relationship. I just don't want to fuck around with someone who is fucking around with ten other people. I guess you could say I have standards. Or, as Craig would say, I have blue balls, thanks to my standards.

"Okay, so what was wrong with the babysitter?" Craig asks, and I feel a shiver of disgust ripple down my thoughts as I tell him all about my evening.

"So, you know how she invited me over to her house last night?" I ask, and he nods, but says nothing, so I continue. "Well... it turns out it wasn't actually her house. She was babysitting this young kid."

"Ohhh, my naughty nanny porn is coming to life before my very eyes," Craig jokes, and I can't help but laugh at his crazy antics.

"Nah, it was nothing like that. I was so self-conscious. I mean, she's supposed to be watching the little kid, who thankfully was asleep the whole time, and yet she was more concerned with the joint she had with her."

"Wait! So, not only did you have a bad babysitter situation going on, she also provided you with weed. I'm failing to see what was wrong with this girl. Did she have a third boob, because at this point, I might be on board with that?"

I flop back so that I am lying on the bed as a loud groan escapes my lips, frustration over my best friend more than clear. "She didn't have a third boob. It just felt weird. We were in a stranger's house, and she was getting high while we were responsible for a little kid. Whenever things were getting interesting and we started making out on the couch, the baby monitor would go off, interrupting us. But that wasn't even the worst part."

"So far I'm failing to hear *a worst* part, but please continue."

"She went to settle the kid down, and as she came back, she had some cash in her hand. I wondered what she had got it out for, and where from—since her jeans were so tightly plastered against her body, I would have noticed if she had a purse in her pockets. And I knew her bag was on the floor in front of me. That's when she told me she found it in the parents' bedroom, and sometimes she helps herself to stuff they won't miss. Then, as she put the money in her bag, she also put what looked to be an ornamental dog in there, too. She informed me she had done some research, and it was worth a couple of hundred. I said surely it wasn't a good idea to steal from her employers, and she just said they're so rich they probably won't even know, and that they should have been paying her more. I hightailed it out of there and never looked back."

Silence fills the room, which is very unlike Craig, so I sit up to look and see what he's thinking. He's stuffing his face with another chocolate bar, and replies with his mouth full of chocolate, which makes my stomach roll as nausea takes hold. "Okay, so you probably did the right thing there. Who are we dating next? What happened to the naughty nurse?"

My mind flicks back to Emmaleigh—or Gertrude, as I jokingly call her. She's the only person on the whole fucking app that knows how to hold a conversation. We had been talking every day for almost six weeks, until a couple of weeks ago. We had finally got to the point where we felt comfortable meeting, and if I'm being honest, I was actually very fucking excited about meeting her. I dread the dates now, wondering what fresh hell I will have to encounter, but there was just something different about her. I had a good feeling, but all that was long forgotten when she blew me off. It was the shittest excuse, too. Something about breaking her foot by falling over a leaf. I mean, she could have come up with something better. I was just sick of waiting. I don't want a relationship where we just text every day. I wanted to meet her, but obviously she didn't want the same thing. So, I told her I was moving on, that I was seeing someone else. But it was her message a day later that broke me.

She told me she really had broken her foot, and that it was never an excuse. Apparently, she really wanted to date me and she was gutted that we can't meet. She wished me every happiness with the girl I was dating, but I could tell she didn't fully mean it. It's like one of those things you say, isn't it? You say one thing, but inside, everything is screaming the opposite. Don't date someone else. Don't be happy with someone else. What happened to giving us a chance? And you know what, I've been asking myself the same thing every day.

It's only been around a week since I got that message from her and I already miss her. Not having her there at the end of the day to message, talk about our day together, and generally someone to have a laugh with. It's actually been unbelievably lonely, which I know sounds absurd. How can you miss someone who has never really been part of your life? Particularly since I've never even laid eyes on her, but it's true—I miss her. But, just like every other fucking thing in my life, I messed things up with her, too.

Craig clears his throat, dragging my attention back to him, and I see he's still staring, waiting for me to answer him. Taking a deep breath, I try to push Emmaleigh from my mind, and tell him to do the same. "I already told you, I've moved on from her. She was making excuses not to meet, and so I started seeing the babysitter."

"Ha, look how well that turned out. What do you mean by excuses?" I can practically feel him rolling his eyes at me, like it's more about my excuses than hers.

"We had planned to meet, but then she said she broke her foot. I don't know. I just got the feeling she was blowing me off so—"

Before I get the chance to finish my sentence, Craig interrupts me. "You would be fucking lucky if a girl blew you off. For sucks sake, Lee. You have got to stop making excuses. And more than that, decide what it is you really want. You say you want nothing serious, that you just want to fuck around, yet you are vetting these girls like you are looking for a wife. If you really just wanted a no-strings fling, all you need to know about them is if they are hot, into you, and looking for sex. You keep going on dates, and then ditching these women because they aren't right. You are giving me fucking whiplash, so I can only imagine what the girls are thinking."

Shit, he's right. I don't know what the fuck is wrong with me. Maybe I just don't have it in me to sleep around. But I sure as hell know I'm not looking for a girlfriend. I can barely deal with looking after myself without having the needs of someone else to think about. Besides, even at twenty-one, I already know that I never want to get married or have children. So, what's the point in looking for a woman to settle down with when I can't—or won't—give them what they are looking for?

"Look," Craig says, as he flops down onto the bed beside me, grabbing my attention from the darkness engulfing me. "Just give the girl a chance. I know you've already blown her off, but it's fixable. Give her a week or two, tell her she's been on your mind, but that you were waiting for her foot to heal. Then ask her out. If you don't, you are always going to keep wondering. In the meantime, what about the swimmer you were talking to?"

He's got a point, I don't think I will be able to just forget about Emmaleigh as easily as I have the other girls. It's only been a few days, and I can't get her off my mind. Craig's right—fuck, I hate saying that—I should give her foot some time to heal, then go for it.

It's been a long couple of weeks, and I'm wondering why the hell I'm bothering going on dates. They are just one failure after the next. I really tried not to think about Emmaleigh. I tried telling myself that I broke things off with her and that I need to learn to live with that, but I just couldn't. With each new person I spoke to on the dating app, I compared them to her. They didn't ask me how my day had been like she always did. They didn't get my humour the way she did. They didn't make me laugh the way she did. So, in the end, I bit the bullet.

Carlos: Hey Gertrude. I hope you are well and your foot's healed. I know you probably never thought you would hear from me again—maybe you never wanted to, in which case you can delete this message. But, I really hope you don't. You see, I thought I could easily

move on and forget about you, since you blew me off—or so I thought. But the truth is, I haven't forgotten about you. I keep thinking about you, wondering what you are up to, and if you are thinking of me. If you've already moved on, then I completely understand that, but if you haven't, I would love another chance. What do you say, will you go on our long-overdue date with me?

I sent that text two days ago now, and I've been glued to my phone ever since. The one thing I fucking hate—and kinda love—about WhatsApp is their delivery system. You can see when someone has got your message, which is a relief, but then you wait for them to read it. Even worse than that is when they read it, but they don't reply. That's essentially what happened to me.

Emmaleigh read the message almost as soon as I sent it, but she hasn't replied. I've been checking every hour, hoping she hasn't been back online, as that would mean she isn't ignoring me. She's just busy. But each time I check and see the time she last logged in has changed, that's when I realised she probably will not reply. It doesn't change the fact that I have been glued to my phone. Every slight notification, every message ping, I'm there in a flash to check if it's her. Then I have to ignore the ache in the pit of my stomach when it's not her name.

I've started talking to another girl, Frankie, and honestly, she seems nice. We have a lot in common, and I probably should just ask her out on a date, but there's something holding me back. I never date or talk to two girls at the same time, it just doesn't feel right, and so accepting a date with Frankie would be like admitting that I've blown it with Emmaleigh. Something I'm just not quite ready to face yet.

HOPE

I'm lying on my bed, just staring up at the ceiling, when there's a knock on my bedroom door. Did I forget to mention that I still live at home with my parents? I know some people would frown upon this, and that they are in a mad rush to get away from their parents, but that couldn't be further from the truth for me. I love my parents, and I have such an amazing relationship with my mum—she's like my best friend. So they give me freedom to come and go as I please, and they treat me like an adult, not a kid anymore, which was important to me. But the biggest factor was that I only have to pay a hundred pounds a week, which means the rest of my wages belong to me. Not a bad price considering I get all my food cooked, washing and ironing done, and all my bills are included, too. Why anyone would want to move out and give up all those benefits is beyond me. But, my number one rule when I decided to stay at home is that my room is my safe space. Nobody comes in without my permission, and especially not if I'm not here. Mum agreed to this as long as I agreed to keep it tidy.

Looking over, I see the sliding lock isn't on, and so I call out for whoever is on the other side to come in. Mum pushes the door open and comes to sit on the edge of the bed.

My mum's only a small lady, probably around five feet tall, and she looks good for her age. All the Zumba classes she goes to mean she has the body of a thirty-year-old, despite being in her sixties. Her shoulder-length brunette hair is always perfectly styled, and her face is always made up to fit the occasion. Even around the house is she rarely without make-up. Her flower, baggy linen trousers and her white flowy blouse make her look smartly dressed, even though I know she isn't going out today.

Mum smiles at me with one that matches my own, and I sit up to hear what she has to say. "So, I want to talk to you about something important, if that's okay?" she asks, her voice sombre, and that's when I see the sadness on her face and that her smile doesn't quite reach her eyes.

"Are you okay, Mum?" I ask, fear gripping me as I wait and wonder what she's going to say.

"I was talking to your sister earlier. Unfortunately, she's had a bit of a falling out with Cain. I think the idea of having a baby became a little overwhelming for him. I told you that he'd been pulling away from Lena over the last couple of weeks, becoming more depressed. Well... it turns out, he's been sleeping with one of the girls Lena works with. Obviously, Lena is heartbroken, and she doesn't think she wants to be with him anymore. But, I think she would have given him a second chance for the sake of the baby, but he has said he's not sure he wants to be with her anymore. He thinks he wants this new girl. So, Lena has asked if she can come home. She will most likely have the baby here and then when she's more settled, look at getting a house for them both. But, I know this will be a big upheaval having Lena back, and having a baby in the house eventually, so I wanted to get your opinion." I can see Mum picking at her hands as she talks, and the minute she finishes talking, she bites at her inner cheek. She's worried I'm going to say no.

Initially, my instinct is to say that I don't want to live with Lena, or have a baby in the house. But, the more I mull it over in my head, the more I realise that's a massive douche move. My sister wouldn't want to move back home unless it was the absolute last resort. She loves having her freedom, and when we were growing up, the more she rebelled, the more she argued with our dad. She couldn't wait to move out, so I'm guessing moving back, particularly when she had her whole future planned out with Cain, is not what she wants.

"Shit, I can't imagine how Lena feels right now. Am I thrilled to have her home, or to be living with a baby? No, of course I'm not. But she's family, and she needs our support, so I can get on board." Before I've even finished speaking, Mum throws her arms around me and pulls me in for the biggest hug. For a little woman, she sure gives big, squeezing hugs, and I love them.

Breathing a sigh of relief, I realise Mum was worried I might kick off. "I was worried you would say no."

Shaking my head. "I know I can be an asshole, but Lena needs somewhere, and I know you would never want to turn her down." Mum chuckles and then playfully whacks me across my arm the way she does every time I swear in front of her.

"Language, Lee. So, you got another date tonight? When am I ever going to meet one of these girls?" she asks with a pout, and I can't help but roll my eyes.

"Oh, I don't know. Maybe the twenty-fourth of never!" I joke, and again she playfully whacks my arm as she laughs. I grab hold of my bicep where she just hit me, and as dramatically as I can, I groan and fall backwards so I'm now laying on the bed. I make it sound like she's injured me and she just laughs. We both know I'm distracting her from answering the date question. The truth is, I don't know if she will ever meet one of the girls. At this stage, it will be a fucking miracle if I actually go on a date with someone I like.

My mind drifts back to Emmaleigh, and I can't help but think about how much I've royally fucked that up before we even had a chance. Thankfully, Mum is here to distract me.

She drags me downstairs for some dinner, which isn't really a hardship. I don't know anyone who would complain about having good, home-cooked food given to them every night without even having to ask for it.

After spending an hour or so just hanging out with Mum, I head back upstairs, realising I'd left my phone on my bed when I came downstairs. I actually had a moment when I thought how refreshing it was to not be staring at the damn thing every minute of every day. But when I pick it up and see the new notification that I missed, I can't help but curse out loud.

Motherfucker. I leave my phone for an hour, and she finally messages me. I take some deep breaths and try to calm myself while I ignore the butterflies in my stomach and the jitter in my hands. Fuck, I'm not a teenage girl. Why am I getting so anxious and excited over a fucking text? What if she tells me to leave her alone? I know she would have probably just ghosted me for that, but you never know.

With shaky fingers, I take a deep breath, and press on the button to read the text from Emmaleigh.

Gertrude: Hey Carlos. Sorry for the late reply. I've been on nights and my body clock is all over the place. Thank you for your message, I've got to say I was a little surprised to hear from you again. My foot is almost healed. I still have a bit of physio to do, but it's getting there. If you still want to go on a date, I would love to.

Holy shit! After all the crap that's gone on between us, I never thought she would ever want to hear from me again. But she does, and she wants to meet me! Looks like I'm going on a date.

Chapter Four

EMMALEIGH

Standing in front of the mirror, I take in my outfit, and my mind runs rampant. My dark skinny ripped jeans cling to my curves in all the right places, and they hold in my flabby bits just right. The off-the-shoulder black top is casual enough for a pub date, but the little display of skin and my bra strap makes it that bit sexy. I've worn my best push-up bra, since, let's be honest, guys love the boobs.

My long dark purple hair is curled and clipped up so that it hangs perfectly around my shoulders, with a few stray tendrils hanging to frame my face. I'm wearing a bit of make-up, including my dark eyeliner and mascara, to make my blue eyes pop even more. The bright red lipstick complements my black attire and makes my plump lips look inviting. I know in my head I look good, but I can't stop the anxiety from getting the better of me.

What if you aren't dressed up enough?

What if he's looking for someone a bit more girly?

Maybe you should wear a skirt?

Do those jeans make you look too fat?

All those thoughts are swimming around my mind, and I can't quieten them. A loud ringing pulls me out of my head, and I turn the alarm on my phone off. I set it so I would know exactly when I need to leave. I have a tendency to turn up to things a bit late, but with him, I can't wait.

Pulling on my Converse, I look over at my heels but think better of it. Not only is my balance more horrendous lately, but my foot hasn't properly healed yet, and I don't want to do anything to hinder its recovery. I pull on my favourite leather jacket, grab my bag, and head out the door.

I arrive at the pub, Floods, just in the nick of time. We agreed to meet outside the door, and when I see nobody standing there, my stomach flips and the nerves begin. I'm glad I ate nothing before I left, as it would definitely make the nausea that's just settling in worse.

Looking down at my phone, there's no message from him. Do I wait here or go and look inside? There's no fucking point me looking inside. I don't really know what he looks like, other than the few pictures I've seen on his profile, and honestly, you never know how accurate they are.

What if he's stood you up?

Fuck off, brain.

I lean against the side of the pub, trying not to think about that possibility. He said he would be here, and so he will. I try my best not to look at my watch, but I can feel the minutes ticking by. Then, suddenly, I hear loud footsteps approaching rapidly, like someone is running. I look up to see Lee running towards me.

He stops right in front of me, taking a few deep breaths

so he can slow his breathing down after his run, and it gives me the perfect opportunity to check him out.

The first thing I notice about Lee is his smile. It's warm, inviting, and it lights up his whole face, with the little dimples he gets in his cheeks that are very cute. His bright blue eyes shine beneath his dark-rimmed glasses—that really do suit and complement his face. He's obviously chosen a pair that is made for him. His short, dark hair is so black it almost has shades of blue and purple when the light hits it.

My gaze rakes over his body and I instantly notice one thing Lee told me he was most self-conscious about. He's only around five-foot-six, which, compared to the average male height of five-foot-eight, isn't all that much shorter, but to him it is. He thinks there are a lot of girls out there who would judge him based on that, but honestly, compared to my five-foot-two frame, he is tall. That's all that matters to me.

The rest of his body is something to behold. Dark jeans wrap tightly around his muscular thighs, and I feel sure that when he turns around, the view of his ass will be incredible. His tight black t-shirt clings to his muscular chest. I can tell that he's a runner because his frame is more lean than bulky. His body is toned and hard, and I know that the view underneath will be quite something.

Focus, Emmaleigh. This is only the first date. Show some restraint!

Lee catches me checking him out, and one side of his smile lifts into a cocky grin and fuck, does he look hotter. We both have that awkward moment where we wonder how we should greet each other. While this is the first time we are meeting in person, we feel like we know each other. We've been texting nearly every day for months now—

minus the couple of weeks when we ended things—so just saying hello doesn't quite feel right. I'm close to doing something socially awkward, like hold my hand out for a handshake, when, thankfully, Lee takes the lead and holds his arms open. He doesn't move in straight away, it's like he's letting me know what his intentions are so that I can pull away if I'm not comfortable. With a nod of my head telling him to continue, Lee wraps his arms around my shoulders and pulls me in for a hug.

The minute he pulls me against him, and I'm enveloped by his scent, I feel myself sag. It's such a weird feeling to explain, but it's almost like I found where I'm supposed to be. Like having his arms around me is all I need to feel safe and happy. I know that sounds totally bloody bonkers, given I've only just met him, but I can't change how I feel.

Eventually, he pulls back, and I try to hold back a groan. With a smile on his face, he finally introduces himself. "Hey, I'm Lee. It's so lovely to finally meet you. You look amazing, by the way. Can I buy you a drink?" It all comes out in a bit of a rush, like he's nervous and the words are coming out quicker than he can organise his thoughts. I know that feeling well.

"Thank you! I'm Emmaleigh. You look great too. Yeah, shall we go in and get a seat?" I ask, raising my arm to point at the entrance.

With a smile, Lee holds out his arm, too. "Ladies first."

We walk into the bar and get settled in the back room, next to the big pool table. I look over the list of drinks that's written on the wall, but I don't know why I bother. I always have the same. "Can I get a cider please?" I ask, pointing at my favourite brand. Lee lets out a little chuckle, and I wonder what's funny about my choice?

"That's exactly what I was going to order. I love the

apple and raspberry flavour," he explains. "Great minds think alike." He winks at me and fuck, I think I actually swooned like a teenage girl watching a boy band live. I don't know what it is about this guy, but I can already tell I really like him.

"What do you say to a friendly game of pool?" I ask, tilting my head towards the empty table beside us. His brow furrows, but his cheeky grin remains.

"Oh, I will play pool, but there will be nothing friendly about it. I know I probably shouldn't let you see this side of me on a first date, but I'm ruthless. I will not let you win. I will take you down," he jokes and I can't help the girly giggle that bursts free from my lips.

"Wow, competitive much?" I tease as he stands and heads to the bar, telling me to save the pool table so that nobody else can grab it before us.

He returns with our drinks, and the balls and cues we need to play with. He takes a sip from his glass before shrugging off his jacket, showing off his muscular biceps. As he leans over to set up the balls on the table, I take the opportunity to check out his ass, and fuck, it looks just as good as I thought it would. Though, as Lee turns around and hands me my cue, it's clear by the cocky grin on his face that he knew I'd been checking him out. I take a gulp of my drink, hoping the movement will hide the blush spreading across my cheeks.

"Shall we make this interesting?" I ask, biting my lip as I try really hard not to come across as too eager. I can see I've piqued his interest, appealing to his competitive side.

"I'm listening."

"How about, each time I pot a ball, I get to ask you a question that you have to answer?"

That cocky grin that makes my stomach flip spreads

across his face. "I like the sound of that. What about if I pot a ball? Will you answer any of my questions?"

Shrugging my leather jacket off and placing it on my chair, I shrug. "Of course."

"Then let's play. Who is going to break?" Lee asks.

I take a coin out of my purse and tell him we should flip for it. I call heads just as it lands heads facing upwards and with as sexy a shimmy as I'm capable of, I go to stand at the head of the table. As I lean over to line up the white ball, I'm suddenly very glad I wore my good bra—and given the direction of Lee's gaze right now, I think he feels the same.

I smack the cue ball with as much power as I can, absolutely no skill involved, just brute strength and sheer dumb luck. Thankfully, two balls with stripes on them go straight into the pockets and I hold two fingers up at Lee, making sure they are the right way around, so he doesn't think I'm swearing at him. "That's two questions you owe me."

He leans against his cue with one hand, while he takes a sip of his cider using the other. "Okay, first question."

I make a big deal, pretending like I'm thinking hard about what to ask him. Actually, I'm not pretending all that much. Obviously, it's the first question, so I can't go in with anything too personal, and I can't turn it sexual—yet.

"Okay, so let's make it an easy one. Tell me a secret that nobody else knows about you."

He ponders that for a moment, and we look at each other in companionable silence while I wonder if he's going to answer or not. "I don't want to be an adult." Well, that's not quite what I was expecting him to say.

"What do you mean? And no, that isn't the second question," I clarify, before he cheats me out of my second question on a technicality. He chuckles like that's exactly what he had been thinking.

"I don't like the responsibility that comes with being an adult. Everyone agrees, but nobody says it out loud. I can barely take care of myself. I don't want the added responsibility of having to look after or care about someone else. That's why I never want to get married or have kids," he says firmly, but I can tell he's a little wary about bringing up such a heavy subject on our first date. I might not know how I feel about his answer, given that I very much do want to get married and have kids, but I appreciate his honesty. I like that I know I'm getting the truth whenever I talk to him.

"Does that mean you aren't looking for a relationship?" I ask. I don't mean to, it just kinda slipped out, and I can't take it back. Fuck, I'm going to look like a stage four clinger asking about relationships when we aren't even an hour into our first date.

Lee just laughs. "If I answer, I'm counting this as your second question," he says, and so I nod my head in confirmation, my heart racing as I wait to hear his reply.

I don't know what it is about him. I mean, I only met him less than an hour ago, and already I've got butterflies in my stomach, and my heart is racing while I wait to find out if he's looking for a relationship. Is that what I want? Do I want to date Lee? What if he doesn't want a relationship? Would I be happy with a friends-with-benefits type situation? Fuck, all these things are going through my head, and I try to quieten them down so I can actually hear his reply.

"Honestly, I don't know. For the right girl, I think I would, but it would take a fair bit to get me there. I would want to just be friends first and see how that goes," Lee explains, and I see his cheeks flush slightly as he answers. I mean, it's not a bad answer. I guess there's always hope for us!

I take my next shots and pot nothing, but when Lee steps up, he nets a ball with a spot on it on his first try, doing a very cute little happy dance to celebrate. "Okay, now I need to come up with a good first question that doesn't make me sound too pervy," he muses aloud, and I can't help but laugh.

"Oh, we can go straight for the sexy questions if you want." I wink before giving him a cheeky grin. Where the fuck did that come from? I absolutely don't need to be telling him about the shittest sexy times that have come before him.

"We will get there, there's plenty of balls, after all." We both laugh at his double entendre before taking drinks from our glasses. "Right, I've got a good one. If your mum could change anything about you, what would it be?"

"What kind of a question is that?" I ask, confused by why I need to tell him about my mum's thought process.

"Well, we all have stuff that we hate about ourselves. So, if I ask what you would change, that would be easy. But mums love everything about their kids, even sometimes blindly. So, I want to know what your mum would change."

I laugh because he's right. I have a list as long as my arm of things about myself that I would change, but Mum loves all of it. Except for maybe one or two things. "I guess it would probably be one of two. She would either say my mouth because I can be incredibly bossy and I talk a lot. Or she would say my clumsiness. My body has this incredible ability to fail me at the worst possible times, leading to me injuring myself more times than I can count. The broken foot was just one in a long line of issues. In fact, Mum used to be scared every time she took me to the hospital that social services would ask questions. In today's world, they definitely would have."

He laughs, and the rest of the date flows easily from there. We spend the next couple of hours just playing pool, asking each other funny or personal questions, having a laugh, and just generally getting to know each other.

As the pool game progresses, we get more touchy feely. I try to distract him by running my foot up his leg, or leaning over the opposite side of the table so all he can see is my cleavage. He retaliates by blowing in my ear, or covering my back with his front, pressing himself against me to put me off. It works.

By the time the date is coming to a close, I know I like him. My face aches from the amount of smiling I've been doing. My heart is racing just from being near him, and I don't want the date to end. I know I want to see him again, but that brings up the awkward question of how he feels about me.

"Would you like me to walk you back to your car?" he asks after I explain I needed to park my car a few streets away because of the parking. I'd only had the first cider, swapping over onto cokes after that first drink, so I knew I was fine to drive. It turns out Lee only lives around the corner from where I parked, so I take him up on his offer to walk me to my car. I'm actually glad about it, as I don't want the night to end yet.

As we leave the pub, Lee takes hold of my hand in his and it's like bolts of electricity are shooting through my arm. My whole body feels like it's on fire, all because I'm near him. I let Lee lead the way; this is his town and he knows it much better than me. I only live about twenty minutes away, and since my best friend lives in this town, I know where I'm going, yet he still seems to show me new routes.

We stop in front of a thin alley that barely looks wide enough to fit us both in side by side. It's completely dark, the moonlight that had been aiding the street lamps on our journey so far is no longer visible. There are no street lamps lighting the way, and the darkness is so pitch black, we can't even see the other end of the alley.

Lee goes to move towards the alley, but I hesitate. He looks between the alley and me, and eventually I see the moment the realisation hits. He can see I'm apprehensive about going down a dark alley, with a complete stranger, who I may or may not be very fucking into. "Okay, so this is the ultimate test. I like to call it the dark alley test. Do you trust me enough to let me lead you down a dark alley, all alone at night? I promise you it will come out right beside the street where you parked your car, but you have to trust my word. Do you trust I'm not lying to you and do you trust me?"

His bright blue eyes fix on mine, and I take a moment to appreciate how beautiful the colour blue is. It's like looking into a beautiful clear sea. I don't know how I know, and I certainly can't explain it, but I do trust him. I'm the girl who never trusts, who never takes a chance on anyone but herself. Yet, right now, I want to go with him.

"Do you often lead young girls down dark alleys at night?" I joke, and Lee laughs.

"None as beautiful as you," he winks, before moving towards the alley, keeping hold of my hand. Though he never pulls me, he just keeps hold to guide me.

I follow behind him, trying to ignore the way my heart raced when he said I was beautiful. The deeper we venture into the tunnel, the darker it gets. I trust Lee, but that doesn't mean there are no other murderers and rapists lying in wait in the damn alley. Just as I'm thinking that, a street light shines on Lee's face and as we come out of the other end of the alley, he throws a bright smile my way.

"You really weren't scared at all in there, were you?"

I can't help but chuckle. "No, I would have taken out anyone who attacked us. I'm feisty like that," I say before pointing at the car behind him. "That's my car, by the way. Thank you for walking me here."

We both stand in front of my car, just looking at each other, waiting for someone to say something, anything. I want to ask him if he wants to go on another date, but his silence has me worried. Maybe he's not that into me. Maybe we have crossed wires. Fuck, I really need to quieten my head sometimes.

Before I have a chance to say anything, Lee takes a step towards me and I'm caught off balance, causing me to stumble backwards. Luckily, I land with my back against my car, and Lee closes the distance easily. He leans forward, his hands on the car roof on either side of my head, caging me in, and he's so close I can feel the heat from his body. His breath fans across my face, causing my breath to hitch. I catch my bottom lip between my teeth to bite nervously, but Lee moves one of his hands and gently tugs my lip free. He then leans over and whispers in my ear as a shiver ripples down my spine. "Don't do that. Only I'm allowed to bite your lip."

Fuck. If that's not the hottest thing a guy has ever said to me, I don't know what is.

While I'm busy considering that, he leans forward and presses his lips against mine. It's soft and gentle at first, but the moment our lips really connect, it's like we are both injected with a bout of passion. My hands fly to the back of his head, my fingers threading through his hair as I frantically try to pull him closer. I can feel his body, his hardness pressed against my front, and I can't hold back the sounds that leave my mouth.

As soon as he hears my desperate moans of pleasure, he pulls his head back, but doesn't leave my space. He keeps his body against mine, and I can feel my core throbbing with need. I don't even care that this is a first date, or that we are in the middle of a very public road. Thankfully, Lee is thinking with his head and not his dick.

"Wow. You do not know how difficult it was to pull away from that. But this is a first date, and you deserve better. How do you feel about a second date?" I can't believe after the way I just lost control kissing him, he still looks unsure of what my answer might be.

"I would love to go on another date with you."

He gives me a little smile before he steps back out of my personal space, and I can almost feel my body throbbing from his absence. A strange, almost sad expression crosses his face for just a moment before his face becomes a blank mask again.

"Em, I have to remind you about what I said in the pub. I'm not looking for a relationship right now. If it turns into one, then so be it, but until then, I only want to be friends," he explains, his voice a little sheepish, like he's worried I won't accept his terms.

I nod my head in confirmation. "I remember you saying that. Now it's my turn to clarify something. When you say you want to be friends, do you mean just friends or friends with benefits?" I feel my cheeks flushing, and I want to look away, but I can't. I don't know if I can be just friends with Lee and not want to kiss him again after that.

"Well, I'm still a guy, and you are a beautiful woman.

So, of course, if you wanted to add the benefits part, then I would be very on board with that. But I would also be happy with just being friends too. I've enjoyed chatting with you every day, even before we met. And I enjoyed talking to you."

I give him a big smile before I lean in and capture his lips for a moment. It's nowhere near as deep and sexy as before, and it's over in a flash, but it was full of passion and spoke a thousand words. Though I made sure he knew exactly how I felt. "So, why don't you come over to mine next time? We can do takeaway and a movie?"

"It's a deal. Bring on date number two," he says, as he captures my lips again for another short but intense kiss.

He helps me into the car, and I can honestly say I don't remember a single thing about driving home. All I could think about is his laugh, his smile, the way his eyes light up. Not to mention how hot his ass looked in those jeans. My heart races and my body tingles from where he was touching me. I can still smell him on me, and I feel like I'm in heaven.

I don't know what the hell I'm thinking, but the one thing I know, Lee has got under my skin. He's burrowing his way under, and I do not know what to think or feel. I want him—badly. I guess we'll just have to see how date number two goes. I'm still struggling to believe a guy like him could truly like a clumsy, accident-prone, bossy, sarcastic girl like me. A girl can only hope.

To be Continued...

Have you enjoyed the start of Emmaleigh and Lee's story? Do you want more?
*Their full book, **I Was Always Yours**, is available for pre-order now!*
https://geni.us/IWasAlwaysYours

Please note - *the date on the pre-order is a placeholder only, this will be brought forward.*
Thank you for reading Emmaleigh and Lee's story of hope. I thoroughly enjoyed diving into this story, even though it's not as dark as I normally write, but I hope it's totally relatable. My aim is that there's at least one character in the story that you can relate to in some way. I've absolutely loved writing this story and I really do hope you enjoy reading it.

Also by
Emma Luna

Standalone

I Was Always Yours

Under the Cover of Darkness: A Twisted Legends Novel

Beautifully Brutal Series

Black Wedding

Dangerously Deceptive

Trust in Me

The Ties We Break

Fighting to Be Free

Managing Mischief Series

Piper

Sins of Our Father Series

Broken Sins

Willowmead Academy

Life Lessons

Finding Hope
by H.A. Robinson

Chapter One

SEVEN YEARS OLD

There it was again—that funny, fizzing feeling right down in my belly.

I knew it well by then, but I had no idea what it was or what it meant. All I knew was that my name on the lips of other people always brought the same reaction, deep inside me.

I was getting ready for a party. Matilda, my best friend in the whole world, was turning seven—just like me—and her party was starting in an hour's time.

The only trouble was, the party was fancy dress and I *hated* my costume—a Captain America costume my mum had bought me.

I didn't like Captain America.

I didn't even like superheroes that much.

They were okay, I guessed, but the costume was so boring. Matilda's mum had got her the best costume ever: the yellow dress that Belle wore in Beauty and the Beast, which swished and floated around her legs as she

CHAPTER FORTY-THREE

flounced around in it. I'd watched jealously as she'd paraded around in it the weekend before, picking at the scabs on my knees through the rips in my boring beige jeans.

I'd gone home full of ideas about matching outfits, excited to suggest them to my mum, only to be met with a slightly sad shake of the head and a throaty reply of, "No, people would laugh, darling."

I didn't understand.

How could I?

Weren't clothes just... clothes?

So there I was, standing in front of my mum's mirror—the big ornate one with the silver lions in the corners that I was convinced would one day transport me to Narnia—frowning at my reflection. The costume was just so... bland. Not party material at all.

"Harvey, come on. We need to go." Mum's voice echoed into the room, setting that strange fizzing alight in my stomach again.

"Coming," I mumbled back, grabbing the stupid plastic shield off the bed.

The costume didn't swish at all, and when I got to the party, three boys were wearing the exact same outfit.

Various accessories flew through the air, which smelled of a mixture of sugar and Matilda's mum's flowers that turned the edges of the garden into a bright rainbow. Matilda's dog, Reggie, a shaggy, brown cockapoo, capered around, enjoying the chaos an entire garden full of children provided.

His teeth closed around the stupid shield clutched reluctantly in my hand and tugged sharply. I didn't even try to stop him. I wasn't that attached to it after all.

"Reggie, no," Matilda shouted, racing across the garden

to rescue the toy. Her Belle dress fluttered dramatically around her as she ran.

"It's fine, Matty. I hate it anyway. He can have it."

She stopped dead, glowering at me with one hand on her hip, which jutted out with attitude. "Captain America is the *best* superhero, Harvey."

Fizz. Crack. Fizz.

I grabbed my stomach against the discomfort that erupted once again at her words.

"Captain America is lame. Superheroes aren't even real," I grumbled back full of anger and hurt, though what exactly I was hurt about, I couldn't have told you.

"Better than Belle. I'm bored of being her now. This dress doesn't come with any toys. It's rubbish."

I eyed the swishy, yellow fabric enviously as she glared at it in disgust. There were layers and layers of gold just asking to be appreciated, and there she was wishing she could wear blue and red lycra instead.

And then the idea hit me—the one that would stay with me forever; the idea that people would still talk about when I was living through the hell of high school; the idea that would haunt me and ensure I knew that I must, under no circumstances, ever, ever, try to be myself.

I grabbed Matilda's hand in mine, beaming widely. "I've got an idea," I whispered in conspiratorial excitement.

"What is it?" she replied, equally excited.

"You'll see, but we need to go upstairs first."

I ran as she swished along beside me, and for the first time all day, I felt excited for real about the party.

My excitement lasted all of about twelve minutes. The moment that satiny fabric began to tickle against my calves, I knew this was the costume I should have worn all

CHAPTER FORTY-THREE

along. I was no superhero and never would be, but dancing around a ballroom in a beautiful dress? That I could do.

I was filled with a different kind of fizz now—the kind you got when something felt just right.

I skipped down the stairs two at a time, almost tripping over the dress in my haste to get back to the party and start enjoying myself.

The sun shone in through the French windows, beckoning me into the garden where our classmates were still rambunctiously playing with all the toys Mrs Bagley, Matilda's mum, had left out for us.

I stood in the doorway and inhaled deeply, feeling a thousand percent myself and ready to play.

My eyes lifted to the bright blue sky, squinting against the sun and grinning widely.

Screams of laughter rang in my ears, drawing my attention away to see what game was causing so much merriment.

Except nobody was playing anymore.

All eyes were on me.

Staring.

Glaring.

Laughing.

As much as I wanted to believe they were laughing *with* me, I couldn't deny the fact those faces were not smiling in a remotely friendly way.

The laughter mingled with a loud ringing in my ears as I felt every single speck of happiness draining into the pit of my stomach where it settled like a lead weight of hurt and confusion.

Nobody had batted an eyelid when I'd been dressed as Captain America. I was no more him than I was Belle, yet suddenly everybody thought my costume was ridiculous, and I didn't understand why.

"What on Earth are you doing?" Mrs Bagley cried out, darting towards us and wagging a finger angrily. "That's a *girl's* costume, you silly boy. Go back upstairs and change. Right now!"

The fizzing in my stomach was tinged with more acid than usual as my chin hit my chest and tears stung at my eyes.

"But, Mum," Matilda protested weakly, but there was no arguing with the steel in her mother's eyes.

Silently, we both trailed back upstairs and swapped our outfits back over.

Matilda seethed in anger, me in confusion. It didn't make sense to me. What was it that made her outfit for girls and mine for boys? How was it fair?

The rest of the party passed by in a blur of taunts from the other kids in our class about how I was 'such a girl', which didn't strike me as much of an insult really. If anything, it felt like a compliment.

And as everybody gathered around the party food table and sang 'happy birthday' to Matilda, loudly and out of key, I stared at the flickering flames on the candles until their shapes distorted and merged.

My eyes watered as I made the same wish I made each time I watched somebody blowing out candles: *please, please, when I wake up tomorrow morning, let me be a girl.*

Chapter Two

ELEVEN YEARS OLD

Somewhere in my mind, the idea of turning eleven felt like this seminal moment—like I'd finally make it to high school and everything would be different. I'd escaped from the tiny primary school that had held me captive for so long, where there were twenty students in a class who all looked and acted like miniature clones of one another, and where anybody who was in the slightest bit different was treated like an outsider.

Lineham High School gates were, to me, a beacon of hope—a shining archway leading to a world of opportunity and diversity. I'd been on the outside looking in all my life, but high school... That was where it would all change. This would be my time.

The school was massive. Surely there would be loads of people in there just like me. I wasn't totally sure what 'just like me' actually meant just yet, but I knew with every fibre of my being that I wasn't quite like lots of other boys I knew.

The only person who 'got me' was Matilda.

She stood beside me on our first day, our shoulders bumping together as we stared up at the towering red-brick school that cast its impressive shadow right across the street.

"This is it," she said, trying to sound excited but with the nerves she'd sworn blind she didn't feel sneaking into her voice.

"The big one."

"The one we always dreamed about."

"The one we—" My words were cut off by a cascade of water that sloshed right over our heads as a school bus whizzed past through the typical British puddles. "Oh. Great."

'The Big One' was starting really well.

Our first day and we'd be starting it soaked to the skin. It was a fantastic look.

I tried to block out the sounds of laughter that battered my brain, but they rang out loud and clear, dragging me right back to that birthday party four years earlier.

I was ready to turn around and try again tomorrow when Matilda let out a hysterical laugh, swinging her long, dark hair and sending droplets of puddle water flying around her head.

I forced an incredulous smile as I watched, but laughter was impossible.

"Is something funny?" I gritted out.

"More to the point, is something *not* funny?"

I gestured at my soaking form to answer her.

"Oh, come on," she went on. "It's like the beginning of every cheesy film ever. The hero always has crappy stuff happen at the start. It's like that saying: you have to get soaked by loads of puddles to find your prince."

CHAPTER FORTY-FOUR

"I don't think that's how it goes."

"Yeah, well, you know what I mean."

"Nobody ever knows what you're talking about. Your entire vocabulary is movie quotes and song lyrics."

"You say that like it's a bad thing."

I opened my mouth to reply, but the loud ringing of the school bell rattled through the air like a death knell.

My excitement hadn't even lasted long enough to see me through the school gates.

"Waheeeeeey!" a loud voice called out when I finally located my form room—the school seemed to have completely changed layout since the introductory day we'd had there before the summer.

I slid into the seat closest to the door on the end of the back row, ignoring the chatter around me until the owner of said voice slapped the desk in front of me, grinning widely.

"It's Puddle Boy, right?"

"Wow, Puddle Boy? That's creative. Did you come up with that on your own, or did your carer help you?"

His grin wavered, and the look in his eyes morphed from cocky to irritated in an instant.

"Pretty arrogant for somebody covered in puddle water." He snarled, his fingers tapping against the desk threateningly.

He didn't scare me. I'd met his type before: the ones who felt crappy about themselves and took it out on other people. He thought I was the weakest member of the herd, but if he was looking for a bullying victim, he'd come to the wrong place.

"You know water dries, right? I'd assume you've heard of evaporation but looking at you, it seems foolish to assume anything. I'll be dry in half an hour, but you'll still be an idiot."

He blinked, and I watched him fight for something smart to say in reply but he failed and simply growled, "Watch it, Puddle Boy," instead before stalking off to find his next victim.

"Okay, good talk," I muttered, chuckling to myself.

I'd learned after partygate not to be anybody's doormat, and I didn't plan to change that anytime soon.

High school was... different, but not the liberating experience I'd hoped it would be. It turned out that, just like at primary school, I didn't quite fit.

I had friends—mostly female—and Matilda was a constant and permanent part of my life, but no matter how close my relationships were, no matter how loved I was, there was still this feeling, deep in the pit of my stomach, that I was all wrong. It was like having an itch I couldn't quite reach, this bubbling under my skin that made me want to rip it off and start again. Start new. Start right.

By anybody's measure, I had no right to feel the way I did. I had fun, spent time with my friends and filled the gaping hole inside me that I didn't understand with as many things as I possibly could. They numbed me to the constant nagging feeling that something wasn't right.

In my heart, I knew what it was that made me feel that way: I knew every time I saw the face of a boy rapidly canonning towards puberty staring back at me in the mirror. I knew because I showered as quickly as possible, unable to bear looking at my own body for fear I'd tear my own skin open just to step out of it. I knew when I walked

CHAPTER FORTY-FOUR

into the boy's changing rooms at school, surrounded by masculine banter and the overpowering smell of Lynx and my stomach turned. I knew every time Owen Wilson called me Puddle Boy because it wasn't the word 'puddle' that bothered me. And I knew every single night when I crawled into bed and still childishly hoped I'd wake up the next morning in skin I could bear to be in—that my chromosomes would magically rearrange themselves overnight and make me into the only thing I'd ever truly wished to be.

I knew because my outside didn't match my inside, and there seemed to be absolutely nothing I could do about it.

It was a Tuesday in the summer term of year eight, which meant lunchtime was filled with Sausage Roll Eating Club. SREC was a genuine school society that we'd created when the school had—some might say foolishly—opened up the possibility for new and different clubs.

We'd always had the standard music and sports clubs, but since neither I nor any of my friends had any discernible talent in either of those areas, we'd decided to create a society for one of our greatest passions: the noble sausage roll—something that was, in our opinion, a massively underappreciated culinary delight.

It wasn't exactly a difficult club to run, and it consisted of just five members: Matilda, Grace, Lacey, Ash and me. Mostly, we sat around in our tutor room—that Mr Filey had allowed us to use on the proviso that we didn't leave pastry crumbs all over his floor—eating sausage rolls, obviously, and chatting.

They were my tribe, my people and those who accepted me for who I was, even when I couldn't seem to do the same for myself.

Grace and Lacey were year seven's only 'out' lesbians, who everybody assumed were a couple because obviously they had to be since they were both lesbians, because that was clearly how it worked. In reality, they were best friends, who absolutely loved irritating the homophobes in school. They would randomly kiss in the corridors or on the yard at break time but actually laughed hysterically at the idea of dating one another.

Ash had sat next to me during our first tutor time in year seven, pulled a battered copy of The Hitchhiker's Guide to the Galaxy from his bag and started to read. He was the strong, silent type who rarely spoke, but when he did, it always seemed to be to say something profound. He was the most chilled out person I knew, always happy to go with the flow and do whatever the rest of us were doing. He was also one of the most decent people I knew, so we didn't mind that he didn't partake in the sausage rolls that formed the very foundations of SREC on account of what Matilda called his 'rampant veganism'.

It was sweltering. Dribbles of sweat ran down my temples as I valiantly forged on with my sausage roll, despite the fact the heat was making me want to tear off my own skin and burn it even more than usual while wishing I lived in Iceland.

Grace, Matilda and Lacey were partway through a particularly violent and competitive game of Uno while Ash was chowing down on some butternut squash monstrosity. Some people thrived when the sun came out; I was not one of those people. Every drip of sweat I shed felt like a personal affront.

I was gearing up for a lengthy rant about how summer was the worst time of year when the classroom door slammed open, hitting the wall with a crack that sent little pieces of plaster to the floor.

CHAPTER FORTY-FOUR

We all jumped in surprise—except for Ash, who I wasn't totally convinced had even noticed.

My stomach tightened when I saw the culprit behind the slamming, and I braced myself for another round of verbal sparring with my favourite caveman and his gang of troglodytes.

"Ey uuuuuup," Owen Wilson called out as he walked into the room like he owned the place. "If it isn't Freak Club. How *are* my favourite gang of losers today?"

"Fuck off, Owen. Shouldn't you be grunting at a cave drawing somewhere?" I asked.

Matilda snickered behind me, slapping down another card onto the table and shouting "Uno!" at the top of her voice in an attempt to show Owen the contempt he deserved.

Owen's knuckle dragging mates—Alfie Mason, James Dickson and Billy Eaton—followed him into the room. More members of the unaccountably popular gang.

They were the 'hot' lads: the ones for whom puberty had enhanced rather than ruined their lives. They seemed to sail through life without a single difficulty and thrived on making other people miserable—especially me and my friends.

Their hair never looked greasy only moments after washing it. They never broke out into embarrassingly large clusters of spots, and their voices never did that thing mine seemed to do all the time where it suddenly jumped from one pitch to another in the middle of a sentence—something, incidentally, I wouldn't have had to worry about if I'd been born in the right skin.

Owen ducked down behind Matilda for a moment before shouting out, "She's got a red five left," to Lacey and Grace.

ELEVEN YEARS OLD

I could see on her face the internal battle she warred as she tried not to show her irritation to him. The last thing any of us needed was for them to know they got to us in any way.

"Wow, Owen, you finally learned numbers *and* colours. Your mum must be so proud."

He shot her a scowl dripping with contempt. "Think you're better than me just because you get As in lessons?" he scoffed.

She snorted, shooting him a derisive glance in reply. "No. I *know* I'm better than you because I don't spend my free time trying to make other people feel like shit. It's this thing civilised humans have come up with. Maybe you'll grow into it one day."

"Yeah, whatever," he muttered, an excellent comeback if ever I'd heard one. Swiping his hand over the table, he sent the Uno deck skittering to the floor. "Least I'm not a massive lesbian."

Every eye in the room that didn't belong to the Flintstone gang rolled instantly. Typical Owen: if all else fails, resort to rampant homophobia. It was pretty much his MO by that point.

"Ha! I wish I was," Matilda replied. "I mean, look what being straight has to offer me." She gestured to them with a wave of her hand, a look of absolute disgust on her face. "Meanwhile"— her eyes turned to Grace and Lacey, who were watching the entire exchange with amused indifference—"here's what I could have won, if nature didn't hate me so much."

I laughed loudly, drawing Owen's attention to me, which I was pretty sure I'd quickly regret.

"Something funny, Puddle Boy?"

I shrugged, smirking. "Nothing you'd understand."

CHAPTER FORTY-FOUR

"Oh, yeah, sorry," he started, advancing on me until I could feel his breath on my face and see the fury in his grey eyes. "I don't speak faggot."

His face took on the expression of somebody who had absolutely had the last word, somebody who knew that they'd played their strongest card, designed for maximum shock, maximum hurt, maximum fallout.

Except his wild card word didn't have the impact on me he expected. In fact, as disgusted as I was by anybody throwing that word around in the twenty-first century, it didn't cut anything like as deeply as it did when he called me Puddle *Boy*.

That word.

The word that stayed with me no matter where I went, how old I got, how many stars I wished upon that something miraculous would happen.

I stood, meeting him glare-for-glare, and ground out through gritted teeth, "If you're going to throw disgusting slurs around, at least use the right ones."

Chapter Three

THIRTEEN YEARS OLD

The sun was setting, painting the sky in fiery shades of orange and pink as we sat side by side on top of the canal bridge in the centre of town. Matilda was munching her way through a family-sized bag of salt and vinegar Kettle Chips while I occasionally risked losing a limb by stealing some from the bag. She was one of the kindest, most generous people I knew, until it involved food. Try to take her food and you were as likely to get a fork through your hand as you were to successfully grab anything.

Our legs dangled down over the road that ran under the bridge. We'd been told a million times not to sit there, but it had been our place for too long to change now.

From up there, we could see both our houses, both still dark. Our parents were all at work, which gave us time to autopsy the day as the sun sank below the horizon, bringing with it some relief from the sweltering heat.

So far, we'd discussed whether or not Mrs Bentley, our

chemistry teacher, was pregnant—spoiler: she definitely was—and then lapsed into a comfortable silence only broken by the rustling of the foil bag beside me.

After a few moments and several handfuls of crisps, Matilda cleared her throat and turned to look at me with a curious look on her face.

"Harves?" she asked carefully.

"Yeah," I replied. "You okay?"

"I am..." Her eyes darted away from me for a moment before locking back with mine. "Can I ask you a question?"

"You just did."

"Ha ha, smart arse."

"Thanks." I grinned, lifting my thigh to pat my backside. "I grew it myself."

"I'm serious, though."

"That seems out of character but I'll allow it, I guess." I chuckled, taking her unusually uncertain hand in mine and squeezing it.

"It's just...earlier on, when Owen was being...well... Owen, you said something and I've been thinking about it ever since."

My eyebrows crawled up my face in surprise. I was tempted to crack a joke about how I was so profound that she was still thinking about it hours later, but her expression was so serious, I couldn't do it.

"Okay... What did I say?"

She swallowed, her fingers curling around mine a little tighter as she looked down at them. "You said... When he called you the F word I won't repeat... You said he used the wrong slur. What did you mean?"

I blinked in surprise, joining her in staring down at our joined hands.

When I'd replied to his reprehensible comment, it

hadn't even occurred to me what I was saying—what I might be implying to anybody who was really listening.

My instinct was to laugh it off and pretend I'd meant absolutely nothing by it, but this was Matilda: my best friend in the world. Until that moment, I'd never really thought about the fact that I had a secret. It had always been a private longing inside me, but it wasn't something I'd ever known how to give voice to, so I'd kept it inside.

"I... I'm not totally sure," I admitted honestly.

"Come on, Harves, this is me. You can tell me anything. You know you can."

"I know I can."

"I never even told anybody about that window you broke in year five, even when they got us all in the hall to interrogate us. I'm a vault."

"I know. I do. I just... I'm not really sure myself. I don't know how to explain it."

"Try?" she asked, her face full of kindness.

"Okay... So, do you ever feel like something isn't quite right, like, inside you?"

"Like you're ill or something?"

"Not ill, no. More like, I don't know... Like you don't quite fit in your own skin?" I hedged, biting my lip to keep it from trembling. I'd never, ever vocalised any of this before.

"Well, I probably won't fit inside my skin if I keep eating these crisps to be honest."

I laughed, nudging her shoulder with mine. "Shut up. You're perfect. But that's not really what I mean either."

Her face creased, her forehead scrunching up adorably as she surveyed me, maybe attempting to make sense of what I didn't seem to have words for.

"Sorry, I'm not sure I follow."

"Yeah, well I'm hardly the Pied Piper of words here. I'm not sure even Google Maps could follow me at this point." I thought for a moment, grateful that she sat beside me quietly, her thumb stroking along mine, waiting for me to be ready to speak again. "Do you remember your seventh birthday party?"

She considered for a moment then grinned. "Was that the one with the psychotic swans?"

"No, that was your ninth. Those swans were definitely government weapons sent to destroy us. But no... Your seventh birthday was the fancy dress day at your house."

"Oooooh... Oh! Captain America and Belle. That one?"

I nodded slowly. "Yeah, that one. What would you think if I told you that those few minutes when I wore that dress were the only time I've felt remotely comfortable in my own skin. Ever."

She was quiet for a moment that seemed to stretch out interminably, but I knew Matilda—I knew when her silences were borne of judgement, and this wasn't that kind of silence. It was more of a processing silence, which I definitely couldn't complain about. I'd had years, and I still didn't really understand myself. I could hardly expect her to get me in a matter of seconds.

"So, do you want to dress up as a woman? Is that what you're trying to say?" she asked eventually, her dark eyes filled with an earnest desire to understand that I could have kissed her for.

"No... I mean, yes, but not exactly. It feels like more than that. Like I was born all wrong and nothing I do makes me feel any more right. I lost count of the number of times I went to bed as a kid and wished to wake up as you and you as me."

Another silence passed while her gaze explored me

carefully, her lips slowly lifting into a tiny, almost indiscernible, smile. "So you're a girl? Is that what you mean?"

Was it what I meant?

I couldn't deny that her words had sent a shiver of something I didn't recognise through me, almost like belonging, or rightness. But I couldn't deny the *thing* between my legs that I despised with every fibre of my being. Hating it wouldn't make it go away or change the fact I'd been born with Y chromosomes, whether I liked it or not.

"I think I'm saying that I wish I was."

She frowned and squeezed my hand a little tighter; I clung back even tighter for fear of losing myself.

"Maybe you are," she replied eventually with a shrug.

"Except..." I gestured to my crotch area, miserably.

She shrugged again like that meant nothing. "Sometimes nature gets things wrong."

My stomach churned as I listened, and my head swam as a thousand and one questions roared into my mind, the biggest of which was, "Sometimes... As in, not just me?"

She laughed as though it ought to have been obvious.

"Not just you. You're not that special, Har—H."

The way she instantly stopped herself from using my name—the name that always brought that hideous fizzing into my gut—filled my heart with warmth that spread out from my chest throughout my entire body.

I looked at her for just a moment with tears stinging at my eyes before throwing my arms around her, almost overbalancing and sending us both falling to the road below. Her hand shot out to steady us before she hugged me back, just as tightly.

It was mind-blowing, the way her words lingered and

took root inside me. The way I could feel years of loneliness uncoiling inside me.

Not just you.

Sometimes nature gets things wrong.

Sometimes...

Sometimes...

Sometimes...

The moment I got home, I locked myself in the bathroom with my laptop and ran the shower so I wouldn't be disturbed. I opened a browser and fell down a rabbit hole that only hours before, I hadn't even known existed.

It seemed that, not only was I not alone in feeling like I didn't belong in my own skin, but there were hundreds of thousands of people who felt just the same way. My mind whirled with new words I'd never encountered before: transgender, gender dysphoria, gender fluid, non-binary, transition, binders... It was a whole new world, but the thing that stood out above anything in my confused mind was the fact that I wasn't alone. I wasn't a freak or a weirdo. I was one of many, and I didn't have to live this half life, lost in my own body, constantly battling against my genetics.

It was a revelation, and I made a mental note to buy Matilda the biggest bunch of flowers I could afford with my pocket money to thank her for the hope that had filled me at the door she'd opened for me.

The internet was an absolute mine of information and advice for what to do in my situation, and I devoured everything I read like a starving man at an all-you-can-eat buffet. One piece of advice that was repeated over and over, though, on practically every website I read, was that it was important to talk to a trusted adult about how I was feeling. The very thought was terrifying, and made my stomach turn over violently. I pictured my parents: kind, gentle, caring, and blissfully unaware that I wasn't who they thought I was.

How would they react? Would they hug me and tell me they loved me no matter what? Or would my experience be the same as the kid I'd read about online whose family had kicked them out when they'd opened up to them about being transgender.

Then there was the fact that telling them was only the beginning. The world was huge and full of people, and everybody in my circle knew me as Harvey. No matter how much that name had never felt like it was truly mine, how was I ever going to be able to change who I was for all those people?

It seemed impossible that I could ever live as the person I truly was inside. The overwhelming mountain in front of me, if I decided to embrace who I was inside, felt insurmountable, and despair punched at my gut, deflating the hope that had tried to bloom there only moments earlier.

Chapter Four

FOURTEEN YEARS OLD

It had been half a year, six whole months since I'd made the discovery that would have completely changed my life if I hadn't been a massive coward. In that time, the only thing that had changed was that Matilda had stopped using my name and continued to call me H. A few people had caught on, including our closest friends. I'd lost count of the nights I'd spent on the couch in the living room, watching endless reruns of Midsomer Murders and Johnathon Creek, taking deep breaths and trying to work up the courage to speak to my parents about how I felt. As it turned out, it was much easier to read the advice on a website than it was to follow it.

I'd had endless conversations with them in my head, role played every possible outcome and talked myself out of a thousand ways of breaking it to them. Some days, I thought they might just be okay with it—those days when we hung out as a family, all smiles and happiness. When everybody was in a good mood and everything seemed to go right. But it always felt wrong to taint the perfection of days like that with the news that their little boy wasn't actually a boy after all. And so I kept my mouth shut, simmering with anger at myself that burned me up inside.

Every single night, shut away in my bedroom, I lapped up every bit of information available. I read every book I could get my hands on, watched films, followed transgender people on social media and immersed myself in the world I wanted so desperately to be a part of. I was probably the most knowledgeable coward in the country by that point, but still I couldn't bring myself to tell the two people I knew I needed on my side before I could even think about taking on the rest of the world.

It was a Monday morning, the first of the Christmas holidays, and I was lying on my bed with a Juno Dawson book open in front of me, waiting for the sound of the front door that would tell me Mum had finally left for the day. She was going last minute Christmas shopping with my Auntie Di, which meant I would have the entire house to myself for the whole day. I planned to spend it going through the bag of clothes I'd rescued from Matilda's front step the previous week. It had been left there ready for some charity or other to pick up, but I'd swiped it as I left, promising myself I'd donate some of my unwanted stuff to charity in recompense.

The bag had been sitting at the bottom of my wardrobe ever since, hidden under shoes and all the clothes that had fallen off the hangers that I was too lazy to hang back up. It called to me constantly, whispering to me in the dead of night to find out what was inside, but fear of being found out kept me rooted to my bed.

Today, though... Today would be different. I had all day, hours and hours alone to be completely and totally myself.

CHAPTER FORTY-SIX

All I needed was the telltale click of the front door and I'd be rummaging through that bag so fast my head would spin.

"Harvey?" Mum's face appeared around my door and I scrambled to hide the book I was reading under my pillow. She raised her eyebrows at me with a knowing smirk borne of the wrong end of the stick before speaking. "I'm heading out. You gonna be okay today?"

"I'll be fine," I replied, unsuccessfully trying to keep my impatience for her to be gone from my voice. I was so ready to have the house to myself.

"Don't forget to empty the dishwasher, will you?"

"Do I ever forget?"

She laughed. "Only every day. Be good, kiddo. Call me if you need anything. Your dad's in meetings all day."

"I know. Now go or you'll miss the train and Auntie Di will be mad."

"I'm going. I'm going," she said with a chuckle, blowing me a kiss across the room that sent guilt churning inside my stomach. The guilt wasn't quite strong enough to douse the fire of excitement the front door slamming closed behind her stirred in me, though. I waited, breathlessly, for her car to disappear down the driveway before dragging the bag out from the tangle of mess it was caught up in. It rustled satisfyingly as I delved into the contents like it was filled with treasure. To me, it was.

Satin, silk, cotton and polyester spilled out across my bed like a rainbow of hope. For a moment, I simply sat amongst the fabric, breathing it in and tracing my fingers over the delicate garments.

It was like being in the most wonderful trance, floating in a bubble as I tried on outfit after outfit. I loved the way the skirts tickled the bare skin of my legs, the way the tops skimmed over the imaginary curves I dreamed of having. I even forced my feet into a pair of my mum's heels, tottering around the house in them.

Just for one day, I was free to be truly myself.

I finally settled on a pale pink dress that belted at the waist, relishing in the freedom to move around the house as the person I was inside. I only wished I had the courage to step outside and show the world, but I was far from ready for that.

As it happened, whether or not I was ready ceased to matter the moment the front door was flung open just as I was bent over the dishwasher, and my mum's voice called out, "Harvey, surprise! I'm back. The trains were all cancelled. Rail strikes apparently, and you know how your auntie feels about replacement bus services."

I froze, my heart slamming against my ribs as the plate in my shaking hand slid from my grip and shattered on the floor. Every sound was amplified, every slap of her feet against the hall floor pounding against my ear drums as she moved closer.

I couldn't look up, couldn't face the look on her face as she stood in the doorway, her silence heavy with confusion.

I couldn't breathe, couldn't move.

This was it. Against my will, the moment had come that would change everything.

I could hear her pulling in several deep breaths as I stared at the shattered pieces of plate on the floor, waiting for her to say something, anything.

"Harvey, sweetheart, I love you more than life itself, but those shoes do not match that dress."

I blinked and ran her words over and over in my head, trying to make them scan, but nothing seemed to make sense to me in that moment.

CHAPTER FORTY-SIX

"I... what?" I stammered out with tears stinging at my eyelids.

She moved across the room until her feet appeared in my view. A finger curled under my chin and gently nudged my face up to meet hers. A soft smile was curling her lips as she caressed my cheek with her thumb.

"Red shoes with a pink dress? Come on, sweetheart. I raised you better than that."

Confusion warred with longing inside me, spiralling outwards in the form of tears, which careered down my cheeks in floods.

"But... aren't you mad?"

"Mad that my own child can't match a simple shoe to dress combo? A little."

Child. Not son: *child.*

"Not really what I meant." I sniffled loudly, and dissolved into more tears the moment her arms closed around me and held me tight.

"I know," she whispered, her hand rubbing soothing circles on my back. "But what you don't realise is that I've been waiting for this moment for years."

Half an hour later, I was still sniffling feebly while my mum hugged me and told me over and over again how loved and cherished I was. Maybe she could sense that I wasn't ready for anything beyond surviving in that moment, because she somehow managed to contain the millions of questions I could see burning in her eyes. Her constant need to have a plan must have been causing her acute pain, but she kept any anxiety she was feeling firmly under wraps to give me what I needed there and then.

"You know what helps me when I'm having a day of it?" she asked eventually, not loosening her grip on me in the slightest.

"Cup of tea?"

She laughed, pulling back just a little to brush a lock of hair away from my forehead. "A hot bubble bath *and* a cup of tea."

Always so reassuringly British, no matter what the occasion. I couldn't help laughing along with her.

"Come on," she demanded after a moment. "I'm going to pour you a bath and you can relax and rest for a while. Then, when you're ready and not before, we'll sit down with Dad and talk about what you want to do next."

I peered up at her with blurry, tear-filled eyes, and saw only love shining back at me.

"That sounds... yeah. That sounds nice. Thanks, Mum."

Her warm hands cupped my cheeks and she dropped rapid fire kisses on my forehead before she whispered, "I'm so proud of you, sweetheart. Always."

"It's happened."

I could hear mum's voice as she whispered to my dad on the landing where she appeared to have set up camp while I lay in the bath, turning more and more pruney by the minute.

"Any chance you can give me a crumb of context?" Dad asked with a chuckle as I held my breath on the other side of the door.

"Harvey. I came home and found him in a dress and a pair of my heels."

"Ooh." He let out a long, low whistle that made my heart thunder. "How did that go?"

"Well... I think it went okay. I mean, he cried quite a bit but he's in the bath now. God, do we even call him *him* now? How am I so unprepared despite seeing this coming a mile off?"

CHAPTER FORTY-SIX

"Ssh." I heard him shushing her as she started to get into her usual overthinking stride, and I could picture him hugging her. "One thing at a time. Let him rest tonight and we can have all those conversations when he, she, they are ready, okay?"

He. She. They.

In three words, the simple door between us spanned out into an endless tunnel with me screaming at one end at how little I'd thought this through.

How was I meant to do this?

To the whole world, I was Harvey. He. Him. Boy. I had absolutely no idea how I was meant to go about changing that. Sure, Mum and Dad were supportive but outside the front door was a whole world of Owen Wilsons just waiting to make life miserable for people like me. I wanted to believe I was strong enough to stand up to that, but mostly I just felt terrified.

Grabbing my phone from the edge of the bath, I tapped out a message to Matilda and hesitated for a moment before pressing send.

Me: You there?
Matilda: In bio homework hell. Why?
Me: Mum knows.

Exactly three seconds later, my phone started to ring.

"Hey," I answered, heart hammering.

"Are you okay? What happened? Do you want me to come over?"

My chest filled with warmth at the concern in my best friend's voice.

"She poured me a bath."

A beat of silence, then, "Are you drowning yourself? You are, aren't you?"

"Oh my god, Matilda, stop. I'm not drowning myself.

She was cool with it. In fact, it kinda seemed like she already knew. Both of them did."

"Is that a bad thing?"

"No, it's just weird. Unexpected, I guess. I was gearing up for a massive blow up, and now I'm in the bath full of all this panicked energy with nowhere for it to go."

She sighed. "I'd hold on to that energy if I were you, H. Plenty of knobheads out there still to deal with."

"Yeah," I murmured quietly. "Plenty of those."

I could just imagine how the bullies at school would enjoy something new to go at.

"You know I'll have your back, though, right? Whatever happens?"

"What did I do to deserve you?"

"Oh, I don't know. Probably saved babies from lions in a former life or something huge." I could hear her grin down the line and I longed to be able to reach out and hug her tight for standing so solidly by my side no matter what.

"Love you, Matty."

"Love you, too, H. Keep that chin up. Everything is going to be amazing."

And maybe it would be. Maybe I could eventually be the person I dreamed of at night when I closed my eyes and saw myself as I felt inside. I just wished I didn't have to claw my way through mounds of hate and bigotry to get there.

Chapter Five

FIFTEEN YEARS OLD

"Aww, look, Billy, you made it cry."

I winced as another blow landed, my ribs screaming at the impact. Tears of anger, pain and humiliation lined my cheeks as I struggled against the grip Alfie and James had on my arms. Billy and Owen were taking it in turns to land blows all over my body. My school shirt was torn open and my skirt lay on the grass only feet away, but it might as well have been miles away for all the chance I had of getting it back.

It was Owen's turn next. He stepped forward and forced his face right up close to mine, flecks of spit showering my face as he spoke viciously through his teeth.

"Fucking pervert. My sister uses those changing rooms and she doesn't want a freak like you spying on her while she changes."

The words landed just as hard as his next blow to my stomach that sent bile flooding into my mouth.

I didn't say anything. Even if I could have spoken, what

would I have said? They'd made up their minds about me, and nothing I said would change them.

To them, I was just that freak, the boy who wanted to be a girl. They didn't see any of the turmoil that tore me apart every day. They didn't see the way I stared at myself in the mirror each morning before school, until my face became a distorted mess of abstract shapes. They didn't see the way my hands shook when I took the medication that was heroically keeping puberty at bay, stopping me from developing into the man my Y chromosomes were so desperate for me to be, against everything I knew about myself.

"C'mon, lads," Owen said eventually, and I instantly found my arms free and falling painfully to my sides. "Think I heard the bell. Let's leave *it* to do its freak thing."

The moment they were gone, I fell to my knees and vomited into the grass of the school field. I couldn't even be relieved that they'd gone. There would no doubt be more of the same tomorrow, and the next day, and the day after that... Since the day I'd had enough of pretending to be somebody I wasn't, it had been the same.

I could surround myself with the friends I knew would go to bat for me at a moment's notice if they needed to. Somehow, though, Owen and his gang always found a way to get me alone, and that always ended the same way for me: bruises and another brick in the wall of my will to continue crumbling to dust on the floor.

Drowning in shame, I crawled the few feet to my skirt and tugged it on, wincing in pain with every movement of my body. I couldn't go to lessons like this. They were careful never to leave marks where anybody could see them, but it was getting harder to conceal the pain.

I couldn't even think clearly enough to tear them down with my words like I once would have. The only thing I was able to focus on was putting one foot in front of the other and hoping that the next second, hour, day would be better.

The only trouble was, it never got any better.

I was tired, so damn tired.

Aching, I gathered up my things and hid behind the humanities mobiles, waiting for the crowds of students to clear before making a bid for freedom.

The school was a 'secure site' with gates like prison bars all around the exits, but I knew the exact location of the gap in the hedge that came out onto a private farm lane behind the school.

I couldn't even speak to Matilda about what was happening. The humiliation of the daily shit show my life had become was too much. I couldn't bear for her to know about it. I couldn't face the pity I knew she'd throw my way if I told her.

Loneliness was an itch way down deep inside me that I didn't have a hope of scratching.

I stumbled my way through the gap in the hedge once the dregs of late students had cleared, and made my way to the canal bridge. Climbing onto the ledge I knew so well was a new exercise in torture; the pain in my ribs was like a hot lance running through me.

Tears flooded down my cheeks as I stared down at the traffic moving below, internally waging war on the emotions running riot inside my head and my chest. There were too many of them to pinpoint a single one. They swirled and battered at me until my mind was almost as painful as my body.

It was too much. All if it was too much.

All I wanted to do was live.

Why was that so much to ask?

I wasn't asking for much—just the right to be myself in a world that seemed to hate my very existence.

Tears blurred my vision as I stared out over the town that had been my home my entire life. I'd never felt out of place there before. It was small and boring, but it was home. Now, though, it felt like the seventh circle of Hell, and I couldn't face it anymore.

I couldn't face any of it.

The endless waiting for appointments, the constant trauma of existing inside a body that didn't feel like my own, the nightmare of living in a world that claimed to be accepting of trans people until one of us was trying to live our life right on their doorstep.

The Owen Wilsons of the world who thought that if somebody was a tiny bit different to them, it gave them licence to make their life even more of a living hell than it already was.

I was done with all of it.

I wanted out.

I couldn't see any way that things were going to change. There was no going back now. My true self was out there, and she had been rejected. I wasn't even sure *I* liked who I was anymore. Time was I'd have cut down Owen and his gang with well-chosen words, but I'd lost all ability to do anything but survive, and I was tired of surviving.

My phone began to buzz in my pocket, and the screen showed Matilda's name when I pulled it out. She was probably wondering why I hadn't shown up to history class but I didn't have it in me to answer. How could I explain my turmoil to her when I couldn't even truly understand it myself? It rang out and the screen went dark for a moment before lighting up again, and again, and again. Sighing sadly, I switched it off and threw it into my bag. I had to be alone. It wasn't fair to drag anybody else down with my spiralling emotions.

Heart thundering and hands shaking, I stood, arms outstretched against the wind. I couldn't have told you what I was doing standing there. The road beneath me swam in my vision, not far enough down to kill me, but somehow enticing nonetheless. All I wanted was to escape from my life, my body, my head, just for a little while.

I just wanted a break.

My vision cleared and the whole world came sharply into focus: the wind on my face that smelled faintly of frying bacon, the familiar sound of the traffic as it passed beneath me, blissfully unaware that I was rising onto my tiptoes high above. The dull grey of the sky stood in sharp contrast to the lush green of the trees lining the road, the summer foliage in full bloom all around. I could hear a mower somewhere in the distance, and somewhere nearby, a dog barked.

"Noooooo! H, no!"

I wobbled precariously on the edge of the bridge at the frantic sound of Matilda's screaming, but I couldn't turn to look at her.

"What are you doing? Stop!" she cried out breathlessly, her voice moving closer until she stopped right behind me, and I felt her hand frantically grabbing for mine.

Her fingers curled around mine and tugged sharply, pulling me back from my tiptoes.

"Just wait," she begged. "Think for a minute."

I scoffed bitterly. "That's all I do is think. Every goddamn minute of every day."

"I get that. I do. It's shit, all of it, but you can't just check out. The world needs you. *I* need you!"

"Maybe I'm tired of being the world's punching bag, Matty. I'm just so tired."

Her hand squeezed mine so tightly it hurt, and my eyes locked on the tears raining down her face.

"You're nobody's punchbag, H. You're a trailblazer. A modern day Rosa Parks."

"What if I don't want to be a trailblazer?" I sniffed. "What if I just want to live, to exist without having to constantly fight? I'm so fucking tired of fighting."

"I know. It's all wrong, and it's okay to need a rest. It's okay to hide away and lick your wounds for a little while and recharge. But giving up? Not an option. You give up and they win. All the ignorant arseholes who think they know everything and make your life miserable... they win. Do you think Rosa Parks woke up that morning thinking, 'you know what? Today, I'm gonna change the world'? Nah. She saw a wrong and reacted to it. She'll be remembered forever. You think the people who made her life hell went down in history? Does anybody remember their names? Do they heck."

"But I don't want to be remembered. I just want it to stop hurting. I just want to live without my existence being up for discussion by people who know nothing about me. I want to go to school without..." I trailed off, scrubbing at my tear-soaked face with my hands.

"Without what?" she demanded fiercely.

I shook my head in response, too tired and ashamed to admit to what was happening.

"I swear to baby Jesus, if Owen Wilson and his gang of shitheads have been messing with you, I will fuck them up."

I said nothing.

"I am going to kill them."

Apparently I didn't need to.

"It's nothing," I lied.

"Yeah, clearly." I could hear the eye roll in her voice. "That's why I'm here literally talking you off the ledge, I suppose? Because of nothing?"

I sighed, my body crumpling painfully in on itself as a sob ripped free from my chest and cut through the air. "I just want it all to stop."

"And it will, because you're gonna take a break, and not the kind that lands you in a full body cast-" she peered over the edge of the bridge "-or a coffin."

She pulled on my hand again, and this time I didn't put up any resistance as she guided me back onto firm land and pulled me into a hug so tight it made me wince at the pain in my bruised ribs.

"You have a choice here, H. You choose to crumble and let everybody out there who thinks you're worth nothing win, or you choose hope and show them what you're truly made of. You come with me now, regroup, take a break, and then come out fighting to prove every one of those idiots wrong. What's it to be?"

Chapter Six

TWENTY YEARS OLD

"Hope, for the love of God, hurry up. We're gonna be late."

I rolled my eyes, dropping my mascara wand onto the counter.

"Do you want this done fast, or do you want it done right?"

"Both, ideally."

Matilda was standing in the bathroom doorway, her foot tapping impatiently against the floor as she watched me meticulously making up my face ready for the party.

She'd have to wait. It was my birthday, which meant I was totally allowed to be fashionably late. Besides, we only had to make it down the stairs.

I inspected my face in the mirror, still hardly able to believe that the face looking back at me was truly mine. That I was really, finally living this life.

I'd chosen hope.

And then I'd chosen Hope again... as my name.

It had been twelve years, and I'd finally come full circle.

"And this definitely isn't cheesy?" I checked again for the twelve hundredth time.

"Oh no, mate, it's cheesy as hell, but it's the good kind of cheesy. Like a good mellow cheddar, not a stinky stilton." Matilda winked, grabbing my hand and twirling me around on the spot.

The yellow satin swished around my ankles and I laughed, happiness washing over me in the way it so often did these days. It hadn't been especially easy to find a Belle dress in my size, but Grace and Lacey were absolute ninjas when it came to online shopping. When they'd realised how badly I wanted it, they'd come up with the goods in hours. I wasn't ashamed to say that I'd cried the moment I tried that dress on and felt fully and wholly myself.

"How do I look?" I questioned, curtseying demurely with a beaming smile.

"Perfect," she replied, offering her arm to me. "Shall we, Miss Belle?"

"Why thank you, Captain America," I replied, grinning and tapping her plastic shield with my finger before linking my arm with hers.

We laughed together all along the hallway and down the stairs to the party, and this time, when I walked in wearing that yellow dress, nobody laughed.

These were my people, my tribe, and with them by my side, I could take on anybody and anything. It wasn't always going to be easy. There would be bumps in the road, bigots to prove wrong and ignorance to challenge, but I was ready to blaze that trail, to give hope to all the ones who came after me.

Also by
H.A. Robinson

Standalones

Butterfly Kisses

The Rarest Rose

The Colwich Lake Series

The Pebble Jar

Chasing the Sunrise

The Protectors of Light Series

To Where You Are

Life Before
by
K A Knight

"Hope is being able to see that there is light despite all of the darkness." —Desmond Tutu.

Chapter One

I stare at my consultant, taking in her sad, knowing smile and glistening eyes, and I know I'm right. I knew it the moment the letter came through the door. They said routine tests, but then two weeks later, another letter came.

It's back.

I guess part of me always knew it would return and recognised the symptoms, but I hoped by ignoring them, it would go away. I had just started living again, finishing up college and starting our lives in our new flat. Glancing over at Summer, I drink in the determination in her familiar brown eyes, eyes reflected in my face. Mine are more tired, wrinkled. Her lips are moving, demanding plans and actions as she tries to think of any way to keep me alive, just as she has since we were kids.

Her cheeks are rosy, her face a perfect heart shape. It's the exact same as mine, only mine shows the wear and tear of cancer. When I look in the mirror now, I almost look double her age, not like her twin. Her chocolate brown hair flows in natural waves to her hips, catching the light, while my own is still short from all the treatments.

She looks like how I imagine I would if I never got sick as a child.

Her eyes flick to mine, and a frown tugs at her lips at my inspection. She squeezes my hand before she straightens in the uncomfortable office chair and carries on making plans with the doctor.

Plans to try and save me *again*.

I know this is the end, I've been feeling it for weeks. I don't know what's worse, watching her fight to save me for the last ten years or knowing it was all in vain. After all, it wasn't just me who suffered through the tests, surgeries, chemo, drugs, and endless bouts of side effects. It was her, always her, alongside me.

The only family we have is each other, and we have stood side by side since we were kids, never needing anyone else.

She will now, I think idly.

She can't be alone, it will kill her.

"The surgery is dangerous," I hear the doctor say, her kind voice interrupting my depressing thoughts, and I swallow, licking my dry and cracked lips. I ignore the sickness rolling through my stomach, the ever-present nausea that has followed me for months.

"No." My voice is strong, stronger than I've heard it in a long time, and I realise then and there I mean it. No more. No more treatments. No more fighting. My time is coming, and I want to spend every last second of it living.

"No?" Doctor Sanchez repeats, frowning at me before sharing a look with Summer.

Squeezing my twin's hand, I straighten in my seat, steel

running up my spine—the same kind that's in hers. She says she gets her stubborn nature from me, and I guess she's right. "No more," I tell them, looking between them. "You say this surgery could kill me, that there's only a five percent chance it will help, so no. I refuse to spend the last few months of my life in a hospital bed. I want to live. Really live. I don't want to suffer and struggle until the end."

"Whinter," my sister snaps, and I almost crack a smile at the stern set of her jaw. "You can't be serious. We have to fight—"

"There is nothing to fight," I reply softly. "It's back and more aggressive than ever. There is nothing they can do, we both know that." I look at the doctor then. "This is just a risk you're willing to take because I'm dying anyway, right?"

"Well, Whinter—"

"No, Doc, give it to me straight. You've never lied to us before. I'm dying this time, aren't I? There's no stopping it?"

Her eyes shutter for a moment before she nods.

Summer springs into action, leaping from her chair as she drags her hand violently through her hair. Her eyes glisten with tears she won't let fall in front of me as if she's scared to hurt me, like always. Summer doesn't want to show me how she's feeling, always more worried about me than herself. I hate that. She should be allowed to feel however she wants without tempering it for fear of how I'm doing. After all, I might be the one dying, but she's the one who has to watch it happen and live after.

"No, no, no," she mutters before whirling to us, her wild eyes darting between us. "You're not dying, do you hear me? You are not allowed to die! You promised! We will fight this like we have the last four times, and we will win. You'll be okay, and we can do everything we planned—"

"Sis." I hold out my hand, and she shakes her head, backing away. I see terror in her eyes. Her hands are clasped tightly together, shaking before her curvy, five-six frame, the opposite of my own willowy body that's been ravaged by the disease. Where she is vibrant and full of life, I am cold and dead. "You cannot fight this. It's okay."

I mean it. I've been living with one foot in the grave for ten years.

I always knew this would happen.

"No, it's not. How can you say this? This isn't fair!" she explodes. "We beat it four times. It can't be back. It can't!" She falls to her knees, weeping as she watches us with a childlike innocence. "Please, there has to be something we can do," she begs the doctor.

"I'm sorry," Doctor Sanchez answers, her eyes welling with tears. She's been the one to give me the all clear four times. She's been with us for years, watching us grow up. She's practically family at this point.

Sliding from the chair, I drop to my knees before my sister, ignoring the pain it causes in my spine. I'm used to it, after all, used to hiding it from her so she doesn't worry. Cupping her cheeks, I press my forehead to hers, her tears falling between us. "It's going to be okay. I promise."

"How can you say that," she croaks, "when you're going to leave me?"

And that's what it comes down to, doesn't it?

Leaving her.

There is no Summer without Whinter, and vice versa, but it seems now there will be. It's something we have both feared since I was eight years old and was first diagnosed with cancer. She slept in my bed that night, and we cried together as she begged me not to go... made me promise to never leave her.

I'm sorry, Summer, but I'm going to break that promise.

I hold her in my arms as I meet my doctor's eyes, and we share a pained look. Her, the doctor who thought she could save that eight-year-old girl who brought her unicorn teddy with her to the treatments, and me, a weary eighteen-year-old who has fought this disease for far too long and is starting to realise that death might not be so scary anymore—if it stops the pain.

Bucket List Six - Run away with the circus... or close enough.

"It's time to get up!" I yell as I kick open the black wooden door of my sister's room. I grin for a moment at the difference between her space and mine. Where her room is all rock posters, messy floor, and band tees scattered everywhere, mine is the total opposite, with windchimes, crystals, flowers, bright crazy walls, and what she calls hippy love clothes, which are neatly organised. We couldn't be more different.

Apart from the fact we love each other.

She's been in bed for five days, not touching the food I made or even showering. I know she's depressed, but I won't let her wallow. I don't know how long I have left, and I refuse to spend it locked in this house crying. I won't let her do that either. If I'm dying, then so fucking be it, but I'm going to live every single second of every single day until the moment I do, and I'm dragging her with me.

This way, when I'm gone, she will remember the adventures, laughter, and love... not just shaving my hair, watching me vomit and pass out, cleaning me up, and helping me when I was sick. I want her to remember me like my room—beautifully bright and happy.

It won't stop the pain when I'm gone, but I'm hoping it will give her something to cling onto. Something other than anger and grief. I accepted that I could die a long time ago, and I tried to live like there was no tomorrow, but she has always been so careful, worried about me getting hurt or getting hurt herself and needing to be there to look after me, so she has never truly lived.

She's spent her life in hospitals, holding my hand and suffering through every day with me.

That ends now.

"Go away," she mumbles, hiding under the black skull quilt.

Laughing, I rip it back and peer down at her. "Not happening, sis. Time to get up, Monkey." I smack her ass, and she flips over to glare at me. Mascara is smeared under her eyes, and her face and hair are greasy.

She's a mess.

"Go away, Muffin," she spits.

The familiar nicknames make me grin, something we came up with one day just before my surgery when I was terrified. It made me laugh then, and it makes me laugh now.

"Not a chance, now get your ass up and shower. You stink. Get dressed and meet me downstairs in thirty minutes." I smack her with the pillow to get my point across. "I mean it."

She sits up, her eyes wide. "Why? Do we have a doctor's appointment?" She scrambles for the calendar next to her bed that used to be marked with medicine times, appointments, and so much more. Worry and guilt eats at me for a moment that my sister gave up so much of her childhood to look after me. I never asked her to, but I didn't need to. I would have done the same for her without question.

But it doesn't stop the pain, knowing the life she wasted on a dying girl.

"No, but if I have to come back up here, I'm going to shave your eyebrows off in your sleep," I warn.

She flinches and covers her perfectly shaped eyebrows protectively. "You wouldn't dare," she hisses.

"Want to bet?" Grabbing her door handle on the way out, I wiggle my own at her. "Thirty minutes, or you'll be drawing on permanently surprised eyebrows for months."

"You want to want?" She gawks, making me laugh as I loop my arm through hers and steer her through the crowd towards the event on the hill. I had been scrolling through Facebook when I saw it this morning, and an idea came to mind. Before I knew it, I grabbed a notebook and started writing as fast as I could.

I call it Summer's Bucket List.

It's a list of things my sister and I have always wanted to do, and we are going to do them together before I die. We are going to live, really live, without caring what anyone else thinks or letting fear win.

I'm going to bring my sister back to life before I go.

She has lived her life for me, and now it's time I do the same.

"Come on, it will be fun."

"No fucking way," she hisses, her eyes wide as she looks

at the crowd gathered up there. "Not happening. I'll fall on my ass and embarrass—"

"Then we both will." I turn to her, letting her see a touch of vulnerability in my eyes. "I need to do this, okay? And I want you there with me."

"Why?" she demands, knowing it's more than that. I can't lie to her, I never could. Our mum used to say it was a twin thing. Apparently we can even speak without words, something I never realised until it was pointed out.

"I'm scared, sis," I admit. "I'm scared of dying without really living. I need to do this. I made a list of things that scare me, things I've always wanted to do but have been too scared to try. I'm going to do them all. I have to. And I want you with me." I take her hands, guilting her a little. It's a low blow, but if it gets me what I need, then it's worth it. "I can't do this alone. Please, Monkey. Let's make however long I have left fun."

"Don't," she whispers, swallowing hard. "Don't talk like you're already dead."

I smile sadly. "I won't if you stop looking at me like I am."

She flinches and closes her eyes but nods.

"I have to do this, and I can't do it without you. It's time we started living. I've had enough of hospital rooms to last a lifetime, haven't you?"

She nods again, opening her eyes which are glistening with unshed tears. "Okay." She blows out a breath. "I'm probably going to regret this, since you were always the crazy one, but okay, let's do your stupid list."

"That's the spirit," I tease and spin. I'm wearing my flared brown trousers with orange flowers and a matching waistcoat. There is no shirt underneath, just golden buttons holding back my skinny chest. I'm unbothered by the scars from the surgeries there. I used to hate them, but every time someone looked at them, Summer would verbally berate them until I felt better, and now I wear them like a badge of honour.

My survival shouldn't make others uncomfortable. I refuse to let it. I get why they stare. It's because they are scared that, one day, it could be them. I remind them of their own mortality, but I won't let that stop me from wearing what I want. My orange tinted glasses sit low on my nose, and my fedora is tilted on my head. Summer is wearing a band T-shirt tucked into black shorts with fishnet tights underneath and a leather jacket over the top.

We look like yin and yang.

With a determined tilt to her chin that surprises me, she lets me drag her up the hill to the carnival in the park. There are face painters, shows, donuts, and shitty food, but I steer us towards the outside ring at the back where people are clapping. Spanning most of the back is a tightrope and some swings which dangle high from the scaffolding, and there's a net below it.

We are going to learn to fly.

I can't stop my grin as I pull us faster towards the sign-up table. They ask a million medical questions once they find out about my cancer, but I manage to convince them to let me try, and after an hour of safety briefings and watching videos, we are led to the instructors for our slot.

"Whinter, I don't know about this." Summer nibbles her lip as we are strapped into the harnesses. Grinning, I take her hand and squeeze.

"Breathe, just breathe," I tell her, repeating the same thing she told me a hundred times before a surgery or treatment when I would freeze in fear. "One moment, remember? One moment of fear."

Nodding, she swallows. "I hate when you use my own words against me," she mutters, but with a bravery that astounds me, she turns and nods. "Okay, let's do this shit."

"Whoop!" I grin at the hot instructor who leads us to the mats. They give us another rundown, which I try to pay attention to beyond my excitement, but it's really hard when adrenaline is pumping through my usually pained, dead body.

Before I know it, we are flying, or that's what it feels like. I ignore the usual aches and pains in my weak body and just fly. I fall through the air, and the instructor catches me by the feet and swings me. Next we walk the tightrope, and I make it halfway before I fall into the net. Summer sprints over with a gasp, worry on her face, but I just laugh as I bounce there before I take her hand so she can help me off.

"Your turn!" I gush.

She nods tentatively, so I smack her side. "Go!" I laugh and then I stand back as she climbs up. She hesitates for a long time before looking down at me. I give her a thumbs-up, and she smiles before stepping out. She's wobbly at first, and the crowd gasps in fear, but she uses their response to fuel her and her steps become stronger. Unlike me, she makes it all the way across.

I guess it's just another representation of our life paths.

I whoop and cheer the loudest, and the smile she gives me is worth it all.

We have a few more goes before I have to sit out, exhausted. I watch her with nothing but pride, taking pictures. When she's not looking, losing herself in the moment, I quickly stick the Polaroids in the journal I'm keeping with some notes, feelings, and the list before closing it when she comes bounding back.

"Did you see that? Oh my gosh, it was amazing!" she gushes before freezing, her face turning pale as all her excitement dies. "Whinter." Her voice cracks.

"What?" I grin, and then when I feel something warm on my lip, I quickly duck my head, grab a tissue, and wipe the blood from my nose. Embarrassment heats my cheeks, but she crouches before me and lifts my chin, checking me over.

"Better than brand new," she says truthfully, squeezing my shaking hand. "Come on, let's get you some food and meds and go home."

"No." I force myself to stand, ignoring the pain shooting through me. I really could do with that, but I want to enjoy today. "I have a better idea."

"Oh God." She laughs as she shoulders her bag. "Usually your ideas get us in trouble."

I can't help but laugh, the bloody nose forgotten in the face of such joy.

Bucket List One - Watch the sunset with Summer.

We have quite the spread of food before us on the grass—pizza, pasta, fizzy drinks, and chocolate, as well as cheap corner shop wine—as we huddle together on our coats. We sit on top of the hill in the park, watching the colours of the sunset cast a kaleidoscope across the sky. It steals my breath for a moment, and not for the first time, I wonder if she will still watch the sunset when I'm gone.

I turn to her. There's a half-eaten slice heading for her

mouth when I take her other hand and she freezes. "I need you to promise me something," I demand.

Chewing her bite, she drops the food and watches me worriedly. "What?"

"Promise me," I insist.

"Hey, whatever it is, I promise," she agrees nervously, and I sag as I nod and look back at the sky.

"Good, you just promised to always watch the sunset wherever you are in this world. I don't want you to be sad or think of me. I want you to think of this moment, on this hill, sitting side by side with the flush of today's fun still in our cheeks." I meet her eyes. "I want you to know that before the darkness, there is so much beauty that it steals your breath... that not all endings are bad."

"Whinter," she whispers, and I smile as I cup her cheek, watching her eyes fill with tears.

"Shh, it's okay to talk about it. I have no regrets, Summer," I tell her truthfully. There is no point in dancing around the subject. She needs to be ready and open.

"Really? None at all?" she asks hesitantly. I take her hand as I sip the cheap wine in my paper cup and grin, but it slowly fades. Swallowing, I turn back to meet her eyes, knowing she deserves my honesty.

"Only one."

"Tell me."

"Leaving you." My smile is watery, and hers reflects mine. Licking her lips, she tries to blink her tears away.

With neither of us having anything to say, we just watch the sun set before the stars appear as we stay huddled together. We sit the same way we came into this world, together, but we will leave separately.

I hate that.

"I want you to do this bucket list with me," I admit. "I need you to, sis."

"Anything for you," she promises instantly. "Even if it scares the shit out of me. We'll do this your way, Muffin, until the very end."

She leans her head on my shoulder, and just like we have so many times before, I press mine to hers and wrap my arms around her. I hold her tightly so that when I'm gone, she will feel me with her.

"I never really asked, but have you ever been in love, sis?" I hum in response, and she carries on. "I don't know why, but it's all I keep thinking about. You've missed out on it—"

"I have," I confess, and she pulls away, her mouth gaping open as I laugh. "It was during those six months you went abroad for school. I met him at the theme park I was working at. I never told him I was sick, and the way he looked at me?" I shiver, still remembering it. "Falling for him was the scariest, most brilliant feeling. Even the hurt at the end and the bittersweet goodbye couldn't take that away. It was like today... like flying, but knowing someone is there to catch you."

"What happened?" she questions.

"It ended like everything does, but just because it ended, that doesn't mean I don't think back on it fondly, don't remember the good along with the bad. Nothing is made to last forever, Summer, not even us, and long past when I am gone, you will remember me the same way I remember my first love."

"You are my first and last love," she responds, tears falling before she looks away. "And I don't know how I will live without you."

"One day at a time," I assure her as I pull her into my arms again. "You will live one day at a time, and when you are feeling alone and lost, just look up at the sunset and remember you are never alone. I will always be there, waiting, watching, and loving you."

"I can't do this without you," she whispers brokenly.

"Yes you can. You can do anything. Look at today. You amaze me, Summer. You always say I'm fearless and strong, and you wish you could be the same, but you are when you give yourself the chance. You'll just need to be stronger than ever before, but I know you can do it, and until then, I'll be here, holding on as tightly as I can."

"Promise?" She holds out her pinkie finger, and I wrap mine around it.

"I promise."

Bucket List Two - Skydiving, baby!

"Seriously, where are we going?" Summer groans, her hands on the wheel as she peers over at me. I just grin at her and turn my head to look out of the window again. My arm is out in the wind, and I slowly move my fingers like I'm caressing it. It feels like a lover's touch as it winds across my skin, cooling the overheated burns from the sun shining down on me.

"Damn it, I need to know. I'm driving," Summer grumbles.

Laughing, I turn my head and pull down my green-rimmed 80s sunglasses to peer at her. "You follow this road until the very end. There is no need for more directions."

"That's not ominous at all. Look, I like you and all—sometimes, at least—but we aren't doing a murder-suicide pact or some shit, okay?" she mutters as I laugh and just crank up the sound of Fleetwood Mac crooning through the car. Usually she would turn off my music, but instead, she just sighs and sits back as she drives.

That in itself tells me her state of mind. She's still feeling sorry for me and letting me get away with shit to make up for it. I can work with that.

Closing my eyes, I let the sun bathe me through the front window as I start to sing along. I blast out the vocals with Stevie Nicks, and when the song finishes, I feel eyes on me. Opening my own, I meet Summer's gaze. Her eyes are soft as she watches me and the road. "You never sing in public. I almost forgot how incredible your voice is."

I freeze for a moment before forcing a smile. She watches me carefully as I look out of the front window. For one second, I allow myself to feel grief over my lost potential and life to fill me. There were so many things I wanted to do, wanted to be. I was going to sing and travel the world. I could have done it, but when I realised I was only going to get sick again, I gave it up. It was a silly dream for a dead girl.

"Whinter?" Summer reaches over and takes my hand, and I shake off my melancholy.

"You are going to lose it when you see where we are going, or should I say where we are." I sit up as she glances up to the gates we are approaching. When she sees the airfield beyond, she gulps before her wide eyes swing to me.

"No fucking way."

"Way." I grin.

"Seriously, Whinter, I can't skydive. I just can't." Summer starts backing away as I drag her towards the reception office to register. I've been speaking to them for a few days, and after lots of back and forth with my doctor, and proof that I'm okay and consenting to it, they agreed. No way is Summer backing out now. "Oh my God, what if I die? What if the parachute fails? What if—"

"You vomit? What if you get the nervous poops? What if?" I grin as I spin to her. "Sis, we're doing this, so get it all out now."

"We are so not doing this!" she screams, her face pale and terrified, even though I know she's always wanted to. It's been one of her dreams for years, I'm just giving her the kick in the ass to finally do it.

"Pussy." I cough.

Her eyes narrow. "What did you say?"

"Pussy." I cough louder.

"Whinter," she whines.

Dropping my head back, I shout, "Pussy!"

Her hand clamps over my mouth. "Shit, okay, stop," she hisses, and I start to drag her again. I make sure to have her arm linked with mine at all times as I register us both, and then we wait. Summer makes an escape to the toilet, and when she comes back, she's pale but determined. I can't help but grin at her. My sister is fearless, because it's not the absence of fear that makes someone strong, it's doing the thing that scares you anyway despite it being there.

After being shown orientation videos and examples, we are led to be suited up. Once we are ready to go, I look over at her and take her hand. "We've got this, sis. Just think, it's the only time in our lives we will ever truly fly."

That makes her grin, and we climb onto the plane hand in hand. After we are attached to our instructors and given more lessons, we soar into the air. Summer is pale but grinning, and I know I'm echoing her expression. After all, I'm absolutely terrified, but when you face death every day, terror starts to become the norm, so when I'm shuffled to the open door, I give her a wink.

"See you on the other side, sis." Then, I'm falling.

I can't help but laugh as the wind tunnels around us. A feeling I could never describe fills me as I look down at the world below me. My arms and legs are spread, and I just let go, closing my eyes as I fly. I hear Summer scream, but it soon tapers off into a laugh, and before I know it, we are on the ground again.

My heart skips a beat, and adrenaline courses through me as I'm unhooked. When Summer is safely down, we race for each other, colliding and collapsing to the ground in a fit of laughter, our identical faces grinning at each other.

"Thank you," she says suddenly over a gulp. "Thank you for always forcing me to be brave, for making me do this."

"I didn't make you do anything. I just held your hand on the way," I reply as I sit up and help her sit up as well. "You have always been brave, sis. Never forget that." I haul her to her feet. "I'm hungry, let's go feed me."

Bucket List Eighteen - Road trip without knowing where you are going.

I knew something was wrong the night we got back from skydiving. Despite the fact that I had been feeling weaker and sicker for days, I never told Summer. I also didn't tell her about the bloody noses or that I'm now vomiting blood. I don't want to scare her. I wiped it away for days, pretending I was okay, but I'm not suicidal, so when I wake up covered in my own vomit and blood, I stumble to her room.

"Summer," I croak, trying her doorknob but unable to make it work. Sliding to the hallway floor, I throw up again, coughing her name between tears. "Summer, Summer, Summer."

I hear a crash before the door flies open. "No more skydiving today—oh my God, Whin!" she screams. Dropping to my side, she instantly puts me into the recovery position while calling an ambulance, knowing this routine by heart as she recites my issues, my illness, and then waits with me while they come.

"Dammit, sis, how long have you been feeling sick?"

"A few days," I rasp. "I didn't want to—" I vomit again. "Worry you."

"You stupid crazy bitch," she spits, and through my blurry eyes, I see tears streaming down her face. "Don't ever do that again, okay?"

"Sorry," I whisper. "But it got you up before dinnertime."

She laughs bitterly. "Don't make jokes right now."

"No? Then it's probably not the right time to tell you I have my sexy underwear on just in case that hot doctor is at the emergency room again."

She laughs again, but then she swallows as she clutches my clammy, weak hand. "This isn't the end, is it, Muffin?"

"No," I promise. "It's just a hiccup. We've done this before," I remind her, and she nods but doesn't seem convinced.

She stays by my side, distracting me and cleaning me up as best as she can, and then we hear the knock at the door and the announcement.

"That's the ambulance." Summer scrambles to her feet but hesitates when she looks down at me.

"Are you planning on letting them in telekinetically?" I joke, but it falls flat when worry flashes in her eyes, so I sigh dramatically. "Fine, how do I look?" I say instead, and she cracks a smile, albeit a small one.

"Sexy as ever," she teases.

"I knew it," I wheeze as she finally hurries down the stairs to let them in, and for a moment, I'm alone. I stare at the wall, wondering if I lied to her for the first time ever. Is this the end?

Fear fills me and tears drip from my eyes unchecked, despite the fact that I try to stifle them.

I don't want to die, not yet, not like this.

She still needs me.

Closing my eyes, I beg, pray, and demand that the fucking universe gives me longer.

I just need a little more time with her.

And for the first time ever, it listens.

After several tests, bloodwork, x-rays, and CT scans, I'm lying in a ward. They want to keep me overnight. They said I'm no worse than before and it's just a progression of symptoms, but they want to check my bloods in the morning. They gave me fluids and my usual meds, and now they just hope the rest will help.

We all know that's a lie.

I'm dying, so the last thing I need is rest.

I need to live, but as the moon shines into the private corner room, I look down at Summer. She's curled up next to me on the tiny hospital bed with her hand in mine, worry twisting her face even in sleep. Swallowing hard, I close my eyes and let the tears fall again.

"Thank you," I whisper to the stars. "Thank you for giving me a little bit longer with her. I promise not to take it for granted." I close my eyes and fall asleep wrapped up with my twin.

I was woken up early for more blood tests, but after I get back and find Summer still asleep, I grab our usual go bag that holds comfy clothes—not the sexy fun ones I need, but beggars can't be choosers. I slip into the loose, flared jeans and tie the band shirt at my waist before plaiting my hair back and shaking her shoulder.

She jerks awake, flopping around like a dying fish before seeing me. "You're dressed," she says, still half asleep.

"Astute of you." I throw the bag at her. "Let's go."

"Where to? We need to wait for the tests—"

"To tell me I'm dying?" I roll my eyes. "We know that. I'm feeling better, so let's go."

"Whinter," she mumbles, rubbing her eyes. She looks exhausted, and I hate that I did that and put the worry there. "You need to be here."

"No. I refuse to wither and die here." She recoils, but I take her hands. "We still have my bucket list. Staying here won't change anything, but this will, so get your ass up, and then let's go home, shower, and head out."

I don't think she'll agree, but then something shifts in her eyes, a knowledge I see in my own. She knows I'm going to die soon, and some part of her is coming to terms with that while the other half rejects it, so she surges towards my hope with both hands. After shouting goodbye to the nurses, I discharge myself and we race back home, laughing.

Life's too short not to enjoy the exciting, small moments we're given.

Bucket List Four - Sleep on the beach under the stars.

We are showered, packed, and on the road in an hour and a half. I'm driving this time, while Summer dances away in the passenger seat to some old-school rock. It's a compromise. I sing along with her at the top of my lungs, not telling her where we are going.

She naps, and we stop for snacks.

We argue and laugh, and by the time I pull up at the beach on the coast, she grins over at me. That excitement is back in her eyes, and although there are shadows still there from yesterday, I promise I will get rid of them. "Last one in the water pays for food!" I shout as I slip from the car, and without looking back, I race down the steps and onto the beach. I hear her swearing and scrambling after me as I laugh.

People look, but I don't care.

It's busy since it's summer and a Friday, but I ignore them all as I kick off my shoes and shuck my shorts and shirt at the water's edge. My bikini is orange coloured with golden beads, and I grin when I see Summer trying to catch me. Laughing harder, I rush into the waves, screaming at the coldness before I dive under and swim. Once I'm farther in, I float there, watching her hurrying in after me, calling out profanities at the cold water. When she reaches me, she splashes me.

"Cheater," she says, but she's grinning.

"Race you!" I yell as I swim.

HOPE

For the next few hours, we race, splash, and relax in the sea, watching people paddle board and surf before we collapse back on the sand and work through the rest of our snacks. Then we sunbathe, soaking up the peace and happiness days like this seem to exude.

Families laugh and play together, and partners flirt and spend the day in love. There is hope everywhere. It overflows like the ocean, refusing to be kept down.

I have no plan for the next hour, the next day, or the next week.

I only have this—the crashing of waves, the burning of the sun, the heat of the sand, and her, my sister, who has been at my side through it all.

Life is good.

I took pictures all day, especially when we played volleyball with some hot uni boys and I watched summer flirt and laugh. After they left, we got some fish and chips and ate them cross-legged as we watched the ocean, the cool breeze making our hair tangle together.

"So where do we sleep tonight?" she finally asks.

"Here." I grin at her. "It's another item on my list, to sleep on the beach. There's a fire area down there where we can set up blankets and sleep under the stars with the ocean at our feet."

She snorts. "Is that even allowed?"

"I don't care. Do you?" I retort, my eyebrow arched.

After eyeing me, she shakes her head. "No, as long as I'm with you, I know everything will be okay," she says, and I swallow the pain her words bring before grinning and leaping to my feet.

"Well then, let's get sorted!"

Hours later, after we huddled around the fire, reminiscing about the good times, I look over to find Summer snoring softly. Her arm is draped over her face, and her bare feet are buried in the sand. She has a blanket tucked around her, and her head is on her bag. The stars shine down on her lovingly, highlighting the face I know as well as my own, sometimes better. Grabbing my camera, I snap a picture and then look back at the ocean. Standing, I dust off my ass and walk toward it, kicking at the water as I wiggle my feet in the wet sand, and then I turn and grin as I take a picture under the stars with the ocean behind me.

Sitting back down, I grab my book and stick the photo in next to hers and scribble down notes about today.

You told me that as long as you're with me, everything will be okay, but for me, the only time in this life when I'm okay, when I'm alive, is when I'm with you. I'm watching you sleep right now and wondering how I'm ever going to live without you. But the truth is, I don't have to, but you do. So whenever you are feeling alone, whenever you hate the sound of the ocean or the feel of the sand in your toes, remember this, remember today and how we felt.

Today, we are carefree, alive, and so happy. This is what I will hold onto at the end, being with you, being happy, not the pain of this life. Life hurts, sis, but when it does, remember the stars will always shine, the sun will always rise, and you can always find me here, at our beach.

Closing the book that I'm working on to help her after I'm gone, I delicately put it away and then wrap a blanket around myself as I move closer and take her hand. She groans but grips me back, and I swallow as I watch her.

"You can't save me, Summer, but I will save you if it's the last thing I do. I'll show you the beauty of life, and I'll give you reasons to keep living when I'm gone. I promise you."

Then, I fall asleep with my sister next to the ocean.

Bucket List Ten - Kiss a stranger.

The next day, we explore the town and go hiking after finding a cute bed and breakfast on the beach to stay at that night, and we decide to go out. I can't remember the last time we dressed up and went out, preferring our nights in, watching serial killer documentaries and eating our weight in junk food. Tonight, though, we are going all out with a bang. I'm going to drink too much and dance too hard and have regrets tomorrow, like a normal girl my age, and Summer is on board. The sun and ocean breeze are doing amazing things for her mental health, but I tell her I think it's the company.

We take turns showering. She complains that I take too long, and I moan at her shit being all over the room. The usual. After doing our makeup, I grin as we stand side by side in the mirror. I've done a smoky brown and orange eye with white corners and doll lashes underneath. I painted my lips a mix of orange and pink, and my cheeks and nose have blush. I put waves in my hair and ten earrings in each ear, a mix of metals and crystals with dangling feathers in one. My necklace is made of layered beads, and I have rings on each finger. My dress is a beautiful shade of lime green with long, flowing sleeves. The back is completely cut out with just a string above my bum to hold it together, and then it flares out to just below my cheeks. The front is layered ruffles with a sweetheart neckline. I pair my look with some kickass cowboy boots, and I feel sexy as hell for the first time in a long time.

Summer is dressed the complete opposite in a leather bodycon dress with a zip up the front and crisscrossing straps on the back. Her knee-high laced up boots make her taller than me, and her boobs look epic, almost spilling from the bust.

Her eyes are a smoky, killer red with winged eyeliner. She wears a dagger earring in one ear with a stretcher in the other, silver necklaces, and a skull ring on her middle finger. She looks amazing.

"Wait!" I grab my camera, and despite her protests, she poses with me as I take some photos. I leave them on the bed as I tuck my camera away, taking it with us tonight.

My stomach suddenly revolts, and while she's packing her clutch, I excuse myself and hurry to the bathroom. I lock it and I fall to my knees, holding my hair back as I throw up. There's blood mixed in, and I groan as I heave, turning on the tap to disguise it. Our music is playing in the room, which helps as well, and when I sit back, panting and sweating, I can't help but hate my condition for a moment.

I wonder, not for the first time, what it would be like to be normal.

"Come on, Muffin!" Summer calls, excitement in her voice as she bangs on the bathroom door. "It's time to go!"

Wiping my mouth, I flush the toilet. I feel guilty for not telling her, but I won't ruin tonight, not when I've ruined so many other nights for her. "Coming!" I yell, and I hear her walk away. I quickly brush my teeth and fix my makeup and hair. I can't do anything about the sheen on my skin, but hopefully she just mistakes it for sweat, so after spraying myself, I open the door and grin at her.

"Let's go get drunk!" I holler, and she laughs, grabbing her phone and tugging me out of the door.

Our worries are left behind for one night.

The club we ended up going to is amazing. It has six different floors, each with a different vibe. My favourite is the old-school pop floor, while Summer's is the rock floor, so we travel between both before collapsing into a booth at the bar on the first floor.

We both have a buzz and have been dancing for hours as we sip our overpriced cocktails. I force us to take more pictures, and soon enough, we are back to dancing. I lose myself in the music as I wind and grind to the beat. For a night, I'm not the sick girl.

I'm not dying.

I'm so alive it hurts, and when hands connect with my hips, I don't even look, I just dance with the stranger before turning. He's cute. He wears black-rimmed glasses and has a sweet, smiling mouth, bright blue eyes, and wavy brown hair. His nose is pierced as well. In another life, I might have even taken this further, but tonight is about the bucket list, so I stand on my tiptoes and kiss him.

I want to taste his health, his soul, and the feeling of being free and alive.

He groans into my lips and kisses me back as he pulls me closer. It's a good kiss, swoon worthy actually, and when it's over, I laugh and turn, carrying on dancing as he kisses my neck. That's when I see Summer flirting. She's leaning into the bar with a guy who is double her height. His massive muscles strain under his leather jacket and plain white shirt, which are paired with black jeans and boots. He sticks out here, with his black hair and the metal in his ears and lips. He's exactly her type, and as she leans into him and laughs, I can't help but relax further.

She's going to be just fine.

We end up escaping the club with our new friends in tow. My guy's name is Tobias, and hers is Hunter. They follow us to the beach where we skinny dip and laugh and flirt, then we watch the sunrise before they walk us back to our room. I kiss Tobias, watching his blue eyes.

"Tonight was incredible, thank you," I tell him honestly.

He takes the hint. I'm exhausted, after all, but he's a gentleman as he kisses me softly. "For me too. If you are ever here again..." When I don't reply, he smiles sadly. "Or your number?"

"Just tonight," I tell him and kiss him again, grinning when I spot Summer making out with Hunter. I wink at Tobias and slip back into the room, giving her privacy. I fall to the bed and the room spins, my body aching more than it ever has.

It's a good ache though, and it tells me I'm still here.

I hear Summer laugh, and I can't help but smile as my eyes close.

They say the good die young, but as I watched my sister tonight, I knew they were wrong. Some of us might, but the ones like her, so full of life and destined to explore this incredible world and experience everything it has to offer?

They live forever, just like I will with her.

Bucket List Thirteen - Bungee jumping.

We rest for a few days after our road trip at Summer's insistence. She can tell I'm tired, and I am. I sleep for days. I go for another check-up, and the news isn't good. I'm struggling to eat now, and I'm in a lot of pain. Not that I tell Summer, but sometimes even walking hurts.

At night she sleeps in my bed, scared she'll wake up and I'll just be gone. Truly, I'm scared of that too, so I try not to sleep, needing to stay for as long as I can, and then one morning she shakes me awake. I'm groggy and slow to come around as I flip over and peer at her.

She's dressed.

That is enough to alarm me, but I struggle to sit up, wincing at the weakness in my body. She watches the struggle with a frown and pain flashes through her gaze before she swallows. "It's time to stop moping and get going. We have more of your list to do, right?"

"I-I don't think I can," I admit as I sit against the headboard, pressing my hand to my spinning head. The simple movement made me dizzy.

"Fuck that," she snaps, and I jerk my head up. "You wanted to do this, so we are doing this. You don't get to stop now because it's not easy. Where is the woman who told me to fight to the bitter end? If I have to, then so do you. So get up and do what you have to in order to feel better, but we are doing this. You're not staying in bed until you die. I won't let you. You are going to experience everything you want to." Her voice cracks then, and she spins on her heel. "I mean it, Whinter. If I have to drag you kicking and screaming, I will."

I know she will too, so despite how much it hurts, I get up. The mountains of drugs I have to consume takes me a while, and I feel sick during the process, but I manage to keep them down. After a shower, which exhausts me so much I almost collapse, I tell myself to get dressed, going with something comfy because I don't feel like dressing up today. It's not what you wear, though, but how you act.

I'm going with her despite the fact that it hurts and I'm so tired.

Who cares what I wear?

I end up in some flared flower trousers and trainers,

with a crop top cami and a denim jacket. I also take a blanket because I'm always cold now. I put my hair in a bun and smear sunscreen on my face. That's about it. But I'm out the door with her. This time she's in control. I read some of the bucket list to her yesterday at her insistence, so she obviously picked and planned one. It makes me smile, even as I fall asleep in the car on the way there.

When I wake up, I'm confused about where we are, but after drinking some water to take the sick taste away in my mouth and swallowing some more meds, she leads me through the area filled with cars. I realise we are in a field, and it's not the field we are here for, but the structure above it, hanging over the cliff with the river below.

Bungee jumping.

It's another thing she always wanted to do. "Come on!" She drags me with her, and I muster up some excitement, which is dashed when they get one look at me and declare I'm not fit enough. I get it, I do, but the disappointment in Summer's face kills me, so I take her hands.

"I'm too scared to do it anyway. Can you do it for me and I'll watch?"

She frowns. "Are you sure?"

"We didn't come all this way for nothing." I squeeze her hand. "Please, sis, do this for me? Let me see you fall." I nudge her then, grinning. "I'll sit here safe and sound and warm in a blanket."

That makes her laugh, but she searches my face one more time. "Whinter," she starts, but I shake my head. After all, this list is a way to make her be selfish and do the stuff she never has because she's spent her life being selfless and looking after me.

"It's fine," I promise and push her to the queue. Once she's there, she looks back at me huddled in my blanket, but I wave and smile, and only when she turns away do my shoulders slump. It's official, I'm too far gone to even do the bucket list with her.

That's a humbling and terrifying thought, but I don't let her know as I perch at the cliff's edge with other spectators. I grab my camera and wait for her turn, watching others before staring at the beauty around us—the craggy cliffs, the peaceful river below, the sun warming the air, and the birds chirping.

It's a beautiful day, and there is something so peaceful about it.

It's so freeing, especially when I hear Summer laugh as she talks to someone in line behind her, the wind carrying it to me. Because she's doing this without me and not letting fear hold her back, I know she's ready.

She's ready to let go of me and live.

Which means it's my turn.

Bucket List Twenty - Stop being scared and let go, it's time.

Can I let go? My body hurts so badly. It's so tired, and so am I.

I am tired of fighting, of being scared, of being in pain all the time. Each breath is agony, and each blink of my heavy eyes hurts. It hurts to be alive, so much so that I know the end is coming. I don't want to fight it and suffer in agony for months and waste away before my sister's eyes. I want to go peacefully. I know that's not my choice, but it could be. If I were ready...

Am I?

I'm scared, yes, but above that fear is peace—peace that my time has come. It's okay, because I fought so hard and long to get to this point. I might not have achieved everything I wanted or done everything I wished, but I did enough, saw enough, and lived enough thanks to my sister.

To my twin.

I will never be rich, I will never have kids or get married, and I will never change the world, but if I impacted one person's life for the better, then that's more than enough. Because when I am gone, I will live on in their heart, and wherever they go, whatever they do, I will always be with them.

All this time, I've been helping Summer tackle her grief, but I've also been helping myself. I feel grief for a life I will never have and she will. I realise now that life can be so complicatedly beautiful, even in a short period of time, and one moment can change it all. One decision. One leap of faith.

So no, I might not change the world, but I did change hers, and mine along with it.

I've lived, I've been in love, I've experienced as much as I can, and in the end, I will have no regrets. Not anymore. Because my life has been good, even if it was painful. I'm not scared to die anymore, nor am I scared to leave her behind.

I'm just at peace with it.

I existed, and I will always be here with her.

I turn my head in time to see her step up to the podium. She is tied in, laughing and joking with those around her, magnetising them with her presence even as mine shrinks away, fading as hers grows. It still makes me smile wide, which hurts, but I let it. I feel every inch of pride, warmth, excitement, and love for my sister.

The sister that has dedicated her life to helping me with mine, who stopped everything for me.

She will finally get to let go and just live.

"Goodbye, Monkey," I whisper, watching her free fall. "I'll be waiting on the other side."

There in the sunshine, with my sister's carefree laughter carried on the wind, I let go, holding the bucket list in my hand, ready for her.

I stop fighting and feel hope fill my chest—hope that even after I'm gone, she will be okay.

Hope that she will live a full, long, happy life.

Hope that we will see each other again.

Obituaries

Whinter Rose died on the 19th of July after a battle with cancer. She passed away at home with her sister, Summer, after only a few days of falling truly ill. It was a peaceful ending, and she felt no pain. Summer said that Whinter was one of a kind, a true force of nature, one that will never exist again. Whinter was a bright light in this dark world, and her sister feels life has dimmed without her. Summer told us about her adventures with Whinter and the lessons she taught her about her strength in the face of death, and the kindness and joy Whinter brought to everyone she knew. Today, the world mourns the loss of such a beautiful soul, and we offer our condolences to her sister and hope that she manages to find happiness in life after…

Summer, this is for you. I want you to promise to complete them all without me. Live for me. I need you to do this, even though it's selfish, so wash your hair, get out of bed, and start to live again, Monkey.
It's time.
Oh, and don't forget to watch the sunset, I'll be there waiting.
Whinter, your muffin.

Bucket List for Summer

1 - Watch the sunset with Summer, always.
2 - Skydiving, baby!
3 - Go to university.
4 - Sleep on the beach under the stars.
5 - Dye your hair.
6 - Run away with the circus...or close enough.
7 - Go to a rave.
8 - Order a dessert for two and then eat the whole thing, you know you want to.
9 - Stop holding back.
10 - Kiss a stranger
11 - Adopt an animal.
12 - Learn a new skill.
13 - Bungee Jumping
14 - Get a passport and go travelling.
15 - Finally learn to play that damn guitar properly.
16 - Kayak on our favourite river.
17 - Don't be alone, surround yourself with others.
18 - Road trip without knowing where you are going
19 - Do something that scares you.
20 - Let me go Summer.

21 - Fall in love.
22 - Do something you've always dreamed of.

Remember, sis, you are never alone, but this world is filled with endless possibilities and the capacity for true happiness if you are brave enough to reach out and take it. When this list is done, write another.
And another.
And another.
And when you have done everything in this world, I'll be there waiting in the stars like always.

There, underneath it all, is the picture of me at the beach with the stars above me.

The End

Also by
K A Knight

Standalones

Alena's Revenge

Blade of Iris

Crown of Stars

Den of Vipers

Diver's Heart

Gangsters and Guns

Nadia's Salvation

Scarlett Limerance

Stolen Trophy

The Standby

Dawnbreaker Series

Voyage to Ayama

Dreaming of Ayama

Deadly Love Series

Deadly Attair

Forbidden Reads Series

Daddy's Angel

Stepbrothers' Darling

Her Monsters Series

Rage

Hate

The Fallen Gods Series

Pretty Painful

Pretty Bloody

Pretty Stormy

Pretty Wild

Pretty Hot

Pretty Faces

Pretty Spelled

The Lost Coven Series

Aurora's Coven

Aurora's Betrayal

Their Champion Series

The Wasteland

The Summit

The Cities

The Nations

Their Champion Companion Series

The Forgotten

The Lost

The Damned

Life After
by Erin O'Kane

"Hope is being able to see that there is light despite all of the darkness." —Desmond Tutu.

Summer, this is for you. I want you to promise to complete them all without me. Live for me. I need you to do this, even though it's selfish, so wash your hair, get out of bed, and start to live again, Monkey.
It's time.
Oh, and don't forget to watch the sunset, I'll be there waiting.
Whinter, your muffin.

Bucket List for Summer

1- ~~Watch the sunset with Summer, always.~~
2- ~~Skydiving, baby!~~
3- Go to university.
4- ~~Sleep on the beach under the stars~~
5- Dye your hair.
6- ~~Run away with the circus...or close enough~~
7- Go to a rave. Party it up, Monkey.
8- Order a dessert for two and then eat the whole thing, you know you want to.
9- Stop holding back.
10- ~~Kiss a stranger~~
11- Adopt an animal.
12- Learn a new skill.
13- ~~Bungee Jumping.~~
14- Get a passport and go travelling.
15- Finally learn to play that damn guitar properly.
16- Kayak on our favourite river.
17- Don't be alone, surround yourself with others.
18- ~~Road trip without knowing where you are going~~
19- Do something that scares you.

20 - Let me go, Summer.
21- Fall in love.
22 - Do something you've always dreamed of.

Prologue

Staring at the lacquered wooden coffin on the pedestal before me, I feel like my heart is about to rip from my chest, bloody and violent. My grief is so powerful that each breath of air hurts. Surviving without her *hurts*. It's agony, and having to do this alone makes it all worse. I shouldn't be here. This was never supposed to happen.

Sure, I'm in a room full of people, half of whom I don't know. I'm not sure how most of them found out that she died, I sure as hell hadn't told them. The gossips had been busy, but I guess the tragic death of an eighteen-year-old is prime news and travelled fast.

Some of our foster parents from over the years are taking up seats behind me, all pretending to care. No, that's not fair. There were one or two who genuinely cared for us after our parents died and left us alone, but we were never there for long and always bounced from home to home. They couldn't cope with the constant hospital stays and operations. Why care for a kid who's probably going to die anyway? We learned to rely on each other. Summer and Whinter. As long as we were together, we could survive anything.

Only, we're not together any longer. She's gone, and I'm left me behind.

Gritting my teeth, I grip onto the chair before me so tightly that my knuckles turn white, the sting of pain anchoring me.

I refuse to cry in front of these strangers. They don't get to share in my grief with me. My eyes burn, but the tears don't fall. The priest drones on, but I don't hear what he's saying over the buzzing in my ears. My eyes remain locked on the coffin. I can't believe she's in there. She's not really here though, just her dead, lifeless body, one that's about to be cremated, her body burned to cinders. It was what she wanted.

I'm not religious, but if there was such a place as heaven, Whinter would be there. She had such a pure soul, there's no way she'd be anywhere else. I'm not even sure I believe in souls, but she did, with all her hippy vibes. She'd look up at a rainbow and say our parents were shining down on us. I'd just smile and nod, seeing how happy it made her, but all I wanted to say was that rainbows are just the sunlight being reflected and refracted by raindrops, producing a spectrum of colours. There was nothing spiritual about it.

The priest steps back with his head bowed, and I realise that something's happening. Blinking, I notice everyone is bowing their heads, and the coffin is slowly being lowered into a space beneath the pedestal, taking it out of sight—taking her away from me.

Fear like I've never known before slams into me. I

thought the constant state of worry I lived in when she was sick was bad, but this is a hundred times worse and all-consuming.

No, I'm not ready for this.

Surging forward faster than I've ever moved before, I hurtle towards the coffin. Crossing the rope barrier, I lay my hand on its surface, as if touching it would make it stop. Eyes wild, I spin and face the priest, refusing to take my hand away.

"No, stop," I demand, my long, chocolate brown hair falling into my face as I vehemently shake my head. Shocked gasps and low mutters fill the room, and I know I'm causing a scene, but I don't fucking care. They won't take her from me. I won't let them. The rational part of me knows she's gone, but I'm not rational right now, and grief controls my actions.

The priest starts to take a step towards me, his face set in a sympathetic frown. Throwing out my other hand in a stop gesture, I bare my teeth at him, and I'm sure I look savage.

"You can't have her. I said *stop!*" I scream, my voice hoarse.

"Summer," he says with that fucking look in his eyes. I've been seeing that look since we were eight and people found out my sister was dying. It's a mixture of false hope and sympathy. He can shove his sympathy up his ass.

He steps forward again, and I know if anyone touches me, I'm going to lose it.

"Back the fuck off," I growl, narrowing my brown eyes at him, the same eyes I used to see reflected back at me in my sister.

He finally stops, realising that I'm not going to let him

any closer. The coffin finally stops descending, the shiny top visible above the pedestal.

"Let's give Summer some privacy," the priest suggests, his voice tight as he ushers everyone out.

I don't move as they leave, and finally, the room is blissfully quiet. Turning to the box containing my sister's body, I lean my forehead against it, clinging onto the lid with all my strength to stop myself from collapsing. The tears finally fall and large, gasping sobs rip from my chest.

"Why did it have to be you?" I whisper brokenly. "There can be no summer without winter."

Feeling like I can't breathe, I close my eyes and lose myself in the pain.

Chapter One

Bucket List Eight - Order a dessert for two and then eat the whole thing, you know you want to.

"Stop looking at me like that."

I glare at the urn on my desk that contains my sister's ashes. Not wanting to look at it any longer, I roll over onto my other side, only for my eyes to lock on the book she left me.

Life without Whinter feels empty, like I'm repeating the same actions over and over each day, but why? What's the point? My whole life was about her. We were twins, so you didn't get one without the other, and now I just feel... hollow.

Even in her death she's trying to care for me. I knew she wrote a bucket list for me, but I had no idea she compiled a book full of notes and letters from her. Photos of the activities we did together are stuck in with silly captions below, trying to remind me of the fun we had together in those last weeks. I've barely looked at it other than to flick through the pages and see what it contained. It was too painful, too raw, so I put it aside.

This isn't what she'd want. I realise now that the bucket list wasn't for her, but for me. She was trying to get me to do more things, to stop worrying about the inevitable future and give me stuff to look forward to once she was gone.

But how can I possibly have fun and enjoy my life without her at my side?

Guilt rides me. I should be carrying out her last wishes, but I'm broken, a shadow of my former self. I don't know how to be Summer without her.

Get up, Monkey, and wash your hair. It's time to get going. I can almost hear her saying it, and it brings a smile to my face. For one moment, I close my eyes and imagine she's here, frowning down at me as she sees the state of my room and my dishevelled form.

Releasing a long, shaky breath, I slowly sit up on my messy bed, still staring at the book she left me. Reaching out for it, I hesitate as my fingers brush the cover. Can I do this? Swallowing against the nausea that could be from all the alcohol I drank last night in my grief, I finally close my fingers over the book and pull it towards me.

I flip the cover open and find the bucket list at the front. Shaking my head, I quickly pass that page and flick through the photos of all the activities we did. I still can't believe we did half of them, but Whinter was always good at getting me to do whatever she wanted. I smile and laugh at the pictures, tears rolling down my face as I go. The further into the book I get, the sicker she begins to look in the photos. I can't take it anymore, not yet. I don't want to remember her rail thin and hollow cheeked.

Reluctantly, I turn back to the front of the book and look down at the bucket list. It's full of all sorts of things, not just the big, scary ones. My eyes snag on one of them.

20 - Let me go, Summer.

Squeezing my eyes shut tightly against the pain in my chest, I take a shuddering breath.

"Easier said than done, Muffin," I whisper brokenly as I open my eyes and shake the tears from my cheeks.

It's been a week since her funeral, and my phone has been blowing up from people pretending to be friends, trying to get the details and "wanting to be there for me." Where were they when she was fading away, at all the doctors' appointments, and when she eventually died in my arms? It's funny how they are all suddenly interested in her and her life when she's no longer around to live it.

It just pisses me off, so I've not replied to any of them, knowing my messages will not be kind.

I can imagine Whinter rolling her eyes at that sentiment and crossing her arms over her chest. *You need to surround yourself with people when I'm gone, otherwise you'll be a hermit for the rest of your life.*

Maybe that's exactly what I want. I've never needed anyone other than her. Now it's time to learn how to be on my own. Money isn't a problem. Apparently, when they were alive, our parents were rich, and their insurance policies just made us richer when they both died. Once we turned eighteen and finally got our own place, we discovered just how much had been left to us. It made it easier when Whinter was sick. I wanted to spend every minute I had with her, not working away in some hot kitchen or behind a till, and this allowed me to do that.

I guess I should get a job now that she's gone. What else am I going to do with my time?

Since the funeral, I've barely left my bed. I know Whinter would be disgusted with me. I suppose I should do something today, like leave the house and get some fresh air.

I glance down at the list again and frown. My eyes land on one of the items, and a slow smile pulls at my lips as I shake my head in dull amusement.

8 - *Order a dessert for two and then eat the whole thing, you know you want to.*

Closing the book, I chuck it onto my pillow and swing my legs from the bed. After a long, hot shower, I look at myself in the mirror. I'm wearing my ripped black jeans and an oversized, off the shoulder band tee. My long brown hair curls slightly and hangs almost to my waist, and a twisted red bandanna with tiny black skulls holds it back from my face. As my brown eyes skim over my face, I have to look away, only seeing Whinter staring back at me.

Stalking from the bathroom, I grab my miniature back backpack, head for the door, and jump into my car. Driving into town, I park and head over to Just Beat It, the local dessert café.

The bell jingles happily above the door, and Michael Jackson plays quietly in the background. The café is empty, but then again, it is mid-morning in the middle of the week. The guy behind the counter calls out a greeting, and I nod distractedly as I climb up onto one of the stools in front of the bar-like counter.

I've been here a couple of times before with Whinter, and every time we came, her eyes would light up at the huge selection of desserts. She always joked we should just order the biggest cake they had and eat the whole thing ourselves. Looking at it now, I flip straight to the section of desserts for two. I peruse the selection, and I instantly know what I'm going for. Placing my order, I fish my phone out of my bag to keep me distracted while I wait.

"Here you go," a male voice calls as a huge plate is placed in front of me.

My eyes widen at the mountain of cake and ice cream. The dessert is aptly named death by chocolate, because that fucking thing is going to kill me. Laughing quietly, I shake my head. How do I get myself in these situations?

"Thank you," I tell the server, still smiling as I take a fork and tuck into the dessert. The first bite has me humming, earning a laugh from the watching server.

Lifting my gaze from my mound of cake, I run my eyes over him. He's cute, more than cute. I can't believe it's taken me this long to notice. I'm off my game. He's at least six feet tall and has sandy hair, which is shaved close on the sides and left longer on top. His bright blue eyes show his intelligence and don't miss a thing, and his strong jaw has a light dusting of stubble. As he moves around behind the bar, I can see the muscles in his arms bunching, which just makes me wonder what he looks like without a shirt...

"Will your sister be joining you?"

His question catches me off-guard, and I realise he caught me staring. It takes a moment for his words to register in my mind, and my brief embarrassment at being caught vanishes.

Before Whinter died, I would have teased him that he's noticed us before, flirted, and tried to get his number, but I'm not the same person I was back then. Everything is different now.

"No," I answer bluntly, dropping my gaze to my dessert which currently sits like lead in my stomach. "She's dead." Distantly, I can hear my own voice, and I note how dull and lifeless it sounds, which I suppose is only right when the other half of me is gone.

From the corner of my eye I catch his wince as he steps forward, bracing his hands on the worktop. "Shit. I read about that in the paper. I hadn't realised it was you two."

I'm glad he doesn't apologise. It seems like the go-to response when people realise, and I have no idea why. They didn't have anything to do with her death, and the endless apologies just make me angry. I'm supposed to just accept them, say thank you, and move on.

"Are you okay?"

"No." I take a deep breath, thinking about Whinter's last wishes for me. Slowly, I look back up at the server, meeting his crystal blue eyes. "But I will be." It's the first time I've acknowledged this to myself, and surprisingly, I find that I'm not lying. Part of me believes it.

He smiles. It's a gentle smile, but his whole face lights up. It makes something flutter in my chest, something I'm really not ready for. I don't have room for anything else with the size of my grief, not now at least. It's too soon.

Needing to change the subject, I raise my eyebrows as I see just how little of this huge dessert I've managed to eat. My stomach lurches at the idea of consuming this whole thing by myself. Huffing out a laugh, I narrow my eyes and look at his name tag. "Right... Mark, grab a fork. I'm going to be sick if I eat all of this by myself."

He barks out a laugh, then realises I'm not joking. Raising his brows, he quirks a smile at me. "I could get fired for that."

I point my fork at him. "I won't tell if you don't."

He snorts and glances towards the door at the back of the shop marked "Staff only," but then he looks at me with a grin. "Fuck it." Grabbing a fork, he leans across the counter and takes a huge forkful.

We work our way through the cake. We don't talk much, and when we do, it's casual, safe conversation, but I feel lighter than I have since Whinter died. We've almost finished the dessert when an idea occurs to me. Pursing my lips, I watch Mark with a pensive expression, trying to decide on my next course of action.

Feeling brave and channelling my twin, I clear my throat and give Mark my best smile. "I don't suppose you have any job vacancies?"

Chapter Two

Bucket List Twelve - Learn a new skill

Stepping back from the sink, I place my hands on my hips and smile proudly at my work. I'm practically soaked through and covered in soap suds, but I just completed my first shift as a dishwasher at Just Beat It, and I surprised myself with how much I enjoyed it—not washing the dishes, but the responsibility.

Knowing I have someone relying on me to turn up gave me a reason to get out of bed and keep my mind busy. I can just imagine Whinter laughing at me, cheering me on from the other side of the bar.

Turning, I find Mark leaning against the doorway, watching me with a smile. He raises his brows as he gestures towards me.

"You're supposed to wash the dishes, not take a shower," he teases.

Today is my first day on the job. Mark managed to

convince his manager to hire me, and he's taken me under his wing. I'm only doing a couple of days a week to begin with, but that's fine by me. I'm not working for the money.

Mark's comment makes me snort a laugh, and I just shrug my shoulders. "I've never had a job before," I explain as he walks past me and picks up one of my plates to inspect them.

"That much is clear," he drawls as he flicks a piece of cake off the plate. He reaches for another and barks out a laugh. "Geez, did your parents never teach you how to wash a plate?"

"Nope. They are dead too," I say evenly, taking the dirty plate from him and scrubbing it in the sink. This topic is a lot easier than talking about Whinter. They have been gone so long that their deaths only cause a twinge of sadness, and it's more of a sadness of what we could have been if they survived, but I don't remember much of them, because we were so young when they died.

Mark stills at my comment, and I feel his heavy gaze on me. "Shit. So you and Whinter…"

Even hearing her name is painful, but I just swallow the lump in the back of my throat and nod. "We only had each other."

"And now you're all alone." The matter-of-fact way he says it makes me turn and raise a brow.

"Thanks for reminding me how sad and pathetic I am."

Realising he misspoke, he winces and holds up both hands in a *don't shoot* gesture. "I didn't mean it like—"

Rolling my eyes, I flash him a small smile. "I know, I was joking."

And I was joking, but there is a part of me that acknowledges he's right. I *am* all alone, and I've been refusing to interact with anyone. Ignoring the calls and messages.

Sure, most of them are people who only want gossip about Whinter, but there are a couple who actually care, like Dr Sanchez, Whinter's doctor, and Mrs Chow, one of our foster parents who genuinely cared about us. Maybe I *am* sad and pathetic, purposely secluding myself away from the rest of the world.

Mark steps up beside me, breaking me from my thoughts and taking the still dirty plate from my hands. "Here, let me help you with that."

Shaking my head, I try to steal the plate back from him. This is my job, and I don't want him helping me because he feels sorry for me.

"It's fine—"

He cuts me off with a look, lifts another plate from the drying rack, and reveals that it's still covered in cake as well. His lips quirk on one side as he looks through the plates, shaking his head dramatically.

"You really are terrible at this, just let me help," he teases. Seeing that I'm about to protest, he holds up his hand. "Look, I'll help you with this, and I'll teach you how to make ice cream. I've got to make a new batch."

I think back to the book, which is lying open on my bed with the bucket list staring up at me. It would be a good skill to know, a tasty one too. Meeting his expectant gaze, I smile and nod. "Deal."

I get home early in the evening. My shift was over hours ago, but I was having so much fun making ice cream with Mark that I stayed on. Now, I stash a Tupperware of extra ice cream in the freezer and try to decide what I'm going to eat for dinner.

With a meal for one in the microwave, I lean against the kitchen counter as I wait for it to cook. My mind turns back to today and what Mark said about me being all alone.

Glancing at my discarded phone on the kitchen table, I slowly approach it as if I'm expecting it to attack me. I type in the code and sigh when I see how many voice messages I have. Gritting my teeth, I listen to them, deleting most of them before the message has even finished.

The microwave beeps, and I know that I should go and get my dinner, that I could easily continue to ignore the people who have been calling. Instead, my thumb hovers over the number on the screen. Biting my lip, I think, *What would Whinter do?*

Decision made, I press dial and lift the phone to my ear. I can barely hear the ringing over my pounding pulse. The person on the other end of the phone answers, and my breath catches in my chest.

"Mrs Chow?" I reply hesitantly, tears pricking in my eyes. "It's Summer."

Chapter Three

Bucket List Five - Dye your hair

"This is a bad idea," I grumble with my head over the side of the bath as I wash the dye from my hair. It seemed like such a good idea this morning when I went out to buy the dye. I've always wanted to do my hair like this, but I was so busy looking after Whinter that it always seemed like a frivolous fancy. Besides, we loved looking like identical twins. Really, we were like yin and yang, our clothing tastes and personalities completely different, but looks wise, we matched perfectly.

"Will you hurry up?" Mark calls from my bedroom where he's sitting on the edge of the bed. "We're going to miss the movie." From here, I can just see the tips of his trainers as his legs swing back and forth.

Rinsing the last of the dye from my hair, I stare at the coloured water that trickles down the drain. Yup, definitely a bad idea. Forcing down the twinge of nerves, I grab the towel from the side of the bath and wrap it around my head.

"I'm almost done. Find something to entertain yourself with," I call distractedly.

It's been several weeks since I started working at the café, and Mark and I have been inseparable, hanging out almost every day. I know he likes me, and I like him, but I can't even think about any kind of romantic relationship right now. Not when my heart still feels like it's shattered and broken. He sometimes helps me forget, though, that the most important person in my life is gone, and I suppose feeling anything is better than the agonising pain of loss, or worse, the numbness I experienced in that first week.

I hear Mark approaching, his presence hovering in the doorway, and my eyes flick up to the mirror to watch him. He's leaning against the doorframe, looking down at something in his hands.

"What's this?" he asks, flicking through the pages, and as his hand shifts, I see exactly what he's holding.

With my heart suddenly pounding in my chest and nausea rising, I spin around and look at him directly. "What are you doing with that?" My voice cracks, and my instincts are screaming at me to rip the book from his hands. Only, my body won't move.

I'm frozen in place, watching in horror.

He must not hear the distress in my voice, as he continues looking through the pages, lifting the book up to examine the pictures with a light smile on his lips. "Is this you and your sister?"

"Yes," I croak.

He looks up suddenly, and I don't know what expression I'm wearing, but his face crumples. "Summer, I'm sorry. I didn't mean to pry—"

"She wrote a bucket list." The words burst out of me, cutting off his apology. "At first I thought it was for her, all of the things she wanted to do before she died, but then I learned that she wrote it for me. She knew she'd never finish the list, and she filled it with things she wanted me to do, wanted me to achieve."

Mark watches me with a careful expression, like he knows if he shows me sympathy that it'll break me. Slowly, he looks back down at the book in his hands. "She wanted you to have a life of happiness without her." He reads the message at the front of the book, the last letter Whinter ever wrote for me, and something flashes in his eyes for a moment, but when he eventually looks up at me, it's gone. "You looked after her for so long, and now it's your turn to look after yourself."

I've heard it all before, but it's easier said than done. Whinter was my whole life. How do you live as an identical twin when the other half of you is gone?

I don't try to hide my vulnerability as I meet his gaze. "I don't know how," I reply honestly. "I feel completely lost without her."

He steps closer, careful not to spook me as he reaches out to pull me against his chest. "I'll help you."

My first reaction is to stiffen at his touch, so different than Whinter's soft embraces. This is stronger, his arms holding me firmly. Allowing myself one moment of weakness, I rest my forehead against his shirt and let myself be surrounded by him. I want to sob into his chest, to shout and scream that none of this is fair, and to accept the comfort he's trying to offer me.

A comfortable silence falls over us, and slowly, I look up to find him staring straight at me. I recognise that look, and my stomach flips with butterflies. If I don't do anything to stop him, he's going to kiss me, and a part of me wants that. Guilt hits me like a freight train. Whinter is gone, she's dead, and I'm about to kiss someone I barely know like it doesn't even matter.

Mark holds me tighter, slowly leaning forward. I want this so desperately, but I *can't*.

"Mark," I murmur, pressing my hand against his firm chest. He relaxes his hold, allowing me to put some space between us, but he continues to hold me. Regret floods me before I've even spoken, and it makes me wonder if I'm doing the right thing. "I like you, I really like you, but I don't know if I can date you."

He's not asked me to be his girlfriend, so I'm massively jumping the gun, but I can see where this is going. If only we'd met before Whinter... No. If I'm honest with myself, even if I'd met him then, I wouldn't have seen him. My whole world revolved around my sister and her cancer—appointments, making sure she was eating right and had everything she needed, and then, in the end, giving her the experiences she wanted before she died. She never asked me to look after her, but it was what we did. We looked out for each other and didn't need anyone else.

Mark has given me something to look forward to each morning. I'm glad I met Mark and so incredibly grateful for him, but I can't be with him that way.

Questions dance in his eyes. My hand balls up in his shirt as if to steady myself, and I know I have to explain. "Everyone I've ever had in my life has died and left me."

He wants to say more, perhaps even tell me that won't happen with us, but he can't promise that. He registers the unshed tears in my eyes and slowly nods, resisting the urge to ask questions he deserves answers for, and I'm grateful for that.

"Okay, friends then," he says easily, smiling as he leans forward and kisses my forehead. It's obvious he feels no animosity against me for rejecting his kiss. Pulling back, he grins and raises an eyebrow before pointing a finger at me. "I'll be waiting though, Summer, and when you're ready for me, I'll be here."

My smile is wobbly, and fear makes my chest tight. "What if that never happens? What if I'm never ready?"

His grin drops, and the smile he gives me is full of endless kindness. "Then I'll still be here."

Blowing out a breath, I quickly jerk my head in a semblance of a nod in the hopes of hiding my relief that's written all over my face. "Let me just dry my hair and then I'll be ready." I force a lightness into my voice that I know he sees through, but he doesn't call me out on it.

"Hurry, we'll be late." He throws a towel at me, and I laugh.

Picking up the hairdryer, I dry my hair, not daring to look in the mirror until it's done. Taking a deep breath, I run a brush through it and sort my side part. I can't help but laugh at my reflection, pressing my hand to my mouth. Leaning closer, I examine myself.

My long hair is now jet black with two bright blue streaks running through the front. It's so different and I love it. For the first time since Whinter died, I'm able to look at myself without seeing her staring back at me. Sure, she's still there in my brown eyes and my puckered lips, but I'm no longer the mirror image of her, and there's something freeing about that.

"I hear laughing, is that a good or bad sign?" Mark asks lightly, his voice getting closer as he walks towards the bathroom.

"Good, it's a good sign." Grinning, I turn around and do a little curtsy just as he steps through the door.

His face lights up. "You look amazing!"

Unable to stop smiling, I turn around and look at myself in the mirror again, agreeing with him.

Chapter Four

Bucket List Seven – Go to a rave. Party it up, Monkey!

I hear the party before I see it, the pounding music reaching me halfway through the forest we're currently trudging through. Mark arrived at my house a couple of hours ago and told me to dress for a party. When I jumped into his car, I hadn't expected him to drive me out to the middle of the English countryside.

"Remind me why I'm dressed like this in the middle of nowhere, freezing my tits off?" I ask petulantly. My tight black leather trousers and low-cut red shirt with off the shoulder sleeves are not exactly the correct clothes for this terrain. My long black and blue hair is curled and hangs down my back, and my makeup is minimal, but my neck is adorned with several layered necklaces.

Mark tugs on my hand, which is currently linked with his, as he leads the way. "You said you wanted to go to a rave." Glancing over his shoulder, he scans my body in that heated way I've been noticing for a while now.

It's been several months since we first met, and we spend every day together. We've been getting closer and closer, but nothing has happened between us since we had that conversation the night I dyed my hair.

"Besides," he continues, shaking me from my thoughts, "you look perfect. Although, you are missing one thing."

Pursing my lips, I arch a questioning brow at him, feeling mildly amused.

"Glowsticks," he says with a grin, whipping out several glowsticks from his back pocket. Cracking them, he shakes them manically, his face lighting up from the glow. He attaches some string to the loop at the top and drapes it around my neck so the fluorescent pink stick rests between my breasts. "Perfect." He winks, and I get the impression he's not talking about my completed outfit.

Snorting a laugh, I shake my head, my hair falling around my face. Something shifts in his expression, suddenly becoming more serious. He steps closer until we're almost chest to chest, and then he reaches out and takes one of my escaped curls, brushing it back behind my ear. My heart beats so hard I'm sure he's going to hear it, but he just continues to stare at my face. No, not my face, my lips. I should stop this before we get carried away and cross that line, but I can't seem to convince my body to move. Tongue flicking out, I wet my lips, a movement he tracks with his eyes. Arousal simmers low in my stomach, and before I know what I'm doing, I reach up and cup the back of his neck, pulling him down.

Hoots and catcalls break the moment, and I spring away from Mark like I've been burnt. Cheeks blazing, I laugh awkwardly and gesture towards where the group of shouting partygoers are now disappearing between the trees. Lights shine through the forest, and I know we must be close. Glancing back at him, I see disappointment written across his face, and regret makes my chest tight.

"Come on, you need to show me your dance moves!" Sliding my hand into his, I pull him towards the pounding bass that vibrates through my body.

He laughs and follows, his fingers tightening around mine.

After weaving through the trees, we finally reach the party. A bonfire is set up in the middle with two huge speakers blasting out dance tunes. People are dancing and raving around the fire, plastic cups in hand.

Mark says something, but I can't hear him. I shake my head and point to my ears. Stepping closer, he leans down and presses his lips against the curve of my ear.

"Wait here," he whispers, the feel of his breath against my sensitive skin making the hair on my arms stand on end.

Nodding, I watch as he smiles and jogs into the crowd. My eyes drop to his ass, which is cupped tightly by his jeans. He's looking particularly fine tonight, and there's an excitement in his eyes I've not seen before that only seems to make him more attractive.

Cool it, Summer. Blowing out a breath, I shake my head at myself and force my eyes to look at something else. Instead, I watch the dancing masses swaying slightly to the beat as I wait. He's not gone long, returning with two plastic cups. Taking the one he offers me, I look down at the frothy, amber liquid and raise my brows.

"It's cheap beer and tastes like crap, but it's free."

He grimaces as he takes a sip, not filling me with confidence, but he's right, free booze is free booze. Raising the cup to my lips, I take a sip and share his grimace before tilting the cup back and chugging the rest of it.

Laughing, Mark whoops and follows my lead. Once both of our drinks are finished, he grabs my hand and starts pulling me towards the other dancers.

"Come on, let's dance."

I want to protest and say I don't dance, but I think about why we're here. The familiar twinge of pain fills my chest as I think of my sister. She was always dancing between the bouts of cancer and would have loved this. She had to stop at various times over the years due to chemo and operations, but whenever she was fit enough, she was dancing.

So, channelling her, I put on a smile and force myself to dance.

After a little while, I find my inhibitions are lowered and I actually start to enjoy myself. With my hips swaying to the beat, I throw my head back, a smile pulling at my lips, and I catch Mark watching me. He's smiling, and that heated look is back in his eyes as he tracks the movements of my body. I should stop and turn away, but the alcohol has given me some Dutch courage, so when he moves to stand behind me and his hands land lightly on my hips, I don't push them away. Instead, I close the space between us so my back is against his chest. I can feel the muscles in his chest moving as we undulate, the orange light from the fire highlighting the movements of our bodies. Swaying my hips back and forth to the rhythm, I allow myself to lean back into the strength of his body. In this moment, this doesn't feel wrong, and I'm not thinking about Whinter. My mind is fully consumed with Mark and the feel of him against me.

I'm not sure how long we dance like this for, but when

he spins me, I don't fight it. Tilting my head back, I smile up at him when I see the question in his eyes. Without letting myself think about it, I push up onto my tiptoes and press my lips against his. He makes a surprised noise in the back of his throat but quickly returns my kiss. My tongue flicks out, and he groans, deepening the kiss, when a high-pitched noise shatters the moment.

The police have arrived.

"Shit!" He laughs, his eyes wide and wild. Grabbing my hand, he pulls me along behind him as he weaves through the panicking ravers. "Follow me."

Giggling and high on lust and adrenaline, I hurry after him through the trees, the blue light of the police cars flickering through the trunks, almost adding to the rave atmosphere.

After finally making it back to the car, we clamber inside.

"Glad that I parked so far away now?" he asks with a grin, his chest rising and falling rapidly from our run.

Laughing, I nod my head in agreement. Getting arrested was not on my list of things for tonight. Glancing over at Mark, I find him watching me again. I can tell he wants a repeat of what happened before the fire, and honestly, so do I. The atmosphere in the car is charged and heavy, and before I know it, I'm climbing across the console and in his lap. Straddling him, I wrap my arms around the back of his neck and kiss him deeply. He makes that masculine grumbling sound in his chest again and holds me close, kissing me back.

We continue like this, but instead of it easing the need I'm feeling, it only spurs it on, fuelling the fire burning within me.

"If we don't stop now, you know what's going to happen."

He's right, I do. We should stop now, blame it on the alcohol, and continue as normal. I don't want to screw up this friendship, I can't lose him too.

"I know. We should probably stop," I reply, my eyes locked on his.

He watches me closely. "You don't want to."

It's not a question, and again, he's right. My need for him *burns*.

Shaking my head, I bite down on my lip, considering my next answer. "No, I don't want to stop."

"Neither do I," he whispers, as if he's afraid of saying the words aloud.

"Then don't." I know he's going to say something else. He's probably going to try and talk me out of this, so I surge forward and silence him with my lips, giving him my answer.

Chapter Five

Bucket List Eleven – Adopt an animal

As the shower shuts off in the other room, I smile as I click enter on the keypad of my laptop. A flutter of excitement goes through me as I shut the lid, but before I can get carried away, the door to the en-suite opens and a half naked Mark emerges.

"Oh, hey." I grin, waggling my eyebrows suggestively, my heart warming at his presence.

Laughing, he throws a towel at me, although sadly not the one wrapped around his waist. "I've got work, I don't have time for that."

Snorting, I roll my eyes and jump up from the bed, picking out my clothing for the day. "I know, I'm just appreciating the view."

It's been a couple of months since that night at the rave in the woods, and Mark has spent most nights here, or I stayed at his apartment on the other side of town. We fuck regularly, which isn't strictly a friends only activity, but I can't keep my hands off him. He makes me feel good, and with him, I almost feel whole again, and each day it gets easier to exist without Whinter. Neither of us have mentioned the whole sex-slash-friend thing, but it's possible to be just friends who have sex, right? The word *naïve* rings through my mind, but I refuse to acknowledge it.

The two of us get ready together before eating a quick breakfast. He notices my excitement and quirks his lips to one side, watching as I bounce around the kitchen.

"Today is the day?"

I look up from my cereal bowl, wrapping one of my curls endlessly around my finger. "Yup. I'm more nervous than I thought I'd be." I know I'm worrying about nothing, but I can't seem to stop myself. "What if they don't like me?"

Mark laughs and then stops when he realises I'm serious. "They are dogs, they like everyone."

We say our goodbyes, and I drive over to the local animal shelter. I feel nervous, tapping my finger against the steering wheel. Mark doesn't think it's a big deal, but for me it is. Some may think that a pet is just an animal, but I'm choosing something to join my family. I've been so adamant that I can't let anyone into my life because everyone leaves me, but here I am, willingly adopting a pet.

Parking outside the shelter, I stare up at the building, biting down on my lip. Whinter would have loved this, but up until we turned eighteen, we were always moving around, so having a pet was never practical. Taking a deep breath and pulling up my big girl pants, I climb from the car and enter the building.

Once I've signed in, a smiley woman named Mary

greets me. "We have lots of animals available for adoption, but I was told you're particularly interested in a dog, is that right?"

I nod my agreement. She smiles and leads me down a corridor. Mary shows me all the available dogs, several of which I squeal over. She lets me take them out into the garden and play with them to see how I get on with their temperaments, and the large chocolate lab, Marco, is my favourite by far, his goofy face making me smile. We're taking Marco back inside when I see another corridor and a sign on the wall warning customers to enter at their own risk.

Frowning, I stop. "What's down there?"

Mary's smile drops and sadness envelops her. "Those are the animals who came in with behavioural issues and we struggle to rehome."

Curiosity sparks in my chest. "Will you show them to me?"

Mary agrees, taking Marco back to his kennel before gesturing for me to follow. As soon as we cross the threshold of the corridor, the barking starts. Seeing dogs so worked up breaks a little piece of my heart, and we quickly pass them, heading down another corridor. In this one, most of the rooms are empty except for one, where a large black cat with half of his left ear missing and a large scar down his face hisses at us.

I kneel slowly, and the creature stops hissing, but his tail flicks angrily behind him. My chest tightens. "What happened to him?"

I don't look away from the cut, but I hear Mary's sad sigh. "He was hit by a car and the owner couldn't afford his medical care. He was abandoned. He's been with us for a couple of months now, and we've been working with him, but he doesn't like people."

He seems alright to me. In fact, he's watching me closely now with no sign of aggression on his scarred face. He's nervous, that much is clear, but he slowly, hesitantly, takes a step towards me. With my heart in my throat, I press my hand flat against the glass.

Glancing up at the woman beside me, I find her watching me closely. "What's his name?"

Mary's mouth twitches. "Mr Whiskers."

Looking back at the cat, a slow smile pulls at my lips. "He's perfect, I'll take him."

Chapter Six

Bucket List Twenty-One – Fall in love

I throw my bag down on the sofa as I storm into the house, leaving the door wide open since I know he'll follow me inside. Striding straight over to the fridge, I pull out a can of fruity cider and crack it open, not even bothering to pour it into a glass. Mr Whiskers trots across the room and jumps up onto the kitchen counter, watching me with a tilt of his head. Slowly, he walks over and butts his head against me until I stroke him.

Mark enters the house, shutting the door quietly behind him. He doesn't come any closer, just watches me and my cat with a pensive expression. Mark and Mr Whiskers don't have the most amicable of relationships, and right now, that works for me because he won't come close while I'm touching the cat. He learned pretty quickly that my cat is like a guard dog, protecting me fiercely.

"Are you going to tell me what I've done to make you mad?" Mark finally asks, breaking the silence.

Raising my eyebrow, I throw him a look. How can he not know? Yet there he stands, completely oblivious.

"You called me your girlfriend."

There's a beat of silence.

Barking out a surprised laugh, he shakes his head in disbelief. "*That's* what this is about?"

I jab my finger in his direction. "Don't make it sound like this is all trivial," I accuse, my voice breaking. "I told you I couldn't get into a relationship with you."

He takes a step towards me but quickly stops when Mr Whiskers hisses at him, the cat's hair standing on end.

"We spend every waking moment together," he counters, gesturing widely. "I practically live here. We sleep together. That sounds like a girlfriend to me, but I'm sorry if I didn't make that clear. Do you need a contract?"

His words hit me hard, making my chest tight. I've never seen him like this, and I know this is his frustration making him lash out. To be fair, I know he's right. I should have stopped all of this before we got too involved and our feelings got in the way. Except, right now, my heart feels like it's breaking all over again.

My anger roars to life within me, trying to protect me. "Fuck you! Don't turn this around on me," I shout, shaking my head, my sight blurry from the tears gathering in my eyes. "I *can't* be with you that way."

"But you have been." Exasperated, he steps closer and leans against the kitchen island that separates us. "We've been together for months now."

Tears start rolling down my cheeks as I hold my cat against my chest, needing some sort of comfort—comfort that I'd usually get from Mark.

His face drops when he sees my tears, and his shoulders droop as all of the fight leaves him. "Don't cry, Summer." He sounds like he's in pain, and his expression reflects it. "Is this about your sister?" he asks quietly. "I'm sure she would want you to be happy rather than be miserable and alone."

My heart is pierced again when he mentions Whinter. I can't have him here any longer, because if he stays, I'll give in and fall into his arms. I need time to think.

"I need you to leave," I say dully.

"Wait—" He cuts himself off with a shake of his head, watching me with sad eyes. He knows that fighting this right now will only result in me pushing him further away. "I'll give you the space you want, but know I'm not going anywhere." His voice is steady and full of promise. "I love you, Summer."

Squeezing my eyes shut at those three words, I drop my head and bury my face against my cat's black fur. I feel him watching me, his gaze heavy, and with one last, long sigh, he turns and leaves.

As soon as he's gone, I can't hold back the tears. Mr Whiskers escapes from my hold as soon as possible, running into the house to hide somewhere. Stumbling across the room, I collapse onto the sofa, pull my legs up, and wrap my arms around myself. Deep sobs rip from my chest as I lean back against the sofa and let myself fall apart.

Eventually, once my head is pounding from crying and I've long since run out of tears, I manage to drag myself to my bedroom. My nose is blocked, I feel like crap, and I enter the room to find stuff all over the floor. At some point, Mr Whiskers must have knocked over a pile of stuff by the bed, and sitting on the top of the mess is the book Whinter left for me.

I stare at the book with a mix of hatred and longing. I met Mark because of Whinter and this stupid fucking book. It's because of her that I'm doing the bucket list and feeling again. After she died, all I felt was pain and grief. Thanks to the list, I've been forced out of my comfort zone, and I've begun to experience life again. It's hard, so fucking hard.

Reaching down, I pick it up and flop down onto the bed. Flipping the book open, I look through the images of us happy together despite the inevitable heartbreak that was heading right for us. She never let her cancer stop her, always pushing on and trying to live the life she had left while I was content to push for more treatments, constantly looking for ways to save her or buy us more time.

By giving me this book and the list, she's forced me to live again. I know that's what she always wanted, for me to be happy.

Turning back to the front where the list is waiting for me, I look through the suggestions, ticking off the ones I've completed. It's not until I get to the bottom that I pause.

Twenty- Let me go, Summer.

Releasing a long, shaky breath, I glance over at the urn containing her ashes.

"I don't know if I can do that, Muffin," I whisper. Closing my eyes, I imagine what she'd say if she was here, and I instantly know her answer.

Watch the sunset. I'll be with you, always.

She's right. I made a promise to her, and I'm doing a shitty job of carrying it out. Opening my eyes, I look down at the next item on the bucket list, and my breath catches in my throat.

Twenty-One- Fall in love.
Mark.

I'm terrified of my feelings for him. What if I lose him too? Well, if I continue to push him away, then losing him is a definite. My feelings for him developed at some point, and now I can't imagine not having him around. If I break things off with him then I'm cutting off my nose to spite my face. I need to decide if I can live without him now or as a hypothetical situation in the future. I'm terrified of him dying and leaving me, like everyone else in my life, but at least we would have had some time together, creating memories like Whinter and I did.

I love him and would rather risk heartbreak after a happy future together instead of pushing him away now to avoid that pain.

Looking at the book one more time, I know what I need to do. I reach for my phone and press the number on speed dial.

He picks up after the first ring. "Mark?" I don't give him a chance to speak, needing to say this before I lose my nerve. "I love you, and I'm sorry I pushed you away. Can we meet up and talk? I've got something I need your help with."

Chapter Seven

Bucket List Fourteen – Get a passport and go travelling. See the world.

The sounds of the busy airport echo around me, but I ignore it as I stare out the large floor to ceiling window. My suitcase is parked at my side and the tickets are clutched in my hands. I've barely been able to contain my excitement in the days running up to this, but now I feel strangely calm.

"Are you ready?"

Glancing over my shoulder, I see my boyfriend walking over with a smile and a coffee in each hand. I gratefully take one before returning to watching the sunset.

We're about to board a flight to Italy, my brand-new passport in my back pocket. Whinter had always wanted to travel, and Italy was one of the places we'd both wanted to visit. With Mark's help to sort all the legal paperwork, my sister was coming with us, her ashes safely packed away in my backpack. She'd hate to know she was just sitting on my desk, and I can't think of a better send off.

Thinking of her still hurts, and being a lone twin is agonising, but she's brought hope back into my life, and although she's not around anymore, she's helping me live again. Having Mark in my life has been a blessing, and although things are still hard, we're going strong and taking each day one at a time.

Sliding my free hand into his, I squeeze tightly as the sun sets, casting our faces in orange light, and I know Whinter is smiling down at us.

Turning to face Mark, my heart full of hope, I smile up at him. "Yes," I reply. "I'm ready."

The End

Also by
Erin O'Kane

Standalones

Hero Complex

Dark Temptations

The Cursed Women Universe

Venom and Stone

Betrayal and Curses

The Shadowborn Series

Hunted by Shadows

Lost in Shadow

Embraced by Shadows

Born From Shadows Series

Demons do it Better

The War and Deceit Series:

Fires of Hatred

Fires of Treason

Fires of Ruin

Fires of War

Fires of the Fae

A Lady of Embers

A Spark of Promise

A Legacy of Hope and Ash

Books by Erin O'Kane and K.A Knight

Her Freaks Series

Circus Save Me

Taming the Ringmaster

Walking the Tightrope

The Wild Boys

The Wild Interview

The Wild Tour

The Wild Finale

Books by Erin O'Kane and Loxley Savage

Twisted Tides

Tides that Bind

When Hope is All You Have
by
KJ Ellis

Chapter One

I walk into the hospital with my head down as the tears I'd been trying to hold at bay tumble down my cheeks.

I need to be brave. Not just for me, but for Thomas too. He needs me right now, and I need to be strong for both of us.

Once I've asked the receptionist sitting behind the desk which room Thomas is in, I hesitantly head that way.

My feet feel heavy, weighing me down, and my head is a jumbled mess.

I spot Thomas's parents, Alison and Julian, pacing the floor outside where I presume Tom is, lying on a hospital bed in pain.

"Oh, Fran. Thomas will be happy you're here for him." His mum grabs me and squeezes me tight.

"How is he?" I'm afraid to ask, but I want to know what we'll be up against.

"It's not looking good, sweetie. The doctors are in there now trying to clean him up so they can assess his injuries." Alison runs the back of her hand over her nose and wipes her tears away.

"He was in pretty bad shape when they brought him in," Julian adds, looking worse for wear.

I round the side of Julian and pop my head up to the little window on the door. I cover my mouth in shock at what I see. The doctors have cut all his clothes from his blood-covered body. He's got wires coming out of him in all kinds of places, for God knows what, and they've placed a breathing mask over his face. What has me panicking the most is how his body hasn't moved, not even the slightest lift of his fingers or a twitch in his toes.

All of a sudden, there's a flurry of activity, and the doctors wheel his bed towards the door.

"Please, step aside!" one of the doctors shouts as he gently but urgently pushes me to the side so they can get through with the bed.

"What's wrong? Where are you taking him?" Alison asks frantically.

"We need to take your son down for a CT scan. Then possibly surgery. He's got an internal bleed in his abdomen. He's experiencing significant pain in his lower back. I'm almost certain he's got a slipped disc or a fracture of the spine. We won't know until we take him for the CT scan, but we need to do it now so we can stop the bleed as well. I'm sorry I don't have any other news for you."

With that, the doctor is off again, getting into the lift with the other doctors and my Thomas.

I can't cope. I'm barely holding it together. I don't know what I would do if I lost him. I can't bear thinking that the last time I saw him may have been the last. I never told him I love him. What if he never hears me say it again?

I need to stop thinking the worst. Thomas is a strong and healthy guy; he'll be absolutely fine and he will pull through this.

I know he will.

Chapter Two

It's been a couple of days since Thomas had his motorbike accident. I've been coming and going from the hospital as often as I can in between college classes. The doctors say he's improving every day, but the damage to his spine has left him immobile. He will need extreme physiotherapy treatment to be able to walk again, but it isn't going to happen for a while. He'll be in a wheelchair during his treatment. The doctors said it'll take as long as it takes. It all depends on Thomas and his mental attitude towards the therapy they give him.

I know this won't be a problem for Tom. He's full of determination and always succeeds in every aspect of his life.

I'm not worried, and neither should Thomas or his parents.

I've finished up at college for the day, so I'm heading to the hospital again. Now Tom is eating solid food, I've brought some treats for him in the hopes it'll cheer him up. His parents are just walking out of his room when I arrive.

With a smile, I say, "Hey, how's he doing today?" My smile soon disappears when I notice the sombre expressions they're both sporting. My body goes rigid. Something must have happened. "What's wrong?"

"He's not having a very good day. The physio is in there with him now. He's running through his treatment plan for when he's ready," Julian explains.

"Oh, I thought you were going to tell me something bad." I release a small breath I didn't even realise I was holding. "Is it okay if I go in?"

"Yes, of course. We're just about to head out and grab something to eat. We've been here all morning and skipped breakfast and lunch," Alison tells me with a rub on my shoulder.

"Thank you." I wave them off, turn, and go in to see Thomas.

"Hi, babe. I've just seen your mum and dad. They say you're giving them hell today. Is that right?" I ask with a soft laugh.

I round the side of his bed the physio isn't sitting on and lean down to give him a kiss. I was aiming for his lips, but I get his cheek.

Wow, he really is in a foul mood today.

I ignore his brush-off. That way, I won't get upset. It's out of character for him to act like that towards me. It's a first, and I'm hoping it's a last. I put it down to him being stuck in the hospital and stress he's feeling right now.

"What have I missed?" I sing as I take a seat.

"Oh, nothing. It's not like I can get up and do anything, Fran," Thomas replies, full of frustration.

I sense a massive change in him since yesterday. One I'm not a fan of.

I keep quiet and let his physiotherapist finish up with his questions. With every question he asks, Thomas gets more and more agitated. The huffing and puffing coming from him is enough to make me feel uncomfortable, so God knows how the physiotherapist feels. He's here to help Thomas. Tom just needs to get his head out of his arse long enough to see that, which doesn't look it'll be any time soon.

Deciding enough is enough, Tom tells him to leave, and the physiotherapist wastes no time rushing from the room.

I felt sorry for the poor man. "That was really rude, Tom. He's only trying to help you."

"What could he possibly do to help me right now? I'm practically bedridden! I can't do the simplest of tasks like using the bathroom or having a wash by myself."

"No, but you will need his help, and he's trying to prepare you for what's ahead."

"What's the point? My legs are useless. I can't even sit up by myself, let alone walk." I can tell he's given up already by the tone of his voice.

He's looking at this all wrong. I know it's hard for him to see the end of the tunnel in his current state, but in time I'm hoping he'll see the bigger picture. He can't give up without at least trying. That's not going to help him recover. I need to put a stop to him thinking about all the negatives.

"You can't think that like, babe. You're stronger than you know. You'll get through this, I promise. It's going to take time, but if anyone can get through this, it's you." I take his hand in mine to show the faith and hope I have for him, but he swiftly pulls out of my grasp.

I'm not going to lie; it hurts like you wouldn't believe. It hurts more than when he dismissed my kiss when I came in.

Then he snaps at me. "What do you know, Fran? It's easy for you to say. You're not the one lying in a hospital bed." I can tell he's using up any reserve energy he has as he's beginning to tire, but he's not finished yet. "Just go."

I take a step back out of pure shock. "Thomas. I'm only trying..."

He swings his irked eyes on me, and I don't recognise the person I'm seeing. "Trying to what? Help? Well, you're not. There's no point in you coming here anymore."

His words cut me deep. He's never spoken to me like this before. He's never even raised his voice at me in the whole two years we've been together.

My eyes well up. "You... you don't mean that. You're just frustrated with your situation. Things will get better if you just have a little bit of hope."

"I've lost all hope, Fran. In myself. In us. I'm done." He looks away from me.

The feeling in my gut tells me all I need to know, but I find myself asking anyway. "What are you say... saying, Tom?" My tears begin to fall like an endless river.

"I think you know what I'm saying. It's over between us. I don't want you coming to see me anymore." I sense the finality in his words.

I take a timid step towards him. "But... I love you."

"Love? How can you love this?" He points to himself.

"I don't care about any of that."

"Well, I do. Being stuck in this place has given me time

to think about a lot of stuff. I realised I don't love you anymore."

I've never felt pain in my chest like this before. I can practically feel my heart breaking into pieces, and there's nothing I can do about it.

"Leave, Fran, and don't come back. I mean it."

My legs almost give way, but I try to stay strong and hope I don't fall to the floor.

I have no words. I feel numb.

So, I do the only thing I can. I turn and run from him. I run from the only person I've ever opened myself up to and who I let steal my heart.

I'm rushing out the main doors, breathless, when I hear my name being called.

"Fran, sweetie. Whatever's the matter?" Alison comes to stand in front of me.

"It's over. Thomas has ended our relationship and he doesn't want me to come back," I cry.

"I'm sure he didn't mean it. He's got a lot to deal with at the moment. He'll be..."

I don't want to listen to her make up excuses for him. "It's definite. I'm sorry, but I need to get out of here."

I wipe my eyes and run away from Tom's parents. Run away from the person I gave my all to, leaving a trail of broken pieces of my heart along the way.

Chapter Three

"I'm in the taxi now. I'll be there in five." I put the phone down on my best friend, Hannah, placing it back in my clutch bag for safe keeping.

Less than five minutes later, I'm pulling up outside the restaurant in town.

It's my thirtieth birthday. Hannah is treating me to a meal and a few drinks afterwards. I party in style, as you can tell. If it was up to me, I'd be at home wearing my winter warmers with a takeaway and a film, but Hannah was adamant I was going out.

I pay the taxi driver and jump out of the cab.

"Hey, you look great." Hannah greets me with a hug.

I opted for a black pair of skinny jeans, a thick, fitted woolly jumper, and black heeled boots.

"You don't look so bad yourself." I pull out from the hug. "It's freezing. Shall we head in?"

"Yeah. I'm starving and in need of alcohol." Hannah walks ahead of me.

I'm looking down at my feet as I walk through the door so I don't trip and fall flat on my face. As I look up, I bump into someone trying to walk out, making them drop a set of keys.

"I'm so sorry." I bend down to pick up the keys at the same time the other person does, causing me to head-butt them.

"Ouch!" I rub my head with my free hand and stand back up.

"Shit, sorry."

I know that voice.

Where do I know it from?

With the keys now in my hand, I lift my head and almost stumble backwards.

"Thomas?"

Of all the people I could bump into, it had to be him.

"Fran? Wow, what's it been?" From his facial expression, I can tell he's trying to work it out.

"Almost twelve years. Look at you."

"Yeah, walking and everything," he says awkwardly.

"I see the physiotherapist worked his magic, then?"

I'm ecstatic that he pulled through and he's back on his feet again. I can't imagine what he must have put himself through to get to where he is now. Jesus, not only is he walking by himself, he's filled out too. The muscles in his arms are screaming at me to touch them. I really want to, just to see if he's real. It's been so long and he's changed a lot.

Part of me feels bitter towards him for giving up on us so quickly. Maybe if he stuck with it and made more of an effort with me, things would have worked out differently.

Regardless of that, I wouldn't take anything away from him and how well he's recovered from his injuries.

"He did. Took a long time, but I got there in the end." He shrugs like it was nothing.

"Good, I'm glad." I hear Hannah calling my name. I hold my finger up to say one second and turn back to Thomas. "It was nice seeing you, Thomas." With a soft smile, I turn and start to walk away, but his hand on my shoulder stops me, along with the shiver his touch left on my skin.

"Erm, Fran..."

"Yep?" I scold myself for the hope I hear in my words.

"Can I have my keys, please?" I look down at my hands. I'm still jiggling the keys.

"Oh, God. Yeah, here." I hand his keys over. The moment his hand touches mine, I feel an electric shock, but the good kind.

"Thanks."

"No problem. Bye, Tom." I don't give him time to reply. I turn away from him again and walk over to Hannah.

All of a sudden, I'm not feeling up to eating.

I can't believe after all these years I still recognised him. I mean, so much time has passed, but apart from his amazing physique, he's the same boy I left in the hospital all those years ago.

Only now, he's all man. And what a man he is.

I feel myself getting hot and bothered thinking about him.

I know I only bumped into him, but I always hoped that I would see him again. Hoped that one day we could at least be friends.

I shake my head. I'm getting ahead of myself.

I sit opposite Hannah at the table. She's already looking over the menu, and thankfully, she doesn't ask about the guy I bumped into, and I'm not telling either.

For the rest of the evening, I put Thomas to the back of my mind and try to enjoy my night and my birthday.

You're only thirty once.

Chapter Four

I wake the next day with the headache to end all headaches. I can't remember drinking that much. I vaguely remember ordering a couple of vodka and Cokes with my meal. I recall flashing strobe lights in the club Hannah dragged me to.

"Oh, God." Flash after flash of shot glasses burn into my memory, making me gag.

The rest of the night is hazy. I don't even know how I got home, or into bed, for that matter.

Speaking of which, the bed dips on the other side of me. I scrunch my eyes closed in horror.

I've brought a guy home. I never bring guys to my house. I don't do the whole one-night stand thing.

I hold my breath while they rise from their sleep.

They throw the duvet back swiftly. "Jesus, my head is sore."

I release the breath I was holding in relief. "Hannah?

Thank Christ. I thought you were a dude." I prop my pillows up and lie back down, facing the ceiling.

"Wow, thanks. I know I feel rough, so no doubt, I look it too. But a bloke, really? I'm insulted." She places her hand over her heart as if I've wounded her.

"I don't remember getting home. I panicked thinking I'd pulled and brought someone home with me."

"Please. You didn't have time to pull anyone. You were too busy telling me all about some... Thomas? Who the fuck is Thomas?"

I cover my eyes with my hands, annoyed with myself for bringing him up in the first place. I vowed never to talk about him the moment I walked away from him. It was twelve years ago.

I guess bumping into him last night brought up old memories. Memories I've never been able to bury.

"I need coffee and paracetamol before I can get into any of that." I groan as I swing my legs from the bed and sit up. "Woah, dizzy much?" I carefully make my way to the bedroom door. "You want a coffee?"

"Obviously. What a stupid thing to ask." Hannah begins to get out of the bed.

We head downstairs with our tails between our legs.

I've not felt this rough in a long time.

I fill the kettle while she grabs two mugs from the cupboard. I reach for the coffee, but when I remove the lid, I don't see any coffee granules.

"Fucking hell. I'm out of coffee," I huff.

"You've not got any paracetamol either." Hannah adds to my misery.

"I can't get through the day without both. I'll die."

"You'll have to go to the shop and grab some. I'll go

make your bed and sort something for us to eat. You go get dressed."

I do as I'm told and get ready. The shop is only a short drive away, but I probably shouldn't drive in my condition, so I choose to walk instead. Maybe the fresh air will make my foggy head better.

I quickly throw on a pair of joggers and a thick hoodie, tie my hair up in a messy bun, and dash to the bedroom to brush my teeth.

I pop my head into the kitchen to Hannah and tell her I'm off, then head out the door.

Chapter Five

I traipse into the shop with urgency, looking around for the aisles I need.

"Coffee, coffee, coffee. Ah-ha." Locating the coffee granules, I put them in my basket and turn in the direction I need for the tablets.

I turn into the aisle with all the medicine, scanning the shelves for the boxes of paracetamol.

They happen to be on the top shelf and, as someone who's only five-foot tall, I can't reach them. I look up and down the aisle, hoping to see a member of staff.

I almost die on the spot when I identify Thomas walking my way. I have to do a double-take, just to make sure.

Yep, it's definitely Thomas.

I lean my body away from him and pretend I'm busy looking for something.

"Fran?" Great. I was expecting him to just pass me by, unaware of my presence.

I plaster on a smile and try to hide just how dreadful I feel. "Oh, Thomas. Fancy seeing you here."

"Yeah, two days in a row. How are you?" I feel him assessing me from head to toe.

"I've felt better," I tell him honestly. I never could lie to him; he's always been able to tell.

"You had a rough night last night, huh?" he asks with a soft laugh.

I shrug. "Something like that."

"Happy birthday. It was yesterday, wasn't it? I'm guessing your head is sore."

He remembered? And how does he know my heading is banging?

"Yes, I... how?"

"You're in the medicine aisle. You never were good with hangovers when you were younger. I see nothing has changed."

"Some things have," I mutter under my breath. I don't know why I said that. I'm not usually that direct or hurtful with people. I hate myself for being so blunt with him. I guess a part of me still holds a grudge against him for how he left everything between us and how easy it was for him to let it go like it never meant anything to him.

It did to me, He meant everything to me, and I would have gone to the ends of the Earth for him if he asked me to.

"What was that?" he asks, leaning forward.

"Oh, I said, could you pass me that?" I point up at the paracetamol on the top shelf because I can't think of anything else to say and I don't want to start reflecting on my wounds that never healed in the middle of a shop aisle.

"Sure. You want one or two?" He has the nerve to smirk at me. As much as I don't want to admit the effect he has on me, it has my insides turning to mush.

How can he still affect me after all this time?

I hold up two of my fingers, having lost the ability to speak.

He pops them in my basket alongside the coffee jar.

"Thank you." I make a hasty retreat, heading for the tills.

Thankfully, he doesn't follow.

I pay for my goods and leave the shop as if my arse is on fire.

Why, of all days, when I look and feel like shit, do I have to bump into him?

My morning goes from bad to worse when the heavens open up on me the moment I leave the shop.

"Great."

I hear my name being called in the distance, so I pick up my pace a bit. I don't need Thomas seeing me as a drowned rat as well as being hungover.

A car pulls up alongside me as I go to cross the road. The window is wound down. "Fran, jump in." Thomas's velvety voice hits my ears.

"That's okay. I'm only up the road," I shout over the pounding rain.

"Just get in the car, Fran. It's pelting down." He's persistent, I'll give him that.

In the end, I give up. I open the door and jump into his car. "Thank you."

He pulls out of the car park and onto the main road. "Where to?"

I reel off my address, not daring to look at him.

The car is filled with an awkward silence.

"So, how have you been?" Thomas asks.

"Erm, fine. You?" I wipe my hand across my face to remove the wet hair from my cheek.

"I've been good. Finally got on my feet—literally—a few years ago," he jokes, as if trying to ease the tension. "I work for my dad's company now. You remember his steel-work company?"

I smile at the thought of Julian and Alison. God, I do miss them. "Yeah, I remember. That's good."

"Yeah, it's taking off at the minute."

"How are your parents?" I steer the conversation to something lighter, and I want to hear about them.

"They're doing well. I told them I bumped into you last night. My mum would love to catch up with you." My tears build at the mention of his parents. The last time I saw them and spoke to them broke my heart. It broke my heart more that I didn't really get to say goodbye to them.

I wear my emotions on my sleeve, and no matter how Thomas and I ended our relationship, I wish I'd stayed in touch with them. "I'd love that," I admit.

"How about next week, then?" I nearly take my neck off my shoulders as I swing my gaze from the window to him. He's watching me, then he looks back at the road again. "What?"

"Nothing. I just didn't think you'd say that." I want to say yes as I've missed his parents something rotten, and it would be lovely to see how they're doing. It wasn't their fault Thomas broke up with me, but seeing his parents again will open up old wounds, and it would mean seeing Tom again.

Would I be setting myself up to be heartbroken again?

I can't go through all that again, no matter how much I find myself wanting to say yes.

"Look, I know I wasn't a nice person the last you saw me, but I had so much to deal with. I didn't want to put you through it all and drag you down with me. I don't regret sending you away. Not back then, anyway."

"Thomas, I..."

He cuts me off. "Wait. Let me finish what I was going to say." I nod my head and stay silent, even if dragging up old memories is the last thing I want to do right now.

"I was in a really bad way after I told you to leave. I got depressed and was all set to give up on the physiotherapy sessions because I wasn't getting any further forward with it. I felt like I was going backwards most days, but do you wanna know what kept me pushing me on?"

I shake my head, not having a clue.

"It was you, Fran. The whole time, I was thinking about you. How I treated you. The look of devastation on your face before you walked out of the room. I know my words cut you deep, but I didn't mean any of them. I never fell out of love with you. I just couldn't let you watch me suffering like that. It almost killed me." I don't miss his knuckles turning white from the grip he's got on the steering wheel.

I'm stunned silent.

"Everything I told you was a lie, but I knew I needed to hurt you to get you to leave. It's because I loved you that I needed to hurt you, Fran."

"I don't get why you're telling me all this now. It's been twelve years."

"I don't know either. I guess when I saw you last night, I realised I needed to give you an explanation. I at least owed you that much, and I always hoped that one day, if I ever did see you, that I would give you that and an apology. I'm sorry."

When I look out the window, I notice he's pulled the car over and we're now outside my house.

"What are you saying, Thomas?"

Yeah, okay, I deserved an explanation, and he's given me that, but he should have given me that twelve years ago, not now.

"I can't go through all this with you again. It took me so long to get over you, Tom. I'm still trying to achieve that to this day. What you did to me broke my heart, and it's still broken now." The tears I've been holding back begin to trail down my face.

"I don't want to upset you, Fran. I made a promise to myself that when I was better, when I was me again, I'd give you what you deserve. It was wrong of me to treat you the way I did, and there wasn't a day that went by that I didn't think about you and how I ended our relationship." He switches off the engine and turns in his seat towards me.

I can't do this anymore. "What do you want from me, Thomas? You caused me nothing but misery back then, and you're causing me nothing but pain now. I gave you my everything when we were together, and you broke me. I don't know if I can ever get over that."

"All I want is to make things right with you. What I did to you, it's been a dark cloud hovering above my head since the day I told you to leave. I guess I just need clarity. I wouldn't ever forgive myself if I never told you how sorry I am, and if I couldn't put things right." He takes my hand in his, rubbing his thumb lovingly over my fingers. "Can you forgive me?"

Can I forgive him?

Can I forget all the pain and heartache he caused me?

Does he deserve my forgiveness?

"Thomas... I... I don't know if I can. I mean, I appreciate you explaining your reasoning behind your actions, but that doesn't suddenly make everything right. I'm not the same person you knew back then. I've changed."

"I'm not asking for you to forgive me straight away. Just think about what I've said. Give me a chance to make it right. Not for me, but for you. I lost a part myself the day you left, and I know that's all down to me, but I did it because I loved and respected you too much to let you go through the ups and downs with me. Please, just try to see things from my perspective. Would you have wanted me to watch you struggling day in and day out? To witness your failure? Having to help you back up when you fell flat on your face? I know you wouldn't, Fran."

When he put it that way, maybe I would have done the same. I would have pushed him away. I guess I never looked at the whole picture until now.

"Fran, if I had let you stay, watching me fail at the most basic of things, I would have ended up hurting you more. Not only that, but you might have found it all hard too. I thought by ordering you to go it would make it easier to get over you. But I guess I was wrong."

"What do you mean?" I lock my gaze with his.

All the hope I'd felt of us finding each other again washes over me like a tidal wave.

"I mean, I still love you, Fran. I never stopped loving you." My breath hitches, getting stuck in my throat. "Seeing you again has only intensified those feelings."

I'm speechless.

I've dreamt about this moment most nights since I walked away from Thomas. I should know what to say to him, but I don't.

I've been living in hope for so long that I can't compute what is happening in front of me. I never thought this day would come.

"I know things will never be the way they were before, but neither of us is the same person we were. All I want is for you to tell me there's hope for us in your future. Even if that means we're just friends. If that's what it takes to have you back in my life, then I'll take it, Fran. Please don't shut me out altogether like I did to you. I don't think I could take it. Not now I've seen you again."

I don't say anything for a long time. I'm trying to digest what he's asking of me.

"You don't need to decide now," he adds.

"Good, because I don't know what to say."

"How about I take you out for lunch next week? Just as friends, to catch up." I hear the desperation in his voice.

I can do that, right?

Have lunch with a friend.

"Okay, just as friends, but I'm not making any promises." I need to make that clear.

"Thank you."

We exchange numbers, and Tom tells me he'll be in touch.

I release my seatbelt and offer him a soft smile, then jump out of his car.

I know I shouldn't, but I'm looking forward to seeing him again.

I can already feel my heart breaking all over again.

Chapter Six

The past four days have dragged by. Whether it's because all I could think about was meeting Thomas for lunch today, I don't know.

Now, all I can think about is what to wear.

"Will you relax? You're giving me whiplash with all your pacing. It's a casual lunch date with a friend," Hannah says.

"It's not a date, Han. You saying it's a date only makes me feel worse about it. You're making me nervous."

I frantically pull clothes out of my wardrobe onto the bed, still not having decided what to wear.

"From what you told me about him the day he dropped you off from nipping the shop, I'd beg to differ."

I stop dead in my tracks. "Why would you say that?" I stare blankly at her, now in a panic.

"What? I'm only stating the obvious. With how you said you left things with him all those years ago to everything he said to you in the car, it makes perfect sense. He's still in love with you, he said so, and no matter how much you try and convince yourself otherwise, you're still in love with him." She starts pulling the imaginary lint off her legs to avoid looking at me.

She makes it all sound so simple. It's anything but.

"It doesn't matter. I can't get my heart broken like that again. I'd never survive him breaking my heart twice. Jesus, it would be broken beyond repair." I start hyperventilating at the thought of going through it all again.

"You're thinking too much into this, Fran. Just go meet him, have lunch, and catch up for old time's sake. There is no expectation from him, so you're worrying over nothing." She shrugs her shoulder.

"Yeah, you're right. I can do this. I can be friends with him. I mean, he was a big part of my life. It would be nice to reconnect with him as just friends." I don't know who I'm trying to convince more, me or Hannah.

"Atta girl. Now *that's* sorted, can we get back to what you're going to wear? I don't think jogging bottoms and an old t-shirt will suffice, do you?"

Forty minutes later, I'm dressed, hair done, with a light layer of make-up on.

I've opted for a pair of denim jeans and a long cream jumper as the weather is still bitterly cold. I finish off my look with a pair of white Converse pumps and I'm ready to go.

On time, the doorbell rings, announcing Thomas's arrival.

"I'll get it." Hannah practically runs for the door, giving me no time to react. "You grab your bag and phone and I'll make sure I give him the best friend speech." She runs off, laughing.

"Don't you dare!" I shout after her. I know she heard me because she laughs harder.

I hear Thomas's carefree laughter coming up the stairs as I make my way down to him.

Hannah must hear me coming, because the moment my feet hit the ground off the last step, she turns and mouths 'hot' at me. I scrunch my eyes up at her. My warning for her to behave. She sticks her tongue out at me and once again mouths 'no fun,' forcing a smile to break out over my face.

"Fran. Wow, you look amazing," Thomas greets me.

"You don't look so bad yourself."

That's an understatement if there ever was one. He looks breathtakingly gorgeous. His jeans hug his thighs, and the long-sleeved shirt he's wearing clings to every single ridge of muscle. He's hot with a capital h.

"You ready to go?" Tom asks, breaking my perving session.

I shake the thoughts from my mind and lick my suddenly dry lips.

"Yes, yes. Sorry, I was miles away. I'm all set. Hannah, lock up after you leave and re-post the keys. I have mine on me," I instruct over my shoulder as I head for the door.

"Yes, boss. You two have fun. But not too much."

I slam the door shut with the hope Thomas didn't hear her little dig.

Thankfully, he doesn't say anything.

And we're off.

Chapter Seven

"Pizza Palace? This is where you're taking me for lunch?" I find myself laughing like a schoolgirl.

"Yeah, why not? I remember you loved pizza when we were together. Has that changed?" He starts to fidget in the driver's seat, unsure if he's made a mistake already.

"No. I love pizza. I just didn't expect to come here."

"Where did you think I'd take you?"

"I don't know." I shrug.

"Come on." Thomas unclips his seatbelt and gets out of his car, laughing at me.

We find a seat in the restaurant and begin to scan over the menus. I'm starving.

"Go crazy. It's on me."

I peer over my menu and see Tom watching me intently. "How did you know?"

"You keep banging your lips together. If I remember correctly, you used to do that when you were starving."

I hide my face behind the menu, trying to conceal my blush. "I do not."

I don't get to hide for long, "And now, you're trying to hide your embarrassment." Thomas pulls the booklet from my face, confirming his theory. "See. You're as red as a beetroot."

"Can we change the subject? What are you having to eat?"

His hand lingers on my side of the table for a long pause before he pulls it away and sits back in his chair.

"We could order a half and half and some garlic cheese melts on the side. If you wanted to, that is?" he asks nervously.

The Thomas I knew wasn't a nervous person at all.

Maybe he's nervous because he doesn't want to mess this up. Maybe he's trying his best so we can be friends.

I decide to just enjoy the afternoon and be in his company. If it goes well, then I can see us being friends. And in time, I can possibly forgive him. I'll never fully forget, but I might be able to forgive him.

"Sounds good. Let's do that," I say with a stern nod. He blasts me with his megawatt smile, almost knocking me off my chair.

Our meal arrives, and the rest of the afternoon goes smoothly.

We had a genuine conversation, where I let him do most of the talking. He asked me what I do for a living, if I still have the same hobbies I had when we were together. And I asked the same things.

It was easy, and not once did he bring up any bad memories for me. I had a blast with him.

I catch a glimpse of the clock on the wall and realise we've been talking for over two hours.

Wow, where has the time gone?

Before I know it, Tom has paid the bill, and we're back in his car, parked outside my flat.

"Thank you for today. I had a lot of fun," I tell him honestly.

"It was my pleasure. So did I. No pressure, but can I see you again?"

My insides flutter. "As friends?" I need to clarify.

"Yeah, just as friends. I don't want you to feel like I'm pushing you for more because I'm not. I just wanna spend some time with you."

I don't hesitate. "Okay, sure. Hannah and I are going indoor rock climbing this weekend. Why don't you tag along? It will be fun." I can hear the enthusiasm in my voice.

"Have you become an adrenaline junkie now?" He swings his body my way.

"No, but I went with Hannah once and I fell in love with it. We make it a regular thing now."

"Cool. What time?"

I tell him where and when and begin to get out of the car, but Thomas places his hand on my arm, delicately halting my movements. I sit back down and face him.

"Thank you. For giving me some of your time. I know it wasn't an easy decision to make, but I appreciate it."

He arches towards me, and without thinking, I touch my lips to his. It's only a brief peck, as he pulls away from me.

"I was going for a kiss on the cheek, but whatever takes your fancy," he jokes.

"Oh, God, I'm so sorry." I cover my face with my hands in complete horror. "I don't even know what I was thinking." I've never been so embarrassed.

"I guess some things never change. Your lips still feel the same as they did all those years ago."

The sultry tone in his voice works wonders on my already throbbing core from just that single kiss.

I need to get out of here.

"I need to go. I'm sorry." I can't even bring myself to look at him.

I swing the car door open, almost taking it from its hinges, and throw myself out, shutting it behind me. I can hear him calling my name in desperation, but I don't stop.

At this point, I'll run until my feet bleed.

Chapter Eight

No sooner am I through the door and locking it does the banging start.

"Fran, open up. Please," Thomas shouts from the other side of the wood.

I can't bring myself to face him. Not after the stunt I just pulled.

How could I be so stupid?

"Just go. Please leave me alone." I run up the stairs and away from the man who has always owned my heart. As I close the bedroom door, I hear shouting one more time.

"I'll leave, but just know, I refuse to let you go again."

I sigh in relief and watch him walk back down the path from my bedroom window.

Why does he have to be so hot still? He couldn't have been fat or bald now, could he?

My head fills with thoughts of what his body will look like now under those tight-fitting clothes. My chest gets tight and my thighs rub against each other. Shit, I need to stop this daydreaming.

It's then I notice he's looking up at me with a worried expression on his face.

Embarrassed, I step back out of view at the same time my phone starts ringing.

"I can hear your phone ringing, Fran. Will you please just answer me?" he pleads, for all the neighbours to hear.

I don't fancy any of the neighbours getting involved, so I release my frustration with a growl and swipe the screen. "Thomas, I don't want to speak to you," I all but shout through the speaker.

"Why? What have I done wrong?"

How is the tone of his voice affecting me so much when I should be anything but turned on right now?

"It wasn't you, it was me. I thought when you leant towards me that you were going to kiss me, so I acted on instinct and... and I got it wrong. I'm sorry." I dare a glance back out the window.

The cocky prick is smirking up at me. "Why are you sorry? Just because we kissed—a very brief but enticing kiss, may I add—you didn't need to run from me." The more I stare at him, the bigger his smile gets.

"This is not funny, Thomas. Stop smiling at me," I bark down the phone, yet I can't stop my lips from twitching.

"Was that a teeny tiny smirk pulling at your lips then, Fran?" I don't need to be looking at him to know his smirk is turning into a laugh. "Look, some of your neighbours are giving me worried looks. Can you let me in, please? I promise I won't laugh or make you any more embarrassed than you already are."

I rest my head against the glass while I contemplate

what to do. He makes a cross over his heart to tell me he means it.

"You promise?"

"Yes, Fran. I promise."

"Okay, fine. But one slight comment and I'll kick you out again." My threat is weak, but I make it anyway.

I turn around on my heel and head back to the front door. When I open it, Thomas is already standing there. We've both still got phones attached to our ears.

"Hi." He speaks into his phone and at me at the same time, earning him a little chuckle.

"Hi back."

Tom pockets his phone, advances on me, and boxes me in between the wall and his huge frame.

"What... what are you doing?" I stutter.

"I have a feeling I might embarrass myself, but it's a risk worth taking. Don't be mad."

"Why would I be m..."

His lips crash down on mine without a second thought.

Chapter Nine

I should push him away. My head is telling me to, but my heart and body have other ideas, and they're taking centre stage.

I drop my phone and wrap my arms around his neck as he lifts me under my arse and walks us into the living room.

He parks his bum down on the sofa with me still attached to him, so I'm straddling his legs.

My tongue dances with his in a frenzy. It's messy but feels so damn good I can't bring myself to stop it.

It's in this moment that I realise no matter how hard I try to keep Thomas at arm's length, being friends with him will never be enough.

I know the more I push, the more Thomas will pull.

Is there any reason for me to drag out the inevitable?

If Thomas is the same person I knew when I was eighteen, then I know for a fact he won't give up on me. When Thomas wants something, he goes for it until he gets it.

From what he's already confessed the two times we've met, he never gave up on me. The only thing holding me back is that Thomas has the potential to break my heart all over again. I don't know if I'll recover from that kind of heartache again.

Tom's hand riding up my top has me halting the kiss. I press my palms flat against his chest, both of us breathless from the heated lip-locking.

"Thomas, I don't think we should be doing this." I see the disappointment on his face as clear as day, but he tries his best to hide it.

"You're right. I'm sorry."

I climb off his lap and sit next to him, my body alight with a slight buzz from being so damn close to him.

"I don't know how I'm meant to feel. My body wants one thing, but my head says to stop before you hurt me again." Getting to my feet, I begin to pace the living room.

"Look, Fran, what we do or don't do now is irrelevant because we both know that now I've had a taste of you, I can't and won't be going anywhere. So, fight it all you want, but I'm sticking around. I know you want me to, too." He comes over to me and wraps his arms around me, stopping me from wearing a hole in the carpet. "Just say we can try. That's all I want. A chance to try. You're the love of my life, Fran. You always have been."

My eyes start leaking and my knees go weak. He must notice because he takes a firm grip on my arms. He steers me back to the couch, where I perch myself on the edge. He parts my legs and sits on his haunches in the gap he created there, wiping the stray tears from my cheeks.

"I know we had something special the first time round, but what if we can't get it back? We're different people now." I don't want to be negative, but if I'm to agree to this, then I need the facts.

With his hands still on my cheeks, he kisses my head, then my cheeks, followed by my nose, and ending with a peck to my lips.

"We can work it out as we go along. I understand now that we're not the same people, but that doesn't mean my love for you has changed. What's to say this time around won't be even better?"

His declaration warms my heart.

"I can't just fall back in love with you, regardless of whether I ever stopped loving you at all. But after seeing you and talking to you, I know I wouldn't be happy again without you in my life. I was prepared to just be friends, but the more I think about it, I don't know if I'd ever be satisfied with that. Especially if you ever had a girlfriend. I don't know how I'd feel about that." Just the thought of seeing Thomas with another girl on his arm fills me with dread.

"The only girl I want to end up with is you, Fran. Please, just say you'll try. I think we'd be great together this time around. We're more mature and wiser now. We know who we want to be and what we want in life. For me, that's you. I thought seeing you and apologising to you would be enough, but the moment I laid eyes on you, I just knew I wouldn't be able to walk away again." He lays his heart out on the line, and I can't tell him I want different things in life than him because I would be lying to him as well as myself.

I bite the bullet and put myself out there, hoping for the best. Hoping he doesn't break my heart again.

"Okay, I'll try. We take this slow. We can't just pick up where we left off, Thomas. Do you understand that?" I swear I can feel my heart beating out of my chest.

"We'll go as slow as you want. Cross my heart."

"None of this." I point from his body to my own to indicate what I'm saying. "I'm not giving you the goodies until we've had at least five dates," I say sternly.

"No sex. Got it. What about kissing you? Do I have to wait for that too?"

My face lights up at his obvious dismay. "We can kiss, but nothing more," I tell him with a smile.

The relief on his features is adorable. "Oh, thank God." With that said, he grabs me by the neck and pulls me towards him. His lips smack against mine deliciously.

Why I made a five-date rule, I'll never know. I don't think I'll last long myself.

Chapter Ten

It's the evening of our fifth date.

I don't know how we managed to make it here, but we did. The whole time we were sitting in the restaurant, neither of us could contain our excitement. It was like being back at school. The butterflies I felt reminded me of my first kiss with Thomas. I was so giddy and full of nerves.

The whole drive back to my place was filled with untold apprehension. The fire I felt in the pit of my stomach was enough to make me want to tear off his shirt and jump his bones.

All the fidgeting Thomas was doing during the meal and now on the drive home is proof that he's feeling the same.

We're just pulling into my street when he speaks for the first time since we started the drive back.

"I have to know. The anticipation is killing me, Fran. It was our fifth date tonight. Not that I want to pressure you or anything, but... fuck, I want you so bad. Your body tells me you want me just the same. Am I right?" I can feel the nerves coming off him in waves. I want to scream out to him, 'YES! Take me. I'm ready and all yours,' but I'm hot and flustered and just as nervous.

"I want you too." My simple reply affects him, as his knuckles turn white from gripping the steering wheel, and he puts his foot down.

Within seconds, we grind to a screeching halt outside my house. The engine is off and the keys are in his hand before I can get my seatbelt off and pick my bag up from the footwell.

My door is swung open and my hand is grasped, pulling me from the car as soon as my first foot hits the concrete.

"Slow down. We have all night," I squeal, but in truth, I'm just as eager.

The front door is barely shut before I'm pushed up against it with abandonment. I'm both excited and a little scared. I've always been a vanilla sex kind of girl, but Tom is showing signs of wanting it a little rough.

Tom throws me over his shoulder fireman-style and carries me straight up the stairs.

"You don't want a coffee, then?" I giggle.

"Not unless it's from your body." I'm unceremoniously dropped onto the bed. "I want to worship you here, now, and always, Fran. You okay with that?"

I nod because I'm lost for words.

The fire burning in his eyes sends them almost black with desire as he strips me of my clothes at lightning speed.

I groan as his fingers slide deftly over my skin when he leans over me, his lips following the same pattern. I grab the hem of his shirt and relieve him of it, then undo his jeans and push them as far as I can down his strong, firm thighs, taking his boxers with them. He kicks them off the rest of the way, then continues working my body up.

"I'm ready, Tom. I don't need foreplay. Just worship me, please."

He spreads my legs and puts himself at my entrance, balancing himself on his arms that are on either side of my head. Looking straight into my eyes, he thrusts in deep, filling and stretching me to accommodate his size.

"Christ, you're so tight. I don't think this first time will last."

I blush as he thrusts slowly in and out in rhythm. It's been a while since I had the cobwebs blown away, but I'll keep that to myself.

"I don't think I'll last either, but there's always round two," I offer out of the blue.

Round two? That's so unlike me. I've always been a once a night kind of girl. Or has it been that I've just not had the right partner until now?

He takes my nipple in his mouth. His hips gradually get faster and faster until they become pistons of destruction, hammering into me deep and hard.

I scream out as the pleasure becomes too much. I'm on the edge of my orgasm as he stops his thrusts completely, taking the orgasmic feeling away. Just as quick as he stopped, he starts to work me back up again. His hand roams my body, making my skin tingle in pure delight. His teeth graze over my sensitive bud before he sucks it back into his mouth, and just like a freight train, my orgasm is within reaching distance. He must feel it too because he picks the pace up. I've got a feeling he isn't stopping this one as he grunts his way home. One... two... three rough thrusts and we both come together, our blissful orgasms taking us off somewhere above and beyond.

"Wow!" is all I can manage.

"Baby, get ready. Round two is definitely coming. This time, I will be taking my sweet time with you and this sinful as fuck body."

And just like that, I'm ready for him to take me all over again.

Chapter Eleven

I wake the next day happy, sated, and oh so satisfied. Last night couldn't have gone any better. The night with Thomas was hot, steamy, and out of this world. He made me feel like I was his everything and then some. He took me to highs I never thought possible.

He was careful, yet demanding.

It was a night filled with passion and so much raw tension.

It felt like we were making up for missing the past twelve years of each other's lives, never mind our bodies.

I can feel the weight of Tom's arm wrapped around me as he softly snores in a deep sleep.

I twist my waist slowly, so as not to wake him. Knowing I've succeeded, I take my time appreciating his devilish good looks.

From his golden blonde hair, his surprisingly perfect-shaped eyebrows, his sharp, chiselled jawline, to his kissable lips. He turns over slightly, taking the cover with him, which gives me the perfect view of his sculpted abs and dusting of chest hair.

Just perfection. I guess he always has been.

It was his personality and caring nature that drew me to him back in high school. His physique is just an added bonus for me to enjoy now.

"I can feel you checking me out. You're making me self-conscious."

I almost jump off the bed in fright, but seeing his lip turn up on one side in a lazy half-asleep smile melts me into the mattress.

"What do you possibly have to feel self-conscious about?" I ask as I drag my finger down his chest leisurely.

"When it comes to you, lots of things. I don't want to be a disappointment or feel like I've failed you." His admission shocks me into silence. "I know I've let you down before, and in the worst way possible, but I promise I'll never do that to you again, Fran."

I feel my heart breaking. I can't let him do this to himself any longer.

"Thomas, that was all in the past. You need to stop blaming yourself for what happened. You weren't yourself; you had a lot of shit to deal with, and you did what you thought was right back then. Stop beating yourself up. If we want this to work between us, for us to have a future together, then you need to forgive yourself. Please. Do that for me?" I plead for him to listen to me.

"How can I forgive myself when you can't? I need to make it right with you before I can do that."

The words are out of my mouth without having to think about them. "I forgive you, Thomas."

The shock on his face is clear.

"You're just saying that. You..."

"I'm telling you the truth. I forgive you. I don't want you to ever mention the day I walked out on you at the hospital again. I shouldn't have given up on you so easily. I've come to realise that I'm partly to blame. I should have fought you on it and not given up so easily. If you can forgive me for that, then I can forgive you for your mistakes."

For the first time since seeing Thomas again, I'm admitting to playing a part in my heart getting broken. But the person who broke it is staring right at me and has the ability to mend and forge it back together again.

He tenderly strokes my cheek with the tip of his finger. "There's nothing to forgive, Fran. I love you so much."

"I love you more than is humanly possible, Thomas. Always have, always will." Then I kiss him with everything I have.

There's hope for us yet.

Also by K J Ellis

The Counterpunch Series

Isaak

Mr & Mrs. Brookes

Owen

Saxon

Don't Hold a Grudge
by KM Lowe

Chapter One

CARTER
TEN YEARS AGO

"You can't always think about yourself, Carter. Your family needs you here. You have a duty to take over the family business!" yells my dad.

I sigh. "How can you stand there and say I don't think about the family? I'm nineteen next week. I've given up all my spare time for you and Mum. I babysit your foster kids whenever you have a business gathering. I don't have a life. But I know for sure I'm not interested in business. Takeovers and mergers bore me to tears. I've been accepted into med school. Why can't you be happy for me?"

"We're your family."

"That will never change, but I am going to med school in September."

I might have been a pushover over the years, but now it's my turn to live my life and do what I want. I want to be a doctor and my dad's controlling won't deter me.

"Don't expect me to help you out!"

My dad storms off, leaving me and my mum.

CHAPTER SIXTY-EIGHT

"I'm sorry, Carter."

"Sorry." I snigger. "Sorry for not sticking up for me? Sorry for not supporting your son? I'm done, Mum. I'm going to stay with Uncle Jack for a few days, because one of us is going to do or say something there's no coming back from."

"Carter..."

I'm walking away because I'm angry. My mother has always been the anchor in this family, but lately, my father calls the shots and no one bats an eye. I can't live my life like that.

Life has changed and I can't wait to leave for university.

Eight weeks later, I'm standing in my Uncle Jack's office to say goodbye. My father's office is directly across from here, and he shakes his head the moment I walk in. We haven't spoken to one another in eight weeks, since the day I left to stay with Uncle Jack. I doubt we ever will agree on this matter. I'm past caring. I've made my mind up, and I'm not going back on it.

"All set, son?"

"Sure am. The car's all packed and I'm ready to set off."

"You know where I am if you need anything, right?" He pats my shoulder.

"I do, but you've already done so much to help me."

"Let me be the judge of that. I'm just glad you have one adult in your life who can help shape your future and let you follow your dreams."

That makes two of us, because without Uncle Jack, I don't have a clue where I would be. I would have given into my dad a long time ago, but with my uncle's support,

I was able to stand up for myself and be the person I want to be.

"Thank you, Uncle Jack. Keep in touch."

"You too, son." He pulls me into his arms.

I turn to leave the office and my dad is showing a man into his. He looks me up and down, enters his room, and closes the door without a word.

I can't believe we've got to this stage, but I'm not giving in to his tactics. I'm not a child anymore.

I can stand on my own two feet. The Cowell genes have some benefits. We're strong, independent people. We don't let anyone stand on our toes. We live the life we want.

Life's for living.

Chapter Two

CARTER
ELEVEN YEARS LATER

"Come on, Doc. You have to do something for your thirtieth birthday in two weeks," says Joe, my work colleague and best friend of several years.

"I'll probably spend it in theatre. There really is no point planning something; you know how it is around here. Work comes first, and there's always someone that needs my attention."

"You're a spoil sport. You're no fun now you're getting older."

"It's called growing up. You should try it." I punch his arm.

We bump into our boss, Steven, just as we round the corner into the ward.

"Glad I've caught you, Carter. Can you do a consult with me today?"

"Sure. What time?"

"Two p.m., but if you drop by thirty minutes earlier, I'll fill you in on any major details."

"See you then."

I look down at my watch. I have two hours to catch up on paperwork, which is rare in this department. I usually have to take a lot home with me just to hand everything in on time.

Since I graduated as a general surgeon five years ago, I've been working under Steven Burke, learning and treating Sarcoma patients. I find the process fascinating and I love helping patients survive rare diseases. No two days are the same, which is one thing I love about my job.

Life is never boring.

I knock on Steven's door and enter his office.

"Hey. Come and have a seat."

I place a takeaway cup of coffee in front of him and sit down.

"I love you, son. I've been dreaming about coffee for hours."

I laugh. "So, what do we have today?"

"Sixty-one-year-old woman. Large fibromatosis tumour wrapped around the bowel and small intestine. I plan on scheduling her surgery for Monday morning, but I want you to meet the patient as well. It's going to be a big surgery. I want you to scrub in too."

"Sure. Is there a family history of fibromatosis?"

"Going from the reports I've had sent to me, no. We'll do further testing on the tumour when we remove it."

"Okay. And we can get clear margins?"

I know only too well that fibromatosis can be a pest to get rid of completely, but Steven is the best doctor we have in Scotland. I'd trust him with my own life.

CHAPTER SIXTY-NINE

"We can. I'll send you all the imaging I've had sent to me."

"Okay then. Let's get this over with." I stand up with my coffee cup.

"We're going to room three," Steven tells me.

Walking through the corridors, I feel hairs rise on the back of my neck. I look over my shoulder, but no one is there. I shake my head. I need a holiday. I eat, sleep, and breathe for this hospital. I can't remember the last time I did something for me. Joe was right; I am no fun now.

Steven knocks on the door and we enter.

"Hello. I'm Steven Burke, and this is my colleague Carter Cowell."

I step through the curtain to introduce myself and feel the blood drain from me. This can't be happening.

"Carter, are you okay?" asks Steven.

I clear my throat and take the file from Steven. "Jessica Cowell is my mother." I throw the file down on the table and walk over to the window.

"I didn't know you work here, Carter," my mum says, and my father keeps his head down.

When I finished my medical degree in Dundee, I moved back to Glasgow to work with Steven. I didn't feel the need to tell my parents I was living near them because they never once supported me.

"That's what happens when you take sides."

"Okay..." Steven steps forward and holds his hands up. "Carter, send Joe in here. He can take your place on Monday. I didn't make the connection with the name. I'm sorry."

"Monday..." my mum and dad say together.

I look at the sheer panic on my mum's face. I pull out a chair and sit in front of her, taking her hands in mine, and inhale a deep breath. I might dislike my father, but I wouldn't wish this on my worst enemy.

"Let's start again." I have a job to do and it doesn't matter what happened in the past. "This is Steven. He's my boss. He's one of the best doctors in Glasgow. He's planning on operating on Monday morning. We'll bring you into hospital on Sunday evening, because you'll be first on the list."

"Are you doing the surgery, too?"

I shake my head. "Not now. Joe will take my place. I'll bring him by on Sunday evening to meet you."

My mum nods. "It has all happened so fast."

Steven rolls a seat over and sits down beside me.

"Fibromatosis - or Desmoid Tumours as you may have had it referred to - isn't common. We only deal with a few cases a year. They may not be cancerous or metastasis, but when they're at the aggressive stage they're the biggest pain in the backside. The best thing to do is remove it where possible. I've looked at your MRI scans, and while the tumour is very large, it isn't connected to any major vessels that will stop us removing it."

My mum sighs with relief. "How long will I be in hospital for?"

"We'll play it by ear, but maybe ten to fourteen days, give or take."

"Okay. What time do I need to arrive on Sunday? It's Mother's Day, and I'd like to have dinner with my family."

"Will we say seven p.m.? Carter, can you arrange for Joe to meet your mum on Sunday evening?"

"Sure. I can pop in around half past seven."

"Perfect. If you have any questions over the weekend, write them down for me, and I'll answer them on Monday

CHAPTER SIXTY-NINE

morning. I know this is all overwhelming, but you're in the best hands."

"Thank you, Doctor."

We all stand up and I open the door to get a nurse.

"Abi, can you do bloodwork on Mrs Cowell, please?"

"Of course." She drops what she's doing and takes the file from me.

"Mum, Abi will take care of you."

"Carter…" She holds her hand out for me and I take it. "Will you come for dinner on Sunday?"

I shake my head. "I don't think that's a good idea, Mum."

"Please. Leave your father to me."

I look over her shoulder towards my dad. He's aged in the years I've been away, but he still holds a grudge. I can see it in his hooded eyes when he looks my way. I always had hope that he would see sense one day.

"I won't make any promises. I'll see what I can do."

"Okay." She sighs. "We'll be sitting down at three."

She wraps her arms around my waist and I kiss her head. I've missed my mum over the years, but it was better for us all that I stayed away. Yet, here we are, and now she's facing a big battle. One I hope she can fight back from and be that strong person I know she once was.

Chapter Three

CARTER

"Oh my God. You're not in scrubs, and your dressed in a shirt and tie. Where are you off to on a Sunday afternoon?" asks Joe.

I roll my eyes at my friend. He slags me off, but he's a workaholic just as much as me, if not more so.

"I'm going for dinner at my parents' house."

I cringe hearing those words leave my mouth. I can't believe I'm doing this. Something inside me knows it's for the best, but I can't ignore why I've been away for all these years.

"I'm glad you've decided to go. I'll see you tonight when you come in with your mum."

"Why don't you come to dinner with me? It kills two birds with one stone and you don't have to hang around until later tonight."

"I don't know, buddy. Maybe you should rip the plaster off and do this on your own."

I shrug. I know he's right, but it makes more sense for

my mum to meet Joe in her own surroundings. "Well, come home and meet my mum and then you can leave. You're only sticking around here because of our meeting tonight. It will be more comfortable for my mum in her own home."

"Eurgh! You drive me crazy. I'll follow you. Meet you out front in ten."

I smile at my achievement. I feel more comfortable having someone with me that I know and trust. I could be walking into the lion's den with my father, and I doubt we'll ever agree on anything now. I made the right decisions for me a long time ago. I don't regret going to med school and living the life I wanted. My dad will either get over it or remain holding the grudge forever.

We pull up outside my parents' house thirty minutes later. I'm nervous about this lunch meeting. I get out of my car and retrieve the flowers from the back seat.

"So, this is where you grew up?" asks Joe.

I look up at the house standing on its own. It's a large house, bigger than anyone needs, but it was home to me once. It was home to a lot of kids that didn't have a family. For that, I must take my hat off to my parents. They opened their house and shared what they had.

"Yip. Come on in."

I walk up to the door, but before I open it, I take in a deep breath. The warmth hits me the minute I step through the door. The chatter and laughter from the living room tells me where I need to be.

The moment I step into the room, the chatter stops, and my Uncle Jack stands up. Before I can say anything, he wraps me in his arms and pats my back. Over the years, my dad and Uncle Jack have got closer. My dad got over the grudge he held over Uncle Jack taking me in, but it appears I'm still in the bad books.

"This is a surprise. It's good to see you again, son."

"Don't act like you haven't seen him in years." My dad stands to leave the room.

Uncle Jack and I have kept in touch. Even more so since I come back to work in Glasgow. It's just a surprise for us to meet here in this house.

"Carter." My mum gasps as she enters the room from the kitchen. She rushes over to me and wraps her arms around my waist. "I'm so glad you could make it."

I hand her the flowers and she smells them like she always does with a flower delivery. "Mum, do you have half an hour to spare? I've brought Joe over to have a chat with you, so you can meet him. He was going to hang around at the hospital until tonight to meet you, but I didn't think you'd mind."

My mum looks over at Joe, and then over at the family sitting on the couches.

"It's nice to meet you, Joe." My mum ushers us out of the room and I wonder what's going on. "I haven't told any of the family yet. I was going to do it over dinner today."

I close my eyes and count to ten. This is just like my mum and dad to leave everything to the last minute or hope that it will go away if it isn't spoken about.

"Jess, the timer is beeping. Do you want me to take the roast out?"

I turn around to see a petite woman standing with oven gloves in her hand. Her long brown hair hangs around her shoulders. Her brown eyes sparkle. She's beautiful.

"Keeley, you remember, Carter," asks my mum.

"Of course. It's good to see you again." She smiles at me.

I'm speechless. Keeley was the foster kid my mum and dad kept after she turned sixteen. She'll probably be about twenty-six now.

"I can't believe how grown up you look. I didn't even recognise you." I cringe. I walk towards her and place a kiss on her cheek. "You look really well."

"Th-thank you. You do, too."

"You kids go and get a drink. Joe, you'll stay for dinner, right?"

"I don't want to impose." Joe steps forward.

My mum waves the oven gloves around. "Nonsense. A friend of Carter's is a friend of mine. Carter, grab some drinks for you and Joe. We'll be eating in ten minutes."

I follow my mum into the kitchen and Keeley and Joe follow me. I grab two beers for me and Joe and hand his to him. We're off the clock and one won't affect us driving.

"Keeley, can I get you a drink?"

"I'm good. I have a juice. I don't drink alcohol."

I nod. I make a mental note to ask why she doesn't drink alcohol, but right now, I just need to get through this awkward dinner.

"How are you feeling, Mrs Cowell?" asks Joe.

"I have my good and bad moments. Right now, I have no pain and I feel like a million dollars. I've imagined Carter being here for dinner for a lot of years. I'm just glad he could make it today."

I look down at the ground sheepishly. I should have known my mum would have tried to guilt trip me. She was always good at that when I was growing up.

"You have a very talented son, Mrs Cowell. I've had the privilege of working alongside him for a lot of years."

I smile at Joe because, no doubt, tomorrow he'll be telling me I'm an arsehole for something.

"Please, call me, Jess." Joe nods. "Now, go and get a seat at the dining table. I'll serve up with Keeley."

I walk into the dining room and my father is sitting at the head of the table. Uncle Jack, and couple of people I don't recognise, all sit down in the seats they clearly sit down in all the time. Uncle Jack notices my hesitance and nods at the seats in front of him. I punch Joe's arm and pull out a seat. That's the type of relationship I have with my work colleagues. I prefer to be light-hearted, because we deal with some tricky situations and our moods can deflate quickly.

"So, how's it going in Glasgow Royal?" asks Uncle Jack.

"Same old. How's things with you?" I take a swig of my beer and sit back in my seat so I can't feel my father's glare through Joe. He's acting as my shield and I'm not sure if he's oblivious, or if he knows and doesn't care.

"Business as usual, son. I can't believe how well you're looking. What brings you by today?"

I wondered when the questions would start. I haven't been home in eleven years, and here I am with a work colleague.

"I saw Mum during the week and she left me little option but to stop by."

"A good day to stop by, it being Mother's Day and all."

I nod. I don't want to keep skirting around the subject of what really brings me here. Uncle Jack would have heard what I said about Joe when I first entered the house; he's just waiting to see how long I wait before telling him the truth.

"Here we go. Everyone can get tucked in. But, before we start eating, can I just tell you how happy I am that I have my full family around this table today? It means more than I can even tell you."

I wink at my mum as she sits down beside my father, and Keeley sits opposite my mother. Does it bother me that she's higher up the table than I am? Maybe once it would have, but not now. I accepted my position within this family a long time ago. Now, I just need to eat dinner and get out of here. If I can do that, I will treat Joe to a few beers in comfort.

Dinner went by slowly. My father made it perfectly clear that he wasn't comfortable with me being here. He hasn't broken breath to me since I arrived. He's chatted with Uncle Jack and Keeley, but the conversation hasn't included me or Joe, which is just rude. We've made our own small chat; we're used to each other's company in the bleakest of moments. This dinner won't alter that.

"We've had a beautiful dinner, we've drunk a few glasses of wine. Are you now going to tell us what's going on, Jess?" asks Uncle Jack.

I fold my arms across my chest and listen to the silence. I'd like to say silence is golden, but in this case, it's anything but.

"Yes, I do have something to tell you all. This week, I met Carter at the hospital. He and his boss were there to see me. Obviously, Carter didn't know I was his patient at that time, but he was there for me when I was in a state of panic."

"Why were you at the hospital, lass?"

Uncle Jack was like a dog with a bone when he started. I sometimes wish my dad was as attentive as him.

"I have a large mass growing in my stomach. Carter, can you fill everyone in for me?"

I clear my throat and sit forward, clasping my hands together on the table. "Before I start, I want you to know that we have everything under control. My boss and Joe will be doing the operation on Monday, because I can't operate on my own mother. My mum has something we call a Desmoid Tumour growing around her bowel. While these tumours are aggressive, they don't spread to other organs. In Mum's case, it isn't growing in a life-threatening place. With some reconstruction and a lot of TLC, she should be back on her feet in six to ten weeks."

"And these tumours won't kill her?" asks Keeley.

"Like every operation or disease, they hold risks. In Mum's case, she should make a full recovery. However, with the type of tumour, we can't guarantee it won't return even more aggressive than before they're removed. Therefore, during surgery, Steve will remove a lot of extra tissue to try and get clear margins."

"And that will prevent it from coming back?"

"We hope so, Keeley. There's never any guarantees, but from what we know, ninety percent of our patients don't have any regrowth."

The questions cease and the atmosphere hanging around us is thick. I don't think anyone knows what to do or say for the best.

Joe clears his throat. "Steve is one of the best doctors in the U.K that deals with Desmoid Tumours. I'd trust him with my life. You're in good hands." He reaches over and squeezes my mum's hand. "We'll be with you every step of the way."

"Excuse me." Keeley scrapes her chair back and leaves the table.

My mum stands up to follow her, but I stop her. "I'll go."

Walking through my parents' house is something I haven't done in a long time, but it hasn't changed any. I make my way out into the conservatory, because it's the place everyone runs off to in here. It has always been that room. It was probably the room my dad ran off to when I walked in today. And it will be the room my dad spends most of his time in when my mum's in hospital. If walls could talk, this room would be able to share a lot.

"Hi." I walk slowly into the room. "Can I sit down?"

Keeley wipes her eyes and nods at the empty space beside her. "I've always imagined that Jess would be untouchable."

I smile. "Yeah. I hear that a lot in my job. People don't expect bad things to happen to their loved ones. Unfortunately, these diseases don't care who they effect. We've just got to be strong for them and be there when we're needed."

"Will you be there, Carter?"

Keeley looks me square in the eyes, tears streaming down her cheeks. I wipe them away with my thumbs. "I'll be there all the way. I won't be operating, but it's my team that's taking over Mum's care. You're not alone."

She falls into my arms and I hold her for the longest time possible. I run my hand down her hair, caressing her back in the process. I hate to see people crying; it's one part of my job that I dislike.

"I'm sorry." She pulls away from me and tucks her long hair behind her ears. "You must be sick of people crying on you."

"I'm afraid it's a part of my job, but you don't need to apologise. I'm just happy I could be here for you. I know I've not been around over the years, but I'd like to be here for you now. If you need me at all, just call me." I reach into my pocket and take out my wallet. I hand her a card with my mobile number and hospital line. "You'll get me on my mobile anytime, unless I'm in theatre, but I'll always return the calls."

"Thank you, Carter."

I place a kiss on her forehead and stand up to leave. I look over my shoulder and see the timid woman curl up into the seat to look out into the garden. I feel terrible that I must leave her here alone, but I need to get back to Joe. He'll be cursing me enough.

"I'm glad you're here for this, son," says Uncle Jack as he walks out of the kitchen.

"Yeah, me too," I lie.

I wish I was anywhere else but here, but my mum needs me. Everything else goes out of the window for that. There is a big part of me that wishes I hadn't been so stubborn, but there's no point dwelling on the past. We need to look to the future, and I know my mum will have a bright future ahead.

When I walk into the dining room, it's only my mum and Joe sitting at the table. Joe has moved to sit beside my mum and has her hand in his. She's laughing at whatever he just said. Joe is one of those doctors that always makes the patients smile and laugh. Even on their death bed, Joe's the doctor you need around.

"I don't even want to know what you just said to my mother." I squeeze my mum's shoulders.

"Just keeping her company." He winks at my mum.

"I feel a lot happier knowing I'm in good hands. You'll all take care of me. How's Keeley?"

"She's okay. I hope I've put her mind at rest a bit. She loves you, Mum, so this is understandable. Where is everyone?" I look around the room.

"Your Uncle Jack is away to the games room to speak with your father. He's taking this harder than I thought."

"He'll be fine, Mum. Just concentrate on yourself. Is Dad taking you to hospital tonight?"

She nods. "Will I see you in the morning?"

"Of course."

"You've made this Mother's Day very special for me."

I bend down and place a kiss on her head. "I didn't do anything, but I really need to be getting off."

She stands up and wraps herself around me. When I was younger, this would have been the other way around. My mum would cuddle me for hours when I was ill. Now the tables are turned, and I need to get her through this, so she can spend many more Mother's Days with us.

Chapter Four

CARTER

I arrived at the hospital an hour early today, just so I can get my ward rounds out of the way, then I can sit with Keeley when my mum goes into theatre. I wouldn't be any use to my work colleagues; I'm as well sitting today out. My team know exactly where I'll be. The ward staff will know how to get me if they need anything. Everyone will be happy.

"Hey, buddy. How are you today?" asks Joe.

"I'm good. What's happening?"

"Not a lot. I'm heading down to theatre to see the list. We're all set for your mum. Everything is ready, all the T's are crossed, and she's going to be fine."

I nod. "I don't doubt you, buddy. I'm just heading to her room now."

"I'll see her before she goes into theatre."

I carry on walking in the opposite direction from Joe. I know my mum will be in safe hands with him and Steve, but it doesn't stop me from worrying.

I knock on her room door and enter. The nurse is checking her vitals, and they look as good as can be expected under the circumstances.

"Morning." I smile.

Keeley is sitting at the side of my mum's bed, holding her hand, and my dad is standing at the window.

"Morning, Dr Cowell. I believe everything is all set for the operation to go as planned this morning. Your mum is first on the list," explains Andrea, our ward sister.

"I believe it is, Andrea. Thank you."

I take off my white doctor's coat and throw it over the back of a chair. I sit opposite Keeley and take in a deep breath. "Did you sleep okay last night?"

"Eventually. I'll just be glad to get this over with."

"The theatre porters will be up for you soon. When you go down, the nurses will take care of you. Joe is going to pop in and see you before the surgery starts. The next thing you'll know, you'll be waking up."

"Good. I guess it's just as well we don't remember anything."

I smile. I know it's just as well, because even as a doctor, it makes me feel sick to my stomach knowing what my mum is about to go through this morning.

"Will she be in theatre long?" asks Keeley.

"A few hours. Steve will come up and speak with us when it's over."

The room goes silent and I look between my mum and Keeley. It's obvious to see they have a bond like no other. I haven't been around for some years, but even I can see how much they mean to one another.

A knock on the door makes me look over. I see Jive and Erik, our porters. They're a big part of our team, and they keep everyone's spirits up on a busy day.

"Morning, Doc. It was weird not seeing you downstairs this morning."

"Yeah, I bet. Steve will keep you on your toes though," I joke.

"Carter, will you take Keeley for a coffee?" asks my father.

I'm shocked that my father spoke to me. I nod and stand up. "Of course. Mum, these two will take good care of you until you get down to Joe and Steve. I'll see you on the other side." I lean over and kiss my mum's cheek.

I hold my hand out for Keeley, but she kisses my mum and gives her a big cuddle. I can see she's reluctant to leave, but my father helps get her to my side of the bed. I nod in his direction. I leave the room with my arm around Keeley's shoulders. I feel her body shaking from the sobs.

"Hey, she'll be okay. I promise."

"It's just that she's been the only person I've been able to count on for as long as I can remember. I don't know what I'll do if anything happens to her."

"Nothing will happen to her today. She'll be groggy and sore when she comes back up to the ward, but she'll get meds to help with it all. Come on. Let's get a coffee."

For the first time in my career, I'm seeing illness from the other side. Usually, I comfort the family and hand them over to the nurses, but this time it's my own family. I don't want to be anywhere other than by Keeley's side.

I place a tray down on the table beside Keeley. There's coffee and pancakes for her, because I know she won't eat unless it's put in front of her.

"Thank you." She wraps her hands around the cup.

"Eat. It will keep your strength up. Time will feel like it stands still today."

"I know what you mean. It already feels like hours ago since I left Jess's room. Tell me something about you, Carter. You look very different to the teenager that left home."

I sit back in the seat and cross my ankles over each other. "I guess a lot has changed since we last saw each other. I followed my dreams. I become a doctor and moved back to Glasgow. I took up this job because my keen interest was in strange tumours. That probably sounds geeky to most."

"Not at all. I think it's very interesting. I never really thought about all the different diseases until now. It must be rewarding when you help people."

I shrug. "It can be when we get a positive outcome. Not everyone we work on gets a happy ever after. We must take the good with the bad, but it's not always easy just to move onto the next patient. Some stick with you longer than others."

"I take my hat off to you, Carter. You're a hero in my eyes." She takes a sip of her coffee and I sit forward and copy her position with my hands wrapped around my cup.

"I'm not too good at taking compliments. Tell me something about you."

"I work in graphic design. Mostly within the book industry. Novels, magazines, websites... It's something I love doing."

I must admit, I never expected her to say that. I don't know what I expected her to do, but that's different. "That sounds like a very interesting career. No two projects are the same. Sounds a bit like here."

"Only I don't save people's lives." She laughs.

Her laugh pulls straight at my heart strings. Women don't usually make me feel like this. I don't know if it's because my parents took her in as a teenager, or if it's something else. I'm not sure I want to know either, but my curiosity will get the better of me.

"Mind if I join you?"

I look up to see my dad standing with his hand on Keeley's shoulder. I gesture to the seat opposite me. He pulls it out and sits down, letting out a long sigh.

"I was going to bring this up to you." I push over a takeaway coffee cup and he stalls for a moment or two before he takes it.

"Thanks. I think I'm going to need a few of these today." He grins weakly.

"Did she go down okay?" asks Keeley.

My dad nods. "I think I was more bothered than Jess. She trusts the doctors and that's all that matters."

"She's in good hands. I don't doubt my colleagues. You guys just need to be strong for her when she comes back up."

My dad looks directly at me. I'm waiting for something smart to come out of his mouth, but he's aged so much since the last time I saw him; even just from last night he looks older and more washed out.

"Is this the type of surgery you do daily?"

"Mostly. As I just told Keeley, I deal with weird and wonderful tumours, but I'm also a general surgeon, so we deal with a lot of other operations like gall bladders, appendix, etc."

"You've done well for yourself, son. I can't apologise enough for pushing you away from your family. It killed your mother each day you were away. She put on a brave face, but deep down I could see the hurt and pain she was going through. I'll never be able to make that right."

"It's over with, Dad."

"No. I need to say this. I should have said it a long time ago, but I let my stupid pride get in the way. If anything had happened to your mother without her seeing you, I wouldn't have been able to forgive myself. I was a terrible father. Seeing you at the table yesterday for Mother's Day, that was probably the best gift your mum could have received. It means a lot to her that you're here today."

I clear my throat. "I wouldn't be anywhere else."

I've waited years for my father to acknowledge his part in our family falling to pieces, but it has taken my mother's illness before it brought us this closure. I won't be grateful that my mother got ill, but I will be grateful that my father could find it in himself to apologise.

"Dr Cowell, can I have a word?"

I nod towards the sister and excuse myself from the table before my emotions get the better of me.

Chapter Five

CARTER

Three hours later, we're all sitting in the family room. We've sat in every chair there is, paced the floors, taken in every piece of scenery out of the window, and now we're clock watching. I know the operation should be over any time now, if it isn't already finished, but I try to hide that bit of information from Keeley and my dad. They're worked up enough now. Anything else will push one of them over the edge.

"Can I get anyone a coffee?" asks my dad as he shuffles towards the door. He's exhausted, but he's as stubborn as they come.

"Sure. Coffee sounds good," I say.

"I'm fine," says Keeley.

The door swings closed behind my father and I sit back in the seat and rest my head against the back rest. I look up to the bland white ceiling. It doesn't help much to keep your mind busy in situations like this.

"We should hear something soon, right?"

My head lolls to the side and I take in the dainty woman beside me. I take her hand in mine and squeeze it tightly. "We should hear something soon."

I keep her hand securely in mine. I feel a little calmer whenever I touch Keeley. I think that's something I'll have to address later.

My phone chimes in my pocket, and with one hand, I fish it out.

To - Carter
From – Joe
All finished. I'll be up soon.

I sit forward and type out a quick response.

To – Joe
From - Carter
All good? No complications? Give me something to put Keeley's mind at rest.

Keeley sits forward and squeezes my hand. "What's going on, Carter?"

To - Carter
From – Joe
All good. Great margins. A couple of minor complications, but nothing we couldn't deal with. Don't worry. It's all good. Better than we originally thought. No bags in sight.

I sigh with relief and place my phone on the table. I feel tears fall from my eyes and I quickly wipe them.

"Joe will be up soon. Everything went well. Even better than they originally thought. They've been able to remove the tumour without dealing with any bowel issues. We originally thought she would need a colostomy bag for a while, but Joe said they got away without it. She'll be up soon."

Keeley throws herself into my arms and I hold onto her

tightly. I'm relieved and ecstatically happy right now.

"What happened?" asks my dad.

I keep Keeley in my arms and manage to look over at my dad, who is suddenly white as a ghost. "It's all okay. Everything is good. I got a text from Joe. He'll be up soon, but it's better than we originally thought."

My dad breaks down in tears and I break free from Keeley to show him some comfort. "It's okay. Let it out." I wrap my arms around him and I feel his arms wrap around my back for support. I don't know who's keeping who standing right now, because I'm overwhelmed to be seeing this side of my father. He was always a hard-faced bastard when I was growing up. This is a side I never thought I'd see... ever.

I guess it's true what they say; when your true love is in danger, it makes you see life from a different perspective.

Chapter Six

CARTER
TWO DAYS LATER

I walk through the ward towards my mum's room. I nod to a few of the nurses and carry on walking. When I reach my mum's room, I'm shocked to see her sitting in her chair beside the bed. For someone who just went through a gigantic surgery, she looks a million dollars.

"Wow! Look at you." I bend down and place a kiss on her cheek. "How are you?"

"All the better for seeing you."

I laugh and pull a seat over to the side of my mum. I take her hand in mine and sit down.

"Have you seen Joe or Steve this morning?"

"Both of them aren't long away. They're pleased with my progress. My bloodwork is good, and it's just a case of recovering now. Less about me, tell me what happened with you and your dad. I thought I was in heaven when I came back to the ward and saw you two together."

"I think you can say that we both had one of those moments that made us realise that life is too short. We spoke for a while when you were in theatre. I don't know what life will be like for us when you get home, but we'll take it day by day. We can only hope that this reconciliation lasts."

"Do you think we'll have a proper family Mother's Day next year?"

"I don't see why not..." says a voice from over my shoulder.

My dad leans over the top of me to kiss my mum. I go to move to let him in, but he clamps his hand on my shoulder to keep me sitting.

"Stay where you are. By God, it's so good to see you looking so much better, honey."

"We'll have you running a marathon in no time," I joke.

A soft knock on the door makes us all turn around and Keeley and Uncle Jack are standing there. Keeley comes in first and kisses my mum's cheek.

"Here, Keeley. Take this seat."

"Thanks, Carter." Her arm brushes mine and I feel goosebumps spread all over my body.

"Never mind next Mother's Day, why don't we have a big family get together when you get home? Something low key, obviously, but we can invite those lovely doctors over. I can get some caterers in."

"That sounds good," says my mum enthusiastically with a big smile on her face.

I feel terrible that it's taken us eleven years to get here, but I'll spend the next eleven years making it up to her. I've learnt that holding grudges does you no good.

"Carter, will you do me a favour?"

"Of course, Mum. What is it?"

"Will you take Keeley out of here? Go for something to eat, have some fun, anything but sitting here with me.

CHAPTER SEVENTY-THREE

You've both been here with me every spare minute you've had. I'm good. I'm going to be fine. Now I need to know you two will be okay."

"Erm..." I look between my mum and Keeley. My dad and Uncle Jack share a knowing look; of what I'm not quite sure. "Okay. If that's what you want. I just need to check on one of my patients and then I can take the rest of the day off. Is that okay with you, Keeley?"

"Y-yeah," she stutters and smiles at me shyly.

I nod and leave the room quickly. Maybe she feels this connection with me, too. Maybe it isn't all one-sided.

Today has been a weird kind of day. Sitting across from Keeley with a bottle of Budweiser while she has some gin drink she likes, it seems like we were born to be sitting like this. It feels right to be sitting here.

"What happened to you telling me that you don't drink," I smile brightly at her.

She shrugs her shoulders. "I guess I should have rephrased that. I don't dislike alcohol, I just need to feel comfortable before I can let myself go. My biological mother was an alcoholic, and without going into details I hated her for it."

"I'm sorry about your mother, but I sense that you don't want to talk about that just now, so what do you say that we lock that discussion away for another day?"

She nods. "Deal. I can't tell you how happy I am to see your mum on the mend."

And just like that the conversation is locked away and we are back to here and now.

"Me too. It's amazing how fast life can be turned upside

down. How people come into your life and things seem to change."

"I know what you mean. It's been good having you around the last few days. I don't know what I would have done without you." Keeley reaches over the table and squeezes my hand. "I guess we'll need to go back to normality soon."

"What is normality for you?" I ask.

"Working around the clock. Spending Sunday with your mum and dad. I have very little time for anything else at the moment. I put a lot of my work on hold when I found out about your mum's operation, so now I'll need to catch up. What about you?"

"Pretty much like you. I work some ungodly hours. The only difference is I have a good team that have taken on my work load while I've been with you guys."

"What about the patient you had to see today?"

"That was a special patient. I've been around that patient since I started here. When you have a patient like that, they become trapped under your skin and you feel responsible for them. I needed to make sure he was comfortable before I took off."

"What about your downtime? What do you like to do?"

"What is downtime? Joe was giving me grief about that just last week. I've not got anyone at home, so it makes sense to keep busy."

"And if you had someone at home..."

"That would be different. Life would be different. Responsibilities would be different."

I study the woman in front of me. I feel something deep within every time I'm around her. It doesn't matter what situation we're in, where we are, what we're doing; I still

CHAPTER SEVENTY-THREE

feel it. She's the first woman I would give up working so much for, and that says a lot about me and her.

"Keeley, tell me I'm not the only one that feels this connection between us. Tell me I'm not losing my mind."

Her cheeks blush slightly. She looks down at her glass before returning her gaze to me. "No. I feel it too. I just didn't want it to come between us. I kind of like having you around, Carter."

"Me too. I just haven't felt this before. It feels weird, but also so good. Like every time I look at you my heart leaps out of my chest."

"What do we do about it though? I have a funny feeling your mum was trying to act as matchmaker today."

I laugh. "Yeah, I got that feeling as well. Look, I'm not saying that I'm an expert in relationships, because I'm anything but. What I am saying is that maybe we should just hang out when we get the time, and see where this goes. I'm a firm believer of letting fate run its course."

"I'm not usually one to just let go and enjoy the moment, but I think you're right. I'd really like to get to know you now. I'd like to see what can come of us, and if nothing else, we can be friends, right?"

"Right." I lift my bottle and clink it against her glass.

As much as I want to agree with her, I know fine well that I'll never be able to just be friends with her, and if she's honest she'll know that too. But, right now, I'll take anything as long as I get to spend some extra time with her away from work and my parents.

Chapter Seven

CARTER

The last few days have been testing to say the least. I can count on one hand how many hours sleep I've had. I've been away from the hospital even less.

I lean over the nurses' station and place a file in the cabinet. I daren't say I'm finished for the day because something always crops up when I'm ready to walk out the door.

I haven't seen much of my mum for a few days; a quick five minutes here and there, but I know she's doing well. Joe was talking about letting her go home on Monday, which is good news.

"You look how I feel," says Joe as he sits down in the swivel chair in front of me.

"That's a great compliment since you look like shit." I smirk. "I'm heading out of here. I can't even think straight."

"Are you going home?"

"I'll call in and see my mum first, but yeah, bed is calling." I back away from the desk and salute to my best friend.

I feel like I'm floating along these corridors. It isn't until I reach my mum's room, when I see Keeley, that all sense of tiredness leaves me. The sound of my mum and Keeley laughing at something is like music to my ears. I'll never tire of hearing them together. The bond they share is like nothing I've come across before. They've clearly shared a lot of burdens over the years.

I walk into my mum's double room and look at her chart first. It's a bloody habit I can't get out of.

"Hi, sweetheart. You look exhausted."

"Thanks, Mum. You look good. Joe said he was thinking about letting you go home on Monday."

"Yes. I can't wait. I feel like a fraud sitting here because I feel fine."

I shake my head and sit on the bed. "You're not a fraud."

I look over at Keeley, whose knee is practically touching mine, sitting across from me, looking as beautiful as ever.

"Doctor, I shouldn't have to tell you not to sit on the bed," says the sister as she peeks her head around the door, laughing.

I stand up like a scalded school child, making my mum and Keeley laugh.

"Anyway, I just wanted to pop in before I go home. Do you need anything?"

"I have everything I need right here." She points to Keeley and me and smiles a big bright smile. "Get out of here, both of you."

"Anyone would think we were kids." I lean over and kiss her cheek.

"You'll always be my baby; don't you ever forget it."

I nod. I have a funny feeling that she's held that thought

in her head all the years I was away from her. I do something out of the ordinary, knowing it will make my mum happy. I hold my hand out for Keeley, and she stands up, puts on her jacket, and accepts my hand. I can feel my mum's eyes watching us as we leave her room. When we're out of her sight, I turn to Keeley and wrap my hands in her long hair then take her mouth with mine. Her warm lips open and give me access to the most amazing mouth I've ever tasted.

"Get a room, you two," shouts Joe.

I flip Joe the bird. I knew who it was without even looking. He's just as bad as my mum, trying to marry me off with the first available woman, but he needs to sort out his own life first.

I lean my head against Keeley's and close my eyes. "I might not be much company today, but what do you say we get out of here and head back to my place?"

She nods slightly, leaning up to peck me on the lips.

I wake up to a dark room, but the smell of something amazing makes me sit up. Suddenly, I remember coming home with Keeley, and now I'm in my room alone. I can't even remember falling asleep, but I guess that's what happens when you've worked around the clock for days.

I get out of bed, pull on a t-shirt, and walk through my flat. The cold floor makes me shiver, but the sight in front of me makes my heart contract, and any remaining walls are gone.

The soft glow surrounds Keeley, making her look like an angel. Her laptop is open, and the concentration on her face is adorable. It's the first time I've seen her with glasses on, and her long hair is pulled back into a messy thing on her head. She looks adorable.

I walk up behind her and wrap my arms around her shoulders, kissing her soft skin delicately. "You should have woken me."

"Why? You need sleep, Carter. You were dead on your feet. Besides, I had my laptop with me, and I have plenty of work to catch up on."

I look at the screen closely. The beautiful art work is amazing. The textures, the tones; they all work together perfectly. It's the first time I've seen any of her work in the middle of a design process.

"That's fantastic. You're very talented."

"Thank you." She closes the laptop and stands up, leaving me hanging over the back of the couch. "I hope you don't mind, I cooked your dinner. I thought you'd be hungry when you woke up."

"Mind? Why would I mind?"

She shrugs. "I don't know. It's only a simple lasagne and garlic bread."

I follow her into my open plan kitchen and take out a bottle of wine from the fridge as she heats up my food. She looks at home in my kitchen. This is probably the most action it's seen since I moved in here.

I sit down at the breakfast bar and push a glass of wine towards her. She passes me my plate and sits down opposite me. My cold foot runs up her warm leg. I feel her pull her legs together, and her reaction to my touch is comforting.

"This is amazing. I could get used to this," I tell her. I have never tasted lasagne like this. It's even better than what I remember of my mum's lasagne, and she can cook well.

"You still look tired," Keeley says over her glass of wine.

"I've taken the weekend off, so I should have plenty of time to catch up. What are your plans for this weekend?"

She shrugs. "I have a party to attend tomorrow night. I have a plus one. I…"

I reach over and take her hand in mine. "Are you trying to ask if I want to go with you?"

She nods, her cheeks giving off a red glow. "It's a client I worked with on design work. It's in the Grand Central Hotel."

"I'll be there. I think we could both use a night out, don't you?" She nods softly again. "Do you fancy staying the night? I mean, of course I have a spare room if that makes you feel more comfortable. I can take you home in the morning to get a change of clothes. It seems a waste to leave this opened bottle of wine."

"Okay. I'd like that. Let me save that bit of work I was doing and I'm all yours."

She jumps down off the stool and I catch her arm. We both lean into one another at the exact time and our mouths collide.

I feel lucky that such a woman walked into my life. I've spent so many years walking alone, and now, I will do whatever it takes to keep her by my side.

Chapter Eight

CARTER

Waking up with Keeley in my bed this morning was amazing. I've had an empty bed most of my adult life, apart from the odd one-night stand. Not that I'm proud of them, but I had needs.

We spent the full day in each other's arms, watching a movie, chatting, even eating lunch practically on top of each other. Now that she's gone home to get her dress for tonight, I feel lost. I feel like my right arm has been cut off. My house feels empty, which seems crazy.

I tighten my tie and straighten it up, taking in my appearance in the mirror. It feels weird to be wearing this attire for anything other than work. I hate formal wear, but I think I've come to accept it over the years.

I pick up my car keys and leave the flat as quickly as I can. I'll be early picking up Keeley, but I can't wait to see her again. For once, I'm looking forward to a night out. I can't remember the last time I went out to enjoy myself.

I take in a deep breath, knock on her door, and wait for her to open it. I can hear the clip clop of her heels before I see her. When she opens the door, my breath is taken away. She's wearing a floor length black ball gown with silver sequins around her neck.

"You look amazing." I lean in and capture her mouth with mine. "We have to go before we never make it to the party."

She nods, picks up her clutch bag, and we leave her house with her arm tucked into mine. The feel of her on my arm is also something I could get used to. It's weird how everything feels familiar when she's around.

We walk into the lobby of the Grand Central Hotel, and as always, it's a hive of activity in here. I let Keeley lead the way, because she clearly knows where she's going.

"Do you come here often?" I ask.

She shakes her head. "Maybe twice a year."

We come to a double door that's shut. I wonder why a big party would have shut doors, but when Keeley looks over her shoulder towards me, her eyes sparkle. Her smile is contagious. I forget all about the shut doors. We step into the large room, the lights go on, and everyone shouts, "Surprise!"

I'm gobsmacked. I can't believe I didn't realise this party was for me. The gold 3 0 balloons float around the room, and Keeley holds my face in her hands and kisses me passionately.

"Surprise."

She moves out of my way and my mum is wheeled over to me in a wheelchair. I bend down on my knees and place a kiss on her cheek.

"Let me guess; this had something to do with you."

"I can't take all the credit." She points over her shoulder and I see Joe raising his glass to me. "Your friend thinks you could really do with this party. I just happen to agree with him."

"But you should be in hospital."

She smiles. "I got discharged this morning. Your Uncle Jack and your father took care of everything, and Keeley kept you occupied." She winks at me and I feel my cheeks flush a few shades of red.

"Thank you for this."

I stand up and my dad is standing a few feet away from me. I feel like we're both waiting for the other to make the first move, but my mum squeezes my hand and I look down at her, smiling. That is the only encouragement I need to move towards my father. He opens his arms to me, and I pat his back several times.

"I'm proud of you, son." I pull back and my dad places his hands on my cheeks. "What you've accomplished in your life... your job, your living arrangements, well... I'm so proud of you."

"Thanks, Dad." Tears well in my eyes and I shake my head to get rid of them.

"That girl is worth ten million dollars. Look after her."

I look over my shoulder to see Keeley laughing with my mum and Joe. I nod my agreement and turn back to my dad.

"I will. She's special. I don't plan on letting her go anywhere."

And that was the truth. That woman would become my

wife and mother to my kids. She would be my best friend. She would be every title known to man.

I walk away from my dad and take the glass out of Keeley's hands. I don't care who is waiting to congratulate me or hand me gift bags; I need to do this before I bottle out of it.

"Carter, what are you doing?"

I hear Joe and my mum whisper something, but that's the least of my worries.

"I know we said we'd take things slowly. I know we said we'd just have fun and see where we end up. But I can't do that, babe. I need you in my life. I need to fall asleep with you and wake up to you in the morning. I need to share my life with you. I'm not going to ask you to marry me right now, because that will be a special moment between us, but I am asking you to share your life with me. I am asking you to take a leap of faith in me. Let me love you. Let me care for you."

Silence.

"Yes," she whispers. "I want all of that, too."

I place my mouth over hers and kiss her like I've never kissed before. This is my promise to this woman. I will never kiss her any less. She will always be my number one.

"I love you, Carter."

"I love you too."

Everyone takes that as their cue to interrupt and congratulate me on my birthday, and my woman. For the first time in my life, I can't wait to see what the future holds.

This is a lesson to anyone... don't hold a grudge, because it might just be keeping you from something special.

Also by
K M Lowe

Standalones

A Christmas Stranger

A Country Escape

A Different Christmas

Celebrations: A Collection of Short Stories

Date Night

Home for Christmas

It Was Meant To Be

One Last Wish

Tidal Love

What Becomes Of a Broken Heart

Burning Hearts Series

Burning Hearts

Burning Hearts: A Dark Loss

Burning Love: A Burning Hearts Novel

Shawland Security Series

Shawland Security: Book #1

Shawland Security: Book #2

The Beautiful Life Trilogy

The Smile

The Smile - New Beginnings

The Smile - Forever After

The Forbidden Duet

Forbidden Love

The Guardian Shifters

Lisa: Coming of Age

Jasper: United Together

Kevin: Always and Forever

Joel: Alive and Kicking

Jasper: Taking Control

Callum: Past and Present

Julian: A Clean Break

The Pastry Warlock

by Laura Greenwood

Chapter One

ELLIE
1 YEAR & 2 MONTHS AGO

The academy feels bigger than it did when I was here for the open day, and I try not to feel too intimidated as I follow the pink-haired witch who had introduced herself as Daphne into the accommodation block.

"Are you excited?" she asks.

I nod. "And nervous," I admit. "This is the first time I've lived away from home."

She smiles reassuringly at me. "I was on my first day at Grimalkin too," Daphne says. "But you're going to have a great time."

"I hope so. I'm not sure what to expect."

She gives a bemused chuckle, though I get the impression it's because of something she's remembering, and not what I've said. "Expect the unexpected," she tells me. "Then you'll be prepared."

"I'm not sure if that's helpful," I mutter.

CHAPTER SEVENTY-SIX

She shrugs. "I can tell you about my first year, but you said you were an only child?"

I nod.

"Then I find it very unlikely that your twin brother will ask you to date a vampire so you can find an old family spell in the vampire part of the academy."

I blink a few times. "That actually happened to you?"

"Believe me, that wasn't even the strangest thing to happen in my first year. My best friend also got cursed and ended up making a load of magical kittens. They're adorable, but a handful," Daphne says cheerfully. "Oh look, we're here. This is your new flat."

I blink a few times, still trying to process what she said. I didn't come to Grimalkin Academy to have outrageous adventures. My intention was just to learn more about magic and have an experience that doesn't revolve around my family.

Daphne pushes open the door to the flat and checks the clipboard. "All right, you're in room five, so this is you." She gestures to her left.

I twist the key and step inside, surprised to find it was nothing particularly special, just a room with a bed, desk, and a small bathroom in the corner with a shower and toilet.

"One second," Daphne says, pulling out her wand. With a quick wave, she summons my boxes from where I stored them outside.

"Useful," I say, though what I mean is impressive. That isn't easy magic.

"It is. All right, I'll leave you to it so I can go and meet my next new student. But if you need anything, my number is here, you can message me." She hands me a small booklet. "There are mugs and hot drinks waiting in the kitchen for everyone. It's not home until you've had that first cup of tea."

"Thanks, Daphne."

"No problem. I'll see you around." She bounces out of the door, full of energy.

Am I going to be like that in another couple of years?

I push the thought aside and head to the kitchen. A cup of coffee sounds like just the right start to my time living here.

The door opens into a surprisingly spacious room with plenty of cupboards and two fridges. Just about enough for the people living here.

Someone turns around as I enter. "Hey," a guy who I assume is the same age as me says, giving me an awkward half-wave.

"Hi," I respond, trying to ignore the nerves fluttering within me at the idea of meeting someone new. This is the part of coming to the academy I've been looking forward to the least.

"Are you new here?"

"Aren't we all first years in the flat?" I ask.

He chuckles nervously. "Sorry, that was a dumb question. Do you want a drink?"

"Coffee, please."

He pulls out his wand, which somehow surprises me despite the fact I already know he's a warlock just from the fact he's here. Grimalkin Academy serves as a higher education institute for witches, warlocks, and vampires, but the latter are housed underground so they avoid the risk of burning to a crisp in the sun.

He waves his wand in the direction of the kettle, switching it on and starting the process of making drinks.

CHAPTER SEVENTY-SIX

"Are you trying to show off for any particular reason?" I ask.

He raises an eyebrow. "How am I showing off?"

I gesture to the kettle. "Most magic users wouldn't do that."

He frowns. "Oh, I suppose they wouldn't. My family runs a bakery, it's just normal for me."

"Ah."

"I'm Ash, by the way." He holds his hand out to me.

I take it and give it a shake, liking the way it feels against mine. "Eloise. Well, Ellie, if we're using our shortened names."

"Oh, my name is just Ash, it's not short for anything. I'm named after the tree."

"I'm sorry, I shouldn't have assumed. Is there a reason?"

He shrugs. "No idea. My sisters are all named after plants too, and our cousin. We think our parents lost a bet or something."

"At least it makes your name interesting."

"True. How do you take your coffee?" He picks up a sachet of instant stuff and dumps it into one of the mugs branded with the academy's logo, followed by a tea bag into one of the others.

"Is it bad to say better quality than that?"

Ash grins. "I'd say the same for tea. Luckily, I can do something about that."

"You can?"

He nods and turns to one of the cupboards, which already seems to be stocked with all kinds of food items.

"How long have you been here?" I ask, impressed by how quickly he's unpacked.

"Since this morning. I just unpacked food first." He

1 YEAR & 2 MONTHS AGO

dumps out the instant coffee and replaces it with some from a fancy-looking caddy. "Milk? Sugar?"

"Just milk," I say.

He nods and pours the water in. It doesn't escape my notice that he uses his hands and not his wand for this part, though maybe it's because I told him I thought he was showing off.

"Do you like gingerbread?" he asks.

I frown. "As in gingerbread men?"

"Yes."

"I do. Why?"

"Oh, I just have some from my sisters' bakery." He pulls out a tin and holds it out to me. "Want one? They're imbibed with settled magic."

"Settled magic?" I echo, eyeing them warily.

He nods. "You know you can put magic in food, right?"

"Yes. Though I've never done it."

"Well, that's what my family's bakery does. They bake feelings into things. It's not enough to change your actual emotions, but if you eat one of these, it'll give you the feeling of being settled. Rowen thought I'd want some with it being my first day."

"And you're sharing them?"

"Of course. It would be rude not to," Ash says with a genuine smile.

There's something about him that makes me feel comfortable. And like he isn't lying about the gingerbread.

I pick one of them up and bite into it, closing my eyes and almost moaning with how delicious it is. It's only once the gingerbread hits my stomach that I realise what he means about the feeling of being settled. It spreads through me, filling me with warmth and contentment. I can tell that

CHAPTER SEVENTY-SIX

it's not really how I'm feeling, but that it's taking the edge off in a way that makes me relax.

"This is amazing," I admit.

"Right? Rowen makes the best gingerbread even without the magic. The bakery is in town, I can bring some more next time I visit if you want."

"Then I'm going to have to think of something I can bring you in return."

"I'm going to need a study buddy," Ash says. "You bring the pizza, I'll bring the cake." He passes my coffee to me.

"That sounds like an offer I can't refuse."

"Then it's a deal."

"Especially if you bring this coffee too," I admit, enjoying the deep and rich smell from it. "Where did you get it from?"

"My cousin's coffee shop."

"I can see that you're going to be a good friend to have," I quip.

Ash gives a good-natured laugh. "I aim to be."

Despite my nerves over coming to Grimalkin for the first time, I have to admit to being put at ease by the friendly face in front of me.

And if he keeps bringing me delicious treats, no doubt our friendship will last for years to come.

Chapter Two

ASH

The delicious scent of baked goods fills the air, and I know Broomstick Bakery will have had an influx of morning customers as a result.

I push through the door, the small bell above it announcing my arrival.

"I'll be one moment," Oakley calls from behind the counter.

"It's just me."

"Oh, hey, Ash. Willow said you might be stopping by."

I chuckle. "I can't do anything without you all talking about me, can you?"

"She said you were bugging her for coffee."

I lift up the bag with the Cauldron Coffee Shop logo on the side. "I was."

"For Ellie?"

"How did you guess?"

"Because you asked for her favourite cupcake flavours again." She sets a box on the top of the counter.

"You used confidence in it, right?" I ask.

"Of course. I wouldn't mess with you and Ellie."

"There's nothing to mess with," I mutter.

"But you want there to be?" She raises an eyebrow and leans on the counter.

I sigh and perch myself on one of the customer stools. "It's complicated."

"I believe I can handle it," she retorts dryly.

"I don't want to ruin our friendship," I admit. "Ellie means the world to me, I don't want to ruin things between us by asking her on a date and making her reject me."

"And what if she doesn't reject you?" Oakley asks. "Which I think is the more likely option given the way the two of you are with one another. Even Dad commented on it after the summer fete, and you know how clueless he can be about those things."

"Wait, Dad said something?"

"Mmhmm. What was it? Oh right, he asked if you were together."

I raise an eyebrow. "And that's all you're basing this on?"

"No, and you know it. If you didn't think there was anything between you, then you wouldn't be worrying about it ruining your friendship," Oakley points out.

"Or maybe we're just that close as friends."

She lets out a small snort of amusement.

"You wouldn't all be saying this if my best friend was a guy," I mutter.

"In this hypothetical situation where the only difference is that Ellie is short for Elliot and not Eloise?" Oakley asks.

"Sure."

"Then we'd be saying exactly the same things, the only

difference would be that I'd be encouraging you to ask him out on a date instead of her out on a date." The expression on her face makes me believe she's telling the truth.

Which doesn't help me get out of them all asking me what's going on with me and Ellie. If anything, it makes it worse.

"I can make you a confidence cupcake too," Oakley suggests. "Then you don't have to worry about it ruining your friendship when you ask."

"You know that isn't how the magic in these works," I counter. "I'll still be able to think rationally, that's why you're allowed to sell them."

She sighs dramatically and leans her head on her hands. "Fine, I'll give you that one."

The door to the kitchens swings open and a tray of perfectly baked macarons appears floating through the air, followed by one of my other sisters with another tray in her hands and her wand gripped tightly against it.

"Will you grab the tray, Oak?" Hazel asks.

"On it." She takes the tray from the air, breaking the spell Hazel has placed on it to make it float. "These look good."

"Only the best for the customers," Hazel says brightly before turning to me. "Do you want the rejects to take back?"

"What's in them?" I ask.

She shrugs and pushes a strand of bright blue hair behind her ear. "The usual. Joy and brightness. It's always the best choice for macarons."

"Sure, I'll take some of them with me."

"I'll go box them up for you," she says, setting down the second tray so Oakley can unpack them into the display.

A vague pang of jealousy flashes through me at the reminder of how well my sisters work together and that I'm not a part of it, even though I want to be. None of them have any idea how much I love to bake. Or that I'm good at it.

It isn't even really their fault. When our grandmother gave over the bakery to them, I was too young to be part of the business along with them. I just wish I had the courage to tell them I want to be a part of this.

One day I'll do it. I'm just not sure exactly when.

Hazel disappears into the back while Oakley finishes putting the macarons on display next to Rowen's gingerbread men.

"Isn't it a little early for Christmas biscuits?" I ask.

Oakley sighs loudly. "You sound like Rowen, she chuntered about it the entire time she was making them. But we get so many requests for them. Besides, the kids don't see them as Christmasy, they just want the fun gingerbread."

"You should do some children's cupcakes," I say offhandedly. "I saw a tutorial video about how to make ducks out of marshmallows and fondant. The kids would love those."

"Hmm, you might be onto something there," my sister agrees.

"And Hazel could make children's macarons. Imagine one of the pink ones with pig ears and little eyes." Excitement builds in me at the thought of all the ways we could make existing products appeal to even more potential customers. If kids want the cakes, they'll drag the parents in and they'll end up buying more.

"They do sound cute," Oakley admits. "I'll suggest it. It can't hurt to try."

"Exactly. Though I'm not sure there's much that can be done to make Clover's baklava kid-friendly."

"Then we'll just work on selling that to their parents," she assures me. "We sell enough of it to keep her busy." The affection in her voice intensifies as she talks about her twin.

"Good point," I say. "Though we could also do with some basics. Hazel barely ever makes croissants."

"There's a good reason for that," Hazel says as she comes back out front and hands me the box of rejected macarons. "They're a pain to make."

I bite my tongue before I say something about how much I enjoy making them. This isn't the right time to tell them I want to join the bakery.

"Ash was just suggesting you decorate some of the macarons as pigs," Oakley says.

"Oh?" Hazel looks right at me and picks up a pink macaron. "What did you have in mind?"

Delight fills me at the idea of getting to show them one of my ideas. I half expected them to dismiss me just because I'm younger and not technically one of their business partners.

I set down my bags and take the macaron from her, pulling out my wand. "Obviously we'd want to make the decorations properly and not with magic."

"Naturally," Hazel agrees.

I conjure up an image of the pig macaron in my mind and wave my wand towards the confection. A small shower of sparks falls onto the bright pink surface, making the decorations spring to life on top of it. I turn the macaron back to her. "Something like that."

Hazel smiles broadly. "Ash, you're a genius."

"Thanks."

"We'll have to run it by Rowen and Clover, but I don't think they'll say no," she says.

"Row will probably be glad there's something to take the pressure off her gingerbread men all year around," Oakley responds.

"Hmm, true. And it could expand the produce for the Christmas Fayre too," Hazel says.

"Then she'll need help manning the stall. Do you think one of us will be able to do it?" Oakley asks.

"I could do it," I volunteer without thinking.

The two of them turn to me, surprised expressions on their faces.

"What?" I ask with a shrug. "I've helped at the fayre before."

"Yes, but we all figured you did that because you had to," Hazel responds.

"It's a fun event. I can see if Ellie will help out too if you think Rowen will need an extra extra pair of hands." I know she'll enjoy the event, especially if she gets to try lots of fun food.

"All right, we'll run it past her when she gets back from the suppliers," Hazel says.

"But shouldn't you be in class now?" Oakley adds.

"I don't have a class until four."

"It's half-three," she responds.

I jump to my feet, trying not to panic too much. "I need to get going." I grab my stuff and head for the door, waving to my sisters while they laugh at my lack of time-keeping skills.

I should just about be able to get back to the academy in time for class. I pull out my phone and fire off a message to Ellie to save my seat.

Chapter Three

ELLIE

I dump my bag the moment I reach my room and barely resist the urge to flop down on my bed and pretend the rest of the world doesn't exist.

Unfortunately for me, that won't get my academy work done, or prepare me for my upcoming internship interview. Most academy students don't do an internship until the summer of their third year, but considering I want to be a designer when I graduate and my parents don't want me to, I know I need to get all the experience I can to make my dreams a reality.

A knock sounds on my door, pulling me from my thoughts and distracting me from the torrent of nerves within me. "Come in," I call.

I'm not surprised when the door opens and Ash steps inside, a tray with two steaming mugs and a cake on it.

I can *feel* my entire face light up at the sight. Somehow, he always seems to know exactly what I need, even when I don't.

"How was your history of magical fashion lecture?" he asks as he places the tray down on my desk.

I sigh and sit down on my bed. "Fascinating."

"Then why do you look like you're about to scream?" Ash asks.

I let out a dry chuckle. "Because I'm tired," I admit. "It's hard that I have to take the lessons I want to on the side."

"I'm sorry."

She shrugs. "You know what it's like. Your sisters expect you to have a career outside the bakery."

"They do," he agrees. "But they wouldn't insist on me taking certain subjects just because they think it's best."

He hands me one of the mugs and I take it, letting our fingers brush against one another as I do. I'm not sure if it means anything, but our friendship seems to be full of moments like it, and a tension that builds the more time we spend together.

The only problem is that I'm too scared to try and do anything about it, and I assume Ash feels the same way.

"It'll all be better once I've had my interview," I promise.

"Tomorrow, right?"

"Do you really need to ask that?" I wrap my hands around the mug and inhale deeply. "This isn't the normal coffee you use."

"I picked some new stuff up from Willow's shop," he responds. "And I got Oakley to make you a cupcake with a hint of confidence in the frosting. You don't have to eat it now, but I thought it might make you feel better about tomorrow."

Warmth spreads through my chest at the thoughtful gesture. "Thank you, Ash."

"You're welcome."

The way he smiles at me makes it seem like I'm the only person in his world. It's times like this I can believe that he feels the same way I do, and that the reason he never goes on any dates is because of me.

But I push that to the side. There's no use letting myself get caught up in a fantasy that can never be real.

"Do you want me to go so you can prep?" he asks, gesturing towards the door but not moving.

I shake my head, knowing that's what he's expecting me to do or he wouldn't have brought himself a drink too. "I'd rather have the company."

"We can watch a show or something to keep your mind off it?"

"That sounds perfect." I set my coffee down on the windowsill and grab my laptop from my bag. "I think there's a new episode of The Magical Sewing Bee."

"Then let's watch that."

"Even if you don't like it?" I ask.

"I never said that. If I remember correctly, what I actually said was that I'd never have started watching if it wasn't for you."

"Mmhmm, and that's just another way of saying that you don't actually like it."

"I like anything that means we get to hang out," he counters.

My heart skips a beat, clearly not on board with the idea that we're just friends.

I distract myself by pulling up the show and trying not to think about it too much. If something was going to happen between the two of us, then it would have happened already. A year and a bit is long enough to know that.

I click on the play button and shuffle back so I can lean

against the group of pillows Ash has set up at the back of my bed.

"Can you pass me the cupcake?" I ask.

He nods and holds it out to me.

"Thank you." I take it from him, our fingers lingering as they brush against one another, just like they did with the mug. If I didn't know better, I might start thinking he was interested in more than being friends.

I clear my throat and pull the cupcake away as the music from the opening sequence of the show starts. I pop the lid of the cupcake box, mostly for something to do to distract me from the complicated swirl of emotions building inside me. There's an appeal in feeling something else, even if the confidence from the cupcake won't cover up my actual emotions.

"Did you not get one for yourself?"

He shakes his head. "Hazel gave me some reject macarons though. I can get them if you want one?"

I shake my head, not wanting him to leave. I swipe my finger through the buttercream and stick some in my mouth. I close my eyes and let out a small hum of appreciation.

Ash clears his throat, though I'm not sure why.

"It's good," I say.

"I'm not surprised."

"Want some?"

"Frosting?"

I swipe my finger through it again and hold it out to him.

His eyes widen and he shakes his head. "I got it for you."

"That doesn't mean I can't share." I eat the frosting off my finger, enjoying the warm feeling of confidence already settling in my stomach. I'm not sure what the best part of

Oakley's cupcakes are, the taste, or the emotion I get after I've eaten one.

She'd probably say that's the point.

"Oh, look, Antoine is struggling this week," Ash says, pointing at my laptop screen. "It's a shame, I was rooting for him."

I raise an eyebrow. "Antoine? Really? His designs are so basic."

"They look pretty good to me."

I shake my head in disbelief. I'm not sure how he can think Antoine's designs are the best when they're clearly inferior to some of the things the other contestants are making, but I suppose I should be glad that he's showing a sign that he actually enjoys the show.

I finish my cupcake and swap it for the amazing cup of coffee he brought. One day, Ash is going to make a great boyfriend to someone.

Sometimes it hurts to know that person isn't going to be me.

Chapter Four

ELLIE

I pat my pocket to make sure I have my wand despite the fact I don't actually need it right now. Sometimes, it reassures me to remind myself that it's there and nothing bad has happened to it. Mum used to always say that no matter what, if I had my wand, then I would be able to get out of any situation.

I'm not sure that's true, but it's always served as good reassurance despite that.

Maybe I should have kept my cupcake for this morning after all. I could use a shot of confidence right now. I pull out my phone, mostly for something to do with my hands. A small smile coming to my face when I see the message from Ash waiting for me.

< Good luck, Ellie. You've got this. >

"Eloise Denning?" a middle-aged woman asks from the door by the reception desk.

I shove my phone back into my pocket and jump to my

feet, clutching my design portfolio close to my chest. "That's me."

"We're ready for you. Please follow me."

I nod and hurry over, trying my best to ignore the nerves fluttering in my stomach. It's going to be fine. Ash thinks I've got this handled, I have to believe in myself too.

The woman leads me into a small interview room with a plain wooden table and six chairs around it. I hope they're not all going to be filled because I'm not sure I'll be able to deal with that level of scrutiny.

"Please take a seat, Miss Denning," the woman says.

"Thank you," I respond shakily, pulling out a chair and sitting down on it. I place my portfolio on the table, but don't open it.

"This is Professor Gregson, I'm Professor Hill," she says, gesturing first to a man in his mid-fifties with round glasses and a plum jacket, before sitting in her seat.

"It's a pleasure to meet you both." My voice shakes ever so slightly.

"We understand that you're looking for an internship with Demarque?"

I nod.

"Can you tell us why?" she asks.

I take a deep breath, this is where I can make sure I shine. "I've always found the Demarque designs to be the perfect combination of timeless and unique. It's something I find admirable and have always wanted to be part of."

"Finding something admirable doesn't mean you'll be a good fit for the organisation," Professor Hill says.

"I know," I assure her quickly. "I also believe that my style and abilities are good fits for the internship program."

"Normally, we accept students from one of the fashion

schools and not from Grimalkin Academy," Professor Gregson says.

"I understand why you would want to do that." I try to ignore the pounding in my chest. "But I believe not being from one of the fashion schools gives me an edge. I'm able to think outside the box when it comes to solving problems."

Professor Hill's eyebrow quirks up, though I can't tell if that means she's impressed, or that she's very much not. I hope the former, but fear the latter. I want this internship.

"I see you brought a portfolio." Professor Gregson nods towards the black folder resting in front of me.

"I did. I know the interview details didn't require it, but I thought it would be better to be able to show examples of what I'm talking about."

An impressed look crosses Professor Hill's face, but it's gone within moments, making me wonder if I imagined it.

"If you would like, I can talk you through some of the designs?" I'm not sure if that's what they want, but it seems like a good start, especially if I want to prove myself capable.

"Be our guest," Professor Gregson says.

I unzip the folder, trying to appear confident. I know I'm good at this, but now I'm having to present it, I'm starting to question everything.

My portfolio is carefully laid out in the order I think best represents what I want to demonstrate about myself, having taken hours of careful planning and compiling With Ash's help, naturally. His sisters even agreed to be the models in some of the photos.

Unsure exactly what the two professors want from me, I start going through things piece by piece, talking about everything from the inspiration behind some of the designs, to particular problems I came across while making them. Every now and again, they ask me a question, but for the most part, they just let me keep talking. I'm not sure if it's a good thing or not, but I'm going to assume it is.

The longer I go on, the more confident I become, the feeling a lot deeper than the one I got from Oakley's cupcakes. That's probably a good thing, I don't think I like the idea of a baked good being able to actually affect my mood.

The interview passes much more quickly than I expected it to, probably because I've had the chance to talk through the various things I wanted to.

"Thank you, Miss Denning, that was most informative," Professor Hill says after another fifteen minutes. The expression on her face doesn't tell me anything about how she feels about my presentation, but I'm hoping she liked it. "We'll be in touch on Tuesday."

I'm stunned for a moment, not realising I'd hear back so soon. But that's a good thing. It means I won't have to spend too long obsessing over how the interview has gone.

"Thank you for the opportunity to interview," I say, holding my hand out to shake both of theirs. "I really appreciate it."

Professor Hill gives me a small smile, a gesture that I hope means she thinks I'll be a good fit for Demarque.

I zip my portfolio and make my way out of the building, ensuring that I say goodbye to the receptionist on the way. If I do end up getting an internship here, then she's probably going to be a valuable ally, and one I want to make sure I make.

I pull my phone out of my pocket and swipe to unlock it, revealing a new message from Ash.

< Meet you at Cauldron Coffee so you can tell me all about it? >

A broad smile spreads over my face and I switch directions. A coffee is just what I need right now.

Chapter Five

ASH

"Want the last slice of pizza?" I ask Ellie.

She shakes her head. "You have it."

"Are you okay?"

She looks over at me, a curious expression on her face. She's cute when she does that. "What makes you ask?"

"You just seem nervous." I can't put my finger on exactly what it is, but something seems off about the way she's acting.

Ellie lets out a loud sigh and leans back against the wall, fidgeting with the edge of my duvet as she does. I don't think she even realises she's doing it. Or how much I like seeing her so comfortable in my room.

"Are you going to tell me, or are you going to sit around pretending you're in a music video with fake rain on the window and a black and white tint?" I ask.

She lets out a soft snort of amusement. "No one makes videos like that anymore."

HOPE

"It doesn't matter, you knew what I meant," I point out as I grab the final slice of pizza and start to munch on it.

"I did. And I don't look like that."

I raise an eyebrow and pull out my wand. I wave it in front of me and project her reflection in front of her along with a filter of rain.

She lets out a light laugh and shakes her head in bemusement. "You're exaggerating."

"And you're deflecting. What's bothering you? Is it the internship? When are they supposed to get back to you?"

"Tomorrow," she answers immediately, telling me I'm right about what's bothering her.

"You said the interview went well, right?"

"I mean, I *think* it did, but maybe I'm just deluding myself."

I move the pizza box and shuffle closer to her, holding out my arm. She comes closer and leans her head against my shoulder. I tighten my arm around her, hoping it offers her the comfort I hope it does.

"You're amazing at what you do, El, and they'll have seen that."

"Maybe." She reaches up and pushes a strand of dark hair behind her ear. "I guess I just want this so much that I hate the idea of not getting it."

"Which is why I'm sure you will."

"Your faith in me is appreciated, but you're not exactly unbiased here."

"Hmm, why is that?"

She turns, bringing our faces closer together than before. My gaze briefly dips to her lips, but I tear it away. I won't ruin our friendship by doing anything as rash as kissing her.

"Because you're my friend," she says, the words lancing

straight through me. I hate that my sisters are right, but there's a part of me that really does want to be more than friends with Ellie.

"But I always tell you the truth, right?"

"Well, yes."

"So why would I lie about this?"

"I'm not saying you're lying," she counters. "Just that you can't see the truth."

"Ellie, I think you're insanely talented, and a wonderful person. And it's not just me saying it anyway, it's my sisters too, and you can't wiggle out of that one by saying that they're biased."

"I could do with one of their baked goods filled with hope right now," she mutters, seemingly half-joking.

But maybe there's something I can do about that. There won't be enough time before to get something from them, but that doesn't mean *I* can't do it for her instead. I know how to do the spells needed, but I've never done them for anyone before.

I look at Ellie and know that this is a worthwhile cause to do it for someone for the first time.

Especially if it will make her feel better.

Chapter Six

ELLIE

The moment my eyes crack open I know I'm not going to be able to go back to sleep. I grab my phone and check the time, letting out a small groan as I do.

Seven is too early to be awake when I don't have a lecture until eleven.

But knowing the call from Demarque is going to be coming in at some point today, I know it's a vain hope that I'll be able to fall back asleep.

I climb out of bed and grab my mug from where I left it the night before. If I'm awake, I may as well go and get myself some coffee.

The moment I leave my room, I'm hit by an eerie silence that I don't normally associate with our flat. There's always someone coming and going to one thing or another. It's kind of nice.

It isn't until I open the kitchen door that it changes. I freeze in my tracks as I stare at the sight in front of me.

Ash is bopping his head along to the music on his headphones while he does something to what looks like pastry.

"Ash?"

He looks up, his eyes widening when he sees me. He pulls his headphones off and sets them to the side. "You're up early."

"I couldn't sleep any longer."

He nods in understanding.

"What about you? I'm sure I've heard you say that before eight is the time for bakers and people who love running."

He chuckles. "It's a good job I'm one of those this morning, then." He gestures to the pastry.

"What are you making?"

A slightly embarrassed expression crosses his face. "I was making you some hope croissants."

I blink a few times as the words sink in. "Oh, Ash."

"What?" he asks.

"It's just a really sweet thing to do," I admit. "And it took me a little off guard."

He grins. "That was the point. I didn't expect you to be awake for another hour or so."

"I wasn't sleeping well."

"No, I didn't think you would."

My heart expands to several times what it should be capable of. I try to get it more in check, but it doesn't happen.

How can it when Ash is acting this way?

"Do you want a cup of tea?" I ask, unsure what else I can say.

"That'd be good, thanks, El."

"Maybe I can help once I have?" I ask. "I might not be any good, I've never made croissants before."

"I'll walk you through it," he promises.

"You don't mind?" I fill up the kettle and switch it onto boil while I get both of our mugs ready.

"Why would I?" There's an earnestness in his voice that makes it obvious the question is a genuine one.

I shrug. "Maybe you like doing it alone?"

"Sometimes, I do," he admits. "But I'm making the croissants for you, partly to distract you from the phone call you're going to get. Making them together will do that."

Together. It's ridiculous how much I like the sound of the word coming from him about us.

The click of the kettle draws my attention back to it and the bubbling water within. I hastily add the water to the mugs, using it as a good distraction while Ash continues to work.

I finish off our drinks and take them over to the kitchen table, setting Ash's tea down where he can easily get it.

"Thanks."

"You're welcome."

"I'm done with the pastry," he says. "It just needs to rest, and I made the frangipane earlier, so all that's really left is putting the hope in. Do you want to do it?" he asks.

My eyes widen. "Are you sure it's a good idea if I do?" I ask. "I've heard Oakley's horror story."

Ash chuckles. "Ah, yes. The infamous thunder incident. She's learned from that one."

"To be more wary of ex-boyfriends?"

"How many times has she told you that story?"

"Only twice, but you've told me it at least a dozen more," I tease.

"It'll be fine. We're not planning on feeding them to anyone but ourselves," he points out. "And we can try on a small amount of frangipane first."

"That seems like a good idea."

He grabs a bowl and scoops a portion of it out.

"It's a good job we can do the washing up with magic," I mutter.

Ash chuckles. "You're not wrong there. Though sometimes I wonder if that's a bad thing."

I shoot him a confused look. "How can it possibly be a bad thing that we don't have to do dishes?"

"It means that we don't think about more efficient ways of doing it." He sets the bowl of frangipane down in front of me.

"We use magic every day, how much more efficient can you get?"

"Speaking of, take your wand out," he instructs.

I do, holding it gingerly over the mixture. A small part of me is still in disbelief that he's going to let me do this.

"What now?"

"Okay, so I can give you the words, or we can try without."

"You want me to try doing a spell for the first time without saying the words out loud?" A small squeak comes through my voice.

"I've seen you do it plenty of times," he reminds me. "Just hold your wand like this." He demonstrates the angle.

I try to mimic it.

Ash shakes his head. "Not quite, you need to...wait. I'll show you." He steps up behind me and takes my arms, moving my wand hand into position.

I know I should be focusing on the magic part of what's happening, but the only thing I seem able to register is how close the two of us are. If I twist in his arms, we'd almost be kissing.

No, I can't think like that. I have to banish all thoughts of anything between us from my head for the sake of our friendship.

"Now what?" I ask shakily.

"You need to feel hope as an emotion and send it into the frangipane through your wand." His voice is barely above a whisper, creating a bubble of intimacy around us that I'm unable to ignore.

"Right. Feel hope," I say, mostly to distract myself from the smell of freshly baked pastry and good coffee, a smell that I always associate with Ash.

"The first few times I did it, I repeated the things I was hopeful about out loud. You can try that?" he suggests.

I nod and close my eyes, finding it sometimes helps me to centre myself on magic.

"What do you hope for?" Ash asks, not moving any further away from me, and not letting go of my hand.

I hope you feel the same way I do.

I don't say it out loud. I can't. There's too much at risk if I do. Instead, I clear my throat. "I hope I have a good call with Demarque later today. I hope I get the internship."

A tingle travels up and down my arm as I keep repeating the words, adding in the silent hope about Ash as I do.

I open my eyes in time to see a small shower of sparks sprinkle over the frangipane. For a moment, it sits there, but then it sinks in and becomes one with the mixture.

Ash lets go of my hand and steps back. I miss his closeness almost instantly.

"That's it?" I ask.

He nods. "But now we try it." He grabs a clean spoon and dips it into the mix, gesturing for me to do the same.

I take a spoon, accidentally knocking my hand against the side of the bowl.

Slowly and rather nervously, I take a bite.

"It's good," Ash says appreciatively. "I'm impressed."

A small blush rises to my cheeks. "Thanks."

"Mine wasn't nearly so good the first time around."

"So now what do we do?"

"We make the rest of it." He gestures to the bigger bowl of frangipane. "And then we roll out the pastry and do the rest of it."

"Coffee first," I murmur, picking up my mug and taking a deep drink, partly because I want some, and partly because I want a chance to compose myself. I haven't quite managed to shake the way it felt to have him so close to me.

I set my mug back down. "Right, first job?"

"You have some frangipane on your cheek," he says.

"Oh." I reach up to wipe it away. "Is it gone?"

He tries to repress a light chuckle. "You've made it worse."

"Eurgh."

"Here, let me." He leans over and wipes it away.

The whole world seems to stop turning as we stare at one another.

Ash pulls away first. "Right, pastry."

I clear my throat, regaining some of my composure. "Just tell me what to do," I say.

We barely say anything as we work, but there's a nice camaraderie about it. Things feel comfortable with Ash, even when we're avoiding talking about the moment which still lingers between us.

At some point, I feel like we may have to actually talk about it.

But for now, we can focus on making the croissants.

Chapter Seven

ELLIE

My phone buzzes and I almost fall off my bed in a hurry to sit up and answer it.
"Hello?"

Silence greets me and I pull it back to check if I've picked up the call right, only to end up disappointed when I realise the buzz is just a message.

I sigh and swipe over the screen. My annoyance disappears when I see it's from Ash, even if it does bring a wave of confusing feelings along with it.

< Croissants are ready, want me to bring you one? >

< I'll come to you. > I type back quickly and grab my coffee mug.

The heavenly smell of freshly baked croissants hangs in the air, and I'm sure it will bring more than one of our flatmates to the kitchen before long.

I push open the door and step inside just in time for Ash to put a fresh cup of coffee on the table alongside the plate full to the brim of croissants.

"We made more than we should have," I say.

"That's the fun bit, we'll be eating them for days. Do you want one now?"

"Do you even need to ask?"

Ash chuckles and gets up to head towards the cupboard with the plates.

Before I can sit down, my phone starts to buzz again. I lift it up, my eyes widening as I see the number.

"Is it them?" Ash asks, freezing in position.

I nod.

"Answer it."

I take a shaky breath and press the green button.

"Hello?" I say.

"Hi, I'd like to speak to Eloise Denning please," the voice on the other end says.

"Speaking."

Ash sets the plates down and comes over, hovering but not coming too close.

"It's Professor Hill from your interview with Demarque," she says. "I'm delighted to be able to offer you an internship with us."

My eyes widen as the words sink in. "Thank you." It's a miracle that I manage to get the words out.

"We'll be sending you an email with start dates and induction paperwork later today."

"I'll keep an eye out for it," I promise.

"Excellent. We look forward to working with you."

"Likewise."

The line clicks and the call ends, leaving me standing in the middle of the kitchen, a little dazed.

"Did you get it?" Ash asks.

I nod slowly. "I did. I got it."

He opens his arms as I step in for a hug, but something

stops us, the air becoming heavy with anticipation of something.

I bite my bottom lip and his gaze flicks down to it. I know what's going to happen now.

So does he.

If we don't stop it, then our friendship may be completely ruined.

Or it could become something even greater.

He leans in and my eyes flutter closed. The moment his lips brush against mine, all thoughts of this going badly are chased out of my mind. It feels right, like the two of us fit together. Which should have been obvious to me.

We break apart but don't pull away from one another.

"I..."

"Don't you dare," I cut him off.

He chuckles. "You don't even know what I was going to say."

"I can guess. Something like you're sorry, or you didn't mean for that to happen," I counter. "And I'd rather you didn't."

An amused smile lights up his face. "I was actually going to say that I've been thinking about that for a long time."

"Oh?" I reach up and tuck a strand of hair behind my ear. "Why didn't you do anything about it sooner?"

"Because you're too important to me and I didn't want to lose you."

"I feel the same," I admit. "So are we going to kiss again, or are we going to pretend it never happened?"

"I know which I'd prefer." He kisses me again, clearly seeing the agreement on my face. I lose myself in it, enjoying the way it feels to finally have my emotions out in the open.

And knowing that he feels the same.

"I guess we didn't need the croissants," he murmurs once we break our kiss.

"That's not true. I enjoyed making them with you," I promise him. "Hopefully you'll teach me to make a lot more."

He chuckles and draws me to the table, plating up one of the croissants and setting it down in front of me before grabbing one of them for himself. "I look forward to it."

"And I'm looking forward to making sure you tell your sisters you want to be part of the bakery. You're too good to not be involved with the family business."

"I'll think about it."

"Ash," I say sternly.

"All right, I'll talk to them," he promises.

"I'm going to hold you to that." I pick up the croissant and pull it apart, popping a bit in my mouth. The flaky pastry melts in my mouth, and the sweet frangipane perfectly compliments it.

The shot of hope enters my system, but it's nothing compared to the real thing simmering within me. My relationship with Ash is finally in a place to take the next step, and I got the internship I was desperate for. Hopeful is exactly how I feel.

Thank you for reading The Pastry Warlock, I hope you enjoyed it! If you'd like to read more from the witches of Broomstick Bakery, you can start the series with The Cupcake Witch (Oakley's story): http://books2read.com/thecupcakewitch

If you would like to stay up to date with new releases & updates on my books, you can download a free collection of paranormal romances here: https://books.authorlauragreenwood.co.uk/74mk3mnxxj

Also by
Laura Greenwood

Broomstick Bakery - Cauldron Coffee Shop - Grimalkin Academy: Kittens - Grimalkin Academy: Catacombs - Grimalkin Vampires - Obscure Academy

Hope Is the Dream

by

Lynda Throsby

Chapter One

"No, please, Jenson. Don't leave me. I couldn't live without you. Please think of that. Think of me and think of our little one. Jenson, choose me. Choose us. Choose hope. If you choose hope, then anything is possible. Hope has always been our dream and our motto. I'm begging you. Things are dark right now, but believe me, there will be light. There will be a big shining ball of bright light. We're pregnant. We've got a peanut in here. Jenson, I love you with everything I have." I sob, holding my tummy, tears streaming down my face as I kneel by him, cradling his head with my hands on my lap. Blood is everywhere. I don't know what's happening or what's going on.

My life is a blur. I found out a couple of weeks ago I was pregnant. I couldn't find him to tell him. There was no replying to texts, his phone was switched off. I had no idea where he was. I was going out of my mind with worry. Not the best way to start a pregnancy.

I fell hard for Jenson the minute I laid eyes on him.

Chapter Two

ONE YEAR EARLIER

I was fresh out of college and needed a job. I got a degree in tourism and travel, but the world had gone to shit with viruses and war, and there were no jobs in the travel industry. I don't have any parents, just an older sister and brother, Tash and Tony, them me Thea. Mum never spoke about our dad. He died when I was six months old. Tony has very few memories of him, and Tash doesn't remember anything about him. Mum brought us up on her own. She worked her socks off to give us everything.

We lost mum five years ago to cancer. Cancer fucking sucks big balls. Tony was away in the army at the time. Mum was so proud of him; he was the apple of her eye. Tash set herself up as a nail technician, initially working from home, then she hired a chair in a local salon. I, on the other hand, didn't know what I wanted to do.

I ended up looking after mum. There were the three of us at home. Mum, Tash, and me. I had the time to look after her since I'd just left school. It was heart-breaking,

ONE YEAR EARLIER

watching her deteriorate from this amazing, independent, strong woman who was full of life to a little frail lady who had no life left in her. I did what I could to make her last months special for her. How I kept it together, I will never know, but you must do what you have to do. I surprised even myself. From diagnosis of ovarian cancer, she only survived three months. It had already spread too much. It was quick, and in one respect, it was a blessing it was quick for her sake.

Tash lived at home with me until she moved in with her boyfriend, Tad, a year ago. I managed to get myself into college months after Mum passed. I wanted to travel and see the world. I had all these ideas I would fall in love in Bora Bora and never come home. I would live the island life in a hot climate, with a hot man near the bluest of blue waters. Yeah, well, that didn't work out.

Fast forward to me finishing college with a distinction, not having my mum around to be as proud of me as she was Tony, and the world going to crap. At twenty-one, I had no choice but to get a job or two. I started working as a receptionist at the salon where Tash worked. The problem was, it was minimum wage, and I had rent to pay, plus bills.

Living on my own was hard. If I didn't pay rent, I'd forfeit the house we grew up in. I managed all through college because I got student loans. Yeah, I'd have to pay them all back when I got a well-paying job, which would probably never happen, so I took them out to help with my rent and bills for the now.

Just before mum died, she told me there is always hope. Make sure to always hope, then anything is possible. That was how I ended up going to college. I had hope and dreams from mum.

I worked the day job, but it wasn't enough. I needed a

CHAPTER EIGHTY-FOUR

night job, and the only thing I could think of was bar work or being a stripper, and that wasn't happening. The place I lived was a bit rough, to say the least, but we grew up there and it was home. No matter what part of England you're in, every town has its rough areas.

The bar I was told was looking for a barmaid was not one I had ever been in before the interview. It wasn't my type of place. If I wore lots of black make-up, had spiky hair, and dressed in a leather, studs, and buckles, I'd have fit right in. Well, I had to do just that. My hair was black and long anyway, so that wasn't a problem. I wore dark make-up. I taught myself from YouTube videos, and I looked hot. I went to the charity shop and bought some gothic clothes. I'm a real girly girl in real life. I love pink, sparkles, high heels, and all things sugar-coated, so this was a complete change for me. I walked into the interview wearing huge platform black boots with lots of buckles up the sides, fishnet tights with holes in them, a short leather skirt, and a black off-the-shoulder holey top, with a tank top underneath to keep my dignity. I wore black and purple make-up, and I had some of my hair up in two messy buns with the rest down my back. I looked fucking good, even If I do say so myself.

My first few shifts went well. I got hit on more times than the till bell rang. I was in training as I had never done bar work before, but I soon picked it up. It was a doddle. I was nervous because the men in the bar were not anything like who I would ever go for. These were mean, rough-looking, but there were a couple of hot, rugged guys amongst the older ones. If Tony saw me working there, he would have flipped. I came to realise this was where the local biker gang hung out. I didn't even know we *had* a local biker gang. I was put in my place and told they don't have gangs,

ONE YEAR EARLIER

it's a club. An MC. A Motorbike Club. I soon learned after being there for a couple of weeks that this was where the clubs hangout was. There were some huge rooms out the back of the pub that were their meeting rooms. The clubhouse, as it was called. I was going to quit because it wasn't something I wanted to be associated with, but Jerry, the bar manager, asked if I would stay. He said the clients loved me, and I was a good worker. He even offered me more money and a full-time job. That, with my tips, meant I would earn a lot more than at the salon and this part-time, so I took it.

Two months into my job, I loved it. I bought more gothic clothes so I would fit in, and I got to know a lot of the regulars. We had good banter; I gave as good as I got from them. They liked that. I learned that the MC had a ranking. There was a president, a vice president, then sergeant or soldiers or something like that, all ranked by birthright or longevity. I laughed at the president and VP. I mean, it was just a biker club. They didn't rule the country or anything.

I soon learned differently.

It was a quiet afternoon when the hottest guy I had ever laid eyes on, walked through the bar doors. I was swooning as he looked around the bar then walked to the entrance to the back rooms. He didn't even notice me. I didn't question who he was. He had a cut on—their term for a waistcoat displaying their club logo—and it wasn't my place to ask. I heard laughing and turned to see Jerry. Was he laughing at me? I turned to look behind me to see if there was something going on there. Nope. I scowled at him.

"Oh, Thea, it happens every fucking time. Jenson only has to walk into a place and all the women wet their panties. Seems you're not immune. You should have seen the look on your face. All dreamy and wishing he would look your way." He placed his hands under his chin and

CHAPTER EIGHTY-FOUR

batted his eyelashes in a stupid mimic of a swooning girl, sighing.

"Did not." I threw the tea towel from my hands at him and stormed off to get some bottles of Jack Daniels from the back. I heard him laughing at me

"Oh, Jenson, please notice me. Please come suck on my titties," he mimicked in a girly voice.

I hated Jerry, but I liked the name Jenson. From what I'd managed to see of him, he was gorgeous. I wanted to see him again.

The afternoon went slowly as usual, but then the evening was buzzing, and I was run off my feet. I think it had a lot to do with Jenson being there. He was the centre of attention, mostly to the women. It was the first time I'd seen him in the time I'd worked there, so he must have been away somewhere.

I kept catching glimpses of him through the throngs of people. Each time, there was a different girl sitting on his knee, sucking on his neck. That put me right off him.

"I'll take a beer when you're ready, love," a deep, husky voice said.

It sent shivers down my spine. *What the fuck is that all about?*

I finished the order I was preparing and turned to give the glasses to Thomas, the guy who ordered them. Somehow, I managed to put the glasses—all four of them—on the bar without dropping them because, as I turned, I looked straight into the most beautiful blue eyes I had ever seen. The face of an angel with blonde hair was staring right back at me. It was him.

My heart skipped a beat and beads of sweat formed on my brow. He just stared straight into my boring hazel eyes. I somehow composed myself and held out my hand

ONE YEAR EARLIER

for the money from Thomas, unable to tear my gaze from Jenson.

"Thanks, Thomas," I squeaked as he told me to keep the change.

I tilled in the order and put the change in my tip jar, then grabbed a pint glass and started to pull a beer as requested. I concentrated as hard as I could on the glass and the tap, my hands shaking. I placed the full glass on the bar in front of him. I couldn't look him in the eyes because I knew I would blush.

I held out my hand. "That's £4.75, please."

He chuckled, placing a note in my hand, but he grabbed my hand and wrapped it around the note. Shockwaves coursed through my body at his touch. He pulled me towards him, only slightly as there was a bar in our way. I had no choice but to look into his face. That close, I could study it. I saw a couple of faint scars; one on his cheek and one above his right eyebrow. He also had a piercing in that eyebrow; a ring with a ball on it. I watched as his lips curled slightly at the corners.

"Keep the change, beautiful." Then he let go and left. He didn't even take his beer with him.

I felt faint. His touch lingered on my skin and the shocks coursed through my entire body. I swear he made me wet. I had never felt anything like that when talking to a man.

I turned to the till to tap in his beer, and when I opened my hand that held the note, I gasped. I'd never seen a fifty-pound note before. He said to keep the change. That was a forty-five quid tip. I couldn't take that. I got the change out of the till, put the twenty-five pence into my tip jar, then headed in his direction, picking up his beer on the way. He had another girl sitting on his knee.

I slammed the pint on the table in front of him then

CHAPTER EIGHTY-FOUR

reached for his hand—the one not wrapped round the girl's waist—and I forcefully laid the notes in his hand.

"Thanks, but no thanks. I couldn't possibly take this as a tip." I turned and walked back to the bar.

"Well, missy, I'm not sure if that was brave or just stupid. Time will tell." Jerry scowled at me, raising his eyebrows.

The rest of the night went by quickly. The devil in disguise didn't come back to the bar. I glanced over at him a few times unintentionally, during the night, and each time, he'd been sitting with no girls on his lap, just staring at me.

I thought back to Jerry's words. Was I stupid? I didn't think so. I was just not taking that huge tip. God knows the money would have been useful, but I felt like it was him buying me, and no one buys me.

The place finally cleared out, all except Jenson. He'd made me uneasy most of the night. I cleaned up the bar with Jerry. He'd been talking to Jenson a little bit but helping me too.

I took my full to the brim tip jar into the back and emptied it into my bag. Grabbing my stuff, I shouted goodbye to Jerry and headed out the back. I usually walked home. A woman shouldn't be out on her own walking late at night, but I didn't live far from the bar, and I'd been okay the last few months. I kinda got the feeling if anything bad did happen to me, that the club would hunt down whoever did it. A lot of the members seemed to be a little protective of me. I think it was because they classed me as a friendly or something like that. I heard a lot of what went on in there, but I took no notice of it. At first, I was a little horrified. They did scare me, and when I asked Jerry why they all had a '1% er' badge on their cuts, he just laughed and said to use the internet. I did just that and it terrified me.

ONE YEAR EARLIER

I was lost in my own world and not far from home when I heard footsteps getting closer behind me. I never wore my EarPods at night for that reason. I had my hand in my pocket on my pepper spray, ready if someone tried anything. Then I heard that voice

"T, wait up. Please, stop." It sent shivers down my spine again. How could just his deep, gravelly voice do that to me?

I stopped in my tracks. One, because I didn't want him near my house, and two, it was his voice. The command made me stop. Also, why was he calling me *T* when we hadn't even been introduced?

He stepped around and in front of me. He was tall. I didn't realise how tall he was behind the bar. I looked up at him and saw his smiling face looking down at me. He adjusted his stance by widening his legs so he was a little lower. "Hey," he said.

I looked into his eyes. It was dark out at nearly two in the morning, but we were by a street light so I could see them clearly.

"Hey," I said back coyly.

"I was waiting for you to come out the front of the bar. I sat waiting, then I asked Jerry. He said you left. I couldn't find you at first."

"So, you found me. It's a bit late to be stalking someone, isn't it? It's a good job you called out or you might have been sprayed." I held out the pepper spray to show him.

He held up his hands, pretending to recoil. "Yeah, I'm glad I shouted to you. I've had that before and it's not nice. I couldn't see right for days. Pops wasn't best pleased, but I didn't do anything to deserve it. The oinks raided one of my garages for no reason and sent in pepper bombs. Fuckers. My pops is my boss. That's why he wasn't pleased."

CHAPTER EIGHTY-FOUR

He didn't have to explain anything to me. I stood with my arms folded over my chest; it was my *back off* stance.

He noticed and stepped back. "I didn't mean to startle you so late. Just, well, I wanted to make sure you got home okay."

What bullshit. I wanted to leave, but I didn't want him to follow me home and know where I lived. He could attack me or something. I needed to lie.

"Well, I'm fine, thank you. I do this every night without any help. I can manage to get home on my own. Besides, sometimes my boyfriend comes to meet me if he's staying over. My sister and brother are home too. Thanks, anyway."

I noticed the surprised look on his face, which seemed to morph into hurt. He looked taken aback. Why? Did he think I wouldn't have a boyfriend?

"Well, if I was your boyfriend, I would make sure I was there every night to walk you home. There is no way I would let you walk home in the early hours on your own."

It was my turn to be shocked. He came across as a pig-headed womaniser from what I'd seen. I'd watched not only the women around him, but the men as well. It was like he was some messiah returned home from a pilgrimage or something. Jerry even commented that was why it was so busy, that it happened every time he returned. Not that I was complaining; my tips jar was full.

"Look, thanks for coming to see I was okay, but I need to get home. It's been a long day and I'm shattered. I've been run off my feet all night." I started to walk around him, and he moved to the side to let me pass.

I didn't look to see if he was following me, and I didn't hear him. I rounded the corner to my road and glanced back. He was still standing where I left him. I practically ran to my house.

575

ONE YEAR EARLIER

Once inside, I didn't turn the lights on, just in case he was outside watching the houses. I climbed the stairs to my room, stripping along the way, and fell into bed in just my bra and knickers.

I'd been at work every day for the next few days and hadn't seen Jenson again. Every time the door opened, I looked up to see if it was him. Jerry clocked on to me looking for him.

"T, I say this because I care about you. I don't think any good will come of hooking up with Jenson. He's a nice kid and I've known him most of his life, but he's a danger to himself and those around him. Tobias has tried to put him right a few times and it's not ended well. He's in line to run the Mammon MC once Tobias hangs up his pres cut. I'm not sure Jenson is ready for it, but I don't think it will be too long. Tobias is already talking about retiring. I think that's why Jenson has come back. He's been away for a few months. I don't know why or what he's been doing. I try to stay out of their business. He just has different ideas to Tobias and Colin. He wants to do things differently. Who knows, maybe if he settled down with a good woman who will stand by him, he might change. I just don't want to see you get hurt or mixed up in it. You're not a biker whore, that's for sure." He laughed. "In fact, have you ever been on a bike before?"

It was my turn to laugh. "Me? God, no. My mum always said they were killing machines and I was never to get on one. I think she knew someone who died in a bike accident." I shrugged. Thinking about it, Mum never elaborated on it. Just a few times out of the blue as I got older she said to steer clear of bikes and bikers. I never really thought about it until then.

God, I missed her. I often wondered what she would

CHAPTER EIGHTY-FOUR

think of me working there knowing it was a biker's clubhouse. I don't think she would have liked it.

It had been three weeks, and still no sign of Jenson. I still looked for him. There was a lot of activity in there yesterday. Something had happened, but I had no idea what. I hadn't seen Tobias—not that I saw him much anyway as he kept himself in the back—but I knew who he was. He was a good-looking older man. He had grey hair and a grey beard, but it was peppered. He also looked tanned all the time. If I liked older men, I would definitely have gone for him. He also didn't seem as intimidating as some of the others, yet the men practically bowed when he entered the room. He was always polite whenever he came to sit in the bar.

Everyone was in the bar, the whole club. They were in and out of the clubhouse. Some frantic, rushing around shouting things, others looking worried.

"Hey, Jerry, is this something we should worry about?" I nodded towards all the comings and goings.

He shrugged. "Who knows? I've seen it like this before, and I'm not gonna lie, we have come under attack here. The guys are good at defending their territory, though." I must have looked surprised. "Don't worry. If anyone attacks, we have a safe bunker out back. The club made it for this purpose and for those working here as we are usually the first in the line of fire."

"Are you talking actual gunfire? If you are, then, fuck. I'm not sure I can carry on working here. I don't want a job where my life is on the line. I only wanted to tend the bar." Maybe I could go back to the salon where Tash was for a while and look for another bar to work in.

"We will be safe, Thea. It's happened before and no one got killed. Just a couple of the club members got injured."

ONE YEAR EARLIER

"Look, Jerry. I'm sorry. I can't do this. There was nothing about working here that said I would put my life at risk. I'm young. I want to travel. I lost my mum, and I don't have a dad. I want to make something of myself. If it starts getting bad, I'm going to leave. I don't want to drop you in it, but I can't do this."

He hung his head and nodded slightly.

"Don't worry, sweetheart. Nothing will happen to you. I will personally make sure you will be safe."

That gravelly voice. Where did he come from? He hadn't been around for weeks, then he suddenly appeared like Houdini. I had those tingles running down my spine again. I didn't turn to look at him because I knew who it was. How could I not with that voice?

"What's going on? Who are you personally seeing to, Jenson?" Tobias had joined in.

God, I felt like a wuss. Jenson explained what he had just heard me saying to Jerry.

"Is that right, Thea? Look, love, nothing will happen to you. We have a first line of defence which will stop as much as we can before it gets here. If it reaches here, you will be in the bunker. I promise you, you are safe. A lot safer with us than not." Tobias winked at me.

Why would he say that? Was I in danger by working there? Was it because I was now associated with the Mammon MC? Fuck, why did I take this job? No wonder he offered me a lot of money. It was danger money with all the shit that could go down. I dropped the towel I was using to clean the glasses and headed into the back. I needed a few minutes.

I went to the bathroom and sat on the toilet lid, head in my hands.

CHAPTER EIGHTY-FOUR

Am I safer here with them? I was perfectly safe before I started working here.

There was a knock on the door.

"Erm, busy here," I shouted. They knocked again.

I sighed and unlatched the door. Jenson smiled then looked at me sitting on the toilet and wrinkled his nose.

I burst out laughing. "As if I would open the door whilst I was actually doing anything on the toilet."

His turn to burst out laughing. I laughed with him. I couldn't help it. If anyone could have seen us, me sitting on the loo and him in the doorway, both laughing. I stopped suddenly and just watched him. I got the feeling he didn't do this often. I don't know why. He wiped away tears from his eyes and looked at me. We just examined each other without the need for words.

Jenson crouched down in front of me. "I promise you, I will make sure you come to no harm. There's just something about you. I love your sass and how you don't bow down to me like other women do. They just want to be part of this life and the pres's other half. You, on the other hand, don't seem to care who I am, or even know who I am. You're just different. Maybe it's because you don't run in my world, but I've fucked other women who don't run in my world before. I just..."

I put my hand up to stop him talking. I didn't want to hear about him fucking other women.

He cocked his head to the side and raised his eyebrow, so I rolled my eyes and huffed, making him laugh again. "See, this is why you're different, and I fucking love it."

I stood and moved past him into the little kitchen area to pour myself some coffee.

"Don't you have urgent business to take care of out there?" I had my back to him, but I jumped when I heard that gravelly voice next to my ear. His hands appeared in front of me, holding onto the counter, boxing me in.

Shit.

"Why would I want to be out there when what I want is right in front of me?"

Oh, no. No way. I am not going there. Jerry warned me.

"Look, Jenson, you're nice and all, but you're just not my cup of tea. Can you please give me some space? I want to drink my coffee and think about what I want to do next. I know you and Tobias said I would be safe, but thinking I could get shot here means this is not my ideal job." I backed into his front, pushing with my ass, trying to make him move, only it did the opposite.

He grabbed my waist with both hands and pulled me tight into him. I swear to God I could feel his hard-on.

My face heated, but I was angry as well as embarrassed. What gave him the right to touch me?

"Jenson, let me go, you buffoon! How dare you touch me like this! Let. Me. Go," I spat, and I poured some hot coffee onto his clasped hands.

Big mistake because it ran down the front of my jeans.

"Ow, fuck! That's hot!" It wasn't the entire mug, just a bit, but it was enough.

Jenson laughed and let me go. I turned as he dabbed his hands with a tea towel. I tried to grab it from him once I saw he was okay, but instead, he raised it above his head so it was out of my reach.

I put my hands on my hips and scowled. Before I knew what was happening, he knelt in front of me and started to pat me down to get some of the wetness off my jeans.

I stepped back in shock and hit my back on the worktop. "Ow, fuck. Look, will you leave me alone and stop touching me, especially where you shouldn't be touching?

CHAPTER EIGHTY-FOUR

Get off me, Jenson." I pulled the towel from his hands and sidestepped him, turning my back on him to pat myself dry.

"Okay, sorry. Look, I'll just go. I'm not used to a woman telling me to fuck off. It never happens. I'm sorry If I overstepped, but please know we will keep you safe. Jerry would hate to lose you, and everyone thinks you're amazing, mainly because you don't take shit from anyone. We like that in a woman."

I listened to him walk away, but suddenly heard lots of shouting, and then... fuck, was that gunfire?

I didn't even know where the fucking bunker was. Panic started to set in. Just then, Jenson re-appeared. He stormed up to me, grabbed my hand, and dragged me to the basement. I had no choice but to follow.

He didn't speak as he pulled me along. He was being gentle but firm, and there was no way I was going to try to stop him, he was in stealth mode. In the basement, he took me to a brick wall at the back. He pressed a brick and a control panel came out. After keying in some numbers, a secret door opened, and he took me inside, where we immediately descended more stairs. My heart was beating so hard it was impossible to hear anything else. My hand grew sweaty in his.

I heard the door shut behind us, and the automatic lights flickered on. Once on flat ground, we walked down a corridor that sloped down. We entered an opening, and it was like being in a posh hotel room. There was a kitchen that looked stocked, a table and chairs, comfy furniture, and a few different doors that were closed. I was in shock this place was even here, never mind it being so nice. I was so busy looking around, I didn't realise he had turned and was holding both my hands, looking at my face.

"I need to get back up there. I will make sure Jerry

ONE YEAR EARLIER

comes down so he doesn't get hurt, then I will come back for you when it's safe to do so. Please stay here. There is a landline phone over there in case no one comes back for whatever reason, and you can phone who you like. Your mobile might not work down here." He leaned in, and to my surprise, he kissed me on the lips, then turned and ran back the way we came.

It took me a few minutes to come around and realise what had just happened. I moved to the kitchen to see what I could get to drink. Preferably something alcoholic. I heard footsteps and turned to see Jerry and a couple of other people appearing in the large room. It was bright in there, even though there were no windows. I breathed out in relief.

"Thank God, Jerry. I was scared. Jenson just dragged me down here."

"Yeah, he told me. We just passed him. We are safe down here, Thea. No one knows this exists. We just need to wait it out. It shouldn't be too long, love."

I was trembling, but I opted for a coffee instead of alcohol; I wanted to keep a clear head. I sat curled up on the couch. Jerry was talking to a woman; I think she was called Geraldine. There were four other women, but I didn't know who they were.

It was sometime later when Tobias came down.

"It's all clear. No fatalities, just a couple of minor injuries. They didn't last long. They knew not to mess with us. They try it on every now and then." He looked at me as he said that. "It doesn't happen often, Thea. This is only the third time in the last five years. It won't happen again."

I just glared at him. "What if another rival MC decides they want to try? Then another and another? It will be nonstop." I turned to Jerry. "I'm sorry, Jerry. I'm going to leave

CHAPTER EIGHTY-FOUR

now and go home. I will call you and let you know my decision on staying or leaving the job. Right now, it's the latter."

I stood up, and just as I was about to walk towards the exit, Jenson appeared. He came barrelling over to me and kissed me again.

I pulled back from him with a quizzical look. "What are you doing? Just leave me the fuck alone! I'm out of here." I stormed past him and headed for the stairs. The door was shut at the top, and I didn't know how to open it to get back into the basement.

I heard him behind me. He leaned around and pressed a brick that opened the door. *Good to know which one it was.* Although, why I thought that, I didn't know. It wasn't like I was going back.

I rushed through the door and up to the kitchen to get my stuff. Jenson followed me, but he didn't speak. I'd probably pissed him off. He pulled me back before I could get out the back door, and I turned on him.

"Leave me the fuck alone. What is your problem? How many times do I have to tell you?" I glared at him, angry, upset, and scared.

He held his hands up as if in surrender. "I think it's best you leave out the front. You don't want to see what's out there." He pointed to the back door.

I frowned. Didn't Tobias say there were no fatalities, just some minor injuries? Why didn't he want me to go out that way? I ignored him, but as soon as I stepped outside, I regretted it.

There were men on the floor, bleeding. I looked at one who seemed to be missing some fingers, and another was missing an ear. Then there was one who looked like he'd got something sticking out of his eye.

What the fuck?

ONE YEAR EARLIER

I stepped back inside and closed the door, turning on Jenson. "Tobias said there were no major injuries. What the hell do you call them? Are they your men?"

He shook his head. "They're from the rival MC. We keep them for a while to send a message. Sorry you had to see that. Fuck, all I seem to do is apologise to you, and for what? You fucking work here, so it's what you will see."

I was taken aback by his tone when all he'd been was nice to me. Was this the real Jenson? Was this him showing me his true colors and why Jerry said to stay away from him?

I didn't speak. I felt sick. I think I was in shock. I just walked past him and headed to the front door as Jerry appeared from the basement. We glanced at each other before I walked out for good.

I knew he followed me home and I didn't care. He more than likely knew where I lived anyway. That was him making sure I got home safe. It was the least he could do under the circumstances.

I'd been lying on the couch for nearly two hours, just thinking about the bar. Was I going to go back? The money was great, but did I want to be where it could be dangerous? Tony would go crazy if he found out, and Tash would too. Not that it was any of their business, but was this the life I wanted? Working in a biker bar? I wouldn't mind if it was in L.A. or something, but I was in dreary England. I didn't even know we had rival biker gangs or gunfights.

I was lost in my thoughts when I heard a light knock at the front door. I bolted upright. Who would that be? No one ever visited, and Tash had her own key and would have knocked then let herself in. They knocked again, then rang the doorbell.

I got up and went to the hallway. I had frosted glass in

CHAPTER EIGHTY-FOUR

the front door so I couldn't make out who it was, and if I got close, they would see my outline.

They knocked again, only a little louder.

"Thea, it's Jenson. I just want to know you're okay."

I rolled my eyes. I didn't want to deal with him. I opened the door, keeping the chain attached.

"I'm okay, Jenson. Thanks for checking in on me."

I began to shut the door. "Thea, can I come in, please? I promise it's just to make sure you're okay."

"Why? We don't know each other. I've only seen you a couple of times and today was the first time we really had anything to say. You can see I'm okay, now you can go."

You would have thought I had just shot him by the look of hurt on his face. He dropped his head and kicked at the step with his hands in his front pockets. I felt mean, and I'm not a mean person. He'd only been nice to me. Now, he looked lost. What difference would a few minutes make? I could make him a drink.

I shut the door, unlatched the chain, then opened it wider for him to come in. The look of acceptance and joy on his face made me smile inwardly. He followed me into the kitchen. It was only small space, and he seemed to fill it.

"Do you want a quick coffee?" I emphasised the *quick,* so he knew not to overstay his welcome.

"Please. White, four sugars."

I stared at him in horror. Four sugars. Yuck. He laughed at the disdain on my face.

I made the coffee and took them both to the lounge where I placed his on a mat on the table, on the other side to where I sat, so he got the message. He did and sat in the chair rather than next to me on the couch. I took my cup and sipped at it for something to do. It felt a little awkward.

ONE YEAR EARLIER

"What did you want, Jenson? You can see I'm okay, so what did you come here for?"

He shifted a little in his seat then leaned forward to take his coffee.

"It's hard, Thea. I never talk to anyone. I never *want* to talk to anyone, but you just seem different. You're not just after me because of who I am." My brow furrowed, and he smiled at me "See, that right there is why you're different. I'm not trying to be big-headed or anything, but most women just fall at my feet. They don't want to get to know me or have a conversation. They just want me to fuck them and fall for them just because they want in on this life. But you don't want this life. It's all I've ever known." He hung his head, then looked up at me. "I just feel like I can talk to you. I have demons, Thea. I have breakdowns. It's why I keep disappearing for months. I don't know if Jerry told you that. I lost hope in life a very long time ago." He took a sip of his coffee, then sat back with his head on the back of the couch, looking up to the ceiling. I watched him closely. I could see the conflict on his face. He was struggling to talk.

"You don't have to tell me anything you don't want to, Jenson, but I'm here if you want to talk, and I'm a good listener. Let me tell you about me, though, if it's easier for you." I told him about my family, how I lost my mum and never knew my dad. He listened to every word and asked me questions.

Since things were going well, I offered him another drink and popped into the kitchen to make it. When I got back, he was looking through a photo album I had on the table at all times. It was the one I used to look at of Mum and my brother and sister.

"You look so happy, and you're just like your mum. She's beautiful."

CHAPTER EIGHTY-FOUR

I blushed. He was saying *I* was beautiful. Instead of sitting back in the chair, he sat next to me on the couch. "Are you quitting your job at the bar? I swear it's not like that most of the time."

I didn't answer him. I sat with my feet up and my back to the arm of the couch so I was facing him. He smiled at me, and I swear, that smile could have melted my panties off. His voice still sent shivers down my spine, but the more I spoke to him, the easier it got.

"I lost my mum too. It was horrible, and I witnessed it. It screwed with me, Thea. I've never been right since. Sometimes I go to a dark place in my head. Only my dad knows, but when I disappear, it's to get help with the thoughts. I had drug problems, but I'm clean now and have been for a couple of years. I don't even drink, which was why I left that pint on the bar. I just wanted to order something from you so I could speak to you. I have a bit of a short fuse, and I could see by your face back in the bar you were worried about who I am."

"I wasn't scared of you, Jenson. I just wondered who was the real you. Were you just being nice before to get into my panties, but then showing your true self? I didn't like what I saw." I would rather be honest than lie to him.

He looks down at the coffee in his hand, then looks me straight in the eyes "No, that isn't the real me. Only on the rare occasions when I'm scared. I never admit to anyone that I get scared. Sometimes, when I go dark, I scare myself with my thoughts. I was only eight when mum was killed by a rival gang. They wanted to get at my dad, so they took my mum. I was in the car with her when they stopped us. They surrounded the car on their bikes. I was in the back and Mum made me get behind the front seat on the floor and covered me with a blanket when she saw them

ONE YEAR EARLIER

approach. They didn't know I was there. I could see through a hole in the blanket as they dragged her out of the car by her hair. She was screaming at them to leave her alone. I managed to sit up and watch without anyone noticing. I think they would have killed me if they knew I was there. They beat her to a pulp after they finished gang-raping her. It wasn't until I was older, I realised what it was they did to her. They cut their MC name into her cheeks to send the warning to my dad. It scarred me for life. I have to go into therapy when I go to that dark place. I never want to get out of control again like I did when I was younger. I never want to be like them. My dad went off the rails, and he sorted them out. That MC is no longer running. He made sure of that."

My heart broke for the strong, tortured man in front of me.

"Thea, I have never told a soul any of this. I trust you. Please tell me I got it right?"

He looked so forlorn. I just wanted to cradle him in my arms. I leaned forward, placed my mug on the table, then scooted closer to him to pull him into a hug.

His body jerked against mine. The strong, beautiful man was crying. I just held him until he was ready.

It took a little time, but he eventually looked up into my face.

"Thank you, Thea."

After that night, I did go back to work in the bar. I figured I would be safe. I trusted Jenson as he trusted me. He was there almost every day, and he would walk me home every night without fail when he was around. The days he wasn't around, he made sure someone else walked me home instead.

On the nights he walked me home, he would come in

CHAPTER EIGHTY-FOUR

for a coffee before leaving. He never tried it on with me, not once. He never even kissed me on the lips since that day at the bar. I was getting a little paranoid, thinking he didn't like me in that way, but I was happy we were friends. We became good friends; we laughed and joked around a lot.

Tobias collared me at the bar when no one was around one day. He squeezed my arm and leaned in to my ear. "Thank you, Thea, for being the light in his darkness. You will never know what seeing him like this means to me. I haven't seen the light in his eyes since before his mum passed away. That's all down to you. You've made my son come alive again. Thank you." He leaned in and kissed my cheek. I had tears in my eyes.

Jenson was home after being away for a week. It was the longest he'd been gone. I'd missed him so much. I caught a glimpse of him in the bar, but he never interfered when I was working. I'd learned he liked cold tea. That was what I served him in a pint glass, just so no one ribbed him for never drinking beer.

At the end of my shift, I grabbed my bag from the kitchen, and suddenly, I was in the air being twirled around. I squealed like a baby, and Jenson laughed.

"Put me down!" I shouted.

He did so slowly, sliding me down the front of his body. "God, Thea, I've missed you so fucking much. I almost screwed up the job because I was thinking about you constantly." He turned me in his arms and held the side of my face with both hands. He smiled that megawatt smile at me, and I returned it.

I held my breath as he leaned in, looking deep into my eyes as though asking for permission. I gave the slightest of nods. He took my mouth ever so gently with his, still holding my face, and I put my hands on his waist. I started to pull him in to me, and the kiss deepened, but then I pulled away. I needed to breathe.

"I'm sorry. Was that okay? Please tell me it was. I've missed you so much. I can't explain it."

I smiled and nodded to reassure him, then kissed him gently on the lips, so he knew it was fine.

He walked me home as usual. Once out of the bar, he took hold of my hand. My heart raced and the tingles started all over again. I smiled inwardly, ecstatic at his affection, finally. Every now and then, he stopped us and took my face in his hands and kissed me very gently. Every time I looked at him, he was smiling.

When we got home, I made coffee, then went upstairs to get my loungewear on. He had never once followed me up the stairs until then.

I had palpitations as I entered my room, knowing he was right behind me. He stood at the doorway, not coming in. I turned and saw the look of trepidation on his face because he wasn't sure if it was okay to do so. I held out my hand to him, giving him permission to come in. The smile of joy spread from ear to ear as he took my hand. He closed in on me, taking my face in his hands and leaning down to kiss me. It was gentle and soft at first, but it didn't take long to intensify.

Our hands moved all over each other. He walked us backwards, where we both fell onto the bed, laughing hysterically. He smiled down at me, and it melted my heart as I looked deep into his eyes. I could see the want, and dare I say the love in them. A tear escaped my eye and gently slid down to my ear. He noticed and wiped it away with his thumb, then looked at me quizzically.

"I'm just so happy, Jenson. I've never been this happy before you."

CHAPTER EIGHTY-FOUR

He stared at me and stroked the side of my head with both hands, pushing my hair back.

"You are the most beautiful woman I have ever met. The minute I laid eyes on you, Thea, I knew we were meant to be. I could feel it, and I know you could. I love you. I've fallen so hard for you. I've never felt like this, ever. I never thought I was capable of it."

Tears filled my eyes. This beautiful tattooed biker with muscles on muscles, who people bowed down to and feared, was telling me he loved me. He pulled back slightly. "Hey, are you okay? I'm sorry. I shouldn't have said that."

He started to get up, but I grabbed his cut and pulled him down to kiss him. My hands wandered down his back to his ass, and he smiled against my lips.

Slowly, he pulled away to stand, and I watched as he started to undress. He smiled the whole time, his face full of lust, and I licked my lips when he exposed his chest and abs. I couldn't take my eyes off him. I noticed he had both nipples pierced. *Wow, that's a new one on me.* I sat upright and played with them both gently. He groaned and widened his stance between my legs. His cock was rock hard and trying to escape his jeans.

I looked up at the giant before me and smiled, trailing a finger down his chest and abdomen to unfasten the buttons on his jeans. I pulled them down to his thighs; he didn't have any underwear on. His cock sprang free, almost hitting me in the eye. It was as big as the man who owned it. I licked my lips again, then took a hold of it, rubbing up and down.

He lifted his hands behind his head and groaned with his eyes closed. I licked his tip, tasting the pre-cum. I'd only ever done this a couple of times and never really enjoyed it, but he tasted good. His breathing grew heavier the more I

ONE YEAR EARLIER

sucked his cock and pumped the base. He suddenly pulled back from me and it popped out of my mouth.

"Baby, I need to be inside you. Is that okay?" he asked with a quivering voice.

I nodded.

I stood and let him undress me torturously slowly. I just wanted him to rip everything off, but he wanted to take his time, and I let him. We'd waited months for this.

With every piece of clothing he removed, he whispered how beautiful I was. He kissed and licked at my body as he uncovered it. He kneeled on the floor to take off my panties and fishnet stockings. With each one, he leaned in and kissed my pussy, and I just wanted to grab his head and thrust it there.

Once I was naked, he gently pushed me onto the bed. He lifted my feet and placed them on the edge, opening my pussy to him. He dived in gently, licking and sucking, keeping his eyes on me the whole time. He then inserted his fingers one at a time while his tongue played with my clit. I pulled his hair, pushing on his head to get in there more. I was going to explode, I could feel it, and I started to writhe.

He pulled his fingers out and looked at
me intensely. "It's time, baby." He lifted me and placed me in the middle of the bed, then climbed on gently, holding himself up with one arm while taking his cock and rubbing it up and down my folds. I was desperate for him to enter me. I thrust my hips upwards and grabbed his biceps. We stared into each other's eyes and nodded.

He placed his cock at my entrance and very gently entered me. I bucked up to meet him. I wanted him to thrust, but I let him set the pace. He needed this. Once inside, he placed both arms at the side of me and smiled into my face, peppering me with kisses "You okay?"

CHAPTER EIGHTY-FOUR

"Yes," I breathed, and he began to move in and out. It didn't take long before I exploded. I was at the cusp to begin with. I screamed out in ecstasy. The feelings of electricity pulsating through my entire body matching his pulsing cock inside me. I gripped his biceps hard; I didn't want it to end.

He smiled down at me, stroking my head. "That was perfect to watch. The hottest thing I have ever seen. I love it. I'm going to make you come so hard just so I can watch it over and over." He laughed, and I slapped his ass.

I raised my legs and he put them over his shoulders before sinking in deep and hard. I fucking loved it. I gripped his bicep with one hand and played with a nipple ring with the other. He became frantic, thrusting as hard as he could. It didn't take long before he was shouting up to the ceiling as he came deep inside me.

I know he should have worn a condom, but I was on the pill, and I knew he hadn't been with anyone for a long time. I watched him intently as he rode it out. It was hot as hell watching him, and in no time, I was joining him again until we collapsed in a heap of sweaty bodies. That was the best I'd ever had. Nothing before even came close.

"I love you, Jenson," I whispered as he lay his head on my chest.

He didn't move or say anything. I suddenly felt water run down my side and a little shudder. He looked up at me with tears flowing down his face. I wiped them away with my thumbs, then leaned up and kissed his cheeks.

"I love you more than anything, Thea. I know it's too soon, but I'm going to marry you one day. I always do as I say. I love you so fucking much it hurts in here." He placed his hand over his heart.

Chapter Three

PRESENT

All the time we've been a couple, we've never been able to get enough of each other. He's told me so many times he's going to marry me. I just laugh it off. I love him with everything I have and could never be without him, but a few weeks back, he started to change. It was right after one of our more energetic love-making sessions and he said he was going to marry me again. I just said there was no rush. I don't even know why I said it because I would marry him today if he asked me. But he never has. He started to withdraw after that. I don't know why, and he's never done that before. Tobias has told me over and over I've brought his son back to life for the first time since his mum died. He asked me last week if I knew what was wrong with Jenson and if we were okay. I told him I had no idea and that we were fine as far as I knew.

It slowly got worse with him withdrawing, and he went missing. No one heard from him.

Also, I knew I wasn't feeling quite right, and my period

CHAPTER EIGHTY-FIVE

was late. I've been on the pill, but I had a fever a few weeks back and I've since found out that can make the pill less effective. I got a pregnancy test, and it told me I was pregnant. I did test after test to make sure. All the same result. I frantically called and texted him. I even asked Tobias if he knew where he was. There was no sign of him.

Tobias called me to the clubhouse. He sounded frantic, which worried me. I ran there from home as I wasn't at work. When I entered, I was ushered to a bedroom. The first thing I saw was Jenson lying on a bed. There was blood everywhere and people were trying to help him. I ran to him and sat on the bed, taking his head into my lap. There was blood on his head, coming from his ears, and I could see there was an open wound they were working on in his stomach. I cried, cradling his head to me and gently stroking his forehead. I kissed his face, whispering to him not to leave us, and that we had a peanut growing inside us.

I stayed with him, whispering for him to come back to us. Telling him to hang on to that hope I knew he had. He told me so many times I was his hope, and that he believed in us. I stayed whilst they sewed him up and cleaned all the blood. I helped clean his head and face. He had sustained a head injury. The doctor said it looked like he had been hit over the head with something. Maybe a bat or a brick. I wanted him to go to hospital, but they told me he was in safe hands where he was. I couldn't argue. I was exhausted.

I stayed on that bed with Jenson for nearly two weeks, each day praying he would wake up. He was responding to the medication and the wounds were healing. Each day, I told him about our peanut and how I was sure it would be a boy and be just like his dad, and that we would get married as soon as he was well enough. One night, as I lay by his side, holding him, he started to murmur. I bolted upright and turned to put the lamp on. I watched as his mouth moved. I took the little sponge I had and dripped water into his mouth. His tongue came out and licked at the drops for the first time.

"Jenson, baby. Can you hear me?"

"Always," he breathed.

I sat crying and holding him, telling him how much I loved him. He went back to sleep, and I sat up, holding his head on my lap and trying not to fall asleep.

"Baby, I love you too. I can't wait to meet our peanut." I heard the whisper and startled awake. I looked down and Jenson was looking up into my eyes with a small smile on his face. He heard me. He heard about our peanut. I burst out crying. He was going to be okay.

It's been three months since he woke up. He couldn't remember what had happened, only that he was starting to drift back into his dark place because he thought I didn't want to marry him, all because I said there was no rush. I chastised him for ever thinking that. He should have talked to me about it. He had gone because he didn't want me to see him go dark. Then he got attacked, but he doesn't know who by. They think it was a rival MC. He heard me telling him every day about our peanut, and he said he tried each day to come back, to tell me how ecstatic he was, but that he just couldn't get the words out.

We are getting married today. We're having a club wedding. Apparently, this is what they do. Tash and Tony were sceptical about the whole thing when I eventually told them, but after meeting Jenson and seeing how much he adores me, they wished us all the luck. Tony has managed to get time off to walk me down the aisle. I wouldn't have it any other way.

I start my walk towards the most beautiful man alive.

CHAPTER EIGHTY-FIVE

My vows talk about hope. Nobody on Earth could possibly feel the way I feel right now. I adore the man standing before me with everything I have, and I know he will look after our family with everything he has. This may not be my dream of a faraway land with a hot guy, but at least I have the hottest guy ever to grace the planet by my side. We stand face to face, knowing our lives are complete.

The End

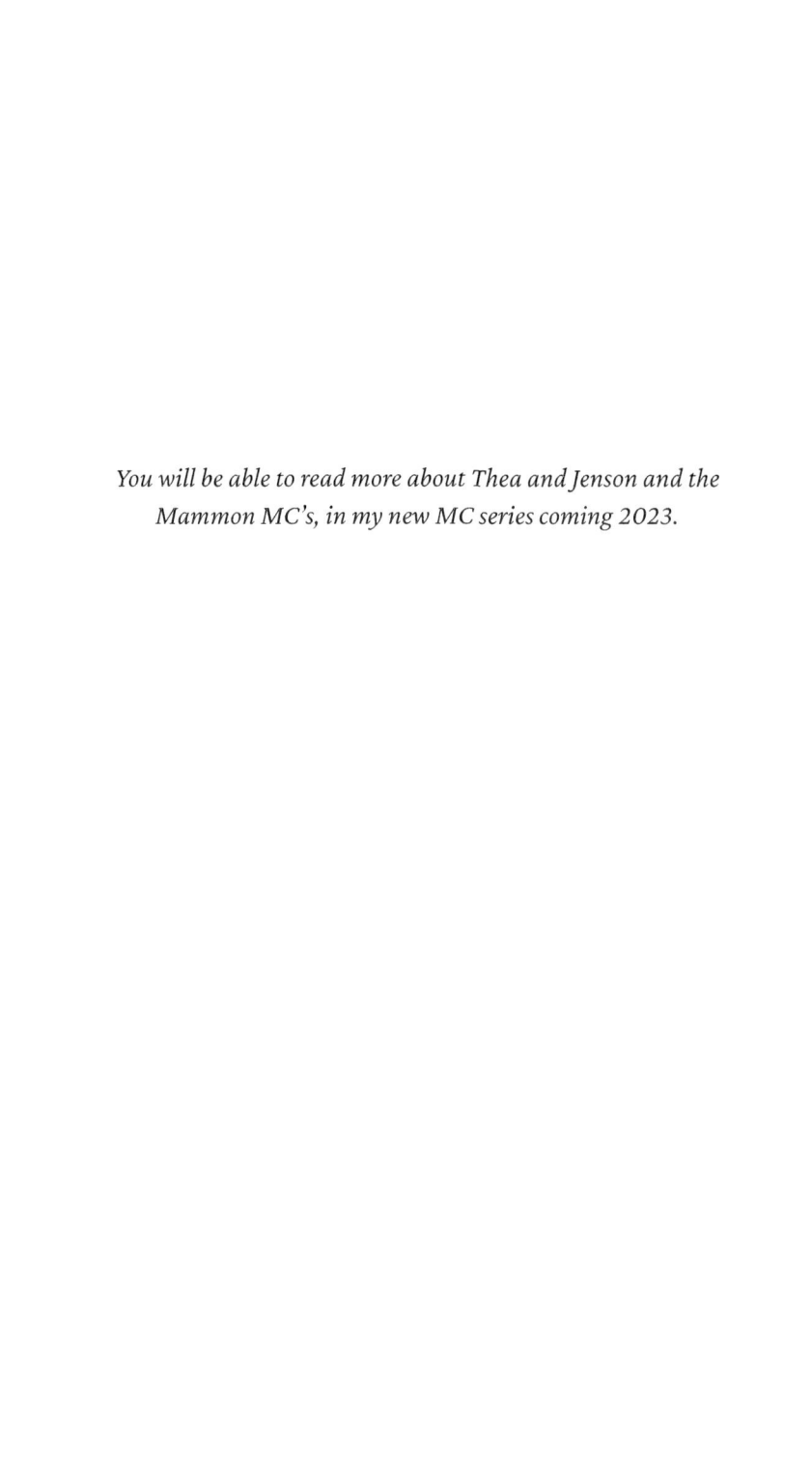

You will be able to read more about Thea and Jenson and the Mammon MC's, in my new MC series coming 2023.

Also by
Lynda Throsby

Catfish

A dark, gritty, romantic thriller (this book contains graphic scenes) for 18+ only.

The Best Day of My Life

A sweet, single dad of twins romance.

Chef

A semi-dark romantic thriller.

A Christmas Wish

A sweet Christmas fairy tale novella

The Pain Series

Book 1 – The Pain They Feel

A dark psychological romantic thriller (this book contains graphic scenes) for 18+ only.

Book 2 – Poppy's Revenge

A dark psychological thriller (this book contains graphic scenes) for 18+ only.

Book 3 – His Rightful Queen

A dark psychological thriller (this book contains graphic scenes) for 18+ only.

Book 4 – You Broke me First

A dark psychological thriller (this book contains graphic scenes) for 18+ only.

Perfect
by Martin Ferguson

Chapter One

MARCUS

*This story came to me in a dream.
It stayed with me for weeks afterwards.*

'Marcus Leigh?' the secretary at the reception desk asks, timetable in hand.

'That's me,' I reply with a forced smile as I look at the campus around me.

It's my first day at this new college. Sixteen years old and I don't know anyone here. All the friends and the life I had before are now far behind me. I'm not happy about it but keep my thoughts to myself. It's not my parents' fault we had to move. My father's job was transferred halfway across the country, so it was either resign or relocate. My mother and I supported him all the way, but now, as I stand surrounded by kids my age, all in their groups of friends, laughing and joking, nerves start to creep in. I stand alone, starting afresh, knowing nothing and no one. The bell sounds, and it's chaos for a moment as students and teachers hurry to their first lesson of the day.

I sign in with the secretary, registering myself as a new student, and I'm handed my timetable for the year. English Literature, Business Studies, and Art. Nice and varied, and the only subjects I have ever been any good at. The secretary gives me directions to my first class before she answers a call on the telephone, waving me away.

I wander the now empty corridors; classes have already begun. Not a great start. The new kid, and already I'm running late. Eventually, I find the Business Studies class—Mr Gilmore's—but I stop outside, taking a deep breath before pushing the door open and walking inside.

'Knock!' Mr Gilmore—tired-looking and dressed in a stained tracksuit and sandals—bellows as all eyes turn toward me.

'Sorry, sir,' I stammer before quickly knocking on the door.

'Not now!' Mr Gilmore yells, drawing a round of laughter from the students. 'Who are you and why are you disturbing my class?'

'Marcus Leigh,' I reply, hurriedly handing over my timetable but dropping the paper before it reaches the teacher's hand. He reaches to take it, banging his elbow against the desk and howling with pain as a swear escapes his lips. The students' laughter erupts again, and as Mr Gilmore recovers, I can't help but take a bow. It's a great way to make an entrance.

'Sit down, sit down,' Mr Gilmore orders as he continues to rub his elbow. 'You've already taken up too much of my time.'

I draw a few cheers of applause as I cross the room, but just as many curious glances. I am the new kid, after all. I find a vacant seat near the windows and am instantly greeted by the lad sitting nearest to me.

'So, you're the new boy,' he says with a grin as he leans over towards my desk. He has spiked-up hair, a big, wide grin, and wears an Arsenal football shirt and bright Hawaiian shorts. 'Welcome to hell!' He chuckles. 'I'm Jason, but friends call me Jace.'

'Good to meet you,' I reply.

'I'm rubbish with accents,' he admits. 'Where you from? Liverpool? Newcastle?'

'Do I sound like a Scouser or a Geordie?' I laugh aloud.

'No talking, new boy!' shouts Mr Gilmore.

'Hell indeed,' I whisper to Jace, drawing a snigger.

Despite the warnings of our miserable teacher, we talk for a bit during that first lesson. He seems easy-going enough and doesn't really care what anyone thinks of him. We share a lot of the same classes, and he says he'll show me around the place. It's great to have already met someone I can get along with, and at lunch, I join Jace and a few other lads in a game of footie. They seem a good bunch and welcome me well enough.

After lunch, we attend the first art class of the year and are assigned our first project, redecorating the outer walls of the school with modern murals, or as the eccentric teacher puts it, *tasteful graffiti*. We're given white overalls to wear that draw a lot of laughs from many in the class, and we're then divided into small groups to work on individual sections of the mural.

Jace and I are partnered with two girls in the class. One is undoubtedly pretty with freckles upon her cheeks, a nice smile, and long blonde hair. Her name is Amy, and she seems popular amongst the class, with Jace especially, as he nudges me with his elbow. An even bigger grin than usual is on his face at the prospect of working with her.

The second girl is Jess, Amy's close friend. She's pale, with bright green eyes and dark hair. She looks young for our age and is also quite short. I'm not the tallest person around, but she is barely up to my shoulders. What I notice most of all, though, is her constant smile... and those bright eyes.

Our first task of the assignment is to assemble the required paints from the supplies room. Inside, arranged on the shelves in dozens of rows, are tubs of paint powder of every colour imaginable.

'So, Amy, how was your summer?' Jace asks as soon as we're inside the room, wasting no time whatsoever.

'Good, thanks, James. A couple of trips away before the boredom set in,' she replies.

'It's Jace,' he says, his cheeks reddening.

'I'm so sorry! I always thought...'

'It's okay,' he says quickly, with mock hurt. 'We've only been in the same classes for four years through high school.'

'Don't tease her.' Jess shoves Jace hard. There is a strength to the girl despite appearances to the contrary.

'To be fair, I've been called far worse,' Jace says, laughing.

'Oh, I'm certain of that,' I add.

'And who might you be?' Jess asks, eyeing me with suspicion in those bright green eyes of hers.

'New,' I simply say.

'No doubt.' Amy rolls her eyes. 'And does *new* have a name?'

'Marcus is his name,' Jace declares as he slaps me on the back. 'I've taken him under my wing.'

'Ha, good luck with that.' Jess chuckles. 'Blink twice if you want us to save you.'

I blink a half-dozen times, drawing laughter from both Amy and Jess.

'You, we like,' Amy says as she looks at me and then Jace. 'And you... we're not sure of.'

'At least I've made an impression.' Jace jokes again.

'Not necessarily a good one,' Jess teases before looking at me. 'So, how did you end up at this college of all places?'

'Parents and work,' I say with a forced smile. 'Spent most of the summer moving house to a place with no friends or family.'

'That sucks,' Amy and Jess reply in unison.

'At least he has me now,' Jace says as he puts an arm around my neck. Now it's my turn to jokingly shove him away.

'Well, as you all guessed, my summer was spent in the sun on a beach in Barbados.' Jess laughs as she stretches out her pale arms.

'Nose deep in books more like,' Amy says.

'Something like that,' Jess replies, though I spot a brief hint of sadness in her eyes.

'Is no one going to ask me how my summer was?' Jace interrupts.

'Fine,' Amy relents. 'How was your summer, *James*?'

'Can't complain. Holiday in Spain with the family.' He gives me a quick wink unseen by the girls. 'I did scuba diving and a bungee jump too...'

'You never did a bungee jump!' laughs Jess as she looks over a few of the paint powders. 'You're afraid of heights!'

'Am not!' Jace argues, perhaps a bit too quickly, his voice a little high too.

'I remember you getting stuck on the climbing wall last

year!' Jess teases. 'Mr Woods had to go up and coax you down!'

'Did not!' Jace says in vain. 'My leg cramped up!'

'I remember that!' Amy giggles, but as she does, her arm catches a full tub of bright red paint that falls and pours down onto her white overalls, covering one entire side of her.

Jace bursts out laughing before he's hit by the contents of a blue tub from Amy and then a yellow tub from Jess, engulfing him in a cloud of paint powder. I'm struck square in the chest by another tub, orange paint powder erupting and engulfing my face. I knock a tub of green powder over and unleash its contents over Jess's head.

'Jerk!' she curses me with a wicked grin and two paint pots in her hands.

Of course, a fight breaks out and only ends when all four of us are covered in powder from all the colours of the rainbow, laughing hysterically. Our teacher does not find it funny.

Chapter Two

JESS

'Detention, really?' I shake my head as we walk down the empty corridors. Our clothes, hair, and skin are still covered in the paint powder, despite many attempts to clean. We are a rainbow mess of near every colour the art supplies cupboard contained. 'We managed one day, and we've got detention.'

'Yep,' Amy says with a heavy sigh. 'I had plans too. Stuck inside the college was not part of them.'

'Please. I don't want to hear about your latest boyfriend.'

'What, Justin?'

'His name was Joshua,' I correct her, as always.

She shrugs. 'I've already forgotten him. Nope, I've written boys off after Justin.'

'Joshua.'

'Yeah, him,' Amy says with a grin and a friendly shove with her shoulder. 'I meant I had plans with others.'

'Your other friends,' I say with a little jealousy in my

tone. It's something I've learned to live with, but Amy will always be my best friend. 'I know you're the popular one...'

'Hey!' She stops me. 'I'll never forget you, bestie. Besides, some of those plans were with you.'

'Well, looks like you're stuck with just me for the foreseeable.'

'Lucky me.' Amy smiles, without a hint of sarcasm.

'You know where...' I begin to ask but pause and stop in my tracks. My head and the world around me begin to spin again, and I fight to stop my lunch from making a reappearance.

'You okay?' Amy asks with concern. 'Another headache?'

'Something like that,' I lie. 'C'mon, let's just get to the room and get this over with for today.'

We reach the classroom shortly after and find that we're the first arrivals. We're greeted by the miserable Mr Clarke, a teacher I'm certain long ago lost his love for the profession, if he ever had any to start with.

'Day one and already I'm stuck with you, Miss Clynne and Miss Townsend,' he bemoans. 'Still thick as thieves. Do try not to touch anything and get paint on it.'

'Yes, sir,' we reply in a monotone.

We ignore him and find our desks before we're joined by the other pair of combatants of our paint powder battle, Jace and Marcus, both as colourful and dirty as we are. Jace, Amy, and I have known each other for years through high school, but the new arrival, with his friendly grin, grey eyes, and short, dark hair, remains a mystery.

'At least we're not on our own,' Amy whispers to me.

'Oh, God. Don't start on them too,' I reply with a roll of my eyes. 'I thought you were done with guys.'

'I am,' Amy argues as Jace slams down his bag and takes

the nearest seat to Amy. Marcus takes a seat just behind us and instantly lowers his head to the desk in frustration.

'Fancy seeing you here,' Jace says with a wide grin, his whole focus on Amy.

'Your friend Matthew is taking this well,' Amy says as she looks at the boy behind us, whose face is still resting on his desk.

'You're getting worse with names,' I tell her.

'Okay, smartass. He's only been here a few hours. What is it, then?'

'Marcus.'

'That's me,' he mutters, his head still lowered.

'Taken note of him, have you?' Amy whispers to me with a wink, but I ignore her.

'Hey, hey! New kid,' I call to Marcus. 'You know, I blame you for us all being stuck in here.'

'Me?' He chuckles before finally raising his head. 'How's this my fault?'

'You're the new kid. You've brought trouble to us,' I tease.

'That's not how I see it,' Marcus says as he leans in closer. 'It's you lot who have corrupted me. I was an innocent before I came here. You're all devils.'

'I did say before,' Jace adds. 'Welcome to hell.'

On cue and with a big smile on his face, Marcus raises fingers to his head to make the horns of a devil.

Chapter Three

MARCUS

Tick, tock, tick, tock, tick, tock. The sound of the clock is maddening as I wait for detention to be over. The four of us sit at desks, the only attendees in detention, all of us incredibly bored... and this is only day one of our three-week sentence. Even the disinterested teacher in charge of us has grown bored of his newspaper and gone outside for a not-so-secret smoke and a couple of phone calls.

'Bet your parents weren't happy, new kid,' Amy says to me. 'Detention on your first day.'

'Yeah, they were mad at first, until I explained why. After that, they seemed happy that at least I'm making friends.'

'Friends, are we?' asks Jess, her focus fully on the sleeping Jace. He has his feet resting on his desk, his chair leaning back as he snores. Covering him are pieces of paper, rulers, pens, and even a couple of books, all gently placed upon him by the rest of us in a game of stealth and balance.

Nothing has disturbed him yet, not even the pencil Jess places atop his lip, just beneath his nose.

'One thing, Mason...' Amy starts.

'Marcus,' I correct her.

'...you need to slow down with those lines.'

'Why's that?' I ask, looking at my page and the endless lines of *I will not waste school resources*, over and over again. 'It's required as our punishment.'

'A punishment from the dark ages,' Jess jokes.

'Two reasons to slow down,' Amy continues. 'One, if you finish those, they will just give you more.'

'And two,' Jess adds, 'you make the rest of us look bad. Besides, it's your turn.'

'And here comes the teacher,' I reply as I see an approaching figure through the window. 'There's only one thing for it.' I stretch out a leg and nudge Jace's chair further back, sending him tumbling off balance and crashing down to the floor in a pile of books, papers, and stationery. The girls and I struggle to contain our laughter as the stern teacher bursts into the room.

'What's happened here?' our prison guard asks.

'Sorry... er, sir...' Jace says in confusion as he pulls himself up and recovers his chair. 'Just... erm... tying my shoelaces.'

'Now, that was entertaining,' Jess whispers to me. 'Keep that up and you and I can definitely be friends.'

'I'll have to think of something to keep us entertained tomorrow,' I reply.

As I talk with Jess, I see the notepad at her desk, the page covered in impressive sketches of words emblazoned in graffiti, skulls in flames, and a lightning storm raging over an island.

'Wow, that's really good,' I say. 'I can see why you're studying art.'

'You think that's good...' Jess snatches Amy's sketchpad from her friend.

'Hey, give that back,' Amy cries, but Jess still holds up the pad, displaying an impressive, life-like sketch of Jace sleeping in his chair.

'Not just a pretty face,' Jace remarks before clamping a hand over his mouth at what he said aloud.

'You think I'm pretty?' Amy remarks as she enjoys Jace's embarrassment.

'Of course he does. They all do,' Jess teases, looking at me. Amy and Jess look at Jace and me in silence, daring us to reply, but both of us fluster until they burst out laughing.

'Sorry, boys. That was mean of us,' Jess says as she and Amy share a guilty glance.

'Cruel,' I say with a smile, though I realise detention with these three won't be so bad after all.

A friendship grows between the four of us over the following weeks in detention. Amy and Jess have been best mates since nursery, and Jace and I form a friendship very quickly, project partners in class and joining the same weekend football team. Over those first few weeks, Amy, Jess, and Jace find themselves leaving their old groups of friends and social cliques.

During classes and in the evenings and at weekends, the four of us spend time together, hanging out at each other's homes, watching films and listening to music, always joking around and teasing each other. Jace is funny and carefree;

Amy pretty, artistic, and popular but not at all big-headed about it; and Jess clever, independent, and quick-witted with a great sense of humour. And then there's me. Thanks to these three, I quickly don't feel like the new kid anymore.

Over the next four weeks, Jess is missing from school a lot, off with a sickness bug or something. The rest of us make sure to visit her when we can to cheer her up and hopefully make her feel better. On one of the days, she asks if we can all go to the beach. Jace, Amy, and I need no excuse to skip a day of college.

The waves calmly roll upon the shore as the sun beams down upon us, heating the sand so that it's warm beneath our feet. We have the entire beach to ourselves, a disposable barbecue cooking whilst music blares from Amy's portable speakers. Jace, always the hyper one, suggests a simple game of catch, one knee two knee, but even that leaves us all laughing loudly as we mess around and dive and roll in the sand.

'That's not fair!' Amy laughs as she kneels down, only able to use one hand.

'You should have been paying attention rather than eying up that handsome runner!' teases Jace.

'Well, I was getting bored of your skydiving story,' Amy replies before sticking out her tongue at him.

'And the runner was wearing very tight shorts,' Jess adds mischievously. She looks pale, even for her, but still she has her ever-present smile. We ask her a few times if she's okay or if she wants to head home, but she silences us by ordering us to simply enjoy the day.

'So, if I wore mine like this,' Jace says, pulling his shorts up high and tight, 'you girls would pay me some attention?'

'Not with that bony bum on show!' Amy teases before she misses yet another catch.

'That's four in a row you've now lost,' I remind her. 'Perhaps this game isn't for you.'

'Another round!' she demands, determined to win at least one game.

'I'll sit this one out,' Jess says. 'You guys keep playing, though.'

Unnoticed by the others, I see Jess stumble and then pause for a moment, taking a deep breath before sitting down on our towels near the barbeque.

'You two play on,' I call to Jace and Amy before walking over and sitting at Jess's side.

'You should carry on. I'm just taking a breather,' Jess tells me.

'Be honest with me, Jess,' I whisper. 'There's something wrong. I can tell.'

'It's just a little bug...' she starts to say before I cut her off.

'Jess, please.'

She turns away, looking down into the burning coal of the barbecue. Keeping her voice low, she says, 'You're right, of course. I'm not well.'

She doesn't sound sad or depressed but almost accepting as she raises the sleeve of her shirt, revealing needle track marks.

'Don't worry, they're from my time in hospital,' she says as her fingers gently trace the scars. 'Although, with the amount of drugs and medications in me and these marks, I could easily be mistaken for an addict.'

'What...' I try to ask, struggling to find the words.

'Is wrong with me?' she finishes, forcing a laugh through a hardened sneer. 'I won't dignify it with a name. I say the name and it becomes all too real.'

'Is the medication working?' I ask.

'It was, but not anymore. They're trying me on another new combination, but... the hospital...' Jess pauses as her words begin to tremor, but when her gaze returns to me, those bright green eyes of hers have a hardened steel to them.

'Basically, I've been warned that my time is coming.'

'You should be resting, giving the medication a chance!' I say in shock.

'Keep your voice down!'

'Sorry... sorry,' I whisper. I look to Amy and Jace, but their attention is solely on each other and their game.

'I've wasted far too much of my life already,' Jess confesses. 'I let it rule me for so long. I can accept that it's winning, but I won't just lie in my bed waiting for the end.'

'Jess, you should tell the others,' I say. 'Especially Amy. She's your best friend.'

'No. I don't want to burden her with it. I don't even know why I'm telling you. There's something about you, despite you being a jerk...' She pauses there as she smiles. '... I feel that you're very trustworthy.'

'Thank you for trusting me,' I say. 'I hate to ask this, but how long do you have?'

'I don't know,' Jess admits. 'I guess it all depends on the medications and if they do anything. But what I can tell you is that I will not let this slow me down. That would be giving in. I will not let it own me, nor will I simply give up. I guess none of us know when our last day will be, so I just want to live my life to the fullest whilst I can.'

'That's good,' I say, not knowing what else to say. 'And I guess there's still a chance the meds might...'

'I still have time and there's always hope,' she agrees confidently. 'I like hope. Besides, I'm not going anywhere. Not yet.'

'Not yet,' I agree.

A quiet settles between us as we watch Amy and Jace playing their game and laughing. My mind drifts to my own family. We have lost loved ones to illness, fading away until they were barely recognisable as the person they once were. Jess, though, is a fighter. I see so much spirit in her. Still, it doesn't help with knowing what to say or do now.

'See, already it's weird between us,' Jess says, her smile returning. 'Let's not talk about this again, and please don't tell anyone. Can I trust you?'

'You know you can,' I reply, forcing a smile of my own.

'Good. Now, changing the subject, tell me about your crush on Amy,' she teases.

'What?' I laugh, shaking my head. 'What on earth are you on about?'

'Now who's lying!' She giggles, prodding me in the side. 'It's okay to like her. Everybody does.'

'No, not everybody,' I say, and I notice a smile flicker across Jess's lips. 'Besides, I've got a *slight* feeling Jace really likes her and... well... just look at them together.'

'There may be more than a spark there,' agrees Jess as we see the pair playfully wrestle each other for the ball in the sand.

'And, between us, I've been trying to help him out in small ways,' I confess. 'Leaving them alone when given the chance, giving him opportunities to impress...'

'He didn't really do a skydive for charity, did he?'

'Nope.'

'That was you, wasn't it?'

'A few weeks before moving out here. My dad and a few of his friends were doing it and they had a late drop-out. I jumped at the chance—literally—out the back of a plane.

With the helmet and gear on, it was easy enough to pass off one of the photos as Jace.'

'I'm not loving the whole lying to Amy thing, but you're a good friend.' Jess takes my hand in hers and gives it a squeeze.

'I try,' I reply as I grip her hand back. 'You ever want to talk about things, I'm here.'

She smiles for a moment before shooting me a serious, stern look.

'That's enough talk, time for a challenge, jerk,' Jess taunts as she stands and pulls me up for another round of the catching game.

Chapter Four

JESS

As the evening draws in, we build a fire on the beach, and the four of us gather and exchange stories. Best holiday, best night out, best birthday, and finally, Amy's chosen subject, first kiss.

'Mine was with an ex-boyfriend, Adrian Stevenson.' She kicks us off. 'He was from the year above, captain of the school football team, and I was the envy of everyone in the school. We dated for a few months after that.'

'And what happened?' Jace asks with a hint of jealousy in his voice.

'I caught him lip-locked with Stacey, one of my former friends,' Amy replies. 'I got my revenge, though, trashing his prized bike and painting his locker with the word CHEAT.'

'Remind me never to cross you.' Marcus laughs, but he's right. I love my friend, but she does have a vicious streak when needed.

'Don't go around snogging my boyfriends and you'll be fine,' Amy says with a wink.

'Now for you, Jace,' I encourage.

'Abby Clarke,' he says with a grin. 'We kissed at the end of the year ten dance. It was a great kiss. Truly unforgettable.'

'And what happened?' Amy asks, repeating his question, her cheeks a little flushed.

'It was, unfortunately, our last kiss. Less than an hour later, she was back with her ex in the cloakroom.' He chuckles at the memory. 'Now you, Jess.'

'Nothing really to tell,' I say, a bit embarrassed. 'I've never had a first kiss. Not a proper one. I'm not usually the one who is seen by the guys.'

'And they are missing out.' Amy supports me as she hugs me tightly. 'How about you?' Amy asks Marcus

'There have been one or two,' he begins before we tease him with a cheer. 'But I would probably say… it would be the girlfriend I had before moving out here. We had been friends for a while and eventually we became more.'

'What was your first kiss like?' I ask. He looks back at me and we hold each other's gaze for a moment as a smile slowly grows across his lips.

'It just felt right,' he replies. 'As if we should have been doing it for years. It was perfect, and that's how I think they should all be.'

'I agree,' I say, his grey, storm-cloud eyes still looking into mine.

'Okay, next subject,' Jace says. 'Favourite film, and yes, I will be judging you on your answers.'

'Says the one whose favourite until recently was…' Marcus begins to say.

'No, no, no. I told you that in secret.' Jace hushes him before he can say more.

'Well, now we have to hear it!' I demand.

'Yep, spill the beans,' Amy encourages.

'Now see what you've done.' Jace scowls at Marcus, but all he does is laugh.

Chapter Five

MARCUS

We catch the last train home, the sun long set in the distance. Jess and I sit together, and Amy and Jace sit across from us. Sleep claimed them less than ten minutes into the journey, leaning on each other in their joined chorus of snoring. I can't help but smile as I see them together, hoping for both their sakes that something does happen between them.

As I check my watch to see how long we have until our stop, I feel Jess's head rest against my shoulder. She must feel my eyes upon her, as she simply whispers, 'ssh' before I can say anything. It's all too clear how exhausted she is, and I can't help but think of the battle she's fighting inside at every moment. Perhaps I should have urged us to return home sooner, to let her rest and recover, but it was her choice to remain and enjoy her time. I couldn't deny her wish.

'Thank you for today,' Jess whispers, her voice tired and weak.

HOPE

It's my turn to take her hand. 'Thank you,' I struggle to say as sadness and maybe fear suddenly claim me. 'Thank you for today and all the other days.'

Though I can't see, I'm sure she smiles before a final whispered, 'jerk'.

Once our train reaches its destination we part ways, heading for home. Of course, Jace volunteers to walk Amy home.

'You don't need to do the same for me,' Jess assures. 'Despite appearances, I'm a big girl.'

'I know. That's why you're protecting me. I've seen and felt that punch of yours.'

She smiles at that, and I think maybe a bit for the company too. In all honesty, despite everything, I don't want this day to end.

'So, your favourite film is John Carpenter's *The Thing*?' I ask.

'And why is that a problem?'

'Not a problem at all,' I say. 'I'm just surprised and impressed.'

'It ticks all the boxes; gore, monsters, nineties heroes with flamethrowers. Everything. *Aliens*, *Terminator*, *Evil Dead*, I love them all.'

'Each one of those is a classic,' I agree, 'and most we are still too young to have seen. I blame the parents.'

'Me too,' she agrees as she laughs. It's a beautiful sound. I see her lips are smiling, as they always do, but I swear her eyes are smiling at me as well.

627

Chapter Six

JESS

We continue to walk home from the station, and although it's really late and my home isn't far, we walk slowly and just keep talking, enjoying each other's company.

'I'm not looking forward to the lecture my parents are going to give me when I get in,' I confide.

'They still going to be up?' Marcus asks.

'Oh, yes. I messaged them that I was safe and would be home soon, but I'm sure they will still be waiting for me to get home. I'll try to sneak in, but they'll catch me out. They always do.'

'How often are you out like this?' he asks with pretend shock.

'Every weekend, of course,' I joke. 'Raving in the clubs until the sun rises.'

'No wonder your parents worry,' he replies with a grin. 'And to be fair, you are out very late with a *strange young man*.'

'Very strange indeed. What about you? Your folks going to be mad?'

'They're both working late tonight so they won't even notice I'm gone.'

'That must be lonely in the evenings.'

'Why do you think I'm in no rush to head home,' Marcus says. 'Especially as I live in the opposite direction to here.'

'And there I was thinking it was just my company keeping you out,' I tease.

'Well, if I'm being honest, I'd rather be here with you. Today has been great and I don't really want it to end.'

'I know what you mean. This is nice. To be fair, most people just see Amy, or they see me as Amy's friend. It's nice to be talked to normally for once.'

'Yeah... sorry, what's your name again?'

'Jerk.' I laugh as I move to shove him, but I'm stopped by a sudden downpour of rain.

I grab his hand and we run, laughing, We're soaked through when we reach my house. Marcus pulls off his dripping jacket and holds it over me.

'You'll get soaked!' I say to him over the loud hammering of the torrent.

'Too late for that!' He laughs before looking at my house. 'You were right. Your folks are still up.'

'Of course they are.' I wipe the rain from my face. His gaze then returns to me, his grey storm cloud eyes looking straight into mine, his smile as big as ever.

'What I said before,' I begin. 'I meant it. I don't want things to change just because you know about me. About what I've been hiding.'

His smile fades away then, as if only just remembering

our conversation. I realise his joy and the way he was looking at me had nothing to do with my illness.

'It's going to be okay,' he says. 'I promise I won't say any more on it, but I have a feeling this won't be the end of you. I'll leave it at that.'

'Thank you.'

The awkwardness of before has returned. He looks at his watch. and I'm certain he's going to make an excuse or remark how late it is and that he needs to leave.

'And just like that, it's a new day.' He cheers. 'You know, we don't have college and I'm free as a bird. What would you like to do today?'

See you, I almost say, surprising myself.

Chapter Seven

MARCUS

I gasp for air as sweat pours down my face and everywhere else. The drills are especially hard today, likely after having missed football training so many times over the past few weeks. Jace must be feeling the same as he collapses to the ground nearby and almost vomits.

'I think...' he struggles to say between much-needed breaths. 'I think... they're... trying to kill... us.'

'No...' I reply, equally exhausted. 'Just... torture us.'

'You wouldn't be so bad if you'd bothered turning up recently,' one of the team members sneers.

'It's 'cos their heads have been turned by girls,' another taunts.

'Whatever.' I dismiss them, not caring what they think.

'No, they're right,' one lad says as he approaches. Tall, handsome, popular. Of course Archie Wright is the captain of the team.

'Leave it out, Wrighty,' Jace says as he struggles to his feet. 'We're here now, aren't we?'

'But I'm guessing you'd rather be sniffing around Amy,' Archie says with a cruel grin. 'You do know Amy's been with half of this team. Probably more.'

'Don't say that,' I warn. 'She's a friend.'

'Speaking of friends,' Archie continues. 'Amy's little friend. Jess, is it? Well, let's just say it's lucky Amy is so popular, otherwise no one would even know she exists. Not that she'd draw much interest anyway. In fact, if she vanished right now, I don't think anyone would notice.' He finishes with a howl, drawing laughter from all the team but Jace and me.

I can't stop myself as my fist launches forward and strikes Archie across the face. The team captain is knocked back and looks on in shock before rushing at me. Jace stops him, standing between us with his arms raised.

'Woah, woah, woah,' he warns, acting as peacemaker. 'Now, can't we all be...' Jace suddenly turns, striking Archie again and sending him tumbling to the ground. '...friends!' Jace finishes as he winces and clutches at the hand that hit Archie.

'Oh, shi...' I begin to say before the whole team erupts into a mass brawl.

Our actions land us in detention again, though, of course, only Jace and I are punished, not those whose words started the fight.

'You got any painkillers on you?' Jace asks me. 'I'm hurting in a dozen places.'

'You didn't need to come to my defence,' I tell him.

'Yes, I did. I absolutely did. I couldn't let you face them alone. Besides, Wrighty deserved it after what he said about the girls.'

'Regardless, thank you,' I say to him. He raises a fist in reply, and I bump it.

'You and me against the world, mate.' He grins before wincing from his split lip, a token of the fight.

'Two weeks,' I say with dismay. 'We only just finished the last sentence.'

'This is going to be even worse than last time without the girls.'

'Speaking of the girls,' I say with surprise as Amy and Jess appear at the door. 'What are you doing here?' I ask as they take seats close by.

'We could ask the same of you,' Jess replies, 'though your black eye is explanation enough, Marcus.'

'I think they broke my nose,' Jace complains.

'It's an improvement,' Amy says cheekily as she gently nudges his shoulder with hers.

'Enough talk!' our teacher orders.

Jess takes a seat close to me and leans in to whisper. 'You gave up your time for me,' she explains with a sly grin. 'So we're giving up ours for you.'

'Both of you,' Amy adds, drawing a big grin from Jace.

'And your crime?' I ask.

'Smoking in the toilets,' Jess replies.

'Really?'

'I didn't realise you're so gullible,' Jess teases. 'No, it was just a light bit of swearing.'

'Light bit of swearing?' I chuckle.

'Only enough to get a week of detention. We'll have to think of something else if we're to join you for the second week.'

'Is this really how you want to spend your time?' I ask quietly and knowingly.

Jess looks to Amy, Jace, and then finally to me.

'I can't imagine anywhere I'd rather be,' she says with bright eyes and a bright smile.

Chapter Eight

JESS

I stop halfway down the steps of the hospital, close my eyes, and take a deep breath. My ears ring, but it's not from the illness, it's from the doctor's words.

'This new combination,' she had explained with an ever-present frown. 'Tests have proven that it has greater effectiveness than those we have tried before. It is your best chance.'

'But?' I asked. 'I can tell by your pained expression there is a *but*.'

'The risks are greater,' she stated flatly. 'The strain on your body alone...'

'Greater risks but greater chance of success,' I summed up, to which my doctor simply nodded.

'Let's do this,' I said, though now, standing on the stairs as another wave of dizziness and nausea hits me, I'm not so sure.

Pulling myself together, I take another deep breath before descending the steps and heading for the exit.

'What's the news?' I hear the familiar voice of Amy call to me from behind. Hearing her brings a smile to me for the briefest of moments.

'Fancy seeing you here,' another jokey voice adds. Jace, of course.

'I tried to explain you needed space, but they wanted to come and show their support,' Marcus explains as Amy hugs me tightly.

'No, we were just in the neighbourhood and...' Jace tries to lie.

'We wanted to be here for you,' Amy explains. 'Marcus accidentally let slip you were here. You should've told me.'

'My bad,' I say regretfully before shooting Marcus a scornful look. He mouths a silent apology, and I can see that he is sorry.

'So?' Amy finally asks. 'What did they say?'

'You're not getting rid of me just yet,' I lie with a forced smile. 'Nothing's wrong. Just a few pills to help with the headaches.'

The three of them cheer and pull me into one big four-way hug.

'We should celebrate!' Amy says.

'Me having headaches?' I chuckle.

'Yes,' she replies, as ever not really needing an excuse. 'What do you want to do?'

'Whatever you guys fancy,' I say, though to be honest, with how I feel right now, all I want to do is go to bed and sleep for a week.

'How about the cinema?' Marcus suggests, and I'm thankful for what should be a fairly quiet celebration.

'Oh, no. Not one of your gory action ones again,' Amy complains as Marcus, Jace, and I cheer at the idea.

'Like you'll notice what the film is,' I tease her. 'You'll be too busy snogging Jace anyway.'

Both of them blush at that as Marcus and I tease them some more.

'Anyway,' Jace says, quickly trying to change the subject. 'Those pills they've given you. Are they going to make you all goofy, or are you going to be falling asleep on us? Or are they experimental and will give you cool superpowers?'

'Yep,' I reply, 'and with my immense powers, of course I will expect you to obey me as your overlord or ultimately be crushed.'

'We obey, Empress Jess!' Amy says as she and the two boys fall to their knees.

'Be merciful!' Marcus implores. 'Take Jace if you need a sacrifice.'

'Yeah, take...hey!' Jace says as he realises the joke.

Chapter Nine

MARCUS

'Wow,' Jace says in amazement as he scans through Jess's music collection in her bedroom. 'You really must be ill if you like some of these bands.'

Jess punches him hard in the arm, drawing a howl from him.

'She's still tougher than you,' Amy says as she hugs Jess tightly.

'No doubt there,' he agrees.

With Jess's illness and her medication, she has good days and bad days. We make the most of those good days with trips to theme parks, the beach, and visiting places Jess has always wanted to see but has never had the chance to. On the bad days, Amy, Jace, and I rally around and help her pull through. After a time, even Amy and Jace knew something must be wrong, and eventually, Jess told them. There were a lot of tears, but as she was with me, Jess was

HOPE

very stern in not wanting anything to change. No fuss or special attention.

After that day at the beach, Jess and I spent more and more time together. I missed school and even more football matches to be there for her. I think of her all the time. Not the illness, but the person. Her smile, her laugh, and the way she always makes me happy when I'm with her. Maybe there's a touch of something more than friendship there, but neither of us ever acted upon it, simply enjoying the time together.

'How about this one?' Amy says as she picks a song, plays it loudly, and begins to dance. Jace quickly joins in, and despite my reservations, I offer a hand to Jess. She smiles at my act of gallantry but knocks away my hand before joining us all in dancing. Her movements are slow and careful, the latest drugs really doing a number on her.

'I may be the sick one,' Jess laughs loudly, 'but I'm not going to lie. Marcus, your dancing is terrible!'

'I couldn't agree more,' I reply with a grin. With anybody else, I would feel embarrassed, but not with this trio, and that it amuses Jess is even better.

Jess shivers, and though she has told me many times not to, I ask if she's okay.

'Cold hands,' she replies, though I expect all of her is cold.

I react without thinking, taking her hands in mine as we continue to dance. Her bright green eyes meet mine, and for a moment, our gaze holds before we both smile, laugh, and look away.

'What song next?' Amy asks after we dance to five or six tracks. 'Jess, it's your pick.'

'You know what, I'm going to sit this one out,' Jess replies, tiredness taking her, her head hanging low. She stumbles, and I quickly catch her, lifting her frail, light body into my arms. I hold her close, her head resting against my chest and eyes fixed on mine. In that moment, everything else is forgotten. The illness, our friends. Everything. I pull her closer still until our lips almost meet.

'I'm sorry,' she whispers, her eyes falling heavy and then closing.

'It's okay. It's getting late anyway,' I reassure her as I carry Jess towards her bed. 'And you should be resting.'

Jace quickly turns down the volume as I lower Jess to her bed and pull the covers over her. Already, she has fallen asleep. I brush the hair from her face and watch her for a moment to make sure she's truly comfortable. When I turn back towards the others, I see Amy is in tears, and Jace is not far off either.

'It's okay, she just needs to rest,' I try to reassure them, though I too feel my emotions threaten to overwhelm me.

'I just wish there was more we could do,' Amy says as she tries in vain to wipe away her tears.

'It's not fair,' Jace adds.

'Hey, c'mon, guys,' I encourage my friends. 'She's the strongest person I've ever met. If anyone can beat this thing, it will be her. Now, let's let her get some sleep.'

'Jerk,' we hear Jess murmur as I close her bedroom door, making the three of us laugh.

'You know you should tell her,' Amy says to me once we have left Jess's house.

'Tell who what?' I reply.

'Jess, and that you like her,' Jace explains. 'Archie is a dick, but you wouldn't have hit him if there wasn't a little something there.'

'And the way you look at her and held her just now,'

Amy adds with a smile on her face as she shares a glance with Jace. 'You like her.'

'She's smart, headstrong, and independent,' I say, more to myself than to them.

'And even now she could still kick your arse,' Jace says, but I ignore him as I look back to Jess's house.

'I think about her all the time,' I say to myself again.

'You've...' Amy begins to say.

'...fallen for her,' I whisper.

Chapter Ten

JESS

'How is it you've only been at half the lessons yet you're twice as good at all this as me?' Amy asks. Two textbooks and a notepad covered in scribbles lay around her on my bed, and she looks at each with dismay.

Amy and I are in my room. We're supposed to be studying. I'm trying to make up for all the time I've missed, but it's not easy. The college has offered me tutors, but I learn better on my own. I wish I could say the same for my best friend.

'You want us to start over?' I offer.

'What I want is to move past this,' Amy says, passing over the textbooks. 'All of this. I'm thinking maybe college wasn't the best idea.'

'Hey, you're not leaving me on my own,' I reply as I twirl a pen between my fingers.

'I wouldn't, of course. Besides, if I want to get into the

art school I have my heart set on, I need to at least finish this year.'

'Art school next, then?'

'Absolutely. It's the only thing I've ever been any good at.' She turns to a blank page in her notepad, draws a pencil from her bag, and then sets to work sketching.

'What about you?' Amy asks. 'I'm guessing uni?'

'With how things are,' I say as I tap my pen across the lids of my many medications, 'I can't really talk about the future.'

'Yes, you can,' Amy says as she suddenly turns to me with a hardened gaze. 'Of course you can. I don't want to hear you talk like that. That's not the Jess I've known since pre-school.'

'I know, but...'

'No. I'm not having it,' Amy declares. 'You're fighting this thing and you will win.'

'Amy...'

'You will. I'm certain of it,' she continues, tears appearing in her eyes. 'You have to. You have to because I... I don't know what I'd do with you.'

The tears run down her cheeks, and we rush to each other, hugging tightly.

'I'm sorry,' I say. 'I'm sorry. You're right I... we... are still fighting.'

'Yes, we are,' Amy agrees as we part, and she wipes the tears away. 'You, me, Jace, and Marcus. We will all face this, all the way.'

'I'm not going anywhere,' I promise. 'Not yet.'

'Good,' she says with a faint smile. 'And no more talk of... you know what.'

Death. I've long gotten used to the word, but I don't blame others for not being so comfortable.

My phone chimes on the desk, and I scoop it up to read the text message.

'I don't need three guesses to know who has just brought a smile to your face,' Amy teases.

'No idea what you're talking about,' I lie.

'It's him, isn't it?'

'Who?' I ask, even though I know my cheeks are reddening.

'Marcus. You like him, don't you? C'mon, I'm not blind.'

'You're crazy.'

'Nope. You may be better at the whole academic side of things,' she says as she waves dismissively at our books, 'but this I can tell. You like him.'

'No, I don't.'

'Yes, you do.'

'No, I don't.'

'You absolutely do!'

'Okay, enough,' I say as a smile betrays me. 'Yes, I like spending time with him. I like talking with him and laughing with him. I like doing pretty much anything in my day as long as he's there. He makes detention bearable and makes me actually look forward to going to college just to see him.'

My joy fades then as realisation hits me.

'It doesn't matter,' I say, with annoyance and resentment rising within me. 'None of how I feel matters because nothing will come of it.'

'Why? Why not take a chance?'

'You know why,' I say with growing frustration.

'No, we said no more talk of... your condition limiting you,' Amy says as she takes my hands in hers. 'Look, Jess, I've known you since we were four years old, and I've never seen you like this over any guy. If you like him, tell him, please. I think you'd be surprised. I've a sneaky suspicion he likes you too.'

'No. Will you just leave it!' I yell as I push her hands away from mine. 'It's not as easy for me as it is for you. You have guys lining up for you, but I'm always in your shadow.'

'I've never seen you like that. You're not in my shadow, you're my friend. My best friend.'

'Then, please, stop with this,' I implore with an angered tone. 'I've always been in the background, and I was okay with that. I was. But now, finally, someone might have noticed me. I like him and he just might like me back... but now I have this...'

I pull up the sleeves of my shirt and display the scars, near every vein picked for tests and taking bloods. I collect up the bottles of my various medications and launch them at the far wall, several breaking open and scattering the pills. Warm tears roll down my cheeks, but still I rage, knocking my textbooks away and slamming weak fists onto my table.

'Jess... Jess...' Amy calls to me frantically, pulling me close in a hug in an attempt to calm me. I try to push her away at first, but she overpowers me until finally I give in.

'It's not fair,' I say weakly as my anger fades. 'It's just not fair.'

'I've got you,' Amy says to soothe me. 'You and me, Jess. I've got you.'

A warm trickle runs from my nose, and when I place a hand to it, I see blood on my fingers.

'Great,' I say as dizziness begins to take me again. 'Can't even get a bit hysterical without my body letting me down.'

Chapter Eleven

MARCUS

It's a Friday afternoon art class, and again, my group is assigned to assemble the required paints from the supplies room, though not without a very stern warning after last time. We have music playing throughout the class and within the supplies room, and away from the eyes of the other students, the girls lead us in a dancing session to the tunes. Amy and Jace are dancing closely at one end of the room as Jess and I mess around at the other. As always, my dancing is the source of much hilarity.

Jess is joyful and laughing. Seeing her like that, all I can do is smile and want this moment to last a little longer.

'Show me those moves,' she teases before suddenly stopping, concern on her face. She grips on to the shelves beside her before managing to say, 'I don't feel right.'

A trickle of blood runs from her nose, and I'm only just in time to catch her as she begins to fall. I kneel down and hold her in my arms. She feels even smaller and thinner than I thought possible. Her body shakes, her eyes shutting tightly as a brief and sudden seizure takes her. Only when her body ceases to tremble do her eyes open again.

'It's coming,' she whispers, looking up and into my eyes, not with fear, but with care and love.

'We need to get you an ambulance,' I say urgently.

'No,' Jess says calmly. 'I only want one thing. Make it special. Make it perfect.'

I remember that word when we sat around the fire on the beach. Memories flood my mind; days together in detention, messing around in class, dancing to awful music, just hanging out and going on day trips to not waste a single day. Her laughter and joy despite everything, her smile, and those always bright eyes, even now as she lies in my arms. Above it all is the happiness she brings me whenever I see her. It all hits me in that moment as I hold this girl for what I realise is possibly the last time... and I'm not ready to let her go yet.

Her hand reaches for mine, entwining fingers and holding tight. I hold Jess closer still, and then, before I can act, her face rises to mine and our lips finally meet.

It feels right. It feels special, and I wish we had done this weeks ago. Our eyes open, both with smiles on our lips before I kiss her this time, and it brings just as much joy as the first.

'Perfect,' Jess whispers before her eyes close again and her head falls back, her grip on my hand loosening and falling away.

I hug her frail, weak body close, tears flowing from my eyes before fear takes hold as I feel her heartbeat slow.

'No. No, no, no.' I panic and try to wake her, but she shows no sign of movement.

'C'mon, Jess. Don't do this now,' I yell as I try to wake her. 'Don't do this to us.'

'Marcus...' Amy calls to me, hands over her mouth in shock as Jace frantically calls for an ambulance.

'No! No, not now,' I plead, tears on my cheeks. 'Come back to us, Jess, please.'

She doesn't move or speak, her chest still and breath lost.

'No...' is all I can whisper, body and mind numb. I hug her tight to me, unable to let go.

Chapter Twelve

JESS

Drifting, falling, deeper and deeper. There's no pain, no suffering, just a growing peace. The only sound is that of my friends; Amy, Jace, and of course, Marcus. I can barely feel his warmth as he holds me, his words distant and almost lost... until...

'Please, Jess... don't leave us. Don't leave me. Not now... not yet...'

It strikes like a bolt of lightning, a longing and need greater than any I have felt before. I don't want to leave him. Flashes of memories, moments, and emotions rise and overwhelm, awakening and lifting me.

On a train, my head resting on his shoulder, smiling and relieved that my secret was finally shared with someone.

Dancing without a care in the world, free.

Paint powder clouds the air and we're covered in all the colours of the rainbow.

Safe and protected in his arms as he carried me.

Running together, hand in hand in the pouring rain.

Shared glances, smiles, and secret notes in detention.

My lips upon his as I finally summoned the courage to show him how I feel.

'Not yet...' I hear his voice, clearer and closer this time. 'Not yet.'

Chapter Thirteen

MARCUS

'Jerk...' Jess whispers with the weakest of voices as she takes shallow gasps of air.

I look at her in utter shock before hugging her tight to me.

'Don't you ever do that to me again,' I say, thanking every possible deity I can think of.

'No... no promises,' Jess replies, her voice still weak and eyes barely open. 'Did... did you kiss me?'

'Maybe,' I say with relief and disbelief.

'About time,' she says with the biggest of smiles.

I hold her close, unwilling to let go. We still have time. We still have hope.

'I'm not...' Jess struggles to say. 'I'm not going anywhere. Not yet.'

'Not yet,' I agree, before kissing her again.

Also by Martin Ferguson

Relic Hunters Series

Eagle of the Empire

Curse of the Sands

War of the Damned

Blood of the Dragon

Origins of the Hunters

The Forsaken Series

The Forsaken: Wraith

The Forsaken: Descent

True Love
by Melody Winter

A Short Story

Rain.

Rain... today of all days.

Typical.

I sighed, glaring at the large heavy raindrops as they pounded the ground outside. They hammered on the roof of the car like a thousand angry birds pecking at the thin metal.

I didn't want to be here, and the weather reflected my nonchalant feelings. I'd hoped this day would never come —not like this—but it was too late now. I couldn't upset everyone. My head swam with voices—everyone's but my own. They all told me to put my doubts aside, jokingly asked if I loved him, told me not to disappoint my mother, our families, and what about all the planning?

It was expected.

Did he feel the same?

I swallowed hard. Six months ago, I'd never have

thought I'd be here. Dressed up and made-up so much that I didn't recognise myself. But maybe that was the point of all this. My mother trying to mould me into the perfect wife. One without an opinion, without a voice. A shadow of the true person that had a beating heart beneath all the camouflage.

But the true me was still there, silent for the moment, but that part of me would never die. You could dress me up in a fancy dress, hide my expression beneath a cartload of make-up, but inside, the carefree spirit, the woman who longed to walk barefoot everywhere, her long hair loose and wild, who wanted to stay out all night with the man she loved, was still there.

Trapped.

Shut down.

Numb.

Weak.

I longed for the person I was to break free, not hide under the skin of a person I didn't recognise.

And I'd let him down.

Would he even recognise me now? I closed my eyes and pushed my memories aside. Today was not the day to reminisce, no matter how strong the urge. Today was a fresh start. Memories were part of the past, and that was where they had to stay.

The noisy clatter of the rain on the car diminished, a sign that the cloudburst had passed. That meant one thing that I would be able to step out of the car and head to the church door. I narrowed my gaze and took another deep breath as I peered out of the polished car window and looked towards the church. A winding path with daffodils and crocuses provided a splash of colour on this dull, miserable spring day. I huffed quietly when I realised my bouquet matched the colours of the daffodils on display. Whites, yellows, and a splash of pale green. Roses, lilies, orchids. All flowers that had no relevance to me—washed-up, pale, and uninteresting. I'd wanted daisies, bright peonies, lilac, tulips—a riot of colour. Me.

It was ironic that I owned a flower shop and wasn't allowed to do my own flowers on my wedding day. Crazy, really, and hurtful. I loved the scents that surrounded me every day, yet my mother hadn't let me prepare anything for today. It would have been too much work for me, and I was just to sit back and let her take care of things. So, there were no daisies, no peonies, no tulips.

My wedding day, or my mother's?

I'd always had a dislike of churches, particularly ones like this—those with graveyards. I couldn't shake the feeling of stepping over dead bodies, as if their arms would reach through the earth and grab me. Today, I would welcome their intrusion. I'd willingly be grabbed and swallowed by the ground beneath me. It would stop this farce of a marriage.

I swallowed my nerves, my excitement, or fear. I didn't know anymore. Months of my mother planning, arranging venues, flowers, food, drinks, guest lists, seating plans, my dress, the groom's suit. Today, it all came to fruition.

I'd known Andrew since we were both six years old. We built mud pies, made rose petal perfume, made promises to always be together, that no one would break us apart. We went on adventures into the nearby wood, built dens, laughed and joked around makeshift campfires, swam in lakes, swung from ropes, and rode for miles on bikes. And as we'd got older, we'd gone on overnight camping trips, eaten toasted marshmallows, and drank hot chocolate whilst snuggled together wrapped in soft, fleecy blankets. He understood me, and I understood him.

With a heavy breath, I stared at the picturesque old church—a perfect venue for photographs after the wedding. Its old tower loomed ominously into the brightening sky, and I couldn't help but think what a beautiful building it was. Such a pity about what was shortly to happen inside.

I stepped from the car, the length of my white beaded lace wedding dress gathered in my arms, and made a dash to the front of the church, dodging the numerous puddles. My father followed, desperately trying to keep the umbrella he'd commandeered over my head. Once under the porch of the church doors, my bridesmaids fussed around me, straightening the dress and train, and lifting my veil to check my make-up was okay. They were bridesmaids I didn't know—his two sisters, and his close female friend. Another unfamiliar face. They titivated my hair, winding stray strands around their fingers to emphasise the curls that had already started to drop in the damp atmosphere. I didn't care, though. I didn't need to look perfect today. Not for him.

My memories flooded my head. His rough, calloused hands sweeping the hair from my face before he kissed me. Our first kiss—sweet, tender, innocent, but not for long. As teenagers, we'd always messed around—a furtive look, a smile just for each other, a wink that no one else saw. But that kiss... that kiss opened a whole new world of glances, smiles, touches, and precious moments neither of us would ever forget. They were memories that would never fade, and I'd cherish their return into my thoughts every time they broke free.

"You ready?" My dad was nervous, anxious about

whether things would go okay. "You can always stop this. Turn around, leave. You don't have to marry him."

I smiled, a gesture that didn't match my demeanour, but I didn't want to worry my father any more than I already had. He cared about me in a way my mother seemed unable to. He didn't bother about appearances, unlike her. He just wanted me to be happy, and he was sure I was making the wrong decision. But was it my decision? I wasn't sure anymore. I'd never had the strength to stand up to my mother when this all started, and I certainly didn't now.

It was too late. This wedding was planned a long time ago in people's heads. It was mapped out over secret discussions, planned without us until he eventually proposed. And even then, I wasn't allowed any input into the day. My day. Our day.

Our plans were nothing extraordinary. We'd wanted to sneak away to be married but knew that neither family would approve. We wanted a bright wedding, balloons, a riot of colour on the wedding cake and in my bouquet. None of the traditional white wedding and white wedding cake. We'd never wanted doves, a large reception with people we didn't know, a choir, or even a church wedding. But here I was.

"I'm ready," I said to my father. Another lie, words that were said to ease the worry of others but did nothing to ease mine. This should have been the time I screamed with all my breath that this be stopped. I didn't want any of it. But my voice failed me, and I nodded, eager to just get this over with. Maybe then I could start to build bridges, plan what to do, fix the mess that had raced out of control.

The church doors opened and the aisle before me became a vortex. I was in the centre of a whirlpool, a spiral of colours that wouldn't release me. I stepped back, my legs shaky, threatening to give way beneath me. I held back a scream as my heartbeat raced and my vision became clouded. Images of being married to him assaulted my mind, and the urge to turn around and run away from all of this attacked my reality.

My father's hand tightened around mine, and the swirling colours, the overpowering scent of old wood and flowery perfume gradually subsided. My heartbeat steadied, and I fixed a smile on my face as I looked at my father and squeezed his hand. It was a silent gesture that would let him know I was okay now. The moment had passed.

I blinked rapidly to clear my vision, but the reality before me was much worse than the panic I'd just experienced. He stood at the far end of the imagined tunnel. Copies of my bouquet graced the end of every other pew. The scent of the roses was sweet, sickly. I could taste them, bitter in my mouth. Their scent was heavy, resting on me with the weight of everyone's expectations. I didn't want to be here. I wanted to be far away, marrying the man I loved. Not a showpiece for everyone to coo over. Not for relatives to see me at my most vulnerable. To have a piece of me I didn't want to give.

Andrew had never liked attention either. We both shied away from it, concentrating on our own little world. A world that no one else could understand. As children, we'd easily settled into drifting away from other children, becoming our own little private bubble. We talked and laughed about anything and everything. We were like an old married couple. As we grew into our teenage years, welcoming but also hating the arrival of hormones and mood swings and the obvious interference of friends, we kept together, stronger, more knowledgeable as each year passed. We were both free-spirited teenagers, difficult to tame, living our dreams, planning for our elevation into adulthood. Andrew was a talented artist, and I had my flower shop. We complemented each other—we believed in each other. We didn't like attention, kept ourselves to ourselves, and didn't crave drunken parties or mixing with others. We were odd teenagers in that sense. But I wasn't averse to creeping out through my bedroom window when my parents were asleep to spend the night at his or wrapped up in blankets in the campervan he'd just bought. We talked so much, chatter that lasted until the early hours of the morning. When he'd drive me home, he parked in the street around the corner so the clatter and splutter from his van didn't wake my parents. Looking back, I was sure my father knew what was going on, but he turned a blind eye. He knew where I was—safe, loved, cared for.

Silence as I waited for the organ player to start the tune that would lead me to my groom.

Time stopped.

I could hear the breath of everyone in the congregation. Every sweet paper rustling, every cough, every shuffling foot. Even the whisper of fabric as people fidgeted… waiting.

My dad's hand tightened around mine as the first notes of the wedding march sounded out. His hand was hot and sticky, his nervousness showing obviously to me, but not to anyone else. Dad was my rock, my best friend, my confidant. He knew how I felt. He knew how desperate I'd become. But I'd never managed to find a way out of the cage that had been built around me.

Every face, young and old, turned to look at me—all except his.

My bridesmaids stepped forward and I took my first

step, following them, knowing my father wouldn't. He didn't want this marriage to happen. He had doubted everything about our union. He'd spoken about his unease to my mother, but nothing had stopped her dedicated planning. My father had even told her that if she liked my future husband so much, maybe she should marry him. Let me be. Leave me out of it. She'd never listened. She'd turned away and continued with her meticulous organisation.

It all started when my family moved here. A new school, unfamiliar faces, being the new girl. Even at six years old, it was difficult. I remember the desperate need to fit in, to want to make friends, to be liked. It was challenging... but only for the first week. My second week at school had started with an unfamiliar cheeky face. A boy with freckles covering his forehead, nose, and cheeks. He'd grinned at me from across the classroom and patted the chair next to him. We'd swapped names, and by the end of the day, we were best friends.

It was all so much simpler back then.

The estate he lived on wasn't the greatest. Hence came the first barrage of disdain from my mother. I wasn't to encourage him to be my friend. I should look to the nice, polite children who she'd be happy to have around to our house to play and have tea—not him, just in case he stole something. Little did she realise that even at the age of six, her words made me dig my heels in. I decided this boy would be my one and only best friend. And he had been.

He'd been by my side every day since we met. When we were little, he'd protected me from the nasty kids at school. When we were older, he'd fought a boy who was pestering me for a date and wouldn't take no for an answer. I still remember the black eye he received and the bruised ribs because of the fight. He'd told me that he'd fight for me again and again, risking black eyes, bruised ribs, a broken nose, and much more.

So where was he now?

When my gran died, he'd been the one I turned to, the one who hugged me as my tears tore me apart. He listened, he never judged, never told me I'd get over it. Grief was a thief who took away all reason, who stripped you of rational thought, who brought out the side of your character that was best left undisturbed. I'd turned on him at one point, wanting someone, anyone to blame for her death. Old age wasn't a reason, it was an excuse. But all he'd done was hold me tighter, let my tears fall, let my angry words punch him repeatedly. And when I'd calmed, he'd continued to whisper words of comfort. We'd taken a road trip—his idea—to all the places my gran had lived or holidayed. We'd lived in her footsteps for two months, touring in his battered campervan. It had been a series of memories that stirred the good times. The times when life was fun, carefree. When I was alive, me, living and loving freely.

Not this.

My breath caught in my throat several times as I walked towards the front of the church. The walk was slow, hesitant, as if each step were a memory being wiped from my mind. The touch of his lips, the sensation of his caress, the love of a man that many could only imagine.

I took a shuddering breath as I observed my surroundings, trying to focus on anything but him. The tall stained glass windows depicting scenes from the Bible. The archways of the lower stone walkways at the side of the church. The simple wooden cross above the altar in front of me.

And then I saw him. Standing tall, his back to me as I faced the vicar who would marry us. Did the vicar know how I felt? Would a man of God see straight through me and stop everything? Why was I relying on a stranger to end this charade? Why couldn't I muster up the courage to stop it all? I knew the answer. Of course I did. I was weak, broken down over the last six months by a force so strong it left me breathless.

Alone.

No one by my side.

Not even him.

Somehow, I managed a sly grin as I imagined the ensuing panic if things were stopped. The manic way my mother would react. Screaming was bound to be part of it, as would her blaming everyone but herself. She'd never think to question the real reason for it all. She had never once considered my feelings in any of this. I was her only daughter, a prize for the most eligible man. The perfect wife for a man who knew how to control a wild spirit. But I would never be tamed. It wasn't who I was. And any man I married would have to deal with that, love me for who I was and not what my mother wanted me to be.

In her world, I should be married at twenty-two. A stay-at-home wife who kept the house clean, prepared home-cooked meals, and waited for my husband to come home from his well-paid job. I should attend to his every need. I should immediately start a family with him. The flower shop business was a hobby, and only one I should continue if my husband agreed. But once I had children, I would need to give it up and dedicate my time to being a mother. Others would be so jealous of the life I lived.

But it wasn't what I wanted. I hated cooking, loathed housework of any kind, and certainly didn't have any desire to have children. Well, not with him. I wanted a partner, one who mucked in with things, not a grown man to look after. I wanted a large garden where I could grow my own vegetables, keep chickens, maybe a goat or two. And I wanted a flower garden. I didn't want the life my mother had planned for me.

Tears. There had been so many tears.

Andrew and I had fought against the plans that didn't include us. We'd argued heatedly, many times, like we never had before. But his arms were always open. His comfort always there. In a way, it had brought us closer. But then it ripped us apart, a reality of the situation that neither of us had anticipated.

He'd walked away.

My world crumbled in a way I could never have thought.

It was as if he'd died, and he'd taken my heart with him.

I became stone, distant from everyone and everything.

The world revolved around me, but I wasn't part of it anymore.

Tears.

Anger.

Frustration.

Blame.

It was all my fault.

But every day since he'd walked away, I'd hoped he'd come back. And every day, that hope had slowly diminished, worn away by the people who had plans for my life that didn't include him. Plans for a life I didn't want. But that hope was always there, a distant flicker of a light that would fade but never extinguish.

I should have stamped my foot, demanded that it all stop. I should have moved out, demonstrated my determination not to do what they wanted. But my mother was a fearsome force when she needed to be.

And his parents were just as bad. Why didn't I want to marry their son? He was young, fit, well. He had a particularly good job in the family business, a role that would become even more important when he married. Of course he wanted to marry me—he got a large pay rise and a promotion. I was his meal ticket, in more ways than one.

Dates were arranged. I was told what to wear and how to behave. And I ignored everything I was told. Unfortunately, he only saw our pending marriage as a means to an end. Many times he'd wanted to get intimate, and each time I'd refused or made an excuse. He'd seemed calm, although I saw the anger behind his eyes at my rejections. But once we were married, I'd not be able to hold him off any longer. He already told me that once we were married, I was his. He'd said he would sneak me away from the reception to 'seal the deal.' It excited him that he'd have me whilst the party happened just a short distance away, within earshot even. It thrilled him that someone might see us. He was turned-on about having sex with me in my wedding dress. He'd described in detail how he'd slide his hands up my legs, push my underwear aside and sink his manhood into me. He said it would be urgent, hard, and quick.

His reward for all I'd put him through.

A prize he'd wanted to claim since the day our engagement had been announced.

His eyes had widened with lust as he'd told me he wanted us standing, my back against a wall as he thrust into me. He didn't care where the deal would happen, but there was no way he was going to wait until the end of the day. A broom cupboard, a quiet corridor, the toilets. All were potential places for him to violate me. The idea elated him—it was his fantasy—one I'd helped create by refusing him.

The church lit in a blinding light and my heart stuttered, waiting for the ominous roll of thunder. When it came, the windows rattled, and the brightening sky that I'd left outside disappeared. The stained glass windows, so bright only a few seconds ago, dulled as the dark downcast clouds rolled over the church. It was as if my lies were seen. That the religious forces saw the charade I'd been acting—they were here to blow the truth wide open. Or had they read my mind, seen the lust-fuelled intentions of my future husband? Was the storm a warning of darker days to come?

A quivering sigh escaped me as I looked forward. He was shifting from foot to foot, his nerves not hidden as well as mine. Was he dreading this as much as I was? Somehow, I doubted it. He was always so sure of himself. So confident, so measured with his responses. A dark wolf in sheep's clothing. I knew what he was like, but others saw only what they wanted to see. It was who he was. Nothing, not even my mother, could change that. Or was he worried I'd cause a scene? Refuse to marry him? Call him out on his dirty fantasy? Having caught sight of his best man and the friends he had invited here today, I doubted they'd be disgusted in him. They'd cheer on, watch whilst he defiled me. It wouldn't surprise me. Rich boys treated women like me as a toy, an item to play with. A vessel to satisfy their manly needs. There was no love—there never had been—not from him, and certainly not from me.

Perhaps I should have given him a chance. Tried to make it work. Not just a show when others were around. Married today but divorced within the year. That was how I saw things. But if I didn't have the courage to stop things now, I was aware I may not have it in the future. And surely ending a marriage would be harder to do than to start one.

I often wondered why he'd agreed to all of this. Were his promotion and money his only reasons? Maybe I should have tried to love him, tried to salvage what I could from a hopeless situation. Maybe it would have been easier, or maybe not. But how could I love him when my heart belonged to another?

My father guided me forward, one shuffling step in front of another. His gaze was fixed forward. I knew if he looked at me, he was likely to break. He thought he understood my turmoil, but no one could. Not even the man I was about to marry. I'd had to keep it quiet, ignore the whirlwind happening around us and focus. Just focus on getting to this part and through today.

It happened so fast, and yet the walk to my future husband seemed to take forever. But once I was there, when his cold hand took place of my father's sweaty one, I cringed inside. The temperature of his hand matched his steely demeanour. It matched his heart. I swallowed hard and refused to face him.

The vicar began talking, a well-practiced speech that was repeated several times a week to unsuspecting couples. He mentioned how we'd met, how our families were united as we ourselves were. He spoke about our commitment to God, and about true love. My eyes misted over, and I zoned out from his monotonous tone.

More memories. This time of when Andrew proposed to me. How we had our own pretend marriage when we were eight years old. My ring was made from several daisies, their stalks split and threaded with another. It was too big and kept slipping off. And Andrew always replaced it, telling me each time that we were married all over again. I skipped everywhere for the following week, dreaming of a time when we could marry as adults, when our relationship would be recognised in the grown-up world we were so desperate to belong to, but so dreading at the same time. We wanted the freedom of being innocent, of not caring that we laughed too much, that we insisted on staying out too late, that we took bike rides to the other side of town and played with the rough kids on the estate where he lived. We had friends who joked that we were like a married couple at twelve years old. But we didn't care. We loved life and we loved each other. Even then, we both thought we knew what love was.

When the late teenage years struck, and our hormones raced, we discovered another way to love each other. And it was the purest, most consuming love I'd ever had, and would ever have. I wanted no other, for I doubted they would ever make me feel how he did. It was natural. It was innocent and yet wicked. It was sinful, raw, edgy, addictive. And he made me feel like that. Him... only him.

I zoned out from the hymn that had started, let the voices of the choir roll over me in waves. How could I stand here and let this carry on? Did I have the strength to stop this? Could I find it within?

I'd always been headstrong, determined with what I wanted, and I definitely didn't want this. I furrowed my brow and closed my eyes, slowly shaking my head.

This wasn't what I wanted.

I didn't want a life with him.

I didn't care that I'd upset my mother, his parents, him.

I clenched my jaw muscles and lifted my vision from the floor.

I became calm and focused as I inhaled deeply and then slowly exhaled.

This was it. My decision was made.

I pressed my lips together as the vicar cleared his throat and spoke my name. So lost in my thoughts, I'd missed the cue to turn to face the man I was supposed to marry.

I struggled to focus on him. He was familiar, of course, but I struggled to recognise him. Piercing blue eyes studied mine. They didn't dance with the mischief of a free heart. His stubble was non-existent, shaved so precisely, not a razor cut to be seen. His blond hair was short, styled to crisp lines, just like his designer suit and maroon tie.

It wasn't him.

Once again, the vicar spoke about the ultimate bond. Love, unity, commitment. A sly grin slid onto my face as I heard the words 'I do' spoken from my groom. And when silence filled the church and I realised it was my turn to utter the words that could never be unsaid, I paused.

The silence stretched out as people held their breath, waiting for me to speak. But I couldn't say the words. They wouldn't form. I wouldn't say them. They weren't true.

I shook my head, my resolve steadfast. My decision was final.

"No," I muttered. Determination flooded through me, and I began to laugh. "No. I do not take this man."

I dismissed all my negative thoughts and the nagging voice in my mind and embraced the resolution of my decision. I held the focus of my groom's eyes, refusing to look away. Holding my chin high, I repeated my word, this time with firm conviction.

"No."

The silence of the congregation was broken—gasped breaths, mutterings, small sniffs. But as soon as I'd had the conviction to say those words it was as if a huge weight had been lifted from my shoulders.

"No, I do not want to marry you," I said, looking directly into his eyes.

My wrists were gripped tight, restraining, as he leaned towards me. "Don't be difficult. This is going to happen whether you want it or not," he whispered angrily.

"No. No, it's not."

I pulled my wrists away from his pinching grip and turned to the vicar.

"I'm sorry. But I won't marry this man. I apologise for wasting your time today."

I was about to turn away, head back down the aisle alone, single, not as a married woman. It felt good, refreshing—I was free. The freedom that had been stolen from me crashed through me as it returned. For the first time in six months, I felt like me. A rebel, a free spirit, a woman who was her own guide.

"Jenni!" The shout was from the doors of the church. Only one man called me Jenni, not Jennifer.

I had no need to look to know who was there—Andrew.

"Jenni, you don't need to marry him. Come with me." Words I'd waited months to hear. Words I feared I'd never hear. All hope of things turning out this way had gone, exhausted when I told him I had to go through with it. He'd walked away, broken that I'd not had the strength to stand up to my mother and the pending wedding.

But he was here now.

He was here to stop this crazy charade.

Never mind that his hand was leaning on the back of a pew, his face flushed red as if he'd been running. He was here.

His skin was tanned, as though he lived his life abroad, and his dark wavy hair stuck to his neck. I could see the stubble on his face from where I stood, as well as the numerous tattoos covering his arms. He was hardly dressed for a wedding—a black t-shirt and paint-splattered jeans. But I didn't care. He was here.

A deep frown pulled at his brow. What was he confused about? Did he really think I'd go through with this? My stomach sank when I realised I nearly had. Guilt careered through me, and I gasped at what I had allowed to happen. How had I let it get this far? Why hadn't I just refused and ran away with Andrew when he suggested it? I took a deep, pained breath and closed my eyes. If only I could have gone back in time and changed things—I'd do it in a heartbeat.

Paul grabbed my wrists again, signs of his controlling behaviour showing once more. His action snapped me from my thoughts.

"No," I hissed.

Turning to the doors of the church, I smiled at Andrew. This was all I'd wanted. Him.

I glanced at my father.

"How did he know?" I asked. "Today... this church?" It wasn't local to us, only to Paul's parents.

He nodded and grinned. "Someone must have told him," he said, eyes dancing with mischief.

I flung my arms around him, tears forming without warning. "Thank you," I whispered, planting a kiss on his cheek.

"Get out of here," he replied. "Quick, before your mother tries to stop you."

I nodded, immediately taking heed of his warning. I threw my bouquet of flowers to the floor and kicked my stupid high-heeled shoes off. I ran toward Andrew, not looking sideways or back. I wanted to greet him with a kiss, but he reached for my hand, and together, we ran out of the church.

The sun was shining, a break in the surrounding storm as he led me to his campervan. It was parked behind the pristine white limousine. The contrast couldn't have been clearer.

Once in the van, Andrew turned to face me. His frown had returned.

"I'm sorry," he said, emotion evident in his voice even over those two words. "I should have come sooner." He shook his head. "I should have never left you. I'm so, so sorry."

"Hey," I said, lifting the veil away from my face and pulling it free from my hair. "I should have stopped it before it even started."

"No," he replied, reaching for my hand. "I should have been there for you. I should have realised that without me there, you'd not be able to stand up to your mother. We needed to be a united front."

"I should have run away with you when you offered." He couldn't blame himself for this. It was all my fault.

He lifted his hand to my face and wiped a tear that, unknown to me, had escaped from the corner of my eye. I closed my eyes as he touched me. This was Andrew. His distinctive scent of turps, linseed oil, and the bitterness of oil paint—all merged with his aftershave. I'd missed this. His touch, his scent, his understanding.

"I've missed you," I breathed, his proximity already affecting me.

"Me too," he whispered, moving closer. He shifted in his seat, twisting to face me.

"You look beautiful," he said, his eyes running the full length of my white dress but stopping on my eyes as he drank me in as if it was the first time he'd ever seen me.

"But I prefer it when your hair is loose. When you look like the free spirit you are. Wild and at one with nature."

I grinned, lifting my hand to his face and running my finger over his stubble. His brown eyes were soft, understanding, and I could see the fire that danced behind them.

"Let's go somewhere quiet," I said, surprising myself with the huskiness in my voice.

His eyebrows rose, and he chuckled.

"Eventually," he said. "But we've got something else to do first."

"What?" I asked, my excitement bubbling, my heart pounding.

"Get married."

My eyes widened. "Seriously?"

He nodded. "Well, you're already dressed for it, and our engagement must be the longest on record. How many years is it since I gave you your daisy ring?"

"You remembered?" I muttered, my words quiet.

"How could I forget?" He leaned closer. So close that our noses were touching. "I made a promise to you. One that I have never forgotten." His fingers twisted a stray strand of my hair and pushed it behind my ear, the roughness of his fingers evident as they brushed against my skin. I breathed the scent of him in. It had been so long since we'd been this close. Too long since I'd drowned in the overpowering strength of him. Like a woman in a lust-fuelled trance, I quietly whimpered as his nose edged along my jaw. Within seconds, his lips were hovering over mine. Instinctively, my hands rose, wrapping themselves in his hair, pulling him closer. It was like our first kiss, but with the knowledge and passion that came from knowing someone intimately. His stubble scratched my face, familiar and comforting. His tongue swept over mine, slow, steady, measured so as not to give too much of himself all at once. I responded, deepening the kiss, needing his reassurance that this was real. I wanted all of him. I wanted to drown in him, lose myself and have him help find me over and over again. I moaned into his kiss, not wanting to stop to breathe but taking my air back through the kiss. He pulled away, desire flaming in his eyes as I looked at him.

"Steady," he said before placing a lighter kiss on my begging lips.

"I want you."

He nodded. "You have no idea how I've longed for this moment. How I've replayed our reunion again and again in my head. But this... this is more than I'd hoped for." His cock-eyed grin appeared. "I hope you slept well last night because you'll not be sleeping much tonight. He tipped his head toward the back of the van. The mattress was already in position and the curtains drawn at the tiny windows.

"That's very presumptuous," I said, my grin making another appearance.

"It's a new one," he said as if making a secret confession. "I thought we deserved it."

I laughed, something I'd not done for months. The sound surprised me and made me laugh even more.

Andrew chuckled, his eyes never leaving me. But then he became serious. I quietened as I noticed the change in his demeanour.

"I just want to make things clear," he said. "I don't want any misunderstanding."

I nodded, frowning at his seriousness.

"Jenni, will you marry me?"

I reached for him, my fingers in his hair again, my mouth against his.

"Yes!" I said when we broke away from each other. "Yes, I'll marry you."

With a cockeyed smile and a wink, he shifted back into the driver's seat.

"Best get going, then," he said, "Before they all come after us." He nodded towards the church and the ensuing crowd of people. With a quiet chuckle, he turned the key in the ignition. The van spluttered to life, and we crawled away from the church.

I didn't look back; there was no need. The last six months had been the worst of my life. When he'd walked away, I'd hoped and prayed every day that he'd come back. I knew that if he'd turned up on any one of those days, I'd have left with him, turned my back on the wedding of the year, and thrown caution to the wind.

Andrew loved me and I loved him. It had always been that way. I should have never gone through with what my mother had planned. It all seemed so easy now. But that's how life with Andrew was... easy. It was natural, nothing forced. It was how it should have always been.

As we pulled away from the busy streets of the city and onto the quiet lanes of the countryside, I knew I'd made the right decision.

And as I took a deep, calming breath, I managed a wide smile. I felt like I was floating. Like a huge burden had lifted. My belly fluttered with excitement, and my limbs tingled. I was free. All the hope I'd had, the desire for Andrew to come and tell me how much he loved me, to stop this crazy wedding and run away with him. It felt like a hopeless dream played on repeat in my mind. It would never happen; I wasn't good enough for him. I'd ruined it all.

But as I turned to look at him, studying his crazy dark curls lapping at his neck, he grinned.

"What are you smiling at?" he asked, not even turning to look at me. He was aware of my gaze even without eye contact—he knew me so well.

"My future," I whispered.

His free hand reached for mine. "Our future."

The End

Also by
Melody Winter

The Mines Series Sachael Dreams

Sachael Desires

Sachael Discovery

The Ascent Series

Iniquity

Adversity

Starshine

A Love Worth Everything

Flamenco Fire - novella

Promise - novella

When All Seems Lost
by Paula Acton

Prologue

"Shut the fuck up."

"Why it doesn't matter, she is blindfolded, no way she going to remember a voice with the drugs they pumped into her."

"Yeah, well personally I prefer not to take chances, just check her over and let's get out of here."

Somewhere in the distant recesses of her consciousness Danielle Wilson-Miller was aware of the voices, and of rough hands checking her pulse and breathing. Wherever she was. and whatever was happening, for now, the sedatives still flowing through her system made waking seem too much like hard work. The only thing that registered was that one of the two voices did not sound friendly.

The next time she roused she was aware that she was laying on an unmade bed, the blindfold stopped her seeing her surroundings, but she doubted she would find herself in the sort of place she was used to. Trying to stretch out, she realised her wrists were bound together, as were her ankles. Her instinct was to try to rub her head against the rough material of the mattress. After a couple of tries she concluded that it was futile. The material covering her eyes was tight enough that it would not move, and thick enough no light could penetrate it.

Her tongue felt thick in her mouth, her lips dry. She was aware of the need to drink, and the need to urinate simultaneously. She clenched her thighs together, trying to piece together what had happened for her to end up here and attempt to distract herself from her body's needs.

She remembered having dinner. She had eaten alone at the kitchen table as Duncan, her husband, was working late yet again. She had loaded the dishwasher then headed into the living room. She had picked up a book and curled up in the chair. It was a good book so she couldn't say for sure how long she had sat there, but then she had been disturbed by the sound of a car pulling up outside.

She had assumed Duncan was home and had headed back to the kitchen. Some nights when he came home, he wanted food, some nights he would just grab a beer before heading to his home office. Lately he had been home so late she was already in bed. Her dog Sukie had run to the back door barking. She had thought Sukie wanted to go out, she had opened the door and let her. Sukie had hurtled across the grass, but she'd kept barking, and she had…

She felt the warmth trickle down her leg. Tears filled her eyes from both the humiliation and the realisation of what had happened. Sukie had run around barking, she had followed her outside to see what was wrong. She hadn't stopped to think, hadn't noticed the automatic lights outside had not come on. She hadn't realised anyone else was there until the arms wrapped round her from behind. She remembered the acrid smelling cloth being pressed to her face and then nothing until waking to those two voices. She had been kidnapped and now the panic began rising him her chest, she was going to die.

Chapter One

"What's your problem?"

"I don't know what you're talking about."

"Like shit you don't! Ever since you saw her you have been up your own arse. So? C'mon let's have it. What the fuck is wrong?"

"I don't like this shit Marcus. I told you before I didn't want to be part of your dodgy deals but no, always one more favour. I know I am your brother, but I want out of this shit. I've bailed you out when you've been broke, when people were after you because you owed them money. I've turned a blind eye to how you make your money. Hell, you have even made me a criminal before now, hiding your stash in my house, but this, this is a step too far."

"I know you don't want a part of this, and you don't have to. Just walk away, go stay at a mates, go away for a few days. Her husband is loaded, he is gonna pay up, and then we can both go on the straight and narrow. I was an idiot, okay! I trusted the wrong person! I was ready to go legit! You know that I didn't ask to be ripped off. This is how I get my money back, once I get it back, that's it, no more. Two of us will be here the whole time. I promise no one is going to hurt a hair on her head while she is under your roof. You don't need to be here."

"Like hell I don't! You think I trust you and your mates? Not only respect my house, but also that woman lying in the cellar drugged and tied up?"

Noah Andrews ran his hand through his dark hair, he noted it need a cut, but for now he had other things on his mind. His brother - or half-brother when he was feeling like this about him - had said he needed to borrow his cellar for a couple of weeks. Marcus had a key to the house so he hadn't paid much attention to what he brought in. When he saw the mattresses, he asked what was going on and Marcus told him it was for soundproofing so he could practise his DJ set down there.

Then, tonight, he had been woken by someone opening the door. A glance at his clock told him it was 2am. He had come down the stairs just in time to see his brother and another guy carry something in and towards the cellar. He'd been about to go to back up the stairs when the long blonde hair fell over his brothers' arm. By the time he had made it down the remaining steps they had shut the front door behind them and started down into the cellar.

Following them he found them laying the woman on one of the mattresses. They had fixed the rest around the room attached the wall as soundproofing, but not for the reasons they had given him. In the corner were two buckets, one with water in and one empty. He had lost it with them, demanding to know what they were doing. He had been thinking the worst of his brother. Though to be fair, when he heard it, the actual plan was just as bad and just as stupid.

Noah walked into the kitchen and opened the fridge. He grabbed a beer, he wanted something stronger, but he also knew he needed to keep his head clear. He shut it again, not offering his brother one, before walking back into the living room and dropping into his oversized leather armchair.

"So, tell me again this bright idea you've had."

Marcus sat opposite him on the sofa. He felt bad about his plan, but the woman wouldn't be hurt, and he would get his money. He kept telling himself he only wanted what was owed to him nothing more. Well, maybe a little more, but that was for the inconvenience of the lengths he was having to take to get it back.

"You remember, the guy I was going into business with? Doug - Douglas Miller?"

"Yeah, what about him? What's he got to do with this?"

"That's his daughter-in-law! She is how I'm going to get my money back!"

"For fucks sake Marcus! You kidnapped his daughter-in-law to ransom her to get your money back? Look, I know losing the money was shit, but I told you we would find another way to make things happen for you. There was no need to do this stupid shit. Do you have any idea what you are doing? Do you know how long you would get sent down for? And don't think they won't go straight to the police and send them straight after you as someone with a grudge to bare? I can't believe you are such a fucking idiot."

"No. Listen, Doug can't go to the police, because then, he will have to explain how he ripped me off for the twenty grand that I gave him as my half of the down payment on the club. He was always bragging about how rich his son was, but he also kept saying that he married her," he nodded his head down towards the floor, "because she had all the money. He reckoned that was the reason that his son married her. So, he isn't gonna want people digging into his business too close either. Trust me, the money I'm asking for isn't worth the aggro going to the cops is gonna cause for him."

"I hope you're right. Because right now, we are all looking at serious time."

"It's all gonna work out. Couple of days I am gonna get my money back, she is gonna be back sleeping on her satin sheets, with all this nothing more than a bad dream. I promise she is gonna be treated like a princess, just one with a blindfold. You go back to bed. I'm gonna make her a sandwich, take her some water, and make sure she is okay for the night. I'll get a couple of hours sleep on the sofa. Honest, I wouldn't have dragged you into this if I wasn't certain it would all work out. Okay? I promise you a day or two and it'll all be done, and I'll never ask anything from you again."

"Yeah, right. I don't like this! I swear anything happens to her and I'll turn you in myself."

Noel got up and took the half full bottle to the kitchen. He poured the remaining beer down the sink and left the bottle on the countertop to recycle the next day. He knew he should be ringing the police right now, but he couldn't bring himself to do it. Of all the screwed up plans his brother had ever come up with, this was the craziest.

He walked back through the living room to the stairs, glancing at the cellar door, before heading up to bed. He could only hope his brother was right about her husband and father-in-law having enough reasons not to call the cops. He had a feeling he wouldn't be getting much sleep that night.

Chapter Two

Marcus watched his brother go up the stairs, he felt guilty that he had dragged him into this, but he was sure his plan would work. If anything went wrong, he would take the blame. His brother had always looked out for him, despite the fact their dad had hooked up with his mum just after leaving Noel and his mum to fend for themselves.

He had only learned he had an older brother when he was in his teens. He had overheard his mum arguing with his dad about the fact they couldn't get married because he wouldn't get a divorce. He had heard his mum say something about her fears he would walk away and leave them just like he had his other family. At that point he had stormed in and demanded to know everything.

He went into the kitchen and grabbed the stuff to make a sandwich from the fridge. As he made it, he remembered the first time he had ever seen his big brother. He had sat outside the homes of three different lots of Knight's in the area his dad had last heard his wife was living.

Each one of them had proved to be a waste of time and he had been convinced that this would be the same. He had decided if this was another dead end he would stop his search, for now at least. He realised he had become obsessed by the idea of an older brother - he had never stopped to consider how his brother might take the news he had a younger brother.

He sat on a wall further down the street, near enough to see who came in and out of the house but far enough away to not be obvious. He had been so engrossed watching the door he didn't hear the footsteps approaching from the other direction. At the last minute he became aware of a presence closing in on him and turned to see a younger version of his dad walking straight towards him.

The young man approaching him was not aware he was there yet, he was engrossed with something on his phone. Marcus had looked around for somewhere to bolt to, but then Noel had looked up and it was too late.

"Hey, do I know you?"

"Erm, no, we haven't met but I'm..."

"Your what? You look familiar."

"I look a little bit like my dad but not as much as you do..."

"What?"

"I'm your brother, well half-brother."

"I don't have a brother, fuck off!"

With that Noel had stormed past Marcus and a few seconds later the door slammed. Marcus had sat stunned. He had never considered that his brother might not be as excited about this discovery as he had been. He didn't hear the door open again or take in the well-dressed woman who walked up to him and put her hand on his shoulder.

"Are you okay?"

"Fine."

"Marcus told me what happened, come on inside and sit down. It was a shock for him, he found it hard growing up without a dad. But he is a good kid and I think the two of you should talk."

She had guided him to the house and called Marcus down to sit and talk with him while she had made them dinner. The three of them had sat at the table and eaten together before she had driven him home. He had got her to drop him off a couple of streets away, not wanting her to see that his dad leaving her had done her a favour. That the quality of life his brother had grown up with was better than his own.

He had built a relationship with his brother slowly, mainly by phone at first, then he had found himself invited to their home more and more often. His parents had not encouraged him in creating a bond with his brother. It had caused rows, right up until the day at seventeen, when he had packed what he could carry in a rucksack and walked out.

Marcus had sorted him out that day. He had sorted his problems so many times, more than he should have to, that was why this plan had to work. He couldn't risk ruining his brother's life.

He made the sandwich and picked up a pack of bottled water. The woman in the cellar had no reason to trust him after the way the had grabbed her but he was determined she would come to no harm. Double checking the front door was locked he made his way down the stairs.

There were three doors between him and his hostage, one at the top of the stair, one at the bottom, then one into the part of the cellar where she was being held. Each one had a lock on it, and he was careful to secure each door as he passed through it. Opening the final door, he entered to see the young woman he had kidnapped sobbing on the mattress.

He placed the paper plate with the sandwich on down on the floor along with the water and moved closer to the woman.

"Hey, please don't cry. I promise you're gonna be okay. I'm sorry I had to do this, but as soon as your ransom is paid you will be out of here..."

The woman on the mattress began to laugh hysterically.

"No one is going to pay for me. You may as well do what he wants now, shoot me and put me out of my misery. He'd love it, me shot laying covered in my own piss."

"Damn, I thought I'd be back before you woke up. I'm going to untie your ankles and your wrists, but don't try moving. I don't want to hurt you, but if you try anything I will need to keep you tied up. Do you understand?"

"What does it matter, you're going to end up having to kill me now anyway."

"Your husband will pay your ransom. He can afford it, it's nothing to him. I don't want you hurt or to suffer for your short stay here."

He moved swiftly; a blade pulled from his pocket sliced through the cable ties freeing her limbs. He now faced an awkward decision - he couldn't leave her sat in wet clothes, but he hadn't planned for her needing a change of clothes. His only option was to strip her off and let her clean herself using the cold water in the bucket. He'd have to strip off his own t-shirt for her to wear until he could wash her clothes in the morning.

He expected her to fight but instead she was docile. She

allowed him to take off all her clothes without protesting. Once she was naked, he passed her a wet cloth and he turned away while she washed herself. He felt guilty that she was having to do it with cold water, but he couldn't waste time going upstairs to refill the bucket. Once she had finished, he had her stand against one wall while he swapped the mattresses round so that she did not have to lie back down on the wet one.

He passed her his t-shirt to put on. It fitted her like a dress and covered everything it needed to. He fed her the sandwich and let her drink from one of the bottles. After she finished, he fastened her hands together again, leaving her legs free to move in case she needed to take care of her bodily functions.

"When I go, I will lock the door, I will bang on it three times then you can take your blindfold off. I have left you more water, there are buckets to wash your hands and to use as a toilet. Get some sleep, you won't be here long. Soon all this will just be a bad dream. But when I am coming back in I will bang three times and I want you to put the blindfold back on. Just because I don't want to hurt you doesn't mean I won't if I need to. Understand?" He walked over and opened the door.

"Yes, but tell me, what are you going to do when he won't pay?"

"Don't you worry about that, he will." The door closed, the lock turned and three bangs on the door followed.

Chapter Three

The three knocks seemed to reverberate around her. Danielle Wilson-Miller reached up to remove the cloth that had covered her eyes. It took a minute for her to adjust to the harsh lighting, A bare bulb dangled from the ceiling as the only source of light. There were mattresses piled against the walls, it looked like some were attached in some way, but one was propped further away.

The tears came again as she realised that was the one soaked with her urine. She was mortified at the memory of not only the act itself but the fact she had then had to strip in front of him to wash herself. Even though it had been humiliating she had decided it was preferable to sitting in her wet clothes with the stench a constant reminder. The fact that her capturer had not touched her had eased her mind a little. She could face death but that idea of the things that could be done to her before death was what she feared most.

Danielle had no doubt at all that she would not be rescued. Her husband would be glad she was gone. Her dad had made her arrange the pre-nuptial agreement. She had been convinced that she didn't need it, and he had been furious, but her dad had been firm, there was either an arrangement, or he would write her out of his will. Duncan had signed eventually. If they divorced before ten years had passed, he got nothing, if she died, well, he would get everything.

Danielle stretched out on the mattress, being alone was nothing new to her. Duncan was rarely home these days. She knew he had a mistress who stayed with him in the Mayfair flat that had been bought with company funds. It was supposed to be somewhere for prospective investors to stay when they visited but she knew better. She had loved him so much when they married, and she believed he loved her.

The first six months everything had been great. They had travelled and enjoyed each other's company. Then there was the accident, and everything changed.

Her parents had been on the way home from the theatre when their Uber was hit by a drunk driver. In one night, she lost her parents, became responsible for her dad's business and, although she hadn't known at the time, she would lose herself and be controlled by the man she loved. At first, everything he did seemed like he loved her and was looking out for her, but it hadn't taken long for her to see things begin to change but she had been unable to fight back.

Danielle shifted trying to make herself more comfortable. If she were being honest with herself, she had always expected to be found dead, but she had always assumed it would be her husband that would be the one to do the deed. She could imagine the smile on his face when the ransom note was delivered, he would probably crack open a bottle of champagne to celebrate her demise.

The first month after her parents' death he'd never left her side. He'd played the supportive husband so well. He held her up at the funeral, he attended board meetings on her behalf, telling her nothing of real importance would be discussed.

In reality he had walked in there and told them all he would be taking her place, that she was too fragile, too distraught to deal with day-to-day business. He told them he would be acting on her behalf just until she got stronger. They had all been sympathetic. They all understood. Not one of them questioned why she hadn't reached out to any of them personally, despite the fact they had known her since she was a little girl.

His next move had been to get her seen by a doctor, her grief had been real and all consuming. She had been devastated but he had insisted that she need medication. Everything had been downhill from there.

Strange, she thought, the fact she knew her time was running out gave her the clarity to see what he had done. Constantly whispering in her ear, driving wedges between her and her friends. Isolating her, then employing 'staff' who would report back to him everything she said or did.

He persuaded her that she was paranoid. He dragged her from doctor to doctor. He would never stay with a doctor once he started talking about weaning her off the tablets or saying she needed therapy rather than medication. No, the truth was, if you had enough money, you could find someone eventually who would write the prescription and not look the patient in the eye.

For a while she had been waiting for him to hand her the tablets to overdose. He would be so happy right now that he wouldn't have to get his hands dirty, and he would get everything.

She believed the guy who had grabbed her genuinely thought that he would get his money. Her husband had covered his tracks far too well for anyone to know the truth about their sham of a marriage. From the outside he looked like the loving husband supporting a wife who had not been able to get over the grief of a tragic accident that killed her parents. It looked like she was the luckiest woman in the world, all the material things anyone could want and an adoring husband.

The truth was she was tired. She had thought about taking her own life before, not because she wanted to die but she didn't want to carry on with this life. Her husband made sure she had no chance to get away from him. He monitored her phone, emails, and made sure she was always with someone. She had no hope of her life ever getting any better. Then, somehow, this guy had got to her and now things would end.

Chapter Four

She passed the night in a fitful sleep. Next morning, she woke feeling like she was hung over. She rolled over on to her front so she could use her tied hands to push herself up. As degrading as it was using the bucket it was better than the alternative. She used the cold water in the other bucket to wash her hands. Picking up on of the bottles of water that he had left she took it back to the mattress.

Opening it turned out to be harder than she had thought. In the end she had to grip the bottle between her knees then turn the lid. The cold liquid was refreshing but did nothing to ease the pounding in her head.

Her first thought was it had to be as a result of whatever had been on the cloth that had been pressed over her face as she was grabbed. It came to her that she had not taken her medication the night before. As much as she hated the fact that she had be prescribed the sedatives, she realised that without them she would go cold turkey.

She tried to think, were her pills in her bag? Did they grab her bag when they took her? She had no idea how long it would be before anyone came back to her. Surely they would be back soon? She looked around the room there was no sign of food. He had fed her last night but not enough to leave her for hours unattended if he was being honest about his intention of her coming to no harm.

What the hell was she thinking? Come to no harm! This was a man who had grabbed her from her own home. Oh god, poor Sukie! Tears filled her eyes. Was her dog okay? Had they shut the gate, or had they left it open so her baby could run out into harms way?

She rolled over and pushed herself back to her feet. She ran at the door, panic for her pet motivated her to action where self preservation had failed. She pounded on the door. She had no idea if anyone could hear her, if anyone was out there. She slammed her bound hands into the door over and over again. After a few minutes her strength failed and she slumped sobbing, her back resting against the door, her bloody and bruised hands in front of her.

She did not register the banging on the door from the other side at first. Only when the door pushed against her did she realise that she had attracted her captor's attention. She tried to remember what he had said the night before. She looked around for the blindfold, but she couldn't see it through the tears that she couldn't stop falling.

"Hey, move to the other side of the room."

"I can't. I lost the blindfold."

Marcus froze on the other side of the door. The pounding below had woken him from an uneasy sleep. Halfway down the steps he had heard crying, now she couldn't cover her eyes. Damn, what was he going to do?

"Look, don't worry just stand facing the wall at the

other side of the room, I will find the blindfold and put it back on you, then everything will be fine."

"Why bother, it doesn't matter if I see you, you are going to have to kill me soon anyway. Has he told you to make me suffer? Has he said to make it look like suicide?"

"What are you talking about? Who is he? I told you yesterday, I just want my money then you will be dropped off near home."

"Yeah right! I know my husband is behind this I worked it out because there is no way you could have snatched me without someone seeing you. I have a companion who is always there, yet she had disappeared just when you grabbed me? Coincidence? Nah, he arranged for you to grab me.

"The woman who was in the house with you was distracted on the phone when we grabbed you. Trust me, we'd been lurking for over an hour waiting for a chance. And the only thing your husband has to do with all this is that he will be dropping off the money for your release."

"No, he won't, he wants me dead."

Something in her tone made Marcus's blood run cold. She really believed that her husband would refuse to pay up. Right now, he needed to get in there and feed her. Then he could go check if there had been any response to the message they had left last night.

"Listen, I get maybe you and your old man have had some sort of fight, but he isn't going to want you dead. Trust me I haven't asked for a lot of money, just enough to cover... well you don't need to know about that. C'mon, just go stand by the wall. I brought you some food, you have to be getting hungry. No one is going to hurt you, I promised you that last night. I know you have no reason to trust me but I don't hurt women."

He felt the pressure on the door release and a scuffling noise that he assumed was her getting to her feet. He counted to ten.

"Are you over at the other wall?"

"Yes." Her voice barely audible.

He pushed the door open slowly. She was stood facing the wall as instructed but she looked so small. The t-shirt he had given her the night before reached halfway down her thighs. He noticed her shiver, or was she shaking?

He closed the door behind him and locked it before looking for the discarded blindfold. Picking it up, he quickly put it back in place then took her arm and guided her back to the mattress. Once she was seated, he fed her the omelette he had brought her. He took the time to really look at her. Despite the fact the cellar felt warm to him she was still shaking. Something seemed wrong. He let his eyes survey the bare flesh he could see, looking for any sign of bruising or injury other than her hands.

He could see nothing, but her hands would require attention. He would go check on the message, then come back and clean them up properly, they could do with being bandaged too. He was angry at her that she had hurt herself, but he couldn't really blame her. Her shaking worried him, it could be shock. He would make her a cup of sweet tea - he had heard that worked for shock.

"What are you going to do with me when he won't pay? Please, promise me you won't make it hurt."

"I keep telling you no one is going to hurt you. It's morning now, I bet anything that you will be comfortable in your own bed by tonight."

"You really believe that don't you?"

"Of course I do, your husband isn't gonna let anyone

hurt you. Now, leave the blindfold on. I will be back in a few minutes to sort your hands out."

Danielle sensed him move away from her. She counted the footsteps to the door, listened to it being unlocked and closed again before she let the tears come again. Whoever her captor was, he was in for a shock. He hadn't allowed for Duncan's greed.

Chapter Five

Marcus logged into the email via the fake IP address. He had it set up so that anyone trying to track it would be bounced between a dozen countries making it almost impossible to trace it back to him. If Duncan Miller chose to bring in Scotland Yard or MI5 they might track him but he doubted that was a real worry. He had only asked for thirty thousand, that was enough to cover his losses to Doug and pay his friend for helping him with the grab. He would use the money to set himself up, maybe he would try Ibiza, one of the smaller clubs.

It only took a few seconds for him to see there had been a reply, and he understood now why his prisoner was so scared.

Do me a favour make sure you dump the silly bitch's body where it can be found quickly. You are doing me a favour she is worth more to me dead.

He stared at the screen in disbelief. The guy couldn't be

serious. He didn't hear his brother approach him from behind.

"Fuck, what a bastard! So, genius what brilliant plan do you have now? You have a woman in my cellar, her husband doesn't give a fuck. You're not going to get your money and it's a huge fucking mess that's gonna land us all in prison."

"Don't panic, he's calling our bluff. I'm gonna reply now adding that if I don't get the money not only will he never see his wife again, then I will expose his dad as a conman and a swindler." He hit send, inwardly praying that this would work. because if not and his brother was right, he was screwed.

"What do you mean he is calling *our* bluff. You promised this wouldn't come back to me, you need to get her out of here, you have me too messed up in this already."

"Please Noah, you know what I meant. I get it, this isn't what I expected. Thing is she keeps saying her husband wants her dead. She even asked if he had arranged her being grabbed. I have no idea what is going on, but she hasn't seen me, she has no idea where she is. Twenty-four hours, and if he still hasn't paid, I will take her and drop her off somewhere safe."

"I can't believe I am even agreeing to this. You mess this up and we are through, you're putting my whole life on the line here, my freedom, my career. I told you I would sort the money for you, there was no bloody need for any of this."

Noah turned his back on his brother and headed into the kitchen. Marcus could hear him fill the kettle and remembered she was waiting for him to return. He closed his laptop and followed in his brothers' footsteps.

"Do you have a first aid box?"

"What?"

"First aid box, I need a couple of bandages, and is there enough water in the kettle to make her a tea.?"

"Why do you need the first aid box? You swore to me she wouldn't get hurt. I swear to God, I will drag you to the police station myself."

Noah stepped towards Marcus who raised his hands in defence. He had learnt the hard way growing up. He might be six foot two, but his older brother had a couple of extra inches on him and was built like a gladiator and could put him in his place.

"She got upset and pummelled the door. I didn't do anything to her!"

"Why did she pound on the door?"

"I am guessing because she is locked up down there, but she ate afterwards. She is a bit shaky, I am guessing shock, that's why I want the tea."

"You would do better to ask her how she is feeling. How much chloroform did you use last night? What are the side effects of that? Is she on any medication? Did you even think to check?"

"I researched how much to use and used less than it said was needed. She does look frail though. Gonna sound stupid but part of me thinks she is safer where she is now than she was at home. The woman on the phone, that was her babysitter by the sound of it. I know that when I set her free, I'll be dropping her somewhere she wants to go, not where he wants her."

"Her knight in shining armour!"

"Don't be a dick. I get that you don't approve of this. Hell, I don't approve of what I did but I swear if you saw her, spent a few minutes with her I wouldn't be the only one starting to feel protective."

Noah slammed his coffee cup down and headed

upstairs. He could think of better ways to spend his day off instead of hanging round his house making sure his brother kept his word. This whole situation was so stupid. He could easily have given his brother the money he had lost if it weren't for his damn pride, and now where was that going to get them. He opened his own laptop and googled Duncan Miller. It took him a few minutes to work out the reason that Danielle Wilson-Miller was shaking. He shook his head. This was why his brother was in this mess, he acted before looking into all the details of a situation.

He took the stairs two at a time and arrived at the top of the cellar steps just in time to stick his foot in the doorway to stop it being shut.

"What the fuck Noah?"

"Shut up and get downstairs now."

Marcus walked down and unlocked the second door. He waited until Noah was through it and then locked it again before rapping three times on the final door and unlocking it. He pushed the door wide enough for Noah to walk in past him but as he glanced inside, he saw Danielle laying on her side. She was shaking more noticeably than when he had gone upstairs. Before he could react, Noah was on his knees by her side, pulling her into his chest and stroking her hair.

"It's gonna be okay, I need you to tell me what you are on?"

"What do you mean what is she on? I haven't given her anything."

"She is on medication for depression. Did you grab a bag when you took her?"

"No, nothing just her."

Noah tilted Danielle's head so she would have been looking at him if she had not been blindfolded.

"Listen to my voice. I know this is all mess, and I know you have no reason to trust anyone here, but believe me, we don't want you hurt or to suffer in anyway. What medication should you be taking?"

"He made me take Sertraline. I didn't want to take it, I wanted to get better, but he kept telling me I wasn't strong enough to cope. It's ironic, I finally get my wish just before you have to kill me."

Chapter Six

Noah shut the laptop closed. He had left Marcus watching her while he had come up and researched the anti-depressant, and the withdrawal symptoms. It was clear not only could she not be left alone, but that he was going to have to risk his freedom by removing her blindfold.

He ran upstairs and grabbed the quilt and pillows from his bed, then added the ones from the spare room to the pile. Pulling open drawers, he grabbed a couple of jumpers and some sweatpants. They would be too big on her, but she needed comfort right now. He couldn't believe he was doing this. He should be throwing her in his car dumping her somewhere and washing his hands of his brother but...

It was that BUT! Something about that girl in the cellar made him feel protective. The minute he saw her there, he wanted to wrap her in his arms and keep her from harm. It was stupid and irrational. But whatever else was going on would have to wait until after she had finished going cold turkey. He was tempted to just bring her upstairs, but the risk was too great. No matter how nice they were to her, they had still kidnapped her, and she might tell the police.

He threw his laptop into the middle of the bundle of duvets and headed back down to the cellar.

"What the hell?" Marcus's eyes widened at the sight coming through the door.

"Change of plan, you go check on what is happening with the money side, and I am taking care of our guest."

Danielle looked up fearfully towards him, were the duvets to wrap her body in? She knew she should fight. She didn't want to die, but she didn't want to carry on living like this. Still trembling she got to her feet, the door was still open she should run, make a break for it. She just needed to make her feet move.

Noah watched the woman from the corner of his eye. She wanted to run he could tell she was thinking about it. He placed the duvets on the floor and positioned himself between her and the door which still stood open. As he closed the distance between them his heart pounded, and he felt the stirring of his cock, *fuck not now*. He couldn't believe he was getting turned on by this woman in front of him and hoped she wouldn't notice the bulge growing in his sweatpants.

This was going to a long couple of days.

"Don't bother thinking about the door. Marcus, you get going and let me take care of things here."

Noah heard the door shut behind him and watched the fight go out of her eyes as she slumped back to the floor.

"Right, just me, you, a load of duvets and Netflix. What do you like watching?"

"What? What do you mean?"

"Let's get the bed sorted first."

He hadn't thought about his words but then he saw the look of horror on her face.

"No, oh my god. I didn't mean that. Fuck. I know you have no reason to trust us, but I am telling you that nothing bad is happening to you on my watch."

He threw a quilt over the mattress, then placed all the pillows against the wall, grabbing the laptop he sank down onto the mattress pulling the other quilt over his legs. He patted the space next to him indicating she should sit, then opened the laptop.

She hesitated, weighting up her options. She could take the space next to him or stay where she was on the hard floor.

The duvet looked so comfortable. She could just crawl onto the corner of the mattress and curl up there, but as she began to move her own body betrayed her. It craved human contact. It had been so long since she had sat next to a man and just watched a film.

How crazy, she thought, that here as a prisoner she was treated better in some ways than in her normal life. As she settled next to him, he placed the duvet across her lap.

"Right, first things first, I know you are Danielle, I am Noah. I have no idea what is going on with you and your husband, but I want you to hear this. Whether he pays or not, you will be released. What's more, you will be released somewhere you're safe, if your husband is abusing you then we'll make sure you are with family or friends. No one is going to hurt you here."

"I have no one. I have no family and he made sure I have no friends left. It doesn't matter where you leave me, he will never let me go. He'll find me, he'll persuade the doctors I need tablets again and keep using that to keep control of all my money and my business."

"Is that what he's doing?"

"It's what he's done since my parents died. He has everyone thinking I am crazy."

"You must have someone?"

"No, no one. There are people who should know me better, but he keeps them away from me, makes excuses so I can't go to events. Please, I just can't talk about it anymore my head hurts. I can't think straight. You said we could watch a film? Please?"

"Hey, I am a man of my word." Noah stretched his arm out and wrapped it around her pulling her closer, he was glad that the duvet and the laptop covering his hardening cock.

"What do you fancy?"

"Something funny please."

"Thank god for that, I was worried you would want a soppy love film."

"I stopped believing in happily ever after a long time ago."

He hit play on the laptop and held her close. She was still trembling, side effects from the withdrawal but he would do his best to distract her and help her through it. Only a few minutes in and her other arm reached across his waist cuddling into him further. He looked down and realised she was asleep.

He moved the laptop and shifted position to lie down. Her head rested on his chest, inhaling he smelt her hair. It was faint but the fresh apple fragrance of the shampoo she had last used still lingered.

It had been a long time since he had felt anything for anyone. There had been plenty of flings but since his last girlfriend had cheated, he had guarded his heart carefully. And yet, this woman, their prisoner, she had awakened something inside him.

He was still watching her sleep hours later when his brother reappeared. The look on his face deadly serious.

Chapter Seven

"Is he fucking serious?" Noah had read the message several times but could still not accept that this guy could be such a douchebag.

"That's what he says, **kill the stupid bitch, you're not getting a penny from me. I really don't care what you do with her. Just do me one favour and make it easy for them to find the body**. I am so sorry Danielle. I should never have done this. I don't know how we fix this but I will. I won't blame you if you go to the police and turn me in but please leave Noah out of it. He didn't know anything until I showed up here with you."

"Can I just stay here?"

"What?" Both brothers spoke in unison. Noah whipping his head around to look at her.

"I know this is going to sound crazy. Maybe it is, maybe I am, but for the first time in years I have the chance to find out. Please let me stay here, just until I get the drugs out of my system and have time to think about what I do. It sounds mad, I know it does, but for the first time in ages, locked in this room, I have had more freedom in some ways than in ages. Well except the peeing in a bucket."

"You want to stay here? Locked in this cellar?"

"Well, I would prefer it if I could just stay in the house, but I will stay down here if it makes you feel more secure. When I woke up in your arms, just for a minute I had something I hadn't had in a long time."

"What was that?"

"Hope! For a minute I forgot where I was, and I remembered what it was like to feel loved and wanted. I want my life back and if you will help me, or even just give me time I will think of a way to get it. If I leave here now he will just have more people watch me so I can't do anything. I need to get the drugs out of my system. Work out a way to prove he is cheating and that he has been taking advantage of me. Then I need to find someone to help me divorce him and get back what's mine."

"That's a lot of thoughts for just waking up?"

"I haven't thought it all through, most of it is coming to me now as I say it. Why did you want the money? How much did you ask for?"

"Shit! I swear, when I took you, I had no idea this would happen. I seriously thought he would just pay the thirty thousand and we would let you go. I never imagined him not paying. I know he has the money, why is he being such a wanker?"

Marcus dropped to the floor, sliding down the wall opposite his brother and hostage. Defeated he dropped his head to his knees. As angry as Noah still was with his brother, he knew that he had never intended to cause pain. Like so many times before his younger sibling had acted without thinking.

"Marcus met a guy, he claimed he was into property, everything seemed legit. I even checked him out myself. He had been saving up looking to either go abroad and work as a DJ or to rent a space to start his own club nights.

This guy, Douglas Miller, he talked big. Bragged about his millionaire son, how he had helped his son make his money and he could help Marcus too. He told him that he knew the perfect property, that it would need seventy thousand to secure it and get it all done out. He would get the licenses and stock. He went along to a club where Marcus was playing a couple of sets, told him he believed in him and wanted to help him, get started. When Marcus said he didn't have that much money, he told him it wasn't an issue, he would invest, be his partner."

"Let me guess Doug ripped him off? Duncan hasn't spoken to his dad for years. I'm sorry to say your brother isn't the first who has shown up looking for Duncan to pay back money his dad has taken."

"You got it in one. He took him to the 'club' it was a warehouse but had potential. Marcus gave him his savings, he kept going back to the 'club' and building work was going on there. A couple of months passed before Doug stopped answering the phone and Marcus found out that the warehouse was actually being made into flats.

So, my beloved brother over there, came up with this crazy scheme in order to get his money back. And now you are sat here in my cellar. The first I knew was when he carried you over his shoulder through my front door."

Danielle pushed the duvet from her legs and crawled across the floor to Marcus. He lifted his head as he sensed her approach. Without giving him chance to pull away or react she put her arms around him and held him tight. As Noah watched from the other side of the room, he could not tell which of them was sobbing harder. A dam had broken and now both were letting all the pent-up emotions flow.

He picked up his laptop and the duvets. Leaving the door wide open he headed up to the living room. If she was wanting to stay willingly then there was no need to keep her trapped in the cellar. If she was telling the truth, she would no longer be their prisoner but their guest.

By the time that Danielle and Marcus emerged from the cellar, Noah had remade the beds and had a quick tidy up. Part of him had wanted to charge down into the cellar to see what was taking them so long. He knew he was being stupid. Hell, if they were shagging on the floor, he had no reason to be jealous, but the thought of it had him wanting to rip his brothers head off. He was wondering if he had time for a cold shower when they emerged. Both their faces were tear streaked.

He looked at the clock it was six already the day had passed in a blur.

"Danielle, why don't you go have a shower? Get cleaned up properly. I will order a Chinese, then when we've eaten, I can get you settled in the spare room. You're probably going to feel rough for a few more days while the drugs get out of your system. Is there anything you fancy in particular?"

Danielle knew he was talking about food but that didn't stop her eyes roving over his body. She had known he was tall and muscular as she had cuddled up to him in the cellar but seeing him here, stood before her in his living room, she realised just how big he was. He made his brother seem just what he was, his little brother.

Her eyes met his and she blushed, had he realised she was eyeing him up? How warped was she? Not only was she about to sit down and eat with her kidnappers but she had the hots for one and felt sorry for the other? She needed to pull herself together and quick. She needed them to want to help her. For the first time in years, she was beginning to feel like she had a future.

"Special fried rice, and Dim Sum, if they have any of the dumplings. That's if you don't mind? I would love a bath if I could?"

"No bath for you tonight. Just a quick shower, I don't want you feeling lightheaded or dizzy laying in the water. There is too much risk of you passing out. Tomorrow you can have a nice long soak if you feel up to it, okay? Marcus show her upstairs, get her a towel and find her something she can throw on after. I'll order food."

"Yeah, I guess you're right."

Noah picked up the phone and began dialling. Danielle followed Marcus out of the room and up the stairs.

"This is Marcus's room and that is the spare room where you will be staying. Bathroom is through here. Towels are in that cupboard there." His arms gesturing as he gave her the guided tour. "While you shower, I'll find something for you to wear. Tomorrow, if you want, I can pop out and pick you up a few bits to tide you over until we work things out."

"That would be nice, and thanks. I know none of us ever intended on ending up here but I am glad I did. I'm sorry that you got ripped off, and I promise, once I get my money back from my husband, I'll repay you."

"Don't worry, somehow everything will work out. And yes, he is single."

"I don't know what you mean." The colour rose in her cheeks as she spoke the lie.

"I saw you checking him out. He's been hurt, he's gonna keep that guard up as long as he can but I see that spark. It ain't just firing one way. But I tell you this, he won't act on it while you're still a married woman. The sooner you get this plan sorted, and we get set on making it happen, the better for all of us. Now jump in that shower. I better get downstairs before he thinks I am trying to charm you. He knows I am far better looking than him."

Marcus winked at her before diving into the bedroom. She could hear drawers opening and closing as she shut the bathroom door behind her. She opened the cupboard and pulled out a bath sheet. She was surprised by how soft it was, maybe the woman that had hurt him was only a recent ex. Looking around she noted how clean and tidy everything was, a place for everything. He seemed too nice to have been single long. She looked in the mirror and shook her head, what did she know? Look how good she had been about judging a man's character the last time.

A wave of nausea overcame her, she clung on to the edge of the sink until it passed. He was right about one thing - a bath was not a good idea. She stripped off the borrowed tee-shirt and shorts. Setting the water to a cooler setting she stood under the spray, she lifted the shower gel and smelled it. This was the one he had been wearing yesterday, sandalwood and something else, she tried to read the label, but it swam before her eyes.

She felt herself sway; a half-strangled noise tried to leave her throat. She was conscious of falling, like it was happening in slow motion. She was going down, then she wasn't, she was in his arms, and he was lowering her into the bath. She was crying apologising for getting him wet, and he was shushing her. Everything seemed so surreal. He had a sponge gentle washing her, telling her it would be okay, they would wash her hair tomorrow. He lifted her out as if she weighed nothing and wrapped her up in the big fluffy towel. He carried her through to the spare room, dried her and dressed her in the tee-shirt and shorts left on the bed before bundling her into a large dressing gown.

"Thank you."

"It's okay, I told you, no coming to harm on my watch. Now, hold on tight I am going to carry you downstairs so we can eat. Then I will carry you back up and get you tucked into bed. No arguments."

An hour later when he returned her to the room and tucked her into bed. She wished he would stay. She remembered the way she had felt with his arm wrapped around her earlier but she daren't ask. The idea he might reject her was more than she could bare and the fact she cared so much about someone she didn't even know confused her.

She was asleep before the door closed. She didn't see Noah standing in the doorway watching her. He was fighting his own internal battle not to climb in beside her before he closed the door and went downstairs.

Chapter Eight

The next day passed quickly. Withdrawal symptoms left Danielle feeling dizzy and tearful. Noah waited on her, sitting in the room with her but keeping his distance from her physically. He thought to himself how easy it would be to slide in beside her and hold her in his arms, but he knew that if he did there would be no going back.

The feelings he had for her were irrational. For all her talk, there was no guarantee that once she was well enough, she wouldn't be out of the door, calling the police to turn them in. He found himself struggling to listen when she spoke. He would become lost watching her lips, wondering if he kissed her would she be soft and gentle or would she match the urgency and desire he could feel building in himself. Even now, when she slept, he sat watching the rise and fall of the duvet, imagining the body beneath it.

When he had found her falling in the shower the day

before he had tried to not look at her but it had been impossible. Every curve and contour of her body was burnt into his memory. She was thin, too thin. She had told them that she had lost weight recently and had no appetite. He wondered if there was a physical reason or if it was just a symptom of the tablets. Her breasts were small but pert. He smiled imagining himself taking her dusky pink nipples into his mouth. Would they be sensitive? Would she arch her back to him?

The sound of the door snapped him out of his daydream. Marcus had been out shopping to get some clothes and toiletries for her. Not the designer labels she was no doubt used to but better than the oversized items of clothing she had been drowned in the last couple of days.

"Did you get everything?"

"Yeah, but what are we going to do now?"

"I don't know. Honestly, the only thing we can do is wait until she feels well enough to tell us what she is thinking. I just hope that it's something that can be sorted quickly. I don't think her being here is a good idea."

"Why not? You worried you might not be able to keep that wall up around your heart?"

"Fuck off!"

"Noah, the bloody chemistry between the two of you is so obvious, Yeah, I get it! Right now, she is a married woman, but for fucks sake don't screw things up because of your ex. Wait until she is free of her husband, and don't roll your eyes at me. After those emails, that woman up there is going to divorce him, no way is she staying after that. You just need to wait, let her know you are willing to wait. Don't push her away."

"I don't know what you are talking about. There is no chemistry."

"Okay, fine. She's a good-looking woman so you won't have a problem with me hooking up with her instead." Marcus turned and walked towards the stairs. He'd anticipated the fist that came flying towards him and ducked it.

"Don't you fucking dare!"

"See no chemistry at all, hey bro?"

Noah collapsed down onto the sofa. Marcus took a seat on the chair facing him. He hated this feeling that he was screwing up his brother's life. But there was a part of him, that was hopeful, that his brother might just come out of this happier than he had been in a long time.

He hadn't liked his brothers ex, Laura had been high maintenance with a capital H. She had accused him of free loading from his brother, but he had known that it was because she knew that he saw through her. He had grown up around people who were selfish and self-centred. He recognised a narcissist when he saw one. Noah's mum had not liked her either, but she had been more diplomatic in her criticisms. He often wondered if he had kept his mouth shut if his brother would have seen through her quicker.

Laura was a personal assistant at the same company where Noah had been an intern at. Maybe, she had overheard him been spoken of as partner material down the road, maybe, she saw him as a plaything, Marcus had never been sure why she picked his brother. But the fact was she had zeroed in on him and Noah had fallen hard. They had made a good-looking couple, both of them could have been models.

Laura had gone on an all-out charm offensive. His brother had always managed to be stylish on a budget, but she had him wearing designer labels. Her Instagram was a merry-go-round of trendy clubs, lunches and shots taken on a sunny beach. At first, she paid towards things but soon

Noah was funding their lifestyle. He bought her an engagement ring and they put down a deposit on a flat in a desirable area. That was when everything came tumbling down.

It turned out that Laura was already married. Noah had found the hard way when her husband had showed up at work. What made it worse was her husband was in the army. He had been deployed abroad for the last eighteen months, he had arrived home a month early and came to her work to surprise her.

Noah hadn't even asked for the ring back. He had walked out of the office and handed in his notice. The deposit on the flat was non-refundable. He'd found himself back at his mum's house determined that no one would ever destroy his heart again. Marcus found it so frustrating because he knew his brother deserved someone to love, someone who would put that carefree smile back on his face again. Someone who could give him back the brother he had looked up to for so long.

Noah had been offered a new position quickly enough. One of the partners at his previous firm had gone out on a limb for him to get him a job, even though it was one of their competitors. A few months ago, he had put down his deposit on this place, a two-bedroom semi-detached. Nothing flashy but plenty of potential to fix it up and sell it on. Nothing had made his brothers face light up the way the woman laying asleep upstairs had.

Danielle had never had anyone wait on her with as much care and attention as she had the last two days. Waking on her third day here she felt more herself. She still had headache but turning to the bedside table saw the painkillers and glass of water left for her.

It was crazy to think that these two brothers who had kidnapped her were responsible for freeing her from her own life. Now it was time for her to take control and plan how to make sure she stayed free.

The house was still quiet, so she crept across into the bathroom and jumped in the shower. Looking around, she noticed a selection of new toiletries, they had obviously been bought with her in mind. She picked up the shampoo, it was a different brand, but like the one she normally used it smelled of fresh apples. Had he noticed or was it just a coincidence?

His brothers' words gave her hope. Was it possible that someone could still want her? Even in this state? Or was he another just after her money? How would she ever be able to truly know, after all she was here because of money, but...

The fact that Marcus had asked for so little money, the fact he only wanted what he was owed - and he believed that he was getting it back from the son of the man who stole it gave her faith in them. They had come into her life in an unorthodox manner, but it was just possible that this could be a fresh beginning for all of them.

Showered and with washed hair she returned to the room. The clothes she had been wearing were clean and ironed but also there was a selection of new items. Her had hovered over her own clothes but instead she grabbed a pair of leggings and a sweatshirt from the other pile. They had obviously checked the sizes before shopping as everything fit.

She made her way to the kitchen, putting the coffee machine on first. She looked in the fridge, it was well stocked. She wondered if that was because she was here, or did Noah keep it full normally. It had been a long time since she had indulged in anything considered unhealthy. Looking at the ingredients she decided to start off her new life with a full English, minus black pudding but that was not something she fancied eating anyway.

Putting the bacon, eggs, sausages, tomatoes, and mushrooms on the table, she searched the cupboard finding the beans. *Right, I can do this*, her next search was for the pans. She was on her hands and knees looking in one when Noah walked into the kitchen and found her.

"You okay down there?"

"Yes, thanks. Where do you keep your frying pans? I want to make breakfast?"

"I don't have one."

Danielle climbed to her feet and let out a sigh.

"I wanted to make breakfast. If I am going to be here for a while, I want to pull my weight."

"We'll do it together." Noah pulled out a cast iron griddle plate from a hidden drawer underneath the cooker, he placed it on the hob and lit the gas. While he tended the food, he directed Danielle around the kitchen. Marcus arrived downstairs just in time to help finish setting the table. Once the food was served, they sat down to eat. There was an underlying tension, each of them attributing it to different causes but no one wanted to address their concerns first.

As soon as they had finished eating, Marcus placed the plates in the sink and began to fill it intending to wash up. He hated doing the pots but the silence between then was becoming unbearable. Finally, it was Danielle that broke it.

"Please, sit down. We need to talk about what happens next."

"Are you going to the police?" The question came out of his mouth as Marcus resumed his seat.

"No, I meant what I said the other night. I want to stay here for now and I want you two to help me get my life back. I'm not going to lie, when you kidnapped me part of me was ready to die, to give in fighting and just let me husband win. He only wants the money, and the pre-nup means, if I divorce him, he gets nothing. He won't let that happen. But now, with you two I can see a future. I can see my hopes and dreams for the life I wanted."

"So, what's the plan?" It was Noah who asked.

"I don't know exactly. I mean I have some ideas, but are you both in?"

"Yes!" The brothers spoke together.

Whatever was going to happen from this point forward, they were each taking control to steer their lives towards a new beginning.

Also by
Paula Acton

Standalones

Disintegration & Other Stories

Voices Across the Void

Queen of Ages Series

Ascension

Choosing Hope
by
Poppy Flynn

Chapter One

"I saw Martha Smith at the supermarket this morning." June Richards chattered as she bustled around the kitchen putting the groceries away. "We were just discussing how nice it would be if you and her Roger went out on a date together. Fancy a good-looking chap like Roger still being single at the age of almost thirty. The two of you would make such a lovely couple."

Hope stopped what she was doing and looked at her mother in alarm. "You cannot be serious!" she replied, genuine horror in her voice. She remembered Roger as a senior in High School, even though she'd been several years younger. He'd been a complete ass. If he was the same now, it was no wonder he was still single. "Mum! Please tell me you did not give her my phone number or something awful like that."

Her mother looked uncomfortable, and Hope knew

damn well the thought had crossed her mind, even if she hadn't acted on it.

She raised a single eyebrow and looked at June.

"Of course not," her mother replied, whirling away under the guise of putting the milk in the fridge. Probably so she could hide the guilty look on her face that Hope had already spotted. "Not after the last time you got so upset about it."

Well, at least something had gotten through back then, she thought with an internal sigh. Hope could still sense a 'but', though, so she crossed her arms and waited.

"Although I might have hinted that I'd text it to her once I had your permission," June finally admitted, her cheeks turning pink, like she was the recalcitrant child in this relationship.

"Just so we're clear, Mum, you do *not* have permission to pass my number to Martha or Roger, or anyone else!" Hope said unequivocally. "How many times have I told you, I do *not* want to date!"

"But honey," June cajoled, turning earnest eyes on her daughter. "You're almost twenty-six. Your youth is passing you by. Don't you think it's time you went out and had some fun? You missed out on all of that when..."

June trailed off. She still didn't like talking about Hope's leukemia. It was as if she didn't mention it then they could all just pretend it never happened.

That there wasn't the shadow hanging over her entire life that one day her illness might return.

If there was one thing Hope herself had learned during those horrific teenage years, it was to take nothing for granted. It could be ripped away from you at any moment.

And while so many people thought that meant she should live the life that had been saved to the full and make up for lost time, what Hope had discovered, to her detriment, was that relationships were... awkward, when you had a potential death sentence hanging over your head.

She'd lost friends she'd never regained when she'd first been diagnosed and started to slog through the trauma of chemotherapy. For a long time, she'd been too ill to notice how her friends kept their distance. And later, when she was feeling better, she simply assumed that they'd naturally lost touch since she'd been out of circulation.

It had taken a very public and very hurtful ordeal for her to realise that some of her so-called 'friends' had chosen to deliberately cut ties.

It had been the twenty-first birthday of Sarah, her best friend from school. Hope had been out of treatment and recovering for the best part of a year and she'd gone around to Sarah's house to deliver a birthday gift.

Hope had been more than humiliated when she realised Sarah was in the middle of a huge birthday party.

A party Hope hadn't been invited to.

She'd been devastated.

She still remembered far too clearly how Sarah's mother had made a botched attempt at an explanation.

"Oh, Hope, how umm... unexpected," Mrs Thomas had stuttered. The older woman looked her up and down, a hint of genuine surprise in her unguarded expression. "And you're looking so... well, too. I didn't realise you were back home."

"Really Mrs Thomas? I've been out of hospital almost a year. Didn't Sarah tell you?"

"I, well, she..." Another pause. There were a lot of those.

Mrs Thomas wrung her hands and looked uncomfortable. Hope could have made an excuse, waved her hand, and said it didn't matter. But it did. She wanted to hear the excuses with her own ears, so she no longer had to play at second guessing.

She waited the woman out.

"Hope, you have to understand, Sarah was devastated by your illness."

Hope pursed her lips and nodded. "Yeah, I was pretty devastated myself," she replied, unable to keep the sarcasm out of her voice as she battled against the hurt that threatened to swamp her. Hurt that hit her tenfold as she spotted a few other so-called 'friends' wander past the door and see her standing there, only to do an abrupt U-turn.

"The thing is, she didn't deal with it well."

Hope turned bleak eyes back to Mrs Thomas.

"Pulling away was one of her coping mechanisms."

"I guess it would have been easier if I really had died, wouldn't it?" Hope said bitterly, jamming her hands in her pockets to disguise the fact that they were balled in impotent rage. "Then Sarah and all those other people I thought were my friends wouldn't have to live with the knowledge that they just turned their backs when I needed them."

"Hope! How could you say such a thing?" Mrs Thomas cried in shock. "That was out of order."

Hope felt like her eyebrows as good as hit her hairline and her mouth fell open. "Really? You want to put this on me?"

God! Why was she even surprised? Tears pricked the back of her eyes, and she scrunched her shoulders up to her ears as she battled against them. "Well, I guess I should apologise for having the audacity to get sick and upsetting all their nice, orderly lives then."

Hope turned to walk away, pain and misery ripping at her.

"But you know what, Mrs Thomas," she added, turning

to look at the woman over her shoulder as she started to close the door. "I hope Sarah never has to find out what it's like to live with a death sentence hanging over her. And I hope she never has to know how it feels to have all the *friends* she has hanging around her today, turn their back when she needs their support, rather than risk their precious feelings."

Mrs Thomas shut the door in a hurry, refusing to look Hope in the eye as she did so.

And Hope walked home with yet another piece of her childhood having been torn away.

When her own twenty-first birthday had come around a few months later, her mother had wanted to throw Hope a party of her own.

She had refused outright.

She didn't want to know how many people wouldn't bother to turn up because they didn't want their neat, orderly lives sullied with the stain of possible death. Didn't want to know how many people thought it was better to cut the ties of friendship rather than risk being bruised by loss.

Sometimes ignorance really was bliss.

Now, as a result, Hope was the cautious one. She'd learned the hard way how much it hurt to lose the people you were closest to. She didn't want to weave together the threads of friendship only to have them severed at the first sign of trouble. She didn't want to be hurt like that again.

And that went tenfold for any romantic relationship.

So here she was. About to celebrate twenty-six years as a virgin. She didn't see that changing any time soon. A few more years and they'd be able to make a film about her.

Chapter Two

"Happy birthday to me," Hope muttered miserably as she walked along the beach towards town.

She'd lied to her mother, and that knowledge was eating at her insides like acid. But she simply couldn't stomach the pitying looks, the forced cheer, and the unsubtle attempts at coercing Hope into a date with Roger, who apparently would love to take her out for a birthday dinner. The thought was so repulsive that she'd told June she was meeting a friend for lunch. But instead of relief at getting her mother off her back, all Hope felt was guilt at the bloom of delighted optimism that had lit up her mother's expression.

Damn it! Why couldn't she just let Hope live her own life? Sure, Hope understood everything her family had been through while she had been battling for her life. And Hope was an only child so all of her parents' focus had been - and still was - on her.

She understood that her mother wanted what was best for her and felt Hope had missed out on so many things after becoming progressively ill throughout her sixteenth year, leading to a diagnosis of leukaemia followed by commencing treatment shortly before her seventeenth birthday. And her father, well, he mostly just kept out of it. Occasionally he would try to run interference if he saw she was getting too overwhelmed by it all. But that usually only happened when Hope threatened to move out and find a place of her own.

So far, she'd capitulated to her parents' insistence that she continue to live with them. It had been a necessity at the start. Her childhood, throughout her illness, had simply extended into adulthood, and Hope had needed her parents' support, both physically, as she recovered, and financially, since she hadn't been able to finish school.

Part of her wondered if that feeling of obligation was what made her stay. Capitulating to their will because she owed them for taking care of her well after she should have become independent.

She'd caught up now. Had taken college classes that were, thankfully, aimed at adults, and was ready to find a job... though her mother continually insisted there was no rush.

But as June also liked to remind her, when she was encouraging Hope to 'get a life', she was five years clear in remission. She'd reached the magic number. That period of time during which everything hung in the balance and where you waited with bated breath to find out if the death sentence you'd been living under had been lifted... at least enough that it ceased to rule every part of your existence.

Her mother couldn't have it both ways. If she was well

enough to seize the day, she was well enough to get a job and a place of her own.

Maybe it was time...

Hope sat and pondered that same thought some more after she'd wandered into her favourite beach front cafe. She treated herself to a rather decadent white hot chocolate with the works, and a huge chocolate fudge brownie with whipped cream. She was getting a week's worth of chocolate fix in one sitting, and she refused to feel guilty about it.

Shame it didn't make her feel any better.

Catrina, the owner of the cafe, and creator of such masterpieces had even stuck one of those sparkler candles in it and Hope watched it fizz and pop with cloudy eyes while it burned down, before giving a heartfelt sigh.

"Well, that doesn't sound very cheerful on what should obviously be a special day."

Hope turned in the direction of the voice that interrupted her dismal thoughts and found a nice-looking guy, maybe a few years older than herself indicating her makeshift birthday cake.

He offered her an endearing, crooked grin when her eyes met his and Hope found herself smiling back.

"So, is it actually your birthday then?" He asked, tipping his head to one side, and raising a single eyebrow in query.

Hope looked back at the birthday brownie and shrugged. "It is," she admitted.

"And here you are, celebrating, all alone."

It wasn't really a question, but she nodded anyway.

"I hate seeing a pretty girl looking so down on such an occasion," the sandy-haired guy said with an engaging smile. "Maybe I could join you, unless you really do prefer to sit there by yourself and play Billy no-mates."

His bluntness had a delighted laugh spilling from her

lips and Hope gestured to the empty seat on the opposite side of her table. "Please do," she agreed, happy for the unexpected company. And in such a nice package too.

She might have steered clear of relationships, but Hope could appreciate a good-looking guy when she saw one.

He put his coffee on the table and raised his index finger. "Just a sec," he said, before he sat. Then he poked his nose back around the door to the beachside verandah where she'd chosen to sit and shouted to Catrina, "Another birthday brownie please, sis."

"Catrina's your sister?" Hope asked, when he returned, an identically plated brownie in hand.

Her new friend nodded and stretched his hand across the table. "She's actually my twin, for her sins," he joked, with a wink. "I'm Curtis Harrison. Pleased to meet you."

Hope took Curtis's hand and was momentarily shocked by the thrill of electricity that sizzled from her fingertips and up her arm. It wasn't that she hadn't looked at him and appreciated his strong face, the thick, wheat coloured hair with its natural sun streaks and those velvety, chocolate brown eyes. She simply hadn't expected to have such a visceral reaction. That was something new to Hope and it took her by surprise.

Her eyes skittered to his. Was it her imagination or had his already dark eyes darkened some more? Certainly, the playfulness had been replaced by a new intensity and Hope tore her gaze away, suddenly flustered. She groped around for something to say.

"I didn't realise Catrina had a brother, never mind a twin," she remarked trying not to wince at the unnaturally high pitch of her voice. But as the words tripped off her tongue, she realised they were true. Catrina was a few years older than Hope and was in her final year of school just at the time Hope had started, but she couldn't help but remember the gregarious girl. And this was a relatively small town, so they'd run into each other outside school too, how could she have not known about Curtis?

She brushed the thought aside as their knees touched, sending another twinge of desire rocketing through her system. She may never have had a lover, but she recognised a healthy dose of lust when it hit her, even if it was a new experience.

"Many happy returns" he said, grinning as he picked up his fork and held up a chunk of his brownie like a toast before digging into it.

"So, are you going to tell me why the birthday girl is sitting all on her own moping into her cake on her big day?"

Chapter Three

Hope hadn't expected it to be so easy to talk to a complete stranger, never mind a guy. Her experience with the opposite sex was limited to her dad, who didn't really say much, and the boys she went to school with… and that was ten years ago. Neither bore much resemblance to the man sitting in front of her, bar gender. But the entire story came tumbling out and Curtis stayed quiet while she ate her brownie and got it off her chest.

"I know my mother means well," Hope qualified, not wanting to come across like an ungrateful bitch. "I just wish she'd leave it alone and let me move at my own pace."

She picked at the crumbs on the tablecloth, dabbing them with her finger and brushing them onto her empty plate. She'd eaten without thinking and finished every bite.

"To be honest, the more she pushes, the more I back off. It's not that I'm deliberately trying to be awkward," Hope confessed, raising her head to meet those comforting eyes.

"It's just that it makes me feel out of control... and so much of my life has been outside my control, I just want to..." She shrugged, searching for the words.

In the end, Curtis voiced them for her. "You just want to be the one who's calling the shots and be in charge of your own destiny, for once."

Her eyes widened and the affinity she was already feeling doubled... quadrupled. "Yes!" she exclaimed. "Exactly that!"

That he understood her just made him all the more appealing and Hope felt an awful lot of the tension and guilt she'd been harbouring - stuff that went back long before today - seep out of her.

It wasn't just that she'd offloaded and got it off her chest. It was his innate understanding, and the fact that she felt she could trust him with her deepest secrets, that washed over her like a balm.

She hadn't even realised just how much she needed that until right this moment.

Hope sighed and pushed her plate aside. "I'm sorry, that was probably way more than you bargained for when you offered to share a birthday brownie with me."

Curtis reached over and placed a hand over the fingers she had clasped in front of her. "Don't apologise," he chided gently, his expression so sincere it made her chest ache. "We all need to feel like the choices we make in life are our own. That we follow the path our hearts and minds are invested in rather than find ourselves simply being battered around by the capricious winds of fate. And when those choices are ripped away from us, it's natural to do everything in our power to take them back."

He squeezed her hand and, without thinking, Hope turned her palms up and gripped hold of him, like he was her anchor. He may have become just that. For so long she'd felt like she was drifting, buffeted around like a storm on the ocean, dependent on the vagaries of tide to sink or swim. And sometimes, even when she swam, it was like the tide was against her, laughing at her pathetic attempts to extract herself.

With just those few words, Curtis had reassured her that it was okay to give herself permission to follow her own path, not the one others thought was best. And in doing so, he'd given her the strength to turn things around and paddle towards her own destiny.

For long moments she just stared at him, losing herself in the depths of those melted chocolate eyes. There were no words. There didn't need to be. He'd said them all. And in doing so they'd forged an unexpected bond that transcended the short amount of time they'd known each other.

He gave her an easy smile and Hope felt her heart do a slow tumble in her chest. One that sped up when he leaned across and tucked one of her wild flame-coloured curls behind her ear.

"You know, you should try and explain to your mother how you feel, rather than bottling it all up," he told her as his hand lingered by her cheek.

Hope couldn't help it, she closed her eyes, tipped her head to one side, and leaned into the warm comfort of his palm like it was the most natural thing in the world. "I don't want her to think I don't appreciate her concern," she began, then opened her eyes with a start at the commotion that intruded into their little bubble.

"Hope..." June's voice trailed off as she took in the cosy scene between Curtis and herself.

"Mum!" Hope sprang back guiltily, and Curtis dropped

his hand. Was it awful that her first thought was that she missed his touch and resented the intrusion?

Her mother was flustered now, wringing her hands, and opening and closing her mouth like she'd forgotten how to speak... And she looked guilty.

Hope narrowed her eyes, then frowned. "Mum, are you checking up on me?"

"I... er... not exactly, I just..."

There was a flurry of movement behind her, and Hope swivelled around to see Martha Smith peering over her mothers' shoulder. "I thought you said she was single?" The other woman said in an accusing hiss. Why would you want Roger..." The loudly whispered words were cut off with an *mmph* sound, as June elbowed her friend in the ribs then tried - and failed - for an innocent smile.

Hope's mouth dropped open in shock, even as a fiery ball of righteous indignation expanded in her chest. "Mother!" She stretched out the syllables in unspoken warning, struggling for calm even though her insides - and her hands - were trembling.

June straightened her spine and lifted her chin in the guise of the self-righteous. "I was just planning a surprise birthday dinner for you..." Her lower lip trembled, and she might have pulled off the feigned hurt if Martha hadn't piped up "...with Roger."

Hope sucked in a breath and gritted her teeth. She didn't want to fall out with her mother today, of all days, but this was getting beyond a joke. She prayed for calm as she exhaled slowly through her pursed lips, but Curtis slipped in and smoothly created a diversion.

"You must be Mrs Richards," he intervened, holding out his hand with that easy charm that seemed to come so naturally to him. "I'm Curtis Harrison, and actually, I was about to issue my own birthday invitation of a weekend at my parents' island villa."

He turned back to Hope and gave her a wink as he issued the invitation.

Surprise stopped her from making an immediate reply, but as she opened her mouth to speak, June took over in her usual obtrusive fashion. "Well really, I'm not sure that's appropriate..." she said primly.

Hope whipped her head around to look at her mother. In all honesty, she had been about to turn Curtis down, herself. She knew he was only trying to provide her with an excuse... not that she needed one. Hope was quite capable of just saying no. But hearing June trying to make that decision for her when she'd been scheming, just moments before, to hitch her up with a complete stranger, had Hope seeing red.

She jumped up from her seat and crossed to Curtis with her blue eyes blazing.

Like the gentleman he was, he rose when she did, and Hope launched herself at him and hugged him tight. "That's so sweet, Curtis," she heard herself say. "I'd love to!"

Chapter Four

"Why didn't you tell me you were seeing someone?" June demanded later on that afternoon when Hope got home.

"I told you I was meeting someone for lunch," she retorted. Okay, so that hadn't been entirely true at the time, but Hope was still angry. While she'd taken on board Curtis's suggestion to explain to her mother how she felt, it didn't change the fact that June had had an entirely different agenda when she'd turned up at the coffee shop. One Hope had already rejected, and she didn't want to be distracted from that.

"I thought you were making that up to avoid going on a date with Roger."

That twinge of guilt surfaced again but Hope held firm; her mother needed to understand that it was *not* okay to keep interfering against her will. "Even if I *was* making it up, perhaps you should have realised that I'm not comfortable with you meddling in my private life. I already told you

I didn't want to go out with Roger! What part of *no* was a problem for you?"

June cast her eyes over at Hope and sniffed. Her lips were pressed together so hard they were barely a line slashed into her face. "There's no need to take that tone with me, young lady," she replied, as if Hope was a recalcitrant teenager, rather than a grown woman who was capable of knowing her own mind.

"I'm not so sure about that," Hope retorted with a scowl of her own. "Clearly whatever I said on the subject before didn't work!"

They were standing in the cheery, yellow kitchen and June scrubbed at an imaginary piece of dirt on the immaculate countertop while Hope paced back and forth in agitation.

Hope decided on a different tactic. "Anyway, you should be pleased that I'm spending my birthday with a friend. Isn't that what you wanted?"

"I still don't think you should be going away with a man I've never met," June mumbled.

"You've never met Roger, but you wanted me to have dinner with him," Hope pointed out acerbically. "And besides, you *have* met Curtis."

"I know Roger's mother," June defended, as if that excused everything.

Hope snorted indelicately and rolled her eyes. "Martha is hardly likely to admit that her son's a jerk, though, is she?!"

June stopped what she was doing and glared. "Well, I trust Martha."

Hope stopped pacing and jammed her hands on her hips. "Oh, so you're saying I can only date people you pick out for me, now?

"No, of course not. I just..."

Hope cut her off. "Good, because I need to go and pack."

She turned on her heel and stalked into her bedroom, but June didn't give up so easily. "I'm just wondering if you know this boy well enough to go away with him, that's all," June threw out there.

Hope paused as she pulled her case out of her wardrobe, because it was a valid point and one she'd wondered about herself. But her mother's concern wasn't all unbiased, and that skewed Hope's perception.

"Well, you know what, mum," Hope replied as she carried the holdall over to the bed. "I know him a damn sight better than I know Roger."

Hope sat down on the side of her bed after she'd shoed her mother out and wondered what the hell she was doing. Was she mad to be considering this? Yeah, she was pretty sure she was. Who the hell went away for the weekend with a guy they'd only just met? Surely that was just asking for trouble.

The sensible part of her didn't much want to listen though and her mind kept coming up with all manner of justifications.

People had blind dates and one night stands all the time; this wasn't either of those things. She'd already met and bonded with Curtis, and she wasn't planning on sleeping with him. He'd already reassured her that there were several bedrooms.

She'd known Catrina, Curtis's twin sister, for over a decade. While Hope might not have been aware of Curtis, she was pretty sure she'd have heard if there was anything sketchy about her friends' brother. People loved to gossip after all.

And Catrina had vouched for him. Sure, Curtis was her

brother, but Catrina was her friend. Hope had to believe that was worth something.

Plus, Catrina knew where she was going to be and, before she left, she'd leave the contact details with her father, too. She wasn't heading off into the unknown.

Hope was even taking her own car; something Curtis had suggested so Hope knew she was in control. She appreciated that thoughtfulness, it said a lot about his character.

And more than anything, the chance to get away, to have time to herself, somewhere completely detached from the life she knew, held more appeal than she could have imagined.

It was something she'd never known she needed, but now the opportunity was there, Hope felt the pull like it was something necessary to her soul.

Maybe it was.

She'd already been feeling like she needed to take stock of her life; make some decisions. This would allow her to do that in a completely neutral environment where she could think about her options without bias and, more importantly, without those who sought to influence her.

She needed to do this, Hope decided, as she got up with renewed enthusiasm to pack her clothes. And she was perfectly capable of making sensible assessments of people, even those she'd only just met, and of arranging check-ins to ensure her safety if things really did go wrong.

With that decision made, Hope finished packing and started to look forward to her unexpected break... and also to the opportunity of getting to know Curtis better.

Chapter Five

Curtis watched Hope with pleasure as she pulled up in her sensible mid-size car. In all honesty, he had surprised himself, as well as her, when he'd offered the invitation. More so when he admitted to himself that he meant it.

Still, there was that small issue that they barely knew each other. He understood how that might make her anxious and had done everything he could think of to ensure she knew she was safe with him.

As she parked in Catrina's cafe car park and climbed out of the driver's seat, he felt obliged to give Hope one last chance to back out.

"Are you sure you want to go ahead with this trip?" he asked, even though he really didn't want her to change her mind.

She smiled and it lit up her entire face, making him grin in return. "I absolutely do," she confirmed without the slightest hint of reluctance. "I really need to make some decisions in my life and having somewhere neutral to do it is perfect. I can think things through without any conflicting influences."

"You know, you could do this on your own, if you want. I don't have to be there."

Hope looked at him in surprise. As much as he wanted to get to know her, he understood the awkwardness of this situation. They didn't have to be together for her to accept him as one of the good guys.

She gave him a small smile, ducked her head, and looked at him from beneath her lashes. "Actually, I'm looking forward to your company," she told him softly, before biting her lip and looking away.

Curtis couldn't help the huge grin that spread across his face and the burst of pleasure that spread through his chest. This felt like the start of something good.

He wouldn't lie, he really did hope it was. But he also knew better than to push. That was exactly what Hope was running from and he was intuitive enough to understand that. For now, he was content to be her friend and hopefully work on building a relationship she would trust.

That was his plan anyway, and it seemed to be off to a good start.

His parents' villa wasn't far away, and neither was it quite as pretentious as it sounded. It also wasn't much different from where Hope lived except it was closer to the sea and on a very tiny atoll with two roads and one shop. At low tide it was possible to cross, on foot, via a land-bridge. Right now though, it was cut off from the mainland and they drove across the old-fashioned viaduct which had originally been intended for a tram but converted to road use before it ever saw another vehicle. It was a single carriageway and they had to wait a fair while before the traffic lights blinked green. It was the kind of thing indicative of the entire laid-back way of life on the islet. Nothing here was hurried. It wasn't possible.

"Wow! This place is like a throwback to a different time," Hope commented as they finally crossed to the island. "I keep expecting to see a horse and cart come around the corner, or something."

"It wouldn't be totally out of the ordinary," Curtis told her. "You'll see a lot of walkers, cyclists, and horse riders here. There's a forty miles per hour speed limit across the island which adds to the 'laid back' feel."

Hope nodded, watching with her window wound down as they drove leisurely past the beautiful countryside, her hair blowing in the gentle breeze. "So do you come here often?" she asked, turning back to look at him.

Curtis coloured slightly, something which didn't go unnoticed by his companion. "What?" Hope demanded, narrowing her eyes at him.

"Umm... I kind of have a confession to make. I should have mentioned it sooner," he said hastily.

"What is it?" Hope asked again, sounding suddenly unsure. He glanced her way to see her biting her lip and a zing of desire shot through his system. He wanted to be the one biting that lip. Damn, he needed to reign himself in before he spooked her completely.

Curtis sighed and returned his concentration to the road. "I've actually been living here. I know," he rushed on before she could comment. "I should have told you that before you agreed to come here and if it's a deal breaker then I'll turn around right now and take you home again."

He sucked in a breath. "But your mother was already so negative about it that I didn't think saying in front of her that I was inviting you to my house was a good idea."

She was silent for the longest time and Josh slowed the car near a passing place, ready to make a U-turn on the single-track road.

"Are we here?" Hope queried, and he chanced looking her way. Her head bobbed from left to right, checking around them, even though there were no houses in sight.

"Not yet. I thought you might want to go back." He pulled into the lay-by and found her gazing at him, seriously.

"I'd like to at least take a look, first," she said quietly. "I understand why you didn't say anything in front of my mother, and I won't deny it has a rather different connotation spending the weekend at your home, rather than your parents retreat, but is it okay if I reserve judgement until we get there?"

Curtis threw her a tight smile. "Of course," he agreed, checking his mirrors, and pulling back out onto the road.

They made the remainder of the trip in silence while he wondered if he'd just blown it.

Chapter Six

Hope walked into the quaint little seaside bungalow with its distinctive roof which earned it the title of villa, not knowing quite what to expect.

Curtis was quiet, pensive, and she knew he was expecting the worst. But she had meant what she said about reserving judgement and as soon as she walked across the threshold into a light, airy white and sand coloured room, she felt completely at ease.

There were sheer drapes at the windows and a comfortable looking couch in a light tan colour with white, lacy throw cushions. The walls were adorned with minimalist watercolour paintings of serene seascapes in muted colours and what she could see of the adjoining kitchen brightened things up with accents of bold blue.

There was a wraparound deck directly onto the beach to the front, accessed through wide double doors, and the sea mirrored the deep blue of the kitchen and sparkled with silver light as the sun glinted off of it.

To the rear was a corridor, undoubtedly leading to the bedrooms, but Hope was certain of one thing.

This was no bachelor pad.

There was little here that shouted Curtis's personality. Not that she knew him well, of course. But the decor here was neutral. Elegant, certainly, but she instinctively knew there was nothing of him within these walls. It might just as easily have been a holiday let.

"I have to admit, I thought you lived above the cafe," she commented, turning to look at Curtis who returned her gaze with an endearingly cautious hope.

He shrugged. "I do stay there occasionally, usually when I'm helping Catrina out," he admitted. "But sometimes Cat likes to bunk there herself if she has a particularly late night, or early morning, so it's not always available."

"So, where's my room?" Hope asked with a small smile, appreciating the way his entire expression lit up at the implication.

"I'll show you," he replied, pushing away from the door jamb he was leaning against and picking up her case that he hadn't quite brought inside.

The bedroom was like the rest of the house, white and sand, with a cool and practical tiled floor. This room had accents of teal and a subtle nautical theme in the wall art of a lighthouse and some sailboats and the macrame potholder threaded with driftwood and holding a trailing beach pea.

The bed itself was a rough-hewn four poster draped in even more gauze which gave it a lavish, romantic feel.

"I'll show you the bathroom," Curtis said as he deposited her luggage just inside the doorway. "And there's one last treat," he added after pointing out his room, the spare room, and the shower room.

She followed him back out onto the verandah which stood on stilts against the high tides and overlooked the sea. "Oh my!" Hope exclaimed when she saw it. "Is that a hot tub?"

He nodded, smiling at her enthusiasm. "It is indeed." He was about to show her the controls, but Hope was too excited. She whirled around and flung her arms around him without even thinking. "Oh, this is wonderful!" she gushed.

Curtis's arms came around her and the effervescence of the moment suddenly calmed, and they were staring at each other seriously.

Curtis ducked his head ever so slowly, giving Hope every opportunity to move away if she so desired.

She didn't, and a second later his full lips landed softly on hers. Gentle at first, just the flicker of a butterfly's wings fluttering against her mouth. He might even have stopped at that, but Hope inched her arms around his neck and curled her fingers into his hair, pressing him closer, making it clear that she welcomed the intimacy. And then his mouth was on hers in earnest, drinking deep and turning incendiary.

Hope might not have been looking for a relationship, but she'd be lying if she denied the chemistry that flared between them.

The only question was where did it go from here?

Chapter Seven

Curtis pulled away and Hope dragged in deep gasps that felt like they'd been robbed of air. She felt light-headed and giddy, almost like she was a little tipsy.

Drunk on lust, she thought, a bubble of happy laughter ready to burst from her throat.

It died on her lips when she stopped to look at Curtis though.

He looked awkward and embarrassed as he dragged a hand through his sun-streaked hair and the next words out of his mouth deflated her even more.

"I'm sorry," he blurted, looking everywhere but at her.

Hope rubbed at her chest stunned at the pain she felt radiating out from there to encompass her whole being. She took a step back from him, her cheeks heating in something that went far beyond embarrassment and into mortified territory.

Desperately, she looked around for her weekend bag.

Thank God she'd brought her own car and could make a quick getaway. This had all been one huge, colossal mistake after all. And even though she barely knew Curtis, she couldn't believe how much it hurt.

Despite everything she told herself, despite all her denials about not wanting a relationship, there had been something there... for her at least. A tiny, germinating shoot that had started sprouting into the anticipation of something more. A fragile kind of hope.

One that had just been crushed like the tiny seed it was.

Tears pricked at the back of her eyes, but Hope forced them back. It was better this way. Better to know Curtis was not really any different from Sarah. Better to get out now before she was hurt by yet another lost friendship. At least this one hadn't gotten too far, even if it did feel just as much of a wrench.

She took another step back, forcing her mind to think about where her car keys were. She heard Curtis suck in a deep breath but she didn't want to stick around for his platitudes.

Hope hurried to the bedroom and grabbed her luggage, blindly. She didn't even wait to check she'd got it all, just grasped what was in sight and hurried towards the door.

"Please Hope, don't go!" Curtis implored behind her. "I really am sorry. It won't happen again, I promise."

She didn't stop as his words tore into her, shredding so much of the confidence she managed to rebuild over the years. Fuck! Why couldn't he just stop talking? Why did he have to add insult to the injury?

She fumbled with the catches on the front door as she juggled her bags and that gave Curtis the advantage.

His palm splayed gently against the white painted wood, not heavy enough to prevent her from opening it, but enough to stop her for a moment. Hope didn't want to hear anything else he had to say though.

"Look, I understand," she said before he could speak again. "I've been through all this before, remember?"

She could feel his heat against her back, but Hope refused to turn around. She didn't want to see that guarded pity on his face and the need to get out while the going was good. "Like I said, it's one of the reasons I don't do relationships because I know what it's like to have them ripped away when the other person doesn't want to have to deal with the possibility of your mortality."

"Then you understand a damn sight more than I do," Curtis growled next to her ear, his hot breath causing the fine hairs there to stand up on end. "Because I have no idea what you're talking about."

Hope screwed her eyes closed and damned her traitorous body for being turned on by his presence; his closeness and the memory of that kiss. "I'm saying that it's okay," she said through gritted teeth. "I accept your apology and I understand why you don't want to be friends. It's my own fault for taking a chance on…"

She didn't finish. Her luggage dropped from her hands as Curtis swung her around and shoved her forcefully against the door, his body pressing and trapping her there while his fingers threaded with hers and held them above her head.

"What the hell?" he hissed through his clenched jaw. "You really think that's what I was apologising for?" he demanded. "That your past illness means I don't want to get to know you better and I regretted kissing you?"

He seemed truly incensed and Hope's eyes opened wide, even as she tried to shove down the thrill pulsing through her veins at his unexpectedly dominant display.

"I was apologising because I promised there were no strings attached to this weekend. Because you took a chance coming here with me and I shouldn't have pressurised you with kisses that weren't supposed to be a part of this. I was apologising because I let my feelings get away from me after saying you were safe here. Because despite all my best efforts, *this* is what you do to me."

He ground his pelvis into her softness and Hope felt the unmistakable evidence of his desire pressing against her stomach, which gave an answering flip.

His chocolate brown eyes speared her, holding her captive just as surely as his hands and body, and Hope felt her mouth go dry. She couldn't move. Her body and arms were both pinned and words had deserted her.

But she could move her head, and his lips were only inches away.

Her eyes never left his, so she had the pleasure of seeing his pupils dilate in the milliseconds before her mouth met his and their eyes fluttered closed as a storm of desire took over and swamped them both.

Chapter Eight

Hope sank into the kiss like Curtis was a lifebuoy and she was drowning. Lips clung, teeth nipped, and tongues tangled, and what she lacked in experience, Hope made up for in enthusiasm.

Suddenly, everything she'd ever believed about herself went out of the window. She wanted this. She wanted Curtis. She wanted him to show her all the joy and intimacy that existed between a man and a woman.

He released her arms so he could grip her waist, rigidly, at first, like he was holding himself back. But Hope speared her newly freed hands into his thick, dark-gold hair and urged him closer, pressing her throbbing breasts against the hard muscles of his chest as she desperately tried to ease the ache he built within her.

His thumb rubbed circles over the thin silk of her top, but Hope wanted more. She wanted his hands on her skin and felt like she might explode if he didn't start putting out some of the fires he was kindling.

The feel of his fingers against the bare skin of her midriff was incendiary when they finally crept under the hem. Hope could only imagine what they would feel like in other, more intimate places, and that imagination was way too limited. Frustratingly so.

Curtis pulled away only when they were both gasping for air and this time he cruised his lips across her jaw to a place below her ear that she thought might be a secret switch for internal combustion because the sensation was burning her alive. He nipped and kissed his way down her throat casting trails of fire in his wake and Hope leaned back against the wall to steady herself. Her short-nailed fingers dug into his shoulders as she held on for dear life and prayed that her trembling legs didn't give way beneath her.

She arched into him in silent encouragement but when his urgent movements slowed, she wanted to scream.

Don't stop! She yelled it inside her head at the top of her lungs.

In reality she was slightly less vocal, but still no less direct. "Make love to me," she whispered raggedly, her voice hoarse with desire.

"Hope, that's not why I brought you here," Curtis groaned, lifting his head, and resting his brow against hers.

What the heck? When did guys get so damned principled? Weren't they all supposed to be horny bastards that humped anything that moved? Maybe it was her word choice. Perhaps the L-word made him skittish.

"Fine, if you don't want to love me, then just fuck me," she retorted, vaguely irritated that he'd stopped doing all those yummy things to her.

"That's not what I meant. Don't twist what I'm saying."

"What are you trying to say then, that you don't want me? Because I thought we just went through all that."

Curtis let out an audible breath. "You know damn well I want you," he retorted. "It's pretty damn obvious, unless you think I've got a rock in my pocket."

"Then what's the problem?" Hope demanded, way more forcefully than she normally would have been. Unfulfilled lust could do that to a girl.

He put a fraction of an inch of space between them and the chilled coastal air that hit her scorching skin brought her to her senses a little. She ducked her head and covered her face with her hands. "I'm being too forward, aren't I?" she said in a strangled voice. "I heard men don't like that."

A bubble of hysterical laughter burst out of her throat, and she shook her head. "And that's got to be the ultimate irony considering I'm still a damned virgin."

Shit did she say that out loud? Stupid fucking mouth!

Hope crossed her arms defensively and hunched her shoulders, wishing the ground would just swallow her up.

Curtis wasn't letting it go though. Oh no, the one time he could do with being a gentleman and letting things slide, he chose to tuck his fingers under her chin and tip her head to look at him.

"All the more reason to put the brakes on, Hope," he said gently. "That's a gift you should be saving for someone special."

Hope closed her eyes and struggled with the sheer mortification. What the hell, she decided, throwing caution to the wind. It couldn't get any worse, so she opened her eyes and laughed humorlessly. "Fat chance of that," she replied, bluntly. "When I can't seem to even give it away."

She rubbed her hands over her face. "Damn you, Curtis. I was perfectly happy being a twenty-six-year-old virgin, until today. It was never something I wanted and never something I offered before. And I guess it's not something I'll offer again, because quite frankly, I'm not keen to repeat this level of humiliation, so I guess that's one lesson I've learned."

Fuck. Now she was starting to babble.

"And now, I really do need to leave. This was a mistake." She looked around for her luggage with a weird sense of deja vu. "Should have just kept going the first time," she muttered under her breath.

"I was trying to be a gentleman," Curtis said quietly from behind her.

"And that would be great if it was a gentleman I was looking for. I'm sorry I'm obviously no lady."

She cursed that her voice broke on those last words, but before she could make herself scarce, Hope found herself scooped off her feet and thrown over Curtis's shoulder.

She yelped and the breath was forced out of her in an audible whoosh as her hair spilled around her face and her ass burned from the shocking slap that was delivered to her unsuspecting rear.

"Don't ever say I didn't warn you," Curtis growled in a voice that had her skin tingling as he stalked off towards a bedroom she hadn't yet seen.

Chapter Nine

Hope bounced on the huge king size bed when Curtis tumbled her onto it. She had the briefest impression of navy and sea green, the dark colours a complete contrast to the rest of the house before he stripped off his shirt and followed her down.

"A man can only be pushed so far, Hope," he growled before devouring her mouth in a kiss more passionate than any of the ones that had gone before.

She didn't believe him for a moment, of course. If she so much as hinted that she wasn't on board with this, she was absolutely certain Curtis would stop.

Not that she wanted to test that theory.

A girl could only be pushed so far, and Hope wasn't taking any more chances on doing or saying the wrong thing.

And right now, she really wanted to get her hands on all the lovely flesh he'd just uncovered.

Her hands were greedy, and Curtis gave her free range

while he did more ridiculously hot things to her mouth and throat, rekindling the fire he'd ignited in her veins.

Hope grazed her fingers over the expanses of smooth, tanned skin, cautiously at first, but gaining confidence as his murmurs of pleasure encouraged her.

She loved the strong, supple feel of his body covering hers, but quickly became frustrated by the clothing that separated them. She wanted more. Wriggling underneath him, she tried to manoeuvre so she could shed the silk t-shirt which had felt so decadent against her skin when she dressed this morning. Now she just wanted it gone, wanted to feel his fingers in its place.

Curtis caught her hands and pushed them above her head and Hope's optimism fell. Please don't say he was going to try and put a stop to this again.

She stilled and looked at him with beseeching eyes, biting her lip to stop her from saying something she shouldn't.

Curtis had that intense look on his face that made her mouth go dry and her tummy churn, but his words, when he spoke, were quiet and simple. "Let me," he whispered, releasing his hold on her arms, and pushing back so he could grasp the hem of her shirt. He drew it up, carefully baring her inch by inch and Hope wished she'd worn something less cumbersome. Something with buttons which was a little more sexy to strip out of instead of a top that had to go over her head. But Curtis somehow managed to make it sexy anyway as he drew it slowly off of her. And he didn't stop there.

For a long moment he sat back on his haunches and took her in as she lay there clad only in her wispy lace bra and tailored shorts. Just when she might have started to feel self-conscious, Curtis swallowed, and his gaze snagged hers and instead she felt beautiful. He shimmied down and his fingers found the button at her waistband, making quick work of it. Hope lifted to help him draw them down her legs and basked in his quiet, indrawn breath. "You're beautiful," he breathed, leaning forward, and drawing his fingertips across the skin he'd just bared. His lips cruised along her collar bone and the swell of her breasts as his hands went behind her to find the clasp of her bra. Then she was gloriously free, and his head dipped, his mouth finding one stiff, aching nipple, and flicking at it with his tongue.

Hope gasped and arched into him. She knew he was being gentle with her; careful... but she wanted more. She wanted everything. And she wanted it right now - with Curtis.

She fisted her hands into his hair and pressed him to her and Curtis obliged by grazing his teeth across the straining tip, making her cry out. "Oh god! Yes!"

He turned his attention to her other nipple and somewhere along the line managed to divest her of her panties without her being aware until his seeking fingers brushed, unencumbered, against her most intimate places. He traced along her seam and Hope bucked against the electrifying jolt his touch sent through her, silently begging for more, straining to get closer. But Curtis took his time, refusing to hurry as his thumb swirled against her needy clit.

Her breath was coming in short pants now and desperation had started to claw at her when Curtis began to steadily kiss his way down her body. She wanted him to hurry and yet, at the same time, she wanted it to never end. She wanted to take every moment of this experience and commit it to memory.

When he settled between her legs, spreading them wide

to make room for his broad shoulders, any thought of embarrassment was gone. All those times she'd overthought these moments when she'd imagined what it might be like, and how awkward she might find it, vanished underneath Curtis's skilled lovemaking and the stark need he'd filled her with.

When his tongue traced the path of his fingers, Hope thought she might combust. She was ready to fly apart there and then with barely any more stimulation.

But his clever tongue dipped and swirled, sending her higher before he found her sensitive nub and suckled on it. The noises that were dragged from her throat were more animalistic than human, but Hope didn't care. All that mattered was the sense of euphoria Curtis had instilled within every atom of her body. One that she was chasing to its completion.

His fingers slipped gently into her soaking channel first one, then a second, readying her, stretching her, and then she exploded. All the colours of the rainbow flared like fireworks behind her eyes and her greedy channel convulsed around his clever fingers.

"Are you okay?" Curtis whispered against the soft skin of her abdomen as he looked up to check on her.

She nodded jerkily. She was better than okay. Everything he was doing just made her want more. "I want you… all of you," she clarified, her voice scratchy and hoarse. "Now!"

She felt his smile against her skin, and he lifted slightly to reach for a condom she'd never noticed him place on the bedside cabinet.

Hope looked at it with a frown as he picked it up. "Do we have to use that?" she asked. Whatever the reason, but this first time, especially, she just wanted to have the entire experience; not some silicone barrier between them. She swallowed when he hesitated. "I'm on the pill. To umm... regulate stuff after my chemo," she explained. "And obviously, this being the first time..." She trailed off, not knowing quite what to say in these situations. "I mean, I'm clean," she told him in a voice that was barely a whisper.

"I'm clean too," Curtis replied, but he still looked torn. "You trust me that much?" he finally asked.

A smile bloomed across Hope's face. "Yes," she told him in no uncertain terms. "I do."

Chapter Ten

Hope had expected it to hurt. She'd read all about having sex for the first time when she'd been younger and thought she was missing something. But when Curtis lined himself up and slid gently home, kissing her tenderly all the while, all she experienced was a glorious sensation of fullness and the feeling that she was somehow whole.

"Fuck, you're so tight," Curtis grated out in a voice that sounded somewhat strained as he buried his head into her neck while he pressed in that final inch.

They let out a collective breath when he bottomed out inside her and he levered himself up, their hands still clasped together beside her head, and asked "Still okay?"

Hope felt like her heart was melting. Whatever Curtis had said about saving herself for someone special, she couldn't have asked for a better experience.

Curtis *was* that someone special and her heart had known it all along.

She smiled up at him, feeling like the sun had just risen on something new and amazing. "Absolutely!"

His lips claimed her once again as he started to move his hips, slowly at first, but increasing in speed and strength with every thrust.

Hope reared her head back and arched against him when his lips found her throbbing nipples and she wound her legs around him, urging him faster, deeper.

Despite the earlier orgasm she felt the heat build within her once again, chasing her to the edge of the peak and suspending her in a fractured moment in time and space as she teetered on the edge of fulfilment, waiting to take that final plunge. Waiting for him to join her.

"Come with me!" she gasped, her short, neat nails biting into the backs of his hands as she sprinted to the edge of ecstasy, ready to fly off.

He lifted his head and their eyes met in a moment so profound it would stay with her forever.

Then the climax took them both and they made the jump together in an incandescent burst of revelation.

Hope gloried in the weight of Curtis's body, heavy against hers, even as she struggled to catch her breath. After a few beats he rolled to one side, taking her with him, still buried inside. Joined in the most intimate way possible for two people to be.

Hope opened her eyes when Curtis reached across and smoothed her hair off of her face, tucking the errant curls behind her ear. He dropped a kiss on her forehead. "How are you doing?" he asked, his lips curling up in a lopsided smile.

"I'm absolutely awesome," she reassured him.

Still, she wondered what the proper protocol was for

situations like these since they'd kind of done everything the wrong way around.

She snuggled against him, not wanting to lose the connection and that lovely feeling of lassitude, no matter how awkward things might get. But she knew the only way to deal with things was head on.

"So... where do we go from here?" she asked tentatively as she pillowed her head on his shoulder. "I mean, not that I expect anything, just because we... you know..."

Her words trailed off. This was more difficult than she anticipated, and she had no experience in how to deal with it.

Curtis crooked his finger under her chin in a move that was already becoming familiar. He was never going to let her hide, she realised. "And what if I do expect something, Hope?" he asked, his eyes steady and serious.

Hope shrugged. "I'm not a good bet," she told him, dropping her gaze away from his intense scrutiny. "My leukaemia might still recur, even though I'm past the five-year mark. I understand not everyone wants to deal with that. I'd understand if you don't want to take that chance."

"If the roles were reversed, would you feel the same way? Would you avoid a relationship with someone with a long-term illness that may - or may not - return?" Curtis asked, his eyes boring into hers like her answer might change the course of their lives.

She opened her mouth to respond straight away, but Curtis placed his finger over her lips. "Think about it, properly," he insisted. "Really think about it."

Hope frowned but gave the question the attention it deserved. Would she have the same feelings as her childhood friends if she was in their shoes? Her gut reaction had been denial, but she gave it deeper consideration.

She still came up with the same response.

Hope shook her head. "No," she said conclusively, realising she had done him a disservice making assumptions about decisions she wouldn't have made herself. "I wouldn't."

He didn't let it drop. "Are you sure?" he pressed.

She nodded. "I'm sure."

She was.

Curtis took her hand and pressed it to his abdomen. His skin was warm and slightly flushed from their lovemaking, and initially Hope thought he was ready for round two, which was fine with her.

But then her fingers encountered a different texture and as she explored using touch alone, she realised it was a long thin scar which curved from his waist to his groin.

Hope pushed up on one elbow so she could see it with her eyes. She stroked gentle fingertips across the smooth, raised tissue. "What's it from?" she asked, raising her eyes to meet his. "A kidney transplant," he told her, pausing for a second for the words to sink in. "I had kidney failure as a child. Ended up on dialysis for five years when I should have been in high school."

It all made sense now; why she hadn't been aware of Catrina having a brother back then. The way he'd understood even the things she'd struggled to put into words.

"Things got pretty dicey for a while, and I wasn't expected to pull through. Then Catrina and I turned eighteen and she made the ultimate sacrifice. She donated one of her kidneys to me. Since we're twins the match was exceptional, and I made a full and unprecedented recovery without the usual complications of organ rejection. But there's still a risk."

Hope scooted down and dropped a light kiss on the

scar, then she looked up and turned a saucy grin on him. "So does this mean you're my boyfriend?" she asked cheekily.

Curtis rolled them both over until she was laying underneath him again, pinned by his pelvis and the grip he had on her wrists which he'd captured above her head again; something he seemed to have a serious liking for.

"That would be my choice, Hope," he replied, those intense, dark eyes boring into her once again and making her shiver. "But there is something else you should know, before you agree."

"What is it?" she pressed when he paused. There wasn't anything she could think of that would change her mind.

"I'm very... dominant," he replied. Well, that was no surprise, Hope had already worked that out for herself. Curtis wasn't finished though. "And when I say dominant, I mean I enjoy sexual dominance. Bondage, impact play..."

"You mean you want to tie me up and spank me?" she interrupted, slightly breathless, her insides turning molten at the thought.

"Something like that," Curtis agreed with a wicked grin.

Hope captured his gaze with eyes that held the promise of years of kinky exploration. "My sexuality is a blank page," she whispered. "You can mould me into anything you like."

He dipped his head and caught her lips, his kiss forceful and passionate and Hope met it with the excitement of new adventures, happy to follow wherever he might lead her.

And the future spread out before them, full of promise now that they had both chosen hope and decided to embrace that future together. Whatever it might hold.

Also by Poppy Flynn

Standalones

On His World

Smokin' Cowboys

Stranded with the Storm Chasers

What Lies Beneath

The Club Risqué Series

Fool's Desire

Fear's Whisper

Ties that Bind

Dark Consequences

Friends with Benefits

Captive Heart

Tormented Dreams

The Club Risqué Collection

The Serendipity Series

Serendipity: Samhain & Sorcery

Serendipity: Yule & Enchantment

Serendipity: Imbolc & Incantations

Serendipity: Ostara & Omens

Serendipity: Beltane & Bewitchery

Serendipity: Litha & Lore

Serendipity: Lammas & Illusions

Serendipity: Mabon & Magic

Masters of Paradise Series

Masters of Paradise

Temptation

Resurrection

Valentine in Paradise

Scandal

Anthologies

New Year, New Me

Secrets and Seductions

Strong Women

Did it Hurt
by R.M. Gardner

Chapter One

As is often the way with these things, the animals felt it first: dogs whimpered to their masters when they walked past the spot; squirrels vacated their nearby homes in search of tree trunks in safer places. Everything down to the last woodlouse fled the area, leaving only a circle of small boulders.

Creatures can feel tremors from far below the surface on which we walk, and if a space becomes suddenly void of all faunas, humans should run: run fast and run far because the animals know something is coming. The humans should have followed the animals' lead, but they didn't.

The humans felt nothing—too busy with their heads in the clouds to notice anything was wrong. They felt it eventually but, by then, there was nothing to be done.

News readers around the county talked of Richter scales that nobody really had the patience for. England rarely had so much as a tremor, so a true-blue earthquake was a terrifying concept for most. The people didn't want numbers that held no meaning. They wanted instructions, reassurances and, above all, for someone else to fix the problem in as short an amount of time as possible.

Scientists couldn't locate where the quake had started. No shifts had been detected that would affect the small island of Britain in such a manner. Panic gripped the public as people fled further afield. Nowhere felt safe. And then it stopped.

Had the animals stuck around, they would have seen the centre of the stone circle collapse in on itself. As if a plug had been pulled the dirt dropped down into the Earth's core, leaving a black hole that allowed the void to stare at the sky.

Had the animals stuck around, they would have seen the rise of bubbling lava, magma spitting out at all angles, sizzling the leaves on the ground where it landed.

Had the animals stuck around, they would have seen that magma subside and drain, only to be replaced by steam and ash that coated the ground and trees like snow.

Within twelve hours, the forest became a black and white photograph from a time long forgotten, the oppressive dust laying claim to everything it could reach out and touch.

If the animals had stuck around, they would have seen hands clawing at the edge of the hole: long fingers that left scratch marks in the dirt and whose nails sent sparks flying as they grazed the nearby rocks.

But the animals didn't stick around, and so Marceline's ascent went completely unnoticed by the mundane world. In complete privacy, she climbed out of the abyss and stood on the mortal plain.

The woman shook her head, letting her hair fall from its perfect French twist. The hole hadn't been wide enough for her to fly out of, so she had scaled her way up—no easy feat, even for a demon of her status. The

only evidence of her efforts, however, was a smudge of ash on her cheek and one broken fingernail that regrew the moment she glared at her hand. Taking advantage of her spacious surroundings, she stretched, allowing her bones to click and her muscles to extend after the climb. She unfurled her wings. The feathery black appendages spread behind her, the span of them enough to create a shadow that reached six feet in front of her. They ruffled behind her, the jet-black shimmering in the sunlight. She flapped them, causing a breeze that sent the nearby boulders flying with ease.

She knew that if she wanted to blend in, she would need to keep them away for the majority of the time, but it felt good to spread them out and she knew she was going to miss the sensation. One never enjoyed restraining themselves, did they?

The sun was low in the sky, painting the horizon with candyfloss pink clouds. Seeing that night was coming, the demon contemplated her options for places to sleep. Anywhere could be comfortable, but what would be most beneficial to her goals?

Appearing to be in need could make things easier for her—give her a jumpstart—but the idea of having one last night to use and abuse her powers was far too delicious a thought to ignore.

Marceline pulled her wings back in and set off on foot out of the woods, following the smell of despair that cloaked every city. Humans were creators of their own folly, and nothing gave a demon greater joy than watching them unravel their lives. There was no better place to do that than a bar.

She followed her nose until she was at the edge of town. Neon lights and cackles of laughter surrounded her—not completely unlike what she was used to down below.

For a while, she just observed the humans, taking particular interest in what they wore and how they spoke. Then, feeling confident in her ability to mimic them, Marceline visualised the outfit she wanted to wear: a tight fitted leather dress that accentuated her curves, bright red with matching shoes.

Full of confidence, she sauntered towards the nearest club. The queue was long, but the beautiful monster had no intention of waiting. Heading straight to the door, she glared at the security guard. "I wish to enter."

"Back of the line, love. Shouldn't be too long now."

"Excuse me?"

"I said, back of the line. You can wait like everybody else." "I am Marceline Chisuke, Princess of the Underworld, Destroyer of Spirits and Torturer of Souls. I do not wait."

The people in line behind her mumbled, giggling like they had some secret that she wasn't in on.

"Well, sweetheart, I'm Mitch, King of the Door and now, you're barred." The boulder of a man brushed her aside and let a trickle of other people into the club.

Marceline felt her cheeks heat up and an emotion she was unfamiliar with made her limbs tingle with awareness.

"You will pay for this disrespect, Mitch of The Door," she spat at him before turning on her heel and storming off. She had caught his scent. He reeked of unearned smugness. She knew she would be able to find him later, and when she did, he would regret crossing her. She could have ended him right there and then, but that would have caused a scene and

she needed to remain inconspicuous whilst she got her bearings in this strange new world.

Marceline made her way to another nightclub, sensibly waiting at the back of the line to be let in. The gaggle of girls ahead of her shot each other alarmed looks as they listened to the curvaceous woman mutter to herself about destruction and death.

Finally, she made it to the front of the queue and was face-to-face with another man who looked like a boulder, but he was slightly hairier around the chin.

"I wish to enter," she told him, prepared for a second altercation. "Right you are, lass. In you go."

"Thank you, good sir." She walked through the door with her head held high, leaving a bemused doorman behind her.

Music blared from every angle, the pounding bass making the disturbingly sticky floor shake beneath the feet of intoxicated dancers. The smell of sickly shots mixed with sweat and a hint of desperation attacked Marceline's nostrils, and she inhaled greedily, feeding off the turbulent emotions.

Standing at the top of a staircase that led down to another dancefloor, she watched the bodies that writhed like maggots. She had no intentions of finding a mate in the nightclub: unsure what exactly to look for in a partner, she was here only for research purposes, wanting to assess what was on offer.

The women appealed to her visually. Their curves were mesmerising—and the elegance of a lady was something she had long marvelled at—but she had tried her hand with maidens below and found that the attraction was purely aesthetic: a delight to look at, but she found no pleasure in being intimate with them. It had been a source of great frustration for Marceline as it would have made her own life much easier if she could have settled with a wife, but alas it was not meant to be.

Sensing that she was getting off track, Marceline turned her attention to the men. It was slim pickings to say the least. There was an array of

contradictory smells coming from the males in the building: insecurity and overconfidence, echoism and narcissism, misery and ecstasy. While she perused the bodies, she noticed the majority of them had a drink in their hand.

Marceline made her way to the bar at the back of the room and settled into a high stool. This was an environment she knew well. Down below, she frequented the taverns and took whatever she pleased. It was her right as the daughter of Hades to take without ever giving anything in exchange. However, her experience with Mitch had taught her that things were different here and her title held no weight. She would need other things to get by on the surface.

She had watched people exchange metal coins and small sheets of paper for the drinks and assumed it was the currency above ground. For the first time since changing clothes, Marceline used her powers and lured a wallet out of the pocket of a man who smelt of entitlement.

"What'll it be?" the bartender asked, in a voice that was confident and husky.

Unlike the other males she had interacted with on the surface, his jaw was strong and true with stubble that she yearned to touch to see if it was as prickly as it looked. His head was shaved at the sides but long on top—jet black except for a few strands of grey towards his temples. The black shirt he wore strained across his pectoral muscles, his sleeves were rolled up and the ends of a crimson tattoo peeked out of them.

"I don't know. What's good?" Marceline purred, the sudden feeling of attraction making her more loquacious than she usually was. "Well, I'm a Fireball guy personally."

"Fireball sounds adequate, thank you." She smiled, handing over the paper with a five on it. Human money was so very basic that even a troll child could learn it within an hour.

The attractive man returned with her drink and leant against the counter, his arms folded over his chest.

"You lose your friends?"

"I did not arrive with friends. I am here in an... explorative capacity shall we say?"

A low chuckle left the man, and Marceline tracked the bobbing of his Adam's apple, wondering what it would be like to trace the outline with her tongue. She shook her head to get rid of the mental image, for this was not the time.

"What are you exploring?"

"My options. So far, I have learnt that I do not like this place. What is your name?" She took a gulp of her drink, and the barman watched her, expecting her to splutter as people often did when they didn't sip it.

"Cas, and I don't like it here either to be frank, but it pays the bills." She drained the glass of its remaining contents. "My name is Marceline. I would like another please, Cas."

The man eyed her cautiously. "This is strong stuff. You might want to pace yourself."

Marceline let out a harsh cackle. "We have much

stronger drinks where I come from. Back home. we would serve this to the young ones when their gums are inflamed." She winked, her long eyelashes dusting her brow bone. She felt comfortable around this man, who seemed as disgruntled with their surroundings as she was.

"Where in the hell do you come from?" he asked with a smirk. "Very far south. Hell is a perfect way to describe it."

Marceline stayed at the bar for some time, watching the humans interact and trying to learn their mannerisms, many of which seemed boorish and clumsy to her.

Cas shot her curious looks between serving drinks. His emerald orbs took in her features with fascination. He knew that she was too sophisticated and poised to be frequenting scuzzy clubs like the one they were currently in. He was about to go to her—to tell her that he knew somewhere better, that he could take her there tomorrow if she would allow him—when an obnoxious voice bellowed beside him.

"Oi, mate. Another beer." The man was younger, no more than twenty-three, and he had the unmistakable air of someone who wasn't used to being told no.

"I'll be with you in a minute, pal."

The young lout rolled his shoulders, a sneer curling his upper lip. "You'll be with me now."

"Wait your turn, man. I'll get to you." Cas rolled his eyes, tired of the arrogant twenty something crowd that the bar attracted.

"Listen here you prick—" The man's hand darted out to grab the bartender by the shirt. He was surprisingly spritely for someone so drunk, but Marceline was quicker.

In one fluid motion, she had pulled him back by the other arm and twisted it behind his back. "You will not speak to my new friend that way. Beg for his forgiveness."

The man struggled in her firm grasp, in shock that a

woman so small could be so powerful. "I'm not begging for shit,"

"You are not now, but you will." Marceline grabbed the hand that was behind his back and pulled. She heard the sickening snap of bone, and he howled as the pain ran up his arm. "Are you ready to beg now?" Cas was transfixed. They were at the end of the bar, in the shadows where no one could see them so no one else intervened. He knew he should probably have stopped her but there was something incredibly sexy about her aggression, and he found himself needing to adjust himself in his pants. "Fuck, I'm sorry. I'm sorry, alright!"

The bartender nodded curtly at the man and the demon dropped his arm. He scarpered immediately, cradling his limp wrist to his chest. Marceline could have sworn she saw a tear as he left.

Once back in her seat, she drained the contents of her glass again and pushed it back to Cas across the bar top. "Next one's on me darlin'. remind me never to cross you."

"English is not my first language. What is a darlin'?" she asked while he poured.

"It's a term of endearment—something you call someone you like," he replied, a slight blush creeping up his neck.

"I think I like it." She smiled, feeling shy for the first time in her life. "Well, if you like it that much, give me your number and I'll call you darlin' tomorrow, too." Cas' emerald orbs sparkled as he handed her the glass, the infatuation sudden but intense.

"I don't have a phone number, nor do I have anywhere to stay tonight. Maybe you could suggest somewhere and I can meet you tomorrow?"

Cas' excited eyes became hungry as he considered his

next move. "You could stay at my place if you like? I would sleep on the sofa of course." His eyes flashed with excitement and something akin to a plea. "I would like that very much, Cas. Thank you."

"I get off in an hour. Can you wait that long?"

"I can wait indefinitely."

Chapter Two

Marceline remained at the bar, watching as Cas worked. She admired the way his arms strained as he pulled pints, his T-shirt was stretched tightly over what she could tell were impressive muscles.

He caught her staring on more than one occasion, but he didn't let her know. Her attention made his skin prickle, and he found himself deliberately trying to flex just to keep her eyes on him.

She was approached multiple times by other men. Their chat up lines were nothing more than an irritating buzzing in her ear. She could have used her powers to keep them at bay, but she liked the looks of jealousy that flashed over Cas' face whenever someone came to her. By the time his shift was over, Cas was desperate to get her away from the pounding music, strobe lighting and horny drinkers, his patience thinning with every passing minute. As they left the club, he placed his hand on the bottom of her back, guiding her out and staring down any man who dared look their way. The urge to press her up against the wall and kiss her senseless—staking his claim to her—was almost unbearable, but he held back. Being a caveman wasn't the way forward, but it was tempting.

"I'm afraid I need to make a quick stop," Marceline informed him once they were outside.

"Where at?"

"Another club. There is a man there who has wronged me, and I must put it right."

"Oh, God. You aren't gonna break this guy's arm, too, are you?" He chuckled.

Marceline laughed: a wicked but delicious sound that came from deep in her chest. "I will not break his arm if you do not want me to, but I cannot let him be disrespectful."

"Then lead the way darlin'," he crooned, his breath tickling the shell of her ear. The sensation sent shivers down her spine.

Cas kept his arm around her as they walked until they were in front of Mitch.

"You've brought your little boyfriend this time, have you?" he sneered. Sweat was beading on his forehead, making his face even shinier. "He is merely here to watch. You will be dealing with me." Mitch's mouth opened, his eyebrows furrowed and he was about to speak when his breath caught in his throat. The words bubbled but couldn't get anywhere, and his eyes bulged as he rapidly ran out of oxygen. No one was touching him, but Marceline's eyes were focused and glowing violet. "You will learn, Mitch of the Door, not to be so disrespectful in future." The man's mouth widened into a silent scream as pain radiated from his crotch. Again, there was nothing touching him, but he felt an unbearable crushing sensation that knocked him sick. Tears and drool streamed down his face as he fought for breath and struggled against the invisible force that was gripping him.

Just as his lips were turning blue, Marceline pulled her powers back and the stumpy man fell to his knees, clutching himself.

"Remember this, Mitch. The next person you offend may not be as kind as me."

Marceline's eyes had gone back to their usual lilac, and she turned back to look at an awe-struck Cas. "I am ready to go now." She thrust her hand out for him to take and he entwined his fingers with hers.

"I don't know what you just did, but that was amazing." His voice was a whisper in the dark, barely reaching her ears.

"Thank you. I may show you more later if you continue to be kind to me."

Cas opened the door to his modest two-up, two-down house. "It's not much I'm afraid but—"

Stepping past him and gracefully sitting herself on his sofa, she looked up at him. "It is very pleasant; I enjoy your decorating." Her living quarters in the castle had always been full of necessities rather than pleasures. Her position meant she needed a number of items that took up most of her space. She planned to move to a larger area of the grounds when she was married so she had more room for comfortable things.

"Like I said, I'll sleep on the sofa; you can take my bed," Cas told her, ruffling his hair and dropping onto the sofa next to her.

"Nonsense. We will share. Unless you would rather I took the sofa?" She tilted her head to the side, trying to figure out whether her bold strategy was going to work. She wanted this man, and she thought he wanted her, too, but her limited interactions with humans had left her at a disadvantage when it came to reading his body language.

"Sharing works for me." His eyes were dark and heavy. Marceline could tell from the sudden smell of arousal that she was right in her thoughts. Cas could be the one to bring home and end all of her troubles.

"I usually eat around now, but you're welcome to go to bed if you're tired. I know my body clock isn't the same as a normal person's." "I will eat with you. I do not need to sleep yet. What will we eat?" "I've been thinking about getting some Chinese food all day. Do you fancy that?"

"I have been told that ribs are good. Would you recommend them?" A grin lit up Cas's face, causing a dimple to form on his left cheek. Marceline touched it with her thumb. It wasn't something she saw on the men back home as they so rarely smiled.

Cas saw his opportunity to make his feelings known and he took it. His hands burrowed into her glossy hair, pulled her head towards him, and he pressed his lips to hers. The taste of Fireball was still there, and it spurred him on as he swiped his tongue across the seam of her mouth, begging for entrance.

She parted her lips and welcomed him in, her tongue sliding against his with confidence. This was something she had experience with, and she was confident she could satisfy him.

Cas sucked her bottom lip between his teeth and bit down. It didn't hurt but the unexpected pressure shot a bolt of excitement through her and a moan fell from her wet lips. Marceline was more than ready to straddle him. Her body ached for a closer connection, but his stomach made a grumble of protest.

With a sigh, Cas' lips stopped their exploration, and he rested his forehead on hers. "Food. Food first, then that."

Marceline shocked herself with a giggle that sounded foreign to her own ears. She had no cause for giggles in her day-to-day life: the perverse pleasure she took from her acts of torture was nothing to laugh about. "Am I ordering ribs for you then?"

"I will have whatever you have."

A shared plate of ribs and rice later, Marceline and Cas were back on the sofa, staring into each other's eyes as if they could see into each other's souls. Their hands wandered: touching, squeezing, soaking each other in.

She had never felt a man so hard yet so soft at the same time. She felt his life's blood flowing through his veins, vital and strong. She'd never experienced a man like him: a man eager to please her. She relished in his attention, his intense gaze making her feel truly seen for the first time in her life.

With a tender touch to her cheek, he said the words she was desperate to hear. "Do you want to take this upstairs?"

Marceline barely had a chance to nod before she was being pulled off the sofa and up the stairs.

Cas' room was surprisingly large with a plush brown carpet, simple oak furniture and a king-sized bed. The smell of his fabric softener lingered in the air, and Marceline sniffed a little, enjoying the freshness of it. She was used to the smell of sulphur and fear, so her lungs sang with pleasure to be filled with something so light and gentle.

She stood still in the middle of the room, waiting for Cas to make his next move. Suddenly, she was unsure of herself. This was a man who was kind. His willingness to help her so easily had shown her that. Did she really want to drag him away to a life within the bowels of hell? She was desperate to avoid the arranged marriage her father had threatened her with, and she had hoped to find a man who would please both her and the king.

While her father was fiercely protective and loving towards Marceline, she had seen how he treated his lovers, and she knew his version of a good husband was very different to hers. To him, wives were to be

obedient, and husbands were to be domineering. She had grown up watching her father use women to fulfil his own desires only to cast them aside with a slap and a harsh word. She hoped things had been different when her mother had been around. Maybe her leaving was what had twisted him into the icy man he was.

With all these thoughts running through her head, she hadn't paid attention to how close Cas had gotten until she felt his hot breath on her face.

"I should not have come here," she breathed, her voice barely audible to her own ears.

"Why?"

"I will not be good for you. You have seen what I can do; you must know that I am not of this land."

He curled a fiery strand of hair around his finger, tugging gently and making her forget why she needed to leave.

"I don't care. I just want you. I'll follow anywhere you want." "You do not even know me." Her lilac eyes were boring into his. Within the space of a couple of hours, she had become enamoured but the guilt of dragging him to the depths below would likely be her undoing. Guilt wasn't an emotion she had felt until now. You can't torture people to the brink of insanity for living if you're going to feel bad about it afterwards. She hated the new emotion—hated the way it made her throat close up and her eyes water. She hated the trembling in her limbs that she had never had before and had no idea how to stop.

"You're right: I don't know you, but I'm dying to, and I know that I love you. I can't explain it, but I swear there is something about you that calls me. You set fire to a part of my soul that I didn't know existed until tonight, and I know that sounds insane—"

"It does not sound insane. I feel the same pull to you. That doesn't make this okay, though. My world is vastly different from yours, and I do not wish to tear you away from your life. It would make you unhappy, no?"

"I would be happy if I had you. If you leave me now, I'll be clinging to the memory of tonight for the rest of my life." His hands were around hers, holding tight as if she were going to vanish on the spot. She could have if

she wanted to, but no matter how hard her conscience tried to scream at her, she was rooted to the spot.

"Let me show you how right I can be for you." His hands left her arms. One went to her waist, pulling her body into his. The other went to her hair, wrapping itself up in there and pulling.

The pain was beautiful, she gasped as he held her in place by her silky locks and kissed up her neck. She felt his teeth grazing against her skin and—desperate for more pain, more pleasure—she panted, "Bite me."

He chuckled in her ear, a low throaty sound that had her rubbing her thighs together in search of some relief.

"Believe me, darlin' I'll bite you. I'm going to leave my marks all over you so that, when you look in the mirror tomorrow, all you will be able to think of is me. And then when we go back to wherever you came from, I'll keep marking you so everyone there knows you're mine."

Marceline loved how possessive he was. She had only ever used lovers before for a brief time, none of them worthy of keeping her attention. Cas was the first man she had ever wanted to stay with. She wanted him to stake his claim, to covet her. It was clear he wanted that, too, if she would only let him.

While they were talking Cas had moved her until her back was pressed against the wall. She enjoyed the feeling of being trapped—of being at his mercy.

Mercy was something people often begged her for, but she never gave any. This was the closest she would get to not being in control and the knowledge that she could easily decimate the man in front of her had completely fallen out of her head.

"How long until you have to go back?"

"Two more sunsets," she whispered, her voice wavering in a way it never had before.

"You won't need the second one. By tomorrow's you'll know that I'm the one to take back with you," Cas vowed, his gaze searing her skin. "And if I don't?"

"Then I'll follow you anyway. It shouldn't be too difficult. You must have hurt yourself at least a little when you fell from heaven."

Marceline laughed and shook her head, her lustrous hair bouncing around her milky skin like snakes. "No, but I did snap a nail when I crawled up from hell."

Chapter Three

Marceline was already sitting up when Cas awoke the next afternoon. They had stayed awake into the early hours of the morning, and he had looked so peaceful in his slumber that she hadn't wanted to wake him. She was gazing out of the window, gnawing on her plump bottom lip. The action sent images through his mind of what he could put between those lips. He was about to attempt to entice her into a little morning fun when she turned to him, her expression a blank mask designed to hide any emotions, executed to perfection.

"You say you wish to come home with me."

Cas nodded.

"Then I must show you something today. My home may be too horrific for you; this will test your resilience,"

"What is it?"

Marceline leant over, covering his lips with her own, coaxing them open with her tongue. "You will see, but I cannot show you here. Can you guide me to a body of water

—somewhere quiet and discreet? This is not something other people should stumble across."

Cas drove for over an hour to get to the river that he knew would be deserted. In summer, it was busy, packed with people barbecuing, people swimming, and people jumping off the aptly named Devil's Bridge. But in autumn it was tranquil and peaceful.

They were both quiet during the car ride, although Cas had spent the whole time with one hand placed possessively on her thigh. To his mind she was already his.

When he pulled over, Marceline was staring at him, memorising his features as he was now: happy and calm. Once she had shown him her true self, there would be no going back to this.

She stepped out of the car and walked to the water's edge. Marceline turned to face him and laid a hand on his cheek. He instinctively leant into her touch and rested his forehead against hers.

"What do you want to show me?"

She knelt on the riverbank and pulled him down with her before turning her attention to the water. She waved her hands over the calm surface, and the water beneath their reflection frothed and bubbled as she whispered encouragement to it.

"*Ostende mihi praeterita, ostende mihi praeterita, ostende mihi praeterita.*" Steam rose from the river, twirling in a non-existent breeze before all movement stopped abruptly. The water's surface turned silver and within it was Marceline's life:

The woman stood at the front door of Marceline's home. She was tall and pretty, but she was also anxious. She had gotten herself involved with someone she shouldn't have, and it was too late now to undo it. Marceline's father stood in the hallway, looking at the woman as if she were something he'd stepped in.

"Please. Marci's watching. Don't do this."

"My daughter has nothing to do with this."

"She shouldn't see us fighting," the woman whispered, her golden eyes flitting to the young girl on the landing. The never setting sun shone a deep red behind her, matching the handprint on her cheek.

"She has seen worse before and she will again." Marceline's father gripped the woman by the throat, easily picking her up from the floor despite her struggling. "I am done with you. You will not come here again." The giant man dropped the slim girl before slamming the door in her face. After taking a deep breath, he turned around to face the child. "My princess, you should be in bed."

"I'm sorry. The noises woke me up." She sniffled, wiping her nose with the back of her hand. She was a tiny little thing really, delicate and fragile.

Her father climbed the stairs to meet her before scooping her up with one hand and holding her to his chest. "Do we need to have another bedtime story?"

She grinned, flashing her tiny fangs and nodding. "I want the one about the queen who cursed that evil man's baby!"

"Well then, that is what you shall have, my little monster."

The picture on the water faded away and was replaced with another—a fresher memory but still a few years old:

Marceline stood in a pair of stiletto heels, leather pants and a matching corset. Her hair cascaded in waves over her shoulders, quivering with her every move. Her eyes had no irises, just large black pupils that glittered like onyx.

She was throwing her head back with malicious laughter, revealing sharp canines. Her wings were spread out behind her, wafting the sulfuric fumes into the faces of the poor souls behind her.

Her attention was fixed on a man chained to a wall. He was a pale, snivelling mess before the demonic princess. Naked and vulnerable, they never had the arrogance they'd had in life when they reached hell. In Marceline's hand was a whip made of silver, the end fashioned into an arrowhead designed to deliver lashings of intense pain.

The man on the wall had clearly been suffering for some time: his face was covered in snot, tears and drool. The manacles holding his arms above his head were the only things keeping him upright, while his sobs echoed through the cave.

Eerie red light filled the rocky shelter, and the nearby creek of lava spat out hot rocks that jumped out at the people in cages who were waiting for their turn with the Princess of Hell. The cage itself was another form of torture. Watching what was happening and knowing it would soon be their turn made the denizens of the underworld manic with fear. They would rattle the bars, some going so far as trying to chew the metal in an effort to escape their fate. Marceline had watched many people break their teeth, deglove themselves and snap their own bones in their attempts to run from her punishments.

The smell of their torment drove her wild. Her cheeks flushed pink, and her mouth watered whenever they screamed.

Her slim arm was reared back ready to deliver another blow when the pathetic worm begged, again.

"No more, please! Have mercy! I can't take another!"

She dropped the whip where she stood and stalked towards her prey, taking his chin in her hand, piercing his skin with her sharp, claw-like nails.

"Fine. I will stop with the whip, but I am not done with you." She pulled a dagger out of her boot and teased it along his

chest, dragging it down his sternum before plunging it between the bottom two bones.

The man howled in agony as Marceline pulled the blade back out and repeated the motion between each of his ribs. Blood gushed from the wounds. On Earth, the man would've died of blood loss, but in the underworld the suffering never ended and so the blood never ran out.

The tendons in the bleeding man's neck stood out, tense to the point of snapping as he rode out the agony. No one could have said the man didn't deserve his punishment: he'd been a prolific serial killer in his life and the bodies of his victims showed him to be a twisted bastard. Everyone's punishment was relative to their own actions on the mortal plane. Some only had toenails ripped out, some were electrocuted, starved or beaten. The worst of the worst was what Marceline dealt with, and she clearly had a passion for her work.

She plunged her knife into the killer's neck. His veins gushed, leaving her coated in blood that she licked off her fingers. The coppery taste wasn't something she craved, but the way her victim's skin crawled when she did it was very satisfying.

The man lost consciousness, making it futile to torture him further, so she turned her attention to the others.

Her eyes shone with excitement. "Who would like to go next?"

The image faded and twisted again until it showed a further scene from five days prior.

Marceline didn't look at Cas. What she had just shown him was the very worst side of her, and she didn't want to see his reaction:

She was at one end of a long table, her father at the other looking sternly at her.

"You have done well in your work, my daughter, but it is time for you to find a husband."

"Why? I am perfectly fine alone," she replied, cool and in control. Inside she was furious.

"I am getting on in years; I won't be around forever. I am not immortal, and the very thought of leaving you here without a companion is unconscionable to me."

"But, Father, I've been alone for this long I'll—"

"You have not been alone: you have had me. You do not know what it is to be completely alone, and I will make sure you never know. You are my only child. My heart beats with the sole purpose of keeping you alive. I need to know that when I am gone you will have another by your side to take care of you."

Hot tears stung Marceline's eyes—partially from anger, and partially from upset. She knew she could take care of herself, and his insistence that she couldn't was frustrating. She also hated being faced with the reality that her father wouldn't always be with her. He was all she had in this world.

"I will find someone for you if needs be—someone strong and capable; someone who can match you in strength and mind." Her spine stiffened. Her father's definition of matching was actually that of dominating. In his head, that was a good thing but Marceline had no desire to be under the thumb of any man.

"The men down here do not please me. Please allow me to go to the surface and find a man of my own choosing."

The king leant back into his chair. His age was creeping up on him, the skin on his neck was loose and liver spots dotted his once capable hands.

"You have three days. If you do not have a partner by then—one I believe will be able to take care of you—I will find you one myself." She stood from the table and walked to the other end, clasping her father's hands in his. "I do wish you would not worry about me so much." The old man squeezed her fingers and *rose, pressing a kiss to her forehead. "I love you very much, my princess."*

The picture vanished, the water was as still as it ever was and Marceline sat, staring at the place her likeness had just been.

Her hands were balled into fists in the dirt, mud had found its way under her nails but she didn't move.

He needed to be the first one to do or say anything.

She didn't want to look at him, sure that she would be met with a face that was contorted in horror at who she was. Her hopes of keeping him were fading fast.

She had performed many dark acts in her life but until now, she had never known any reason to be ashamed of her actions. In hell, she was idolised for her savagery, but humans were different on Earth. For the first time, she was questioning her whole morality. The man beside her had been kind and gentle with her. Surely he would not continue to be after seeing that. She had put so much hope into the idea of him loving her and she hadn't even realised it.

A hand reached out across the ground, curling around her small fist. The warmth felt good against her cold skin.

She still wouldn't look at him, so he shuffled himself around her until she was sitting between his open legs. He buried his face in her neck, losing himself in her thick waves of hair. His strong arms were locked around her waist, holding her to him.

She let the heat of his embrace seep into her bones, but she felt no relief until he finally said something.

"When do we go?"

"The sun will set soon. I must return home by tomorrow's sunset, or my father will send people to come looking for me."

"Then we should go sooner rather than later."

"How can you still wish to come with me after what you have just witnessed?"

Cas brushed her hair over one shoulder and moved so his lips were brushing against the shell of her ear. "I already told you: I will follow you anywhere. I will enter hell with you. I will win your father's approval, and I will have you, just like you have me."

"If you stay for more than a week, you will never be able to return to this place, you know?"

"If you stay down there with me, I'll have no reason to come back. Now, take me to meet your father and marry me."

Chapter Four

Marceline opened the gates to hell. A crack in the Earth opened up, bigger than the one she'd crawled out of. Smoke billowed from the crater, and the smell of burning rock took over the air.

Once again, all creatures had fled the damned place, leaving only the man and the demon.

"Do we have to climb down that?"

"Not if you don't want to. We could just jump."

"Would that not be more dangerous?"

Marceline laughed at him and shook her head. "No, *amica mea*, I will open my wings before we hit the ground and we will land safely. Hold onto my waist, and we shall descend."

Cas did as he was told and wrapped his strong arms around her. He closed his eyes after they jumped, the wind and smoke making them sting and stream. His stomach leapt into his throat as they fell but was jolted back into place when Marceline extended her wings. Together, they glided to the ground.

When he opened his eyes, the woman beside him didn't have a single hair out of place.

For the first time, he looked at her wings. The span of them amazed him. He was sure that if he held his arms out his fingertips wouldn't even reach the edges of them.

Enjoying his inspection, Marceline curved the feathered appendages around them both, cocooning them in soft darkness. He ran his fingertips along them, stroking with awe, and listened to her hums of satisfaction as he did so.

Moving his attention to her face, he traced her high cheekbones and kissed her. It was a kiss that she felt from the tips of her wings to the tips of her toes.

"I must change before we see my father."

"What's wrong with this?" he asked, gesturing to her casual jeans and cardigan ensemble.

"I have a reputation to uphold. Here, I am royalty, and I must present myself as such. Only *you* get to see me in pyjamas and such like." His face softened as she spoke, and liquid warmth flew through his veins knowing he was the one person she was willing to be vulnerable in front of.

In the enclosure of her ebony wings, Marceline changed her outfit. The jeans and cardigan transformed into a shiny, black latex dress with matching thigh-high boots. Atop her head sat a tiara of silver spikes, glittering with blood red jewels. A spiked choker was around her neck and there were cuffs around her wrists to match.

Cas stared at her, slack-jawed.

He was attracted to her in normal clothes, but there was no denying how phenomenal she looked when she was in her element. "You should change, too."

His jaw snapped shut. "Why?"

"So that people can see you are obviously with me and treat you with the respect that you are due."

Heat tingled across his skin, and he looked down to see his jeans turning tight and black. Heavy boots had formed around his feet, and his casual shirt had also turned tight and black, with buttons that matched Marceline's red gems.

"I did not think you could be more attractive than the day we met. I was wrong," Marceline purred, running her hands up his chest and over his broad shoulders.

He dipped his head and pressed his lips to her, playfully nibbling on her lower lip. "Let's do this!"

The couple strolled through the rocky stretch of land, their fingers entwined tightly. Subjects dropped into deep bows as Marceline passed. She greeted them politely but didn't stop to chat with anyone.

"Do they always do this?" Cas asked, uncomfortable.

"Yes. My father rules his land with an iron fist. I will rule fairly and keep the people's respect, but I do not intend for things to remain so intensely formal."

Two guards stood to attention as they reached the doors of the Great Hall. Hades sat atop a throne made of bones. Skulls stared blankly from beneath his colossal hands. He pushed himself off the throne at the sight of his precious daughter.

"My child, you have returned so soon. Is something wrong?" Still clasping Cas' hand, Marceline rushed to meet her father. "Nothing is wrong. I just didn't require as much time on the surface as I was anticipating. This is Cas; he is who I will marry."

The king looked the human up and down. "How do you know he is worthy to sit beside you as you rule?"

"I feel it in my heart; I just know."

The king opened his palm and blew into it. A bright blue flame erupted on his skin. He stood directly in front of Cas and stared deep into his soul. "If you can hold this Hellfire in your bare hands for an hour, I will give you my blessing to marry my daughter."

Cas opened his mouth to respond, but Marceline beat him to it. "This is ridiculous. The fact I have chosen him should be enough for us to have your blessing!"

"I am sorry, Marcie"—the king hoped his use of her nickname would tamper down some of her ire—"but he must prove himself before I can trust him with the most important thing in my world."

Marceline's face softened at his words, but she was still unwilling to allow the man she loved to be hurt.

"Cas you do not need to do this, I can still take you back to the surface—"

"I'll do it." Cas' eyes narrowed in determination. "I'll hold it forever if that's what it takes to stay here with you."

Hades' lips twitched slightly as if to pull into a smile.

Marceline's offer had sounded like she was in control, but in her eyes Cas saw her heart breaking at the thought of being parted, and he felt the exact same way.

Fighting all of her natural instincts, Marceline watched as her newly betrothed spent an unbearable sixty-minutes holding the hottest flame in the universe.

He endured the pain without a sound, but the torment was evident in his face. His strong hands shook violently, sweat streamed down his face mingling with tears caused by pure agony. He watched Marceline the whole time, his eyes never straying from hers. She was worth it. She was everything he would ever want or need and he needed to have her, no matter what the cost.

Her small hands were clenched into fists, her knuckles white like the bones were about to break free of the skin, as she forced herself not to intervene.

When the hour was finally up, the Hellfire extinguished and Cas staggered forward before sinking to his knees in front of his fiancée. She dropped down with him, cradling his damaged hands in hers. His skin had completely burnt away, exposing his muscles and tendons. The smell of burnt flesh was one she was used to, but it was different coming from the man she loved and it triggered white hot rage within her.

Emotions she didn't have a name for wrapped their hands around her throat.

He flinched as she set her palms over his.

"I'm sorry *amica mea*; it will only hurt for a moment," she promised in a wobbly voice, resting her forehead against his.

He looked into her lavender orbs, his own eyes wide and full of pain and trust.

A glow emitted from her hands, and when she took them away, Cas' skin had regrown and healed as if nothing had ever happened. His pain was gone but the fatigue from his ordeal remained, and he swayed on his knees. His vision blurred as a giant figure moved behind Marceline. He wanted to pull her closer to him—away from the shape—but black spots began to dance around his vision until he fell, head first into Marceline's lap.

"Marceline, he will be fine. Please calm yourself," a firm voice spoke from somewhere in the room.

"I know he will be fine. That does not mean I want to see him suffer!" Marceline whisper-shouted from near his head.

He could hear a hiss in her words that he'd never heard before, and he knew she was upset.

Her fingertips brushed over his forehead and down his cheek making him feel sleepier than ever, but he forced his way through the seductive darkness.

Peeling back eyelids that felt like they were glued shut, he twitched his hand, searching for her, desperate to ease her worries. "Marce—" "I am here. You are okay. I am right here," she whispered. He turned his head towards her. "Where are we?"

"We are in my bedroom. You passed out after I healed you." "Yeah, I remember that part." Cas looked around and realised he was laid on a very comfortable bed with Marceline knelt on the mattress next to him.

She swooped down onto him, her face buried in the crook of his neck, "Do not do that to me ever again. You scared me half to death." Cas let out a raspy chuckle and rubbed soothing circles on her lower back. "Sorry, darlin', I'll make it up to you."

A man cleared his throat in the corner of the room.

Cas' eyes drifted to the King of Hell, but Marceline's focus didn't shift. "You were very impressive in your determination. I will gladly hand my daughter over to you." The men nodded to each other in the way that men often do. It shows little but means everything.

Once the door had closed behind Hades, Marceline swapped their clothes for something more comfortable and laid down on the bed, her head on his chest as he stroked her hair. She should have known her father would have created some ridiculous test to challenge whoever she intended to be with, but she had hoped her confidence in her choice would be enough.

"I am sorry for what my father did. If you no longer wish to stay, I—" The words stalled on her tongue. "I can still take you back." "Are you trying to get rid of me?" he teased, stroking his fingers up and down her bare arm.

"Of course not. I am just... It doesn't matter." She snuggled in closer to him, throwing her leg over his waist. She was irrationally worried that saying it would make it true.

"Tell me."

"I am just worried that now that you have seen the realities of my world with your own eyes you will no longer want to stay here with me. You are more than I had ever hoped to find when I set out on my search. I cannot help feeling like I do not deserve you." Marceline's heart became a lead weight as she said the words.

Cas shuffled into a sitting position and pulled her up with him, turning to face her. Her lilac orbs were downcast, so he lifted her chin, forcing her to meet his gaze.

"When you sat down in front of me at that bar, I was completely blown away. You are walking perfection, and I knew I wanted to fuck you. When you knocked back drinks like there was no tomorrow and threw your head back with that sexy laugh you have, I knew that one night with you wouldn't be enough. Then that arsehole came along, and you defended me so fiercely. We'd only just met but you were so protective. That was the exact moment that my heart became yours. Walking back to my house with you, all I wanted to do was wrap you up in my arms and hide you from the rest of the world so I could have you all to myself. Every second I've known you, I've fallen further and further in love with you so, no, I do not want to go anywhere if you aren't going with me. When I said I would hold that flame forever if that's what it took to be with you, I meant it. I am so unconditionally in love with you, and I will not let us be parted."

Marceline's lips had parted with a gasp half way through his speech and she didn't notice to close them. Her eyes flashed violet with overwhelming passion. "I love you just the same. I will love you until Hell freezes over."

The End

Also by
R.M. Gardner

Teach me to Live: A Stargazing Novel

Printed in Great Britain
by Amazon